PERCEVAL'S SECRET

A Novel of the Future

by

C. C. Yager

PERCEVAL'S SECRET

Copyright © 2014 Cinda C. Yager

ISBN: 978-0-9914967-2-3

First Paperback Edition July 2025

https://ccyager.wordpress.com

Licensing Notes
All rights reserved. No part of this book may be used or reproduced in any manner whatsoever without written permission except in the case of brief quotations embodied in articles and reviews.

Cover: Christopher Bohnet, cargocollective.com/xt4inc
Editor: Patricia Weaver Francisco
Paperback Interior produced by BookNook.biz.

This is a work of fiction. Names, characters, places, and incidents are products of the author's imagination or are used fictitiously and are not to be construed as real. Any resemblance to actual events, locations, organizations, or person, living or dead, is entirely coincidental.

To the memory of

D. D. Shostakovich

Chapter 1

"Maestro Quinn?" said the stage manager behind him at the stage door.

Evan Quinn adjusted the gold cufflinks he'd inherited from Joseph Caine so his arms could move freely in his white tie and tails. He felt exhilarated and anxious about conducting music forbidden in America: Joseph Caine's Fifth Symphony "Summer Wind." Uncle Joe would approve of his defiance. He'd defied the ruling New Economic Party and its Arts Council too. Evan heard the muffled voices of the audience in the concert hall. The lights clicked off leaving him in darkness. He imagined the sound of the first note, visualized the score's first page. A man's bass voice spoke from memory:

"You are a true son of America."

No, not now. He must think only of Uncle Joe's music. Why think about the deal he'd made with them now? Why not now? He was on the threshold of his future. But not now! He turned to the stage door as he pushed that voice back into his memory's farthest closet. He must think only of Uncle Joe's music – his heart and soul. That's all that mattered in this moment. The audience waited for it.

He inhaled a deep breath and handed his half-full water bottle to the stage manager. The door swung wide. With brisk confidence, he strode on stage through the cello section, his shoulders squared and chin up. Applause rippled the air.

At center stage, Evan bowed, taking in the mass of faces, the giant sparkling crystal chandeliers overhead and the serene gold goddess statues at regular intervals along the walls of the Grosser Saal of Vienna's Musikverein. Not your usual work place. But *his* usual job and where he was at home. Smiling, Evan leapt up onto the podium and faced the Vienna Philharmonic Orchestra, baton in hand, the symphony's score open to the first page on the waist-high conductor's stand. Above and behind the orchestra, burnished organ pipes extended to the ceiling. The applause subsided into the silent, energized anticipation he loved.

Evan gave the downbeat for the basses and cellos to begin the Caine symphony's brooding introduction. His arms winged wide as if to embrace the violins. Their bowing mirrored his fluid movements.

He knew the grief in this music. Moving his left hand like a seagull riding a gentle air current, Evan quieted the strings as the main theme's taut melody emerged. The violins played over a menacing line in the cellos, basses, and bassoons where he heard Caine's musical voice again. His sense of time faded into Caine's musical time which pulsed through his body and guided his hands.

Wood smoke and oranges. He had been four when Uncle Joe had pulled him out from under the grand piano, his favorite place to listen to Uncle Joe play or compose music, and stood him before the keyboard. Uncle Joe had smelled of wood smoke and oranges that day. He'd taught him the correct fingering and arpeggio chords for the C major scale. His first music lesson.

Uncle Joe's music swelled, and with it, Evan swayed up on his toes and down. Strings and woodwinds keened the return of the introduction. Evan nodded for the brass to enter. The music ascended out of its sorrow but then descended into a grim ostinato. He controlled this angry lamentation, the pizzicato strings, the piano's brash chords, and the acceleration into a caricature of itself as Caine intended. The galloping rhythms vibrated within his body. He thrust his arms up as if to release them out over the musicians. They were all of one mind, one body: Joseph Caine's.

Music had been his home since before that first lesson with Uncle Joe. Music had filled the Caines' house. He had felt loved there, safe and protected. He had wondered if he had been born into the wrong family.

Evan brought his arms close in to his body to restrain his beat for the dirge that diminished into the whisper of the first movement's final notes. After the cut-off, he brushed a lock of his hair from his eyes and allowed himself a wry smile, catching the eye of the principal flute player. Conducting both humbled and empowered him. Uncle Joe had told him once that music was the brandy of the damned.

After an energetic downbeat, Evan prodded the Scherzo's droll rhythm out of the basses and cellos as if goading a recalcitrant circus bear. The melodic line in the woodwinds skipped over the lilting, clownish line in the lower strings. The higher voices of the violins taunted them all. Under his breath, Evan sang snatches of the mocking music. He caught the eye of the principal cellist whose mouth twitched with amusement.

A solo violin picked up the cheeky melody, echoed whimsically by a flute. Evan heard Caine's acerbic snickering in the music. His father's sardonic laughter. His dead father. Bile flowed into his empty stomach, its sour vapor rising to his throat. The music fell like a guillotine blade to its end. His body rigid, Evan slipped a handkerchief from his pocket and wiped sweat from his face. The silence pressed against his back.

To begin the Largo movement, Evan leaned toward the violins, his eyes intent on them. Each note of the sad theme drew him back to the summer up north at the cabin the year before Caine's arrest when Caine was composing this symphony. He, Paul, and Uncle Joe had fished every day, and after they'd set their fishing lines at night, Uncle Joe became their giant cave troll, his long blonde hair falling over his face. He growled and chased them through the shadowy birch, aspen and pine grove behind the cabin until they had fallen into a pile of screaming giggles.

His throat muscles tightened. This musical elegy climbed to a sharp dissonant peak where it hovered unresolved. He listened and watched the musicians and when he turned to the cellos, a shadow of Harold's face leered at him from above their heads – Harold Smith, Vigiciv gang leader and terror of their neighborhood. The music wailed the shadow away and its sorrow reminded him of his mother's melancholy face, the pain in her eyes. His movements and beat delicate, he flowed with the strings through to the Largo's tentative end.

Without a pause, he plunged them into the Finale, into Caine's summer wind – not the gentle, early morning lake breeze up north, but the hammering gusts of a Minnesotan thunderstorm that demolished barns, ripped up trees and peeled off cabin roofs. Carried by its intensity, Evan moved from side to side. His mind raced ahead while his heart and blood beat in tempo. He must cue the trumpet, breathe with him: Caine's single trumpet sounded a call defying power and oppression. Strident strings echoed it, and Evan brought them all to a grinding halt.

Exhaling through pursed lips, he directed the movement's inner section, the violins' line poignant with memory of loss, the harmony in the violas and cellos tense with grief's disbelief. His mother had said this music would kill her. His choice to conduct it without AC approval could kill him. His American reality.

Clarinets and oboes played the defiant main theme at half tempo to introduce the Finale's last section. Evan cued the flute. The strings, trumpets and horns joined the woodwinds. He stooped as if to lift the orchestra and straightened with the music's long crescendo back into Caine's muscular summer wind. He fixed on the timpanist's eye, beating out the deliberate tempo like heavy goosesteps, and the timpani pounded with it through to the end. Evan flung his arms wide to hold the last full-orchestra chord, twisting his body for the cut-off as if to hurl that note at the organ pipes above the musicians.

"Hurrah! Bravo!"

A massive eruption of sound rolled over him in waves. After shaking hands with the concertmaster, who pushed him forward, Evan faced the hall. The audience cheered and applauded; the undulating hands above heads dizzied him. Smiling, he bowed low, whirled back to the orchestra and, with a flourish, motioned them to stand with him. After another bow, he left the stage. The stage manager handed him a towel and his water bottle. Richard, his AC escort waited there too, arms folded across his chest. Evan stuck out his tongue at Richard who grinned and wagged a finger at him.

As usual, Evan wanted to run to the solitude of his dressing room as fast as he could to preserve the music in his mind, but the roar in the hall called him back for bows again and again. The orchestra twice refused to stand with him, applauding as he stepped back into their midst. Several people handed red roses up to him which left him breathless with surprised pleasure. No one gave conductors flowers in America anymore. The audience responded to Joseph Caine's music, not him. They loved Caine's music.

Each time he left the stage, he saw Richard enter something in his palm-sized PDA. Of course, Richard counted his bows. Of course, he'd noted his change in the former AC-approved program here in Vienna, especially that he'd conducted a banned symphony by Joseph Caine. Of course, Richard would make his report.

Giddy and grinning, Evan strode off stage for the last time and directly to his Arts Council escort. "Here, Richard. Thought you might like these to give to your Austrian girl-friends tonight." He laid the two dozen red roses on top of Richard's hands and the PDA.

"This better not be a bribe, Quinn."

"You wouldn't think to buy a woman flowers, would you?"

Richard gave him a sheepish look. "Thanks. This won't change my report."

"*Ausgezeichnet*, Maestro! Excellent." Robert Waldstein, the concertmaster, embraced Evan. "An unforgettable tribute to your father and to Joseph Caine. Come, please. One last time, Maestro."

They went downstairs, Richard four steps behind. Musicians bustled in the corridor, putting away their instruments, talking and laughing. Evan paused to talk a moment with each musician, thanking each, telling each how much working with the Philharmonic had meant to him. They smiled at him, hugged him, thanked him for conducting the Caine symphony with them, and wished him a safe trip home the next day. Back upstairs, his other escort, Dave, leaned against the wall a foot left of the conductor's dressing room door. Evan nodded in greeting to him. Dave only stared.

"Maestro, the reception?" Robert said, grasping his arm.

"Wouldn't miss it. I'll change first, Robert."

Post-concert receptions gave him the cringes. Not many in America and most often for the Hartleben Quartet. He preferred to hang with musicians or go for a run. However, this was the last night of his tour and about half of the musicians planned to attend in his honor. He could never refuse musicians. They were his family. He changed out of his white tie and tails and into khaki-colored chinos and a navy-blue sport jacket.

Voices and laughter spilled out of the Green Room into the hallways and nearby Brahms Saal, the smaller, more intimate concert hall and tonight a garden of floral perfume and wine. For the non-musicians, Evan slipped on his public persona – gracious, calm, helpful and smiling with a mental warehouse full of nice, noncommittal phrases to say. He skirted people in formal attire, the women dripping diamonds, rubies, and pearls, and collided with a robust red-bearded Austrian who pumped his hand. Other hands brushed across his back, squeezed his shoulder, and patted his arm.

The first musician he encountered, the bearded timpanist, offered him a glass of champagne with the comment, "The watchdogs are letting you out to play tonight."

"Yeah, it's the last night in Europe. They want to play too. No alcohol for me, thanks, Bruno," Evan said, looking around for a server.

"Really? But why not?" the timpanist said, taking a sip from his own glass. "We celebrate you tonight."

"Food allergy," he said with an apologetic shrug. This explanation had usually proved more useful than the truth; that is, his mother had been a sweet drunk, had overdosed intentionally on pills and booze, and he believed that his genetics predisposed him to become an alcoholic too. Alcohol caused a loss of control, caused mistakes and unclear thinking, created chaos in life, and killed the brain and liver. He must be clear and in control of himself at all times.

"You are certain they have not reported our telephone calls and the score we sent to you in London?" Robert Waldstein said as he joined them. Robert glanced at Richard across the room, helping himself to the sumptuous buffet.

"Positive." Evan smiled. "I told them you needed to consult me about the program. They lost their chance to stop it at the first rehearsal. I appreciate your concern, but I'm fine."

"We have heard about the American Arts Council's punishments," the timpanist said.

"I've been a good boy. I've made millions for them on this tour." He heard the sarcasm in his voice and took a deep breath. "They understand the concept of public demand. They will understand the public demand for Caine's music here. They'll profit from it. Of course, the NEP profits handsomely somehow from everything."

Robert grasped Evan's hand. "I know I have said it before, Maestro, and the musicians, also, but you cannot imagine our joy that you wanted to play Joseph Caine's music with us and you chose his 'Summer Wind' Symphony. Especially with its dedication to your father."

"I've wanted to conduct the Caine Fifth since the first time I read through the score, a month after Caine's arrest. Given the opportunity the Vienna Philharmonic offered, nothing was going to stop me."

The timpanist grinned. "You know, we had a pool going on whether or not your watchdogs would let you come to this reception after conducting the Caine."

"How much did you win?" Evan said, returning the timpanist's grin.

Robert grunted. "*Ja,* and another pool to invite your two escorts to play."

"Really?" Evan glanced at Richard stuffing his face as he ogled the women in the room. "Did they fall for it?"

"The friendly one, him." The timpanist nodded toward

Richard as two more musicians joined them. "The other only wagged his head."

Evan nodded as the Japanese flutist touched his arm. "Evan, have you followed the Chinese-American talks here?"

"No. First heard about them when I arrived in London." He noticed a familiar head of white hair above the crowd. "Will you excuse me?"

"Of course, you must mingle, Maestro," Robert said.

"Come back and say good-bye, Evan," the timpanist said.

Evan weaved around people toward the tall man with the abundant white hair swept back from his high forehead and skimming his collar. Nigel Fox. Artist Manager. Evan had met him after his first concert in London. Fox carried himself like a military officer in his custom-tailored navy-blue pin-striped suit. The London musicians had told him that Fox was the best artist manager in Europe with contacts and connections all over the world and a stable of clients that included Anders Zukav. Evan had heard a *lot* about Zukav the last three weeks.

"Good to see you again, Nigel," Evan said, shaking his hand.

Fox's hawk-like face softened into a smile. "I loved the Caine, Evan. Brilliant."

"Thanks. In town on business or pleasure?"

"To hear you conduct the Caine. But my offer still stands. If you decide to work without the Arts Council, you'll need representation and I'd—"

"And protection. The AC would never allow it. But I'll keep your card."

"Maestro! Maestro Quinn!"

"I'll leave you to your public, Evan," Nigel said with a chuckle.

A short wrestler of a man in his twenties cut through the crowd, his gait bouncing with energy, his shoulder-length blonde curls shimmering around his face in which wide-set large blue eyes flanked a prominent wolfish nose. A gold earring, a small hoop in his right earlobe, evoked a jolting memory for Evan – the glitter of a gold earring in Uncle Joe's right ear, the same sunny exuberance, the same craggy face, prominent sharp nose curved off center from a childhood break, and the same long blonde hair. A statuesque African woman pursued this physical reincarnation of Uncle Joe. She collided with him when he stopped and smoothed his navy-blue tunic before speaking.

"Maestro Quinn," the Reincarnation said with a deferential bow of his head. "I loved Caine! Fan*tas*tic! And to hear Caine symphony under your baton, American conductor so close with composer—"

He recognized the Reincarnation's accent. He'd known Juilliard students who spoke with the same accent. If Joseph Caine had been Russian, this guy would be him. Goosebumps raised the hairs on the back of Evan's neck.

"Vasia," the African woman said, her accent German. She grabbed his shoulder, with a quick glance at Evan. "The Maestro—"

"My God! So rude of me. Please allow me to introduce – I am Vassily Vladimirovich Bartyakov. I am pianist. I study at Hochshule für Musik. Here. In Vienna."

Evan shook Bartyakov's hand. "Pleased to meet you, Vassily. I'm always happy to meet a musician. Do you know Caine's Piano Concerto?"

"Of course! I love it! We play it together, yes? A true honor for me to meet you, to talk with you – here, I give my phone number and—"

"Vasia, please let the Maestro—"

Bartyakov handed him a slip of paper. "Please you can call me anytime. Oh, so sorry. May I to introduce my girl-friend, Greta Fasching. She works for radio station Österreich Eins."

Evan cleared his throat as he shook her firm, dry hand. "I've been listening to your station while eating breakfast every morning this week, Ms. Fasching. Nice to meet you."

Serenity radiated out of her ebony eyes and warmed him. She smelled of roses. Her black hair fell in a thick braid down her back over a white silk Cossack blouse.

"I loved the concert, Maestro. Especially the Caine."

"Thank you. I've wanted to travel to Africa. What country are you from?"

"Austria, Maestro." She smiled. "My mother emigrated with her parents from Somalia when she was a young girl. Maestro, we wish you might remain here with us."

Evan nodded. "I'd *love* to stay in Vienna. Definitely."

"Maestro Quinn!" A Viennese matron of indeterminate age, dressed in teal brocade and her face thick with make-up, pushed past Greta and Bartyakov. She grasped Evan's hand and looked up at him. "You are the *greatest* conductor in the world!" the woman said in a loud, vibrato voice. "You must come to dinner tomorrow. You *must* hear my granddaughter play the violin."

He glanced past the woman to Richard, PDA in hand, leaning against the wall across the room.

Chapter 2

"Man, did you *see* her? She was a tank! All she needed was a string of Christmas lights to go with all those fake diamonds." Richard laughed.

"Be kind, Richard," Evan said. He shifted the garment bag containing his white tie and tails from one shoulder to the other. He, Dave, and Richard walked from the Musikverein toward the Ring Boulevard. The night sky had an orange tint; the air smelled of dust, flowers and perfume left in the wake of the elegant people who'd attended his concert and reception earlier.

"Ah, man, you are too nice to those people. I don't know how you do it."

"Exactly the way I do it for the two of you. You're human beings, right?"

"Duh. Yeeaah. But those people? I mean, they don't even speak English."

Evan smiled. A gentle, warm June breeze caressed his face and hair. His mood still soared on Caine's summer wind. "Sure, they do, Richard. They just don't want to speak English with you."

On Evan's left, the ghost of a smile flickered across Dave's lips. What time tonight would Dave stop by his room for the usual bed check?

Every concert night, Richard had waited with the impatience of a kid promised his favorite candy for Evan to go on stage, after which he'd sneak out to drink. He preferred to maintain close surveillance on women rather than Evan. Dave guarded the concert hall outside so that Evan could not slip away before or during a concert. Evan would never slip away from the audience or from music, especially Caine's music. He detested his AC escorts, but he respected Dave, his silence, the real danger he represented. To Dave, he was only another object for surveillance and control.

"OK, so why won't you come to my party tonight? We'll have non-alcoholic drinks for you. And lots of girls."

Richard, the party animal from Hoboken. Richard liked him too much to be a serious physical threat. Evan smiled. "I don't want to disappoint Dave. He works hard to hide them."

The smile settled on Dave's lips.

"You *got* to be kidding me! You're going to look for bugs *tonight*? If you're with me, some luscious little Fräulein will bug you."

"I'm tired, Richard. Wiped. I'm going to bed. Why not invite Dave? You both should enjoy your last night in Europe."

Dave grinned. They turned the corner onto the broad Ring Boulevard where the late evening bicycle, motor scooter and occasional sedan sped past with the clanging bell of a sleek silver streetcar.

Richard moaned in exasperation. "You are really too nice to people, Quinn. Someday, you're gonna wish you hadn't been so nice."

Dave laughed as he opened the Imperial Hotel's front

door. In the opulent and chandeliered lobby, Evan said good night to them. Richard headed for the bar, Dave for the hotel's concierge to re-confirm their flight the next morning and order a cab to take them to the airport as he'd done every night before a travel day, and Evan for the elevator and his room.

He dropped the garment bag on the king-sized bed covered by an ivory and pale gold spread that dominated his classic imperial style room on the fourth floor. Of course, the AC had refused to pay for a suite. He hadn't wanted one anyway.

Was he playing chicken with Murphy's Law tonight? The deal hadn't come with instructions. Anything could go wrong. He was nervous, afraid. He wanted freedom. He wanted music. He wanted to live, to feel alive. The watchdogs could never understand. They'd understand the means to achieve the end. One of his father's favorite sayings – by any means possible. Now, take the final step now. Make his move, now.

"*Fernseher.*"

The forty-inch LCD television embedded in the pale gold silk-draped wall opposite the bed flicked on projecting a holographic car that careened down a city hill into the room's air. The car struck a tanker truck at the bottom of the hill in a spectacular explosion.

"*Lauter,*" Evan said. "*Dreimal.*"

The volume increased, drowning out all other noise. Evan pressed a button in the wall between the TV and the computer monitor. A keyboard slid out of the wall under the monitor. He preferred to type, not touch screen. He'd been shocked to discover in London that European computers also responded to voice or touch screen commands. He'd heard rumors of such possibilities in America, but not for musicians. Way too expensive and government regulated. Only for the New Economic Party elite, the Neppers. He wasn't a gadget man anyway. He liked the European approach, the emphasis on humans rather than technology. A room service order for one bottle of Scotch whiskey appeared on the screen. He clicked on "submit." The order disappeared, replaced by "Thank you for your order. Time of service: 20 minutes." Yeah, he liked the Europeans' approach: you could choose what you wanted, and also choose not to have anything.

In each city on his tour, he'd declined web cam activation for his hotel room so that Dave could not watch him. When Dave objected, Evan had cited the high cost and the insurance each hotel charged to free them from any liability connected to the Web cam's use. The money saved had paid for Richard's parties.

Instead of a web cam, Dave had planted collar button-sized nearly transparent listening devices in weird places, hard to find places, challenging him. Changing cities, changing hotels often must have frustrated him. He couldn't install any of the newest generation semi-permanent bugs. So, he relied on the older types, the kind he had to attach to an object. Dave would never have thought to not plant any devices. His mind worked in a literal, straight line that followed orders to the letter. However, he suspected that Dave had made it nice and easy for him tonight. Not that "nice" could ever describe the guy.

Evan found the first bug inside the crystal chandelier.

He searched all the usual places: under furniture, telephone, behind pictures, inside the ivory and gold drapes, along the top of the bathroom and closet doors. He found four more bugs and dropped them on the table. Dave's favorite number: five.

He walked through the TV hologram, now a group of SWAT cops running toward a warehouse. European television had astounded him with not one, not five, but a *minimum* of one hundred *free* channels with a menu of anything you'd want to watch from movies, news and sports to shopping, games, and gambling. In America, the NEP wanted people working, not watching TV. He'd heard a fanciful rumor that at one time a paid television service had existed in America for everyone called "cable" that offered hundreds of channels. Evan had heard also that the rich NEP elite owned state of the art SAT HD digital televisions and the necessary chips to access the world. He wanted to believe that their access matched exactly what he'd enjoyed during the last month, especially the movie channels. He loved movies.

A room service waiter arrived with his Scotch. He accepted the tray at the door and signed the order slip. The waiter walked down the empty corridor. No sign of Dave.

Where to hide the Scotch? He opened the full wet bar. No room for a liter bottle. The mini-refrigerator. By laying the bottle on its side, he could slide it in next to a supply of real butter and containers of milk and yogurt. Dave had checked the room refrigerators at times, but probably not tonight. He'd shown Dave with his past behavior that he never touched their contents.

He ordered the TV to decrease its volume and switch off

the holographic function. He undressed. Following his habit, he left the light on in the bathroom and the door half open, the TV and bed stand light on. He slid under the bed covers.

"Europeans are *crazy* for classical," his Minneapolis AC rep had laughed when he'd assigned him the tour to London, Berlin, Paris, and Vienna. Yeah, the audiences had shown their craziness and appreciation, approval and love by filling the halls for his concerts. Europeans loved classical music. That intoxicated him with its possibilities. Nothing remained for him in America. The AC strangled classical music life in America with its arbitrary rules and demand for profit above all else.

Behind his closed eyelids, an image of the woods near his father's Minneapolis house came into focus like a movie on a screen. He and Paul Caine had played there often. Harold and his Vigiciv gang had ambushed them there often. Not a good memory.

October 2037. His national conducting debut with the St. Louis State Symphony as the assistant conductor. The guest conductor for the concert's global television broadcast had fallen ill (actually ISS had arrested him) and, as the cover conductor, he'd stepped in to conduct the concert. The cameras had creeped him out for the first five minutes, but then the music took over. The broadcast earned high global ratings. His profit potential increased one hundred percent for about a year which had not warranted a pay raise, according to the AC. The new Leonard Bernstein, the AC-approved critics had trumpeted. A real superstar for American classical music. Such as it was. Now, he let memory of the orchestra playing the cheerful opening of Beethoven's

Sixth Symphony under his baton lull him, soothe him into sleep.

The whiss of a keycard swipe at his door woke him. For a second, he forgot his plan and reached to turn off the light. He remembered, however, before the door opened and relaxed into a mimic of sleep.

Dave slid into the room, walked over to the bed, hovered by Evan for ten seconds. Dave sighed. He moved over to the table and Evan heard Dave scrape up the five listening devices. He turned off the bed stand light.

"You really need to stop watching this shit," Dave said in a stage whisper. "Television off."

Dave brushed past the bed. The door clicked closed. Evan opened his eyes. He was alone. His digital watch read 2:23 a.m.

"You are a true son of America." That bass voice spoke loud and clear from memory and propelled him out of bed.

He arranged the plump extra pillows and blankets from the closet in the bed to resemble a sleeping body. From his suitcase, he pulled an old brown tweed sport jacket, old canvas bush hat he'd worn fishing, and a yellow shirt. From the refrigerator, he took the Scotch.

In the bathroom, he dressed, ripping one sleeve of the tweed sport jacket at the shoulder. Standing in the bathtub, he doused his clothes with the Scotch, sprinkling it over his hair. Scotch dribbled down his neck, chest and back when he straightened. The bathroom stank. He switched on the ventilation fan and rinsed out the bathtub.

Back in the bedroom, Evan closed his suitcase, set it in the closet under the garment bag. His white tie and tails. His work clothes. Well, he needed a new one anyway. He closed the closet door.

After counting his remaining per diem money, he tucked the brown envelope into his inner breast pocket, along with his passport and a dog-eared black and white photograph of Joseph Caine standing next to a smiling Randall Quinn at a rough-hewn pine table cluttered with papers and books. He collected the quarter-full Scotch bottle from the bathroom and turned off the fan. At the door he surveyed the room, the "body" in the bed, satisfied everything appeared the way Dave had last seen it.

In the empty corridor, Evan listened. The elevator down the hallway groaned as a car passed the floor. He sensed no presence nor heard any footsteps softened by the brown and gold carpet. He headed for the back exit stairs.

On a deserted, shadowy Bösendorferstrasse, the vermilion and beige Musikverein concert hall loomed opposite the rear of the hotel. He checked to his left. On the street, stacked, bulging canvas bags supporting metal beams surrounded a mound of gravel and dirt. Beyond the dirt the hotel's three large garbage dumpsters stood like open fish mouths pointed at the night sky.

He stepped over the metal beams and rubbed dirt from the mound all over his face, hands and clothes. The first dumpster held recycled bottles. Paper and cardboard containers filled the second. The third stank and offered what he wanted: food waste. Thank you, Imperial Hotel, for collecting compost. He hid the Scotch bottle behind the dumpster and hoisted himself up and over its side, his feet sinking into the squishy muck. The hotel's back door burst open. He ducked down.

"*Scheisse*," a woman said.

Evan peered over the dumpster's side. A mini dress of transparent gold material shimmered over the woman's otherwise naked body. She riffled through her purse, muttering to herself, swaying on stiletto heels. Probably one of Richard's *Fräuleins*. She stumbled across the street, still looking in her purse, and headed away from him.

The garbage. Holding his breath, Evan smeared the rotting, slimy food on his face and rolled in it. When he climbed out of the dumpster, his eyes watered from the stench and he felt queasy. He retrieved the Scotch bottle.

Evan peeked around the hotel's corner. Halfway up Dumbastrasse, Dave leaned against the hotel, wearing the internet eyeglasses he'd bought in London and smoking an e-cigarette, nonchalant, confident, the only other human on the street. Although Evan had imagined this moment calmly many times, the reality cramped his stomach in terror. If he was wearing those gadget glasses and surfing the internet with a blink of his eyes, maybe Dave wouldn't notice him. Dave blew a cloud of nicotine vapor into the air.

A snatch of music came into Evan's mind, something his mother had sung to him in German when he was a boy. She'd told him it came from **Die Dreigroschenoper**, **The Three Penny Opera,** by Bertolt Brecht and Kurt Weill, and the dirge-like ballad told the story of a dangerous man, a shark of a killer. At Juilliard, he'd learned the song's jazzy American version in English: "Mack the Knife."

Evan pulled the old bush hat down on his forehead and

stooped as he ambled like a drunk across the sidewalk under a streetlight. He sang in German about the shark with razor teeth. Out of the corner of his eye, he saw Dave straighten with interest.

"Hey!"

Evan swayed across the street, swinging the Scotch bottle, slurring the song louder, the part about a corpse on the street and a shadow flitting around a corner, as he reached the opposite curb.

"Hey, you bum!" Dave laughed. "How about some action?"

First time he'd heard the guy laugh. So this was entertainment to this watchdog. Whatever he'd been watching on his gadget glasses must have bored him. Dave's jogging footsteps approached. He couldn't react, couldn't show his face. Dave shoved him to the ground. The click of Dave's switchblade punctuated his glee.

"Let's rumble, man."

Evan hid his face, whimpered into his hunched shoulder as Dave grabbed him.

"Oh! You stink!" Dave released him and backed away with, "Drunken shit. Back home, I'd call a street cleaner van for you." He slapped his hand on his jeans, rubbing it against the denim.

Evan's heart hammered his sternum sending pain through his chest. His whole body had gone weak and wobbly. He crawled to the next corner where he used a building wall to steady himself as he stood. He looked back. Dave walked toward the hotel, throwing stones at the Musikverein. The gadget glasses flashed light from the street lamp. Dave had believed he was a drunken bum. Evan breathed deeply and walked slowly to calm his heart. Shadows. Everywhere shadows.

The dark matter of souls leaked into shadows. Street shadows stretched out, grabbed at him, caressed his face. The streetlights deepened their blackness, elongated them, threw them into corners and against walls, but never disconnected them from the buildings, window ledges, and doorways. Shadows hid the secrets of the past, the memories. Evan wanted to forget, sever his past, the shadows in his mind, and abandon them behind closed American borders.

He'd wanted to leave America since the summer he was ten years old, the summer of Uncle Joe's arrest and death, to be free to conduct Uncle Joe's music. Away from the shadows. No more shadows.

"Your son's dead the minute he steps back onto American soil." The ISS cop had been clear on the audio recording that Dave had played for him in London. The proof of his father's death. He wouldn't give them the satisfaction of his own death.

Evan arrived at the brighter Ring Boulevard, curved and tree-lined, it encircled Vienna's oldest district. The State Opera House stood diagonally left across the boulevard, its French Renaissance façade decorated with rectangular red-and-white banners billowing in the gentle night breeze, just like the photo in his tour guide. First time out alone in Vienna, on his own. Evan stumbled over streetcar tracks as he crossed to the other side where he stubbed his toe on the curb. At this time of night, nothing traveled on the boulevard. The world felt strange, surreal to him. Well, the middle of the night will do that to a city.

At the first decorative garbage bin on the Ring, Evan tossed in the Scotch bottle. He needed an information kiosk. Heading north, he found one by the Volksgarten, a park opposite the Greek Revival Parliament building. The tall, circular kiosk's computer sensed him and lit up. He checked around. He was alone.

"*Guten Abend. Ihre Frage, bitte?*" the computer's female voice said.

Out of the corner of his right eye, Evan spotted a white van driving toward him. It appeared old, like from the 1990's, and he hadn't seen any old vehicles like that before in Vienna.

"Where is the nearest police station?" he asked the kiosk computer. He felt lightheaded, separate from the moment and himself as if he occupied a stranger's body.

The white van approached as the street shimmied in front of him, wobbling the ivory Parliament, the green City Hall Park and in the distance, the dark gothic City Hall, on a sea of asphalt, stone, and glinting streetcar tracks. He closed his eyes, shook his head to clear his vision. When he opened his eyes, he saw the van, its black windows, like in a dream, no sound, slow motion. A street cleaner van. He ducked behind the kiosk. They had street cleaner vans here?

"The nearest police station to this location," the kiosk computer said in English, "is through the Volksgarten on your right to Löwelstrasse, and turn right on Löwelstrasse and walk thirty meters. The police station is on the left. Thank you for your inquiry. Good night."

Evan peeked around the kiosk. The white van backed up toward him as if his past backed up to snatch him off the street and make him disappear. He turned to run and collided with a young, fair-haired Viennese cop, crisp and clean in his dark river blue uniform.

"*Na, ja? Was ist los?*" the cop said.

Evan glanced back. The white van had disappeared. The street appeared normal. He took a deep breath.

"*Sind Sie betrunken?*"

Evan landed a right hook on the cop's left jaw. The cop fell back, catching himself by grabbing a chrome ledge on the kiosk.

"*Sind Sie verrückt?*"

"Arrest me." Evan massaged his hand. That right hook had hurt.

"You speak English. You are English? Are you drunk? What are you doing? You know it is serious offense to hit a policeman?"

"I'm counting on it."

The cop sniffed at Evan's garbage and Scotch-soaked clothes. His nose crinkled up. "*Mein Gott.* Your identification, please."

"I'll show my identification to your supervisor. At the station."

The Viennese cop, rubbing his jaw, shook his head. "Your papers, please."

"Your supervisor."

Across the street, a couple with matching purple hair in spikes walked past the Parliament, gawking in their direction.

"Look, Officer. I hit you. Take me in."

The cop grabbed his arm but thought better of it, smelling his hand, shaking bits of garbage off it. "*Mein Gott.* You

English are crazy. Out drunk on the street when you should be home sleeping in bed. Come with me."

The Viennese cop led him to the police station on Löwel-strasse. In America, it's easier to enter a police station than to leave one, thanks to Internal Security Services. Had Austria its own Internal Security Services? Probably, if they had street cleaner vans. He must keep his thoughts to himself, not say more than necessary.

Their footsteps echoed in the station's reception foyer. Behind a gleaming white counter, a uniformed cop frowned at them. He wore the experience of street fights on his face.

"*Na, ja, Fritzi, was ist los mit ihm?*" the counter cop said as they stopped in front of him. He caught a whiff and winced at Evan.

"I defect," Evan said. "*Ich möchte politische Asyl.*"

The young cop stared at him open-mouthed.

"*Was ist los*, Fritzi?"

"*Er hat mich mit der Faust geschlagen.*"

"Yeah, I hit him to make certain he brought me here and he'd protect me. I'm not drunk. My name is Evan Quinn. I'm an American, a musician. I request political asylum." He slid his passport across the counter. "Please do not call the American Consulate or Embassy."

"But you are English," Fritzi said. "Not American. And you speak German. Americans do not speak foreign languages."

"Of course, Fritzi," the older cop said with the sarcasm reserved for youth. "Americans speak only Amerikanish." He opened Evan's passport. His eyes widened. He looked at Evan, and back at the passport. "Come with me."

Chapter 3

The interview room smelled of lemon disinfectant. Evan sang the opening theme of Beethoven's Sixth Symphony to himself as he squeezed a lemon slice over his steaming mug of tea from the breakfast tray a uniformed cop had brought in two minutes earlier. The cops had made him a Semmel roll sandwich to accompany the tea.

They had insisted he shower to remove the foul garbage, then had given him pale blue pajama-type shirt and pants to wear with terry cloth slippers. In response to his questions about the process for political asylum, they had said, "Inspector Leiner will talk to you." Their deference had surprised and unnerved him. He'd expected a good roughing up as American cops would have given him.

He expected also that the mirror spanning the opposite wall provided a view of him seated at the gray metal table to anyone behind it in the adjacent room, a room he imagined as bare and celadon and devoid of character as the interview room.

They had brought him there to wait for the Inspector. He took a bite of the Semmel sandwich. His stomach cramped as he chewed. He'd had no sleep, but felt wired and his nerves buzzed. Singing Beethoven calmed him. He faced the unknown. He needed to remain calm and alert. Focused.

This may be the most important interview of his life. Freedom waited on the other side of it. He must convince them, reassure them that he was an orchestra conductor, a musician, and nothing else. He must keep his secret – the deal he'd made – to himself. He could not fail. If the Austrians deported him to America, it meant death. He expected the Inspector would want to deport him. He'd fight the Inspector's skepticism, suspicion, and the need to protect Austria's national security with the truth and cooperation.

The Semmel sandwich tasted good, a tough chewy crust and tender bread inside with sweet salami and Swiss cheese. Mustard would have topped it off with a delicious zing. He ran his fingers through his damp hair. His index fingertip touched a tiny lump behind his left ear. No one could see it without first knowing it was there. The replacement Nepper tracking chip for the one a doctor had inserted when he was twelve years old in the school nurse's office. His father had raged about it but every Underground doctor had told them not to remove it. His father could be arrested for removing it. The chip had entered Evan's existence into the Nepper tracking system like everyone else and contributed to establishing his clean civic status as he matured.

He studied the mirror. The people behind it – how many? – couldn't know what he'd touched behind his ear or his thoughts. They must never know about the chip. He hoped that the Americans at the Embassy wouldn't think of it. One of the first tasks after the Austrians released him: find a doctor to remove it. Under the table and in secret. He sang Beethoven again to calm his nerves.

The door opened. A trim, ordinary man with blonde

hair in need of a cut and a dark blonde moustache entered. He wore a gray suit and stood five feet eight or nine inches tall but seemed taller with his confident bearing like someone who had mastered his own shadows and lived in light. His intelligent gray eyes betrayed world-weariness behind their alert interest. Evan guessed his age as mid- to late forties. "Good morning, Herr Quinn. I am Inspector Klaus Leiner."

A faint British inflection smoothed Leiner's German-accented English and his tenor voice. He didn't appear threatening, but Evan felt wary, looking for signs of a trap.

"Are you with Internal Security Services?" Evan said.

"We are security but not the same as the American ISS. We have heard of the ISS and its methods and I can assure you that we have no organization like it here. My section is responsible for all police situations that involve foreigners in Austria." Leiner unbuttoned his suit jacket and sat down opposite Evan. "So. Your case has been referred to us. How are you feeling, Herr Quinn? Do you require a doctor?"

"No, I'm fine. I was hungry, but the cops here made me breakfast."

"Good." Leiner pulled a palm-sized computer from his jacket pocket and tapped its screen. It lit up. He tapped on it for a minute, then set it on the table to his right. "Inspector Klaus Leiner present at seven-thirty-three on Sunday morning, June 14, 2048, with Evan Quinn, passport American, who has requested political asylum from Austria. Is that correct, Herr Quinn?"

"Correct. I request political asylum." Evan glanced around the room. "Where's the audio recorder? I don't see anything that—"

"The entire interview room is programmed for recording, audio or video. You will not see any equipment, Herr Quinn."

Evan nodded. "Did the cops call the American Consulate? I asked them not to."

"They called me, Herr Quinn." Leiner sat back, his gray eyes focused on Evan as if studying a new species. "They told me you needed clothes and now I see that for myself. They're using your room keycard to retrieve your luggage at the Imperial Hotel. Please state your full name, birth date, place of residence on your passport."

He'd forgotten – must have pocketed the room keycard out of habit. The cops must have gone through his clothes.

"Evan Quinn. May 11, 2013. Minneapolis, Minnesota, in America. What about my Arts Council escorts?"

"Ah. Yes. They reported to us, and I assume the American Embassy, that you had disappeared and they suspected someone had kidnapped you."

"Kidnapped," Evan snorted. All his good behavior on tour had fooled them. Even Dave.

"Not an unreasonable conclusion, Herr Quinn. Especially with the Chinese-American talks occurring now in Vienna. The Americans have requested our assistance."

"Please tell them I've defected and I'm never going back to America. I want to be free."

Leiner nodded, his eyes on Evan. "The night shift officers reported that you spoke and understood German. Where have you learned German?" His eyes bore into Evan's.

The cop's sharp tone warned him. Careful. Leiner wanted to test him, his honesty. To protect Austria's security. "Are you a native Austrian, Inspector?" He smiled, leaned forward to show his interest.

Leiner's eyes widened slightly. "I was born in Vienna and have lived here all my life, Herr Quinn. Have you lived in Austria or Germany?"

Evan shook his head, no, and sipped his tea before answering. "My mother studied in Munich during college. She taught German in high school until the Neppers restricted foreign language instruction. She spoke German to me from my birth. She wanted a bilingual child."

"Wasn't that dangerous, Herr Quinn?"

"When she began, no. After the Neppers consolidated their power, when I was about five, yeah. We kept it secret. My father knew, the Caines knew, no one else."

Leiner sat back in his chair. "How old were you when your mother stopped your German instruction?"

Evan frowned. "It's in my bio. I was eleven when she committed suicide." His chest tightened. Twenty-four years after her death he still felt the pain.

"You ended your German study?"

"My father found a guy who had taught German at the University of Minnesota. They made an exchange. The Professor continued my secret German lessons for a regular supply of a certain drug the Medical Council had denied his wife. My father got it for him from Canada through his connections. We kept my studies secret until I entered Juilliard. By then, I only needed to maintain my German. The AC and Education Council wanted to know, of course, like you, how I could speak German. They knew my mother's background. I told them about her instruction but not the

Professor's. They accepted it. They couldn't punish her. She was dead. The barn door was already closed."

Leiner had not moved during Evan's explanation. Now he frowned, shifted in his chair. "The barn door?"

"An expression."

Leiner sighed, smoothed his moustache in two quick sweeps of his fingers. Leiner's hands were clean but rough, familiar with manual labor. "Yes, Herr Quinn, I have read your bio, but I read nothing in it about your proficiency in German. What other languages do you speak?"

Evan shrugged. "I studied Italian for a year at Juilliard for my music. That's it. I don't really read or speak Italian very well."

"*Prima*. Fine. What I don't understand, what is quite odd for someone of your position, is the two-year gap in your professional activities, from 2044 to '46. Where were you, Herr Quinn?"

He must convince the cop. Evan sipped his tea. He would go insane without music. "A problem, Herr Quinn?"

It felt like Leiner's eyes had grasped his throat. Evan shook his head. "It's not a pleasant memory," he said. His eyes met Leiner's. "I was incarcerated."

"Why?" Leiner sat up. "Where?"

"You can see why it's not in my bio, Inspector. The Arts Council demands a façade of respectability which doesn't include the truth if the truth might hurt them. I was under strict orders, and guarded closely by my AC escorts, not to talk about it during interviews on the tour."

"Why were you arrested, Herr Quinn? We know that

your father is a leader in the dissident Underground. Were you also in the Underground?"

"My father wouldn't allow it." He pushed back his chair and stood up, walked over to the mirror. His reflection showed a pale face with the shadow of a black beard. He spoke to whoever stood behind the mirror as well as Leiner. "The past and my name makes me nothing in America."

"You are a human being, Herr Quinn," Leiner said, his tone warm and firm. "You cannot believe—"

Evan laughed, pivoting to face the Austrian cop at the table. "Because of my father. It was like a mark on my forehead, the mark of unacceptability. I give him credit for one thing: he kept his promises to Uncle Joe, you know, Joseph Caine."

"Also, Caine was a leader in the dissident Underground."

"With a big mouth. He taunted the AC, the NEP, the ISS, in public and with his music. He was fearless, totally out there. And he paid for it. But he made my father promise."

"Promise what?"

He believed he'd captured Leiner's essential emotional and intellectual attention. Leiner would comprehend and believe the truth now. "My father promised Uncle Joe that he'd distance himself from me, protect me by demonstrating our only connection was biological, so I could pursue music. It began even before Uncle Joe's arrest. My father insisted that I do what I was told, attend civic meetings, join LOT – 'Leaders of Tomorrow,' like a junior NEP – and join the New Economic Party."

"You are now a New Economic Party member?"

Leiner's tone had sharpened again. Evan paced around

the table. "Yes. In order to work. A membership of convenience. I don't agree with their ideology or policies. But membership is crucial for a clean civic status. My father's goal, Inspector. That I maintain a clean civic status, unconnected from him." Evan spun on his toes to face Leiner. "I don't need it anymore. If I had my wallet, I'd gladly surrender my NEP card to you."

"Your father must have been quite unhappy when you were arrested." Leiner's tone taunted him.

Evan noted Leiner spoke excellent English, even picking up on nuances. A surprise Leiner had chosen English for this interview and not German to test him. Evan placed both hands flat on the table opposite Leiner and leaned toward him. "He was furious. All that hard work down the drain." Evan threw up his hands. "There hadn't been an opera company in Chicago for twenty years. A young composer I knew, Timothy York, had written an opera of Shakespeare's **As You Like It**. A good opera. Following the rules, he submitted it for AC review and approval. While he waited, he showed it to the Met but they didn't want it. He decided to re-establish an opera company in Chicago where he lived. He invited me to conduct. He found a theater, backers, singers, and we had put together an orchestra and crew when the Arts Council got wind of it."

A knock on the door interrupted him. A uniformed cop entered carrying his garment bag, suitcase, and a clear plastic bag of his personal belongings they'd taken from him the night before. Leiner waved to the corner. The cop deposited them there and left. In the silence, Evan listened to his pulse pumping in his ears. He sat down opposite Leiner.

"Go on, Herr Quinn. The Arts Council?"

"Found out about it." Evan smiled. "We were all arrested."

"But why arrest you? The punishment does not fit the crime."

"Exactly." Unable to sit still, Evan got up and paced to quell his nervous energy. "In America, everyone's crazy about Shakespeare, Inspector. Theaters produce at least two, often three, of his plays each season in the major metro areas. State television airs shows based on his plays. Wedding classical music to Shakespeare created the potential for a surefire hit, we thought. The AC disagreed but only because they hadn't thought of it first." Evan laughed, the sound soured by bitterness. "They arrested us for our individual innovation and initiative."

"Yes, we have observed the American belief that their way is the only way," Leiner said. "They are right and everyone else is wrong. They have all the best people, culture, products, research, *und so weiter*, in America and anyone else's is inferior. Common American thinking and behavior since the middle of the last century. Of course, sometimes they are right."

"But it's not America, it's the Neppers, Inspector. In 2018, when they established a permanent majority in the government, they acquired the power to do whatever they wanted which included banning music, books, art or plays they didn't like or wasn't profitable for them. Or blacklisting artists like Uncle Joe and my father, who hasn't published in America since I was four years old. Samizdat of his books circulate underground. But you see why I request political asylum? I cannot live under the oppression and persecution of artists that exist in America now. I cannot work as a musician and conductor. I fear for my safety, my security and my life."

Leiner nodded. Evan thought he glimpsed sympathy in his eyes. "After the ISS arrested you, what happened?"

Evan continued his circular tour of the room as he spoke. "Yeah, finish the story, Quinn." He laughed, a nervous bubbling sound. "Tim – the composer – hanged himself in jail before his arraignment. Broke my heart. He was a talented musician, a good friend. The rest of us had the usual speedy trial in front of a judge, no jury, with inadequate defense, and were packed off to prison. I resided at the Redfield Federal Penitentiary in northern Minnesota until June 2046."

"Isn't it NEP policy to blacklist an artist after his release from prison? Why allow you to return to your job at the Minneapolis State Symphony?"

Evan nodded, glancing at the mirror. "They haven't blacklisted all ex-cons in the past. I hadn't been the organizer, only a participant. My civic status was clean. I'd behaved well in prison. I'd done what I was told to do. But I was surprised the NEP cleared me for a European tour. Then the ISS arrested and executed my father which doesn't make sense."

"What?" Leiner froze in his chair, his expression a mixture of shock, disbelief, and horror. "Nothing's been reported in—"

"I know." Evan sat down opposite Leiner and encircled his mug of cold tea with his hands. "The AC escort who joined us in London played an audio recording for me. The day I left Minneapolis for London, the ISS went to our house and arrested my father for treason. They had to have concrete evidence, so they must have obtained it elsewhere because my father kept nothing about the Underground at home. Although they found a safe behind a picture in his study. It held papers but no one on the recording described them. My father fought them but I don't believe he had a weapon. On the recording, two agents shouted first he went for ISS Lt. Harold Smith's gun, then he had a knife. But I don't believe that. I believe they carried orders to murder him, and made it sound like he had a weapon." Of course, ISS Lt. Harold Smith, Sr. was there. Harold's dad. Like father, like son.

"*Gott im Himmel.*" Leiner shook his head. "Why not tell us this earlier, Herr Quinn?"

"I didn't think you'd believe me until I'd had a chance to tell you all the other stuff. There's been nothing official announcing his death and probably won't be until it's safe and profitable for the NEP." A memory of running so fast his chest hurt from gasping air, running down the path in the woods to the curve by the yellow birch, running away from Harold and his Vigiciv gang, running away from the clearing where they'd tied him to a tree to burn him alive. Please, believe me. This interview was harder than he'd expected. Had they sensors in the room to monitor his physical condition? He looked at Leiner whose eyes rested on the mirror.

"We will need to verify everything that you have said, Herr Quinn."

"I understand."

"I have read your father's poetry, his novels, his memoir of Joseph Caine. He was a popular, bestselling writer in America before 2017."

"The people protected him for years because of that. Uncle Joe told me once that my father had sold more books with his first novel, **Revolution**, than Stephen King had with his first five books."

"Your father's work remains popular – profitable – in the global community." Leiner's wry smile underscored his sardonic tone.

Evan smiled. "The NEP will find some way to get that profit."

"You are right." Leiner heaved a deep sigh. "It makes no sense to kill him. Arrest him, yes. Use him as a hostage to insure your return. Killing him insures nothing."

"Except his silence," Evan said. He sipped cold tea. "One other thing on that recording, Inspector. An ISS cop said I'd be dead the minute I was back in America."

Leiner nodded, but regarded him with skeptical eyes. "But you made money for them. You could make more."

The laugh came slow and steady, from the core of Evan's chest, gaining speed and rising like an arpeggio. He left his chair again to walk around the room, glancing at the mirror, as his laughter subsided into a sigh.

"That's true, Inspector. It doesn't make sense to reasonable, rational people. But killing my father made no sense either, except – and only – in terms of the insurgency they're fighting and his Underground activities. I'm sure they'd find some way to charge me with treason. I conducted banned music here. Or maybe they'd create the evidence they need. I'm not as popular as my father. The NEP hates me, too, I expect."

Leiner nodded as if his head were almost too heavy. The skepticism, however, had disappeared from his eyes. Evan sensed success.

"Herr Quinn, why have you waited so long? Why not defect in London?"

Evan returned to his chair, extended his arms out on the table toward the cop. "I couldn't disappoint all the audiences in Berlin, Paris and here. If I'd defected in London, the NEP would have cancelled the rest of the tour. My AC watchdogs would've expected me to try something in London because of my father's death. I needed to build their trust and confidence in me so I could slip away like I did here."

"Why should Austria grant you asylum?"

The question angered Evan. "You mean, besides the fact that ISS has threatened my life and killed my father?"

"Where is this audio recording, Herr Quinn? Where is your evidence?"

"I asked for a copy of it but my request was denied by Washington. I have no proof, Inspector. Only my word that I'm telling you the truth. If you ask the Embassy, I'm sure they'll deny everything. At least until Washington can plausibly announce my father died of natural causes or was caught in the crossfire of a convenience store robbery." Maybe he hadn't convinced the cop after all.

Leiner nodded, his eyes glancing to the mirror. Someone behind the mirror must be checking what he said as they talked.

"Have you other family in America?"

Evan shook his head. "They were killed during the First Purification resisting the Neppers." Evan sat back in his chair and picked up his mug. "Look, about my hitting that cop last night. What do I need to do to resolve—"

Leiner waved his hand as if swatting a fly. "No charges. I understand that you apologized to the young officer."

Evan nodded. "My request for political asylum?"

"We have a process, Herr Quinn. The process requires time. I am concerned about your security. Would you agree to remain in our custody for a week or two?"

"I'm concerned about my security, too, especially staying out of the Americans' hands. My defection will embarrass them. They'd snatch me back or kill me if they got the opportunity. So, yeah, I agree. Here in this police station?"

"No. We will move you to a safe house in the country." Leiner tapped the palm-sized computer's screen. "Interview with Evan Quinn terminated by Inspector Klaus Leiner at nine-sixteen in the morning, Sunday, June 14, 2048. Transcript copy to Dieter Aschenbeck at the Interior Ministry. *Danke*."

"Have you also videotaped my interview, Inspector?" Evan flashed him one of his public persona smiles.

Leiner shook his head, but something flickered in his eyes as he smiled back. "If you need anything, please tell the officer outside the door."

"Could I get fresh hot tea and another sandwich? Maybe a place to change my clothes and take a nap?"

"I'll tell them." Leiner held out his hand to Evan. "I loved the Caine symphony last night, Herr Quinn."

"Thanks, Inspector." He shook Leiner's hand and watched him leave. The first interview was done. Had the Austrian cop believed him? He felt that he hadn't measured up to him. No hope or reassurance from the guy. He had answered all the questions and volunteered nothing that might decrease his chances for freedom. He hated not knowing for certain if he'd succeeded.

A knock on the door and a uniformed cop entered carrying another breakfast tray.

"*Na, ja*, Klaus, what do you think?"

Leiner closed the door to the room behind the mirror, a comfortable conference room with subdued light, where Dieter Aschenbeck had observed the interview. He looked at the Interior Ministry lawyer seated at the table, sipping coffee by a laptop computer.

Aschenbeck's precision in all things showed in his perfectly styled auburn hair, trimmed beard, and his impeccable suit.

A tray of assorted pastries dominated the center of the table. Leiner picked up a lemon-filled croissant.

"Klaus. What would Eva say?"

Dieter's clipped German was also impeccable. He'd never hear a word of *Wienerisch* out of Dieter's mouth. "She would remind me of my cholesterol level and tell me to work out more." Leiner ate half the pastry in one bite. "You ordered them?"

"No. Gert has me on a low-carbohydrate diet. No sugar."

"Our guest thought we would videotape him. An interesting thought, *nicht*?"

He and Dieter looked at Evan in the interview room, eating the Semmel roll sandwich.

"I checked his parents on the internet, Klaus. His black hair and brown eyes resemble his mother, as I suspected. She was half Spanish. So, he is a legitimate son of Quinn's."

"*Why* would he ask about videotape if he's innocent?" Klaus smoothed his moustache, ignoring Dieter's triumphant smile. Klaus now owed him twenty euros.

"He's a brilliant musician and conductor, Klaus. He has had experience with media interviews. Why wouldn't he ask about filming the interview? He did not ask if we monitored his physical responses. That would have been quite different."

"Ah, my friend," Leiner sighed. "We know, *we know*, who the NEP in America allows to learn a foreign language and who not. He admitted he's an NEP member, but he's not a foreign service diplomat, not working for the Commerce Council. That leaves—"

"The CIA. Impossible."

"He speaks German, Dieter. He has a two-year gap in his life when he says he was in prison. He could have been trained during that time. He must have made a deal with them in order to regain his life and career. And we know, since the NEP took over America thirty years ago, every American defector has been a spy. This one is no different."

"Not every American defector. What about Martin Block in France? Hanna Yager in London five years ago? What motivation does Evan have to spy for the Americans? You heard him, Klaus. The ISS threatened his life. They arrested him for involvement in an opera, *mein Gott*." Dieter nodded to the computer. "Ottawa, Los Angeles, and Mexico City all verify what he told us. Except about Randall Quinn's death. Their sources say Randall is alive and well in Minneapolis."

Leiner shook his head as he sat down. "Even his incarceration?"

"*Ja, ja*," Dieter said. "He's right that they would not release news of his father's death in order to protect themselves. They've done it in the past with others. I'll process Evan's asylum request myself."

Leiner watched Evan lift his suitcase onto the interview room table. He'd ordered the two cops who went to the hotel to search the luggage. If they'd found anything, they would not have delivered it. Evan emptied the suitcase on to the table, singing to himself. "Dieter, I want to find out what this American is doing here and stop him before he causes any damage."

Dieter shut the laptop. Leiner looked at him, eyebrows raised in question.

"Your operations to catch spies in the past have been successful and quick. For the usual security reasons, investigate Evan Quinn as you would any émigré."

"*Prima*. Fine."

"You will need irrefutable, concrete evidence. You have the summer. Personally, Klaus, I doubt you'll find anything. What is he singing? Beethoven?"

"They all made a mistake. This one will, too."

Dieter stood up, tucking the laptop under his arm. "Additionally, I will contact the American Embassy and inform them of his defection. Which safe house?"

Leiner watched Evan choose a pair of jeans and a T-shirt from the pile on the table. "Neusiedl am See."

Chapter 4

"He has real bullets?" Evan eyed the plainclothes cop that sat in a wood chair on the back door's threshold. A shoulder holster cradled a gun under the long white sleeve of his left arm.

"For your protection," Leiner said, buttering toast. "As I said last night when we arrived, you are not to leave the house unless one of us accompanies you."

Evan and Klaus Leiner sat at the square table covered with a red and blue floral vinyl tablecloth in the safe house's clean but cramped kitchen. The safe house reminded Evan of a cabin he, Paul, Uncle Joe and his father had used on fishing and hunting trips but this cottage contained furniture, old appliances, and window shades.

"Are you or any of the guards runners?" Evan said, lifting a fork of fried egg to his mouth. "I usually run three to four miles every morning. We're out in the country. I'm sure it'd be safe to run if a guard ran with me."

"No." Leiner bit into his toast, spraying crumbs onto his pale-yellow shirt.

"Well, if I can't run, I need to get back to work. I could phone Vienna Philharmonic musicians or an artist manager I know in London. They could send me scores."

"No." Leiner set down his coffee cup. "You won't be here for longer than a week or two."

"There's no TV or radio, no computer, no books, no piano. What am I supposed to do?"

Leiner chuckled, a giddy, boyish sound. "Your comment reminds me of something my youngest daughter would say, Herr Quinn. We shall keep you quite busy with your debriefing."

"You'll live here, too?" Leiner's comment about his youngest daughter irritated him but he hid it. In fact, this whole safe house scene irritated him, but he must keep his cool. He'd expected at least a piano he could play to pass the time.

"Yes, Herr Quinn. I shall live here with you to insure maximum time for our talks."

"Terrific."

After breakfast, Leiner settled in the front room to work his phone and the guard, who said his name was Marco, took Evan outdoors. Marco showed him the surveillance shed, a small barn-like structure without windows and painted robin's egg blue like the cottage. Inside, two technicians monitored an array of screens on one wall showing different exterior angles to the property and cottage, including the access road. The opposite wall's screens contained interior views of the cottage, including Evan's bedroom. They wanted him to feel safe. They'd videotape his life and the Inspector's debriefing sessions with him. Would they monitor his physical responses as well like the ISS?

Just breathe. Stay calm. They knew a lot but not his secret. He focused on what he wanted: music and freedom, thinking these words over and over in a mind mantra.

Behind the shed stood a grove of maple, oak and beech trees with underbrush, the only concentration of trees nearby. Green vineyards flanked the property. The faint breeze wafted the scent of newly mown grass. In the front yard, they stopped by a glass and black iron patio table with black iron chairs arranged under a massive oak tree. Beyond the gentle grassy slope below them, Neusiedl Lake reflected the cottony cumulus clouds in the sky like a mirror this hot June morning. He liked being near water, the lakes of Minneapolis, the Mississippi River, and the lake up north in Minnesota, but vineyards and a fence blocked access to this Austrian lake a quarter of a mile away.

Farther away, at the lake's north end, a white haze of humidity paled the blue sky over the town of Neusiedl am See. They had driven through the town the afternoon before. He'd seen a whole pig dangling snout down and dripping blood surrounded by a bounty of meat in the window of a butcher shop; window boxes full of red, white, blue, yellow and purple flowers against walls of gray stucco with fresh white trim; green grocers, clothing boutiques, and book stores; and sidewalk vendors selling flowers, ice cream or grilled sausage from carts under red and white striped umbrellas. All signs of abundance and prosperity that affirmed he was no longer in America, now known as the land of sacrifice and scrounging, and still the land of the American Dream, the illusion fed to people that they could succeed and join the wealthy Nepper elite as long as they worked hard and obeyed the rules.

Uncle Joe had told him when he was eight about the "American Dream." Far in the past, it had been a true dream for a better life and possible to achieve. People had worked hard to keep a good job with security and financial success, to own a house, and enjoy the comforts of family and friends, all in freedom and safety. Anyone could achieve the American Dream if he worked hard enough and saved his money.

Over time, the dream had become corrupted, as relevant for illegal drug dealer entrepreneurs as for legitimate businessmen, and from there had become a dream only of obtaining wealth and a position of domination. Money was power. Uncle Joe had told him that hunger for power had killed the "American Dream."

Evan's dream had never been American, that is, about money, but Music, a country without land or borders, the country of sound and passion. At his first orchestra concert when he was six years old, the conductor had mesmerized him, his hands painting the sounds right before his eyes, and he'd known in his bones that he wanted to do that too. His father had wanted him to study music but become an accountant, a profession that held the keys to every Nepper's favorite bank account. Only Uncle Joe had believed in his dream of Music.

The light breeze off the lake ruffled his hair. He closed his eyes to visualize Uncle Joe at the piano, his baritone voice singing with the Gigue, a flash of blue from his eyes and gold from his ear. His kind, calming smile. He had hunched over the keyboard, his long, lean body curved in a capital "C." Uncle Joe calmed him. He had felt safe and loved always with him. The Gigue's angular fugue theme from Bach's Sixth Partita played as Uncle Joe's long, bony fingers depressed the piano keys in his mind.

"Herr Quinn?" Marco's voice interrupted the music.

Evan opened his eyes, turned around. He saw the Inspector standing in the open doorway, a mug in his hand.

The cottage's front room contained a worn couch upholstered in midnight blue corduroy and positioned under the bay windows that faced the lake. A threadbare carpet of variegated blues covered the floor. Evan plopped down on the couch and watched Leiner tap on the palm-sized computer and set it on the coffee table in front of him. He apparently needed to cue the recording with the palm-sized computer. The Inspector followed the police interview procedure with precision: names of participants, date and time, and the note that they also filmed the interview.

"Are you comfortable, Herr Quinn?"

Evan nodded. "This place smells musty. Who cleans a safe house? You can't hire just any cleaning service, right?"

Leiner's eyebrows rose. "I can assure you, Herr Quinn, all the rooms in this house are quite clean." He opened the side window and the front door opposite to catch the fresh breeze.

"That's better. Thanks. What do you want to know this morning, Inspector? I can tell you that music deprivation will drive me crazy. What about a radio? Please?"

Leiner sat down in a plump midnight blue corduroy wing chair opposite Evan. "A radio perhaps. Herr Quinn, your relationship with your father."

"What relationship?"

"He wanted you to have a clean civic status. He protected you."

Evan snorted. "I suppose. We weren't close."

"When you talk about him, often you sound angry."

"I don't want to talk about him. He's dead. His murder was a warning to me."

"Were you ever in the care of a psychiatrist?"

"NO!" Evan's loud vehemence made Leiner start in his chair. "Are you kidding? The Neppers use them and psycho-therapists for brainwashing. If you're not thinking the way they want you to think, behaving the way they want you to behave, they give you a psych sentence at a mental hospital which is really a prison. I did what I was told. I kept my mouth shut and I never, ever let anyone know what I really thought or believed. I wanted to conduct, so I focused on working toward that goal, inside and outside of school." Did Leiner believe the NEP had brainwashed him? He wouldn't be caught within fifty miles of a mental hospital or a psychiatrist.

Leiner shifted in his chair, his eyes alert and locked on Evan. "Who were the informants?"

Evan shrugged, stretched out his legs. "Not me. Vigiciv gangs, snitches at work. But everyone watched everyone else to a certain extent as a matter of survival. The NEP ordered people to report terrorists or suspected terrorist activity, insurgent or Underground activity. You never knew who around you whispered into the long bunny ears of power. Then the street cleaner vans could snatch you off the street. If you informed, sometimes you could bargain for a better life. But I knew that I couldn't do that and still work toward my goal. Everyone knew how brutally the Underground dealt with snitches if they caught them."

Evan felt a surge of impatience. Leiner's expression never

seemed to change. Why was the Inspector asking him *these* questions?

"Tell me about the street cleaner vans." Leiner nodded to Marco as he set a tray of tea pot and mugs on the coffee table and poured each of them a mug of fresh hot tea before leaving.

"You have them. I saw one in Vienna the night I defected."

Leiner went completely still.

"You already know—"

"No, Herr Quinn. We do not have street cleaner vans. You must have seen a van that appeared similar."

Evan stared at Leiner. Yeah, right. Of course he couldn't tell him. Or maybe the Americans operated one without the Austrians' knowledge.

"Please tell me about American street cleaner vans."

"OK. The ISS preferred white vans with all the windows painted or tinted black, front and rear. No other markings. The ISS used them to snatch up drunks, transients, anyone living on the street. Or anyone the ISS called a criminal or a fugitive. Anyone. The people disappeared forever. The official ISS story claimed a substantial decrease in crime as a result." Evan lifted his mug, blew on the steaming tea to cool it. "I saw too many street snatches."

"Were you interrogated after your arrest in '44?"

Evan looked up in surprise. "Of course."

"Was it physical?"

"You mean torture? No. They roughed me up, but they didn't torture me."

"There was no need to torture you?"

Evan studied Leiner over the rim of his mug. "What do you mean by that?"

"It appears, from your descriptions earlier and now, that the ISS treated you well for someone who had worked against the Arts Council."

"We tried to set up the Chicago opera company to show the Arts Council that it would earn profit for them. We worked *around* them, not against them." He couldn't believe Leiner hadn't understood that.

Leiner smiled. "Yes, and the ISS were lenient, the Arts Council quite understanding despite their disapproval of what you'd done. Why?"

He realized what the Inspector implied with these questions. Leiner regarded him as guilty until proven innocent just like in America. "Understanding? I spent two years in prison as a result of their understanding, Inspector. No leniency. No special treatment. And no, I was *not* a snitch working for them."

Sunlight the reddish gold of a fresh peach streamed in through his open bedroom window and onto the worn sage green carpet next to his bed. Dust swirled in the light, a universe unto itself, immune from his world and Leiner's questions. He wished he lived on one of those dust planets instead of here. The Austrian rat terrier had clamped down on him and refused to let go. He shook and shook him, not to kill him like a rat terrier would, but to try to catch him in a lie, or trick him, or shake what he wanted from Evan's mouth.

The Austrian's dogged and creative persistence, and his obsession with his two-year incarceration, frightened Evan. Leiner held his life and his future in his hands. Evan feared slipping, giving the wrong answer, not convincing Leiner, not measuring up. Would Leiner conclude that he was a worthless piece of shit and deport him back to America? He forced himself to focus on the opening notes to the Finale of Caine's Fifth Symphony, Uncle Joe's summer wind. Uncle Joe's defiant music.

The floorboards squeaked outside his door, a gentle knock.

"I'm awake," he said.

The door opened and Leiner, in faded blue jeans and a white short-sleeved shirt, stepped into the room. "Good morning, Herr Quinn."

"You don't like to waste any time, do you, Inspector?" Evan threw off the sheet and sat up on the edge of the bed. "Now you want to debrief while I'm doing my morning exercises?"

Leiner smiled. "If you will forgive me for not joining you."

"Oh, no. You don't get off so easy, Inspector. You have to do sit-ups with me." Evan stretched his six-foot-three-inch frame by reaching for the ceiling. He towered over the Inspector.

"If I didn't know otherwise, I would think you had talked with my wife, Herr Quinn. She insists that I need more exercise. She wants me to take a Pilates class."

"Well, come on, then." Evan led the way out to the front room. For five days, he'd done his stretches, sit-ups, push-ups, and running in place alone every morning in his bedroom while it was still cool, but his bedroom was too small for both of them to exercise there.

Evan, in pale blue boxer shorts, sat on the floor. Leiner joined him, much to Evan's surprise. But what better way to earn the trust of someone than to share experiences or do what you say you're going to do? The cop never stopped working.

For the first ten minutes of stretches, only Evan spoke, describing the moves, counting the holds. After the first twenty-five sit-ups, Leiner stopped. He breathed hard. Evan continued.

"I must be careful, Herr Quinn. I am not accustomed to such rigor." Leiner scrambled up on to the couch. He pulled out the palm-sized computer and their first session of the day began.

"Where's Marco?" Evan paused at sit-up number forty-five.

"In the kitchen, cooking our breakfast."

"Do you know how to cook, Inspector?"

"Yes, I love to cook. My specialty is Chinese cuisine. My wife loves to cook Italian and Greek food."

Evan glanced at the kitchen, lowered his voice to a stage whisper. "Cook for me."

Leiner laughed, shook his head. "Marco loves to cook. But Johann...*ja*, perhaps I will cook dinner one night. And you, Herr Quinn, what is your specialty?"

"Not cooking." Evan resumed his sit-ups. "Never learned."

Leiner sat back, recovered from his exertion. "Were you ever beaten in prison, Herr Quinn?"

Evan counted his brisk sit-ups out loud until he reached seventy-five and stopped, his breathing only slightly faster than normal. "Roughed up. I wouldn't call it a beating. Guards liked to shove prisoners around, kick them, prod them with metal rods, slap them." He flopped over on his stomach for push-ups.

"Were you ever raped in prison?"

Evan froze, his eyes on the worn variegated blue carpet under his face.

"Unfortunately, rapes occur in prison. If you were raped, we could provide help to you for the psychological trauma. Were you ever raped, Herr Quinn?"

"No." He pushed his rigid body off the floor and began counting push-ups.

"What was your deal with the NEP? Observe someone in prison for them in exchange for early release?"

"My sentence was two years. That's what I served." He had lost count, but continued with his push-ups to avoid Leiner's eyes. These questions made him uncomfortable. Leiner was too close. He had made a deal with the NEP, but it wasn't what Leiner thought. The smell of brewing coffee reached his nose. Marco moved around in the adjacent kitchen.

"And the assigned work? What did you do?"

"I told you the other day. First, I cleaned the communal bathrooms. After a year, I worked in the library."

"Because of your good behavior." Sarcasm tinged Leiner's tone.

"Yeah. But they wouldn't let me do anything musical, like give music lessons or form a choir."

"After your release, what instructions were you given?"

"I was on probation. My instructions were to maintain a clean civic status. Be obedient. No individual innovation and initiative. Work with the Minneapolis AC rep on my concert programs for the Minneapolis State Symphony. Be thankful I survived."

"What did they tell you to do regarding your father?"

Evan shivered and stopped, swung his legs around to face Leiner. "It's been what – five days now, Inspector. You've asked me the same things, over and over. What do you want from me? I've told you what I know. Don't you believe me?" His pleading eyes met Leiner's cool eyes. "There's not much more I can say. What you see is what I am." He got to his feet. "No questions in the bathroom, if you don't mind. I'd like some privacy."

Leiner nodded, his mouth a tight line under his moustache. Evan turned for the bathroom. Leiner followed.

"Your father."

"There's a housing shortage and I'm poor, an ex-con," Evan said over his shoulder. "So I couldn't buy a place or build one or rent an apartment yet. I argued with the Corrections Officer because they refused to put me in a halfway house. They assigned me to my father's house. I've already told you this. I suspect they wanted to save money on surveillance – you know, kill two birds, him and me, with one stone. Or punish me further by forcing me to live with him. So, to get my job back, I did what I was told. That's it."

"You were watching your father for them?"

In the bathroom doorway, Evan pivoted to face Leiner.

"I told you. They were watching me and they were watching him."

The cop's questions pricked Evan's patience. The cop wanted him to blow up. To say something he didn't want to say.

"And what were your instructions for Vienna, Herr Quinn?"

"Conduct the AC-approved program. But I changed it." He closed the bathroom door on Leiner's scowling face.

"My wife and I loved your concert with the Vienna Philharmonic. We loved especially the Caine symphony. We look forward to hearing you conduct the Philharmonic again, Maestro." Dieter Aschenbeck cleared his throat, and with his right hand, pushed his auburn beard out from under his chin toward Evan, who grinned at the lawyer's odd gesture.

Evan raised his bottle of mineral water in a toast. "Thank you, Herr Aschenbeck. I'm glad you and your wife enjoyed it." He squinted in the bright sunshine at Leiner sitting across the patio table next to Aschenbeck.

Leiner poured tea from a beat-up brown teapot for Aschenbeck and himself. The Interior Ministry lawyer had brought a *Guglhupf*, a small bundt pound cake, announcing that his wife had baked it for them from a special low-carb recipe. Leiner had chuckled but said nothing.

"Now," Aschenbeck said, opening his leather laptop case in his lap. "I expect a decision within a week regarding your political asylum. Additionally, the media has bombarded my office with interview requests. We suggest a press conference would provide an efficient method for you to deal with all of them. Perhaps in two days, that is, Wednesday afternoon?"

Evan nodded. Aschenbeck's voice reminded him of an oboe. His precise English with a German accent underscored his almost compulsive fussiness that Evan found reassuring. Nothing got past this guy. "A press conference sounds fine. I'll make a statement about my decision to remain in Austria and then accept questions for a brief period."

"Additionally," Aschenbeck tapped a silver pen on his open palm. "I have had contact with Larry Morgan, the Cultural Attaché at the American Embassy."

"I'm not interested in talking with him." He noticed Leiner scrutinizing him.

"Of course. However, a meeting may serve your best interests. I mean that everyone will have an opportunity to answer all questions and clear the air. At your convenience, of course, Maestro." Aschenbeck smiled, revealing even white teeth.

"In your best interests, too, right? To maintain a friendly relationship with America and get them off your back."

"Naturally. Also get them off your back, especially if afterward you release a public statement. I offer you my office for it, Maestro, and if you would like me or Klaus present, we will be happy—"

"Can we hold off until after the press conference? Maybe next week? And please, call me Evan. Maestro is for work and I'm not at work right now thanks to Inspector Leiner." He glared at the cop.

"I suggest, Evan," Aschenbeck said. "If the press conference is on Wednesday, that you meet with the Americans next weekend."

Evan understood that Aschenbeck wanted a reasonably quick resolution and an empty city on a quiet summer weekend to ensure security. "Your office, please, with both of you there." He flashed a grin. "The Inspector holds my calendar at the moment. Please set it up with him. Will Morgan be the only one from the Embassy?"

The two Austrians chuckled, exchanging a look. Aschenbeck said, "I am happy to hear you making jokes, Evan. This process can be especially frustrating. I expect Herr Morgan will bring his deputy with him."

Leiner said, "The Americans have cancelled all cultural exchanges and artist tours in response to your defection."

Evan sighed. "I hope that doesn't last long." Evan caught a whiff of burning charcoal from the grill near the cottage door. He hoped for steak but feared Johann planned something like the dried-out barbeque chicken he'd grilled two nights ago.

Aschenbeck cut slices of *Guglhupf* for each of them. "Additionally, Henley Martin at King Brothers, your father's publisher in London, contacted me. He would like to speak with you, Evan."

"He'll have to get in line behind the Inspector, the media and the Americans."

Leiner frowned. "Your business in this moment is your application for asylum. Your life. If Herr Martin can assist you, as he has your father and his work for many years, I suggest you speak with him as soon as possible after you leave our custody."

He scowled at Leiner's paternal tone. "Why didn't he contact me when I was in London a month ago? What does he want, Herr Aschenbeck?"

"He waited for you to contact him. Herr Martin wants to know if your father has any instructions for them, or any manuscripts he may have sent with you. They have not had any specific communication from him since '29." Aschenbeck took a bite of cake.

"They were in communication with him?" Evan was dumbfounded. His father could not have had communication with anyone in Europe after the NEP had taken over. They closed the borders and restricted computer and internet access and telephone usage. "How?"

"You don't know, Herr Quinn?" Leiner shifted in his chair. Evan thought he detected sympathy in his expression. At least it wasn't his usual alert rat terrier look.

Aschenbeck swallowed a sip of tea. "Beginning in 2020, a man named Redfield contacted King Brothers and Maximilian & Monk, your father's and Joseph Caine's publishers in London, and delivered manuscripts for publication from them. Through Mr. Redfield, Joseph Caine instructed his publisher to establish a trust fund for you and pay his royalties into it. Your father instructed his publisher to establish a similar trust fund for his royalties, again through Mr. Redfield, but your father made himself beneficiary. If your father is dead, then you inherit this trust. Over almost thirty years, Evan, the two trusts have accumulated a substantial amount of money."

Evan saw the answer to a question he'd been afraid to ask: Why choose him for the European tour? The Neppers wanted that money in London. His father was dead. Now he was the only obstacle. He had a terrible feeling, like he'd just listened to a judge sentence him to death. He watched Leiner eat a forkful of cake. "Who's Redfield?"

"No one ever knew his true identity," Aschenbeck said. "Henley Martin believes he was a diplomat, but he could also have worked for the Commerce Council. Mr. Redfield's body surfaced in the Thames River in '29 with no identification. A professional execution, according to the police. Herr Martin saw the story on television news. Redfield had not arrived for their scheduled appointment. Herr Martin notified the police and was able to identify the body only as he knew him: Mr. Redfield, an American. The Americans claimed they had no passport record of him."

Evan shook his head. "During the tour, after concerts, people showed me books my father wrote after '29. I thought the Neppers had confiscated and published them."

"There was a break of five years, and then Herr Martin received the novel, **When You See Her**, from a Canadian contact. More manuscripts followed." Aschenbeck paused, took a bite of *Guglhupf*. "Mr. Redfield had left his trench coat in a men's toilet at Heathrow. Someone turned it in to the Lost and Found Department. Several weeks passed before anyone examined the coat. They discovered the manuscript of Joseph Caine's Fifth Symphony on a flash drive sewn into the lining."

Evan gasped. "That was in '29? Six years after his death. That would have been the last of Uncle Joe's completed music." Evan stared down at his untouched slice of cake. His father had smuggled his own and Uncle Joe's work out to the world, an incredible, heroic, and dangerous feat. His stomach knotted in a spasm of fear. "Was Redfield's murderer ever caught?"

"The murder remains unsolved." Aschenbeck lifted a hardcover book from his laptop case. "Herr Martin sent this for you."

Evan accepted the copy of his father's second novel **The Distance Between Two Points**. The front photo of the shiny new cover jacket depicted an eerie night street scene like in spy movies. An old photograph of Randall dominated the back. He fanned the hemp paper pages, inhaled the smell of fresh ink.

"Have you read it, Maestro?" Aschenbeck asked.

He shook his head no. "I haven't read any of my father's books. He gave me Caine's music to read."

"An excellent story, one of my favorite novels. And movie."

Evan gazed out at the lake glittering like a field of diamonds in the sunlight below them. Four sailboats skimmed the water in a dance with the wind. He felt that a stranger, an alien, looked out of his eyes, and he stood inside behind the stranger. He and the stranger wore his physical body like medieval armor. He'd experienced this sensation often. Someone else spoke, not him inside the body, and so if he was stupid or didn't measure up it didn't matter. He felt certain Leiner and Aschenbeck regarded him as their poor little American, cut off from the rest of the world in a paranoid country, unable to read the same books, see the same movies, do the things they had done all their lives.

"Evan, were you in the military?" Aschenbeck's reedy voice jolted him back to the moment. He shook his head no.

"But we had understood the NEP required military service because of the insurgency." Leiner leaned forward, his gray eyes intense.

"The Arts Council arranged for an exemption when I applied to Juilliard."

"So you have had no military training?" Leiner said, sitting back, lifting his fork to his slice of cake.

A new and unexpected line of questioning. The stranger looked out his eyes.

"Well, would martial arts count? I was touring a lot with the Hartleben Quartet, you know, the string quartet I played violin in, staying in awful motels in the bad sections of cities. It's all we could afford. I wanted to learn some martial arts to be able to defend myself." He shoveled a forkful of cake into his mouth.

"You took a class?" Aschenbeck said.

He chewed for about fifteen seconds and swallowed. The cake tasted lemony delicious but a little dry. "Martial arts instruction wasn't available to the general public. I'd noticed a guy one day in our neighborhood. He was in excellent physical shape, clearly had had military training by his bearing and good diet. The guy who ran the gas station told me the stranger was on leave from the Navy. The stranger approached me, asked to meet my father. As he put it, he wanted to see the world. I introduced him to my father. Afterward, I told the guy I wanted to be able to defend myself when I toured. He taught me the martial arts moves that I've used more than once to defend myself. They've saved me."

"Did the Navy man get what he wanted?"

Evan nodded as he used his fork to cut another bite of cake. "He told me the Underground had found a route for him to the Rocky Mountain States. He wanted to fight with them against Washington." Evan pushed back his chair. "Do you want to see some of the moves?"

Leiner shook his head as Aschenbeck spoke. "Evan, what is a Vigiciv gang?" Aschenbeck's forehead furrowed in a concentrated frown. "You had experience with them yourself?"

Evan turned toward the lake, stretched out his long legs. The breeze cooled his sweaty face, rustled the oak branches above them. He smelled the lake, a slight salty, fishy smell. He smiled at the lawyer. "The official title is 'Volunteer Civilian Security Service Groups.' They're part of the national volunteer service and supervised by – or more accurately, take their orders from – the ISS via the local police force. They're civilian vigilante gangs, formed out of the junior and senior high school civic groups, and they patrol their assigned neighborhoods, keep people under surveillance, harass residents, often beat up people, sometimes kill. They collect evidence against someone the ISS wants to arrest, for example. Harold Smith was the leader of the Vigiciv gang in our neighborhood when I was a kid. And yes, I had personal experience with his gang." Evan squinted toward the lake. One sailboat had broken away from the group and headed north toward Neusiedl and the marina. He could feel the Austrians' eyes on him. He couldn't recall ever talking about life in America like this. The stranger inside him was gone.

"Harold Smith?" Leiner gestured toward Evan's empty mineral water bottle. Evan nodded and the Inspector signaled Marco who lounged in the open front doorway. "Lt. Harold Smith from the audio recording of your father's arrest?"

"No, the Lieutenant's son. Harold senior was a cop when Harold junior led the Vigiciv gang. I was ten. Harold was seventeen."

"And your volunteer service, Evan?" Aschenbeck said.

"At Juilliard in New York, I was assigned to a civic group responsible for backing up the regular garbage collectors. We worked in teams of two or three in assigned neighborhoods. I picked up garbage in the South Bronx."

Marco arrived with a cold bottle of mineral water. "Thanks, Marco." The cop nodded and headed back to his perch in the doorway.

"How were you able to attend Juilliard, Herr Quinn? Especially when the NEP discourages music studies?" Leiner's gray eyes seemed curious rather than scrutinizing.

"Connections. Beginning with Joseph Caine, although the Arts Council would never have admitted that. The Minneapolis Arts Council rep had been watching me and he recommended Juilliard, not only for music study but also to remove me from my father's influence. I think the NEP thought they could make money off me in some way. I have not disappointed them. Even the Hartleben Quartet made money for them."

"You will *not* need to collect garbage here, Maestro." Aschenbeck checked his pocket watch. "*Ach*, Klaus. I am late for my meeting at the Ministry." He reached for his laptop case on the ground next to his chair.

"It was nice meeting you, Herr Aschenbeck." Evan extended his right hand.

"Oh, I have forgotten." Aschenbeck pulled a conductor's score from his laptop case. "The Vienna Philharmonic's concertmaster, Robert Waldstein, asked me to give you this score. Mahler's Fifth Symphony. He thought you would like to begin work on it."

"Yeeees!" He snatched the score out of Aschenbeck's hand. "*Thank you, Robert Waldstein.*"

Leiner said, "And Dieter brought for us two radios to use here."

"Thank you, Herr Aschenbeck. But why did Robert send this particular—?"

"Of course. I apologize. Too many subjects in my mind today," Aschenbeck said, rising from his chair. "The American scheduled to conduct the Philharmonic in September has cancelled. They would like you to conduct those concerts."

His first gig on his own, free. "The American had programmed Mahler?"

"No, no, Maestro. Herr Waldstein said that you and he had talked about Mahler. He told me to tell you it is like London. He said you would know."

Evan nodded, examining the score in his hands. "Yeah, this is the best news." He looked at Leiner. "May I call—?"

"Not yet."

"I can telephone Herr Waldstein, Maestro, if you would like it." Aschenbeck finished repacking his laptop case.

"Please tell him, he was right to pick the Mahler Five, and I'm intensely interested in their offer. I'll call them as soon as I'm finished with this process. And please, thank him a million times for me." Evan hurried to the cottage with the score and his mineral water. He couldn't wait to start work.

Leiner watched Evan almost run to the cottage. Aschenbeck sighed next to him.

"Look how excited and happy he was to receive that music," Aschenbeck said. "He forgot his father's book. I have never seen anyone so restless and tense. He is quite frustrated with you. Also, on the debriefing tapes."

Leiner patted Aschenbeck's shoulder and they walked together toward the lawyer's car parked in back of the cottage. "Please tell Gert that her *Guglhupf* tasted delicious, as usual."

"I have seen also the tapes of your sit-ups with the Maestro. Eva requested copies."

They chuckled together as they rounded the corner of the cottage. Leiner thought of his daughters. Anna in particular would laugh at him grunting and groaning on those tapes. Often enough he'd explained that he wasn't fat, simply he was not in the best physical condition, and there was a difference. She loved to tease him and he loved her teasing.

"He was surprised I began exercising with him," Leiner said. "He'll relax."

Chapter 5

"They are waiting upstairs," Leiner said.

The Inspector and Marco set a fast pace through the vast, busy lobby of the Hilton Hotel on Landstrasse Hauptstrasse in Vienna's Third District. Evan saw people with suitcases at the registration desk, a line of people at checkout, others passing through or lounging on the lobby's plush cinnamon-colored sofas and chairs. No one behaved in an unusual way or focused on them. No potential American attackers here that he could see. Potted palms and ficus trees drew his attention up to convex skylights. Dieter Aschenbeck waited by a broad curving staircase.

On the mezzanine, they turned down a wide carpeted hallway to a security checkpoint with X-ray arch, three guards and a table for examining briefcases, bags, and equipment. Leiner conferred with the guards.

"You control this press conference, Evan," Aschenbeck said after they'd passed through the X-ray arch. "End it whenever you wish."

They continued on to smoky glass double doors. Evan peered through them at the undulating movement inside. Like worms in a fish can, he thought, sliding around twigs and stones, in constant motion with no place to go until a chance for the big hook grabbed them.

"They are all credentialed press, Herr Quinn," Leiner said, grasping one of the door handles. "Except for Nigel Fox, an English artist manager, and the Assistant Cultural Attaché from the American Embassy, Bernard Brown."

"I know Nigel," Evan said. The Brit's presence reassured him. Not so, the American's.

"Mind the cables on the floor," Marco said, pulling on the other door handle.

Aschenbeck ducked into the room as if dashing for cover. Evan, as if walking on to a concert stage, strode in after him with energetic confidence, negotiating the cables and the platform steps with ease. The air held the faint aroma of cooked popcorn. He heard clicking noises, beeps, susurrant voices, a persistent whirring and rustling paper. As soon as he turned toward the seated reporters, they erupted, shouting "Maestro Quinn" over and over, hands waving in the air. The human voice, music's first and oldest instrument, normally produced melodious sounds, but not when the media yapped.

Aschenbeck raised his hands for quiet. Marco clipped a lapel microphone to Evan's collar and handed one to Aschenbeck before positioning himself on the platform behind Evan. Leiner guarded the entrance, his gaze moving over the reporters. A half dozen uniformed security guards ringed the press corps. Behind them, in front of a row of curtained bay windows, stood the tall, elegant, white-haired Nigel Fox. Evan nodded to him and he smiled. Nine feet away from Fox, a lean, athletic man with hair the color of mud, thirty-five or maybe a youthful forty-five years old, leaned back against a bay window, his arms folded across his chest, a smug expression on his rough, unshaven face. Despite his fashionable ivory linen suit, he looked like a street punk fresh from a fist fight showing up in designer clothes without a shower first. The suit was too rich for a cop. So, Bernard Brown from the American Embassy.

"Ladies and gentlemen," Aschenbeck said in English. "For security reasons, we are filming and recording this press conference. Maestro Quinn has a brief statement and he will afterward answer your questions. Maestro Evan Quinn."

Evan gave the uplifted faces and television cameras his brightest public persona smile trying not to squint in the bright TV lights. "Ladies and gentlemen, I'm here today to kill a rumor and clarify my actions." Evan opened a sheet of paper and read from it. "First of all, I have requested political asylum from Austria of my own free will. No one kidnapped me, no one coerced me and no one has held me against my will here. I was arrested, that's true. I punched a Viennese policeman to insure he'd take me into custody so I could defect in the safety of the police station. Maybe unnecessary, but it worked. I apologize again to that policeman today, and I hope he understands my reason for hitting him."

"Maestro, why Vienna?" a dark-haired woman in the second row asked.

"Were you an informant, Maestro?" a blonde man with a German accent shouted from the back.

Evan held up his hand. "The brass doesn't come in until the finale, OK? I'll cue you."

Laughter crackled through the room.

"To continue," Evan said, returning to the statement in

his hand. "I had wanted to leave America since I was ten, when my teacher and mentor, and close family friend Joseph Caine was arrested and killed. My reason for defecting is simple. Music. My heart and soul. I want to learn and conduct whatever I want whenever I want, including all the music that's banned in America, especially Joseph Caine's. I want to live and work in freedom, with choices and opportunities, without government harassment, persecution, and control. I plan to live in Vienna, the life of a musician, in the international family of musicians."

Out of the corner of his eye, he saw Leiner move toward the back of the press corps and a uniformed guard nod to him. He glanced down at the reporters. He commanded their complete attention.

"I decided to defect," he continued reading, "the day I arrived in London on my tour. My Arts Council escorts informed me at that time that my father, Randall Quinn, had been killed resisting arrest."

A collective gasp pierced the air. A British reporter spoke up.

"Maestro, forgive me, but the Americans—"

"I know. The NEP government hasn't made an announcement and won't until they can attribute his death to something not involving the ISS or them, such as a heart attack, like they did with Joseph Caine." Sarcasm sharpened his tone.

"Monsieur Quinn, have you confirmed his death from an independent source?"

"I have no reason to doubt what I was told. My Arts Council escorts were plugged directly into Washington. I have a meeting scheduled with American Embassy officials and I plan to request a copy of my father's death certificate. My request to the Americans right now, here today: tell the truth to the world about my father's death."

A moment of silence followed. Sad faces looked at him. Their unexpected emotional reaction made him uncomfortable. "Next question, please," he said, pocketing his written statement. Evan nodded to a blonde man in the rear of the group.

"*Vielen Dank*, Maestro," the reporter said. "I would like to ask, were you an informant for the government at any time?"

"I chose not to grab that opportunity for a better life although many do. I chose to maintain my integrity and self-respect, to live in poverty and struggle every day to find food, clothes, and the necessities of life. You trust family, sometimes friends you've known for a long time. But there's always the possibility that someone close to you is an informant. The Housing Council forced my father to accept strangers into his house because of the communal housing laws. We concluded that the housekeeper assigned to us and the two couples who moved in with their kids reported on us to the ISS."

A hand went up on the far left and he swung toward it, nodding.

"Maestro, could you tell us please about your father's—"

Gunshots popped in Evan's ears. He ducked down as voices shrieked and he felt the puff of air from a bullet missing his ear. Two uniformed guards lunged for an Asian man holding a camera on his shoulder. Marco pulled Evan to the floor, lay on top of him and covered his head. He heard screams, shouts, the thumps of chairs hitting the carpeted floor for what seemed like an hour.

"Now, Evan," Marco said in his ear.

Marco's strong hands lifted him up. He glanced around. The reporters had scattered away from the platform, some lay on the floor, arms protecting their heads. Nigel Fox remained by the window, his hawk-like features sharpened by concern. Bernard Brown straightened from a defensive crouch near him. Leiner aimed his gun at four uniformed guards who sat on top of someone. Evan stretched but couldn't see whom they sat on as Marco maneuvered him off the platform, over the cable-strewn floor and out the double doors.

He'd never been shot at before. He'd hunted deer and squirrels, had shot and killed at least a dozen rabbits he and his father, Paul and Uncle Joe had eaten in stew or roasted over a fire. Today, he had been the deer, the squirrel, the rabbit himself. It had happened so fast, so unexpected, he couldn't remember how many shots were fired. Their sharp, loud cracks echoed in his ears without pause. His entire body trembled.

"You are safe now, Evan," Marco said.

He eyed the cop by the door. Marco had pushed him into this small, windowless conference room down the hall.

"How do you know, Marco?"

"No one can pass me now," he said, teeth clenched.

"You're the boss, Marco." He paced around the oval table and its brown velveteen upholstered chairs. The smell of stale cigar smoke and bratwurst lingered in the air. He wanted to scream, to run, to hide behind the furnace at home with his mother as they had when his father exploded into one of his rages. At the same time, a cold calm seeped into his mind, reminding him to stay alert, detach, observe. He had no control over the situation. The familiar disconnected sensation of an alien looking out his eye sockets returned.

Someone knocked twice on the door and Marco opened it. Aschenbeck slipped in. "Maestro, are you hurt?"

Evan shook his head, no. "Shaken, but not stirred."

Marco grinned, but Aschenbeck gave him a puzzled look. "We wait here for Klaus. The police secure the room now and our exit route."

"Was anyone shot? I'd hate it if someone was shot when I was the target," Evan said. "The Americans would want to eliminate me, try to keep me from talking. The Embassy guy was here to witness it."

"Fortunately, no one was shot. We need facts, Evan. We do not yet know who shot at you or how they carried a gun past security," Aschenbeck said, pulling out a chair and sinking down into the plush velveteen. "You must know about all the terrorist groups who target Americans, Westerners, anyone who disagrees with them." Aschenbeck shrugged, one hand pushing out his auburn beard.

"Terrorists? You mean I'll have to look over my shoulder all the time for some terrorist, too? I want protection. I want to be safe." Evan increased the speed of his pacing as he spoke.

"Please calm down, Evan. You are safe in Vienna."

"Someone just tried to kill me, Herr Aschenbeck. In *Vienna*." Evan had picked up a chair and slammed it back down on the last two words. "I left America so I could live free and safe. So I wouldn't have to worry about street cleaner vans, ISS informants, and Vigiciv gangs. I wouldn't have to worry about being beaten up, shaken down, snatched off the street, and constantly threatened."

"Evan, please, we protect you."

Another quick knock on the door and Leiner entered. He nodded to Marco.

"Klaus. What is happening?"

"Herr Quinn?"

"I'm fine. I want—"

"They were not Americans. Two Uighurs from The Right Path terrorist group." Leiner walked around the conference table to Aschenbeck.

The lawyer sighed, chin in one hand. "The Chinese-American talks."

"Exactly." Leiner sat in a chair next to Aschenbeck and regarded Evan with cool gray eyes. "One asked for political asylum and told me they had slipped into Austria from Italy using Nepali passports. They had forged Nepali press credentials. They modified one camera and one hand microphone to hide guns. The modifications made them inaccurate, *Gott sei dank*. Now we know this method and we will add it to our database."

"Why me? I've never heard of these terrorists before." Evan sank down in a chair at the far end of the table.

"You are a high-profile American," Leiner said. "They

believed that killing you would disrupt the current Chinese-American talks here in Vienna."

Evan laughed. "I don't think so."

"Wars have begun over far less, Herr Quinn."

Evan leaned back in his chair, drumming his fingers on the table. "Herr Aschenbeck tells me many terrorist groups target Americans."

Leiner and Aschenbeck exchanged a look.

"When I'm finally on my own, I won't enjoy your protection but the threat remains. I'll need my own protection. Which is why I want a gun."

Leiner's face reddened. "No. Absolutely no. We have not and will never grant gun licenses to defectors."

Evan jumped up and walked around the table toward Leiner. "I hunted with my father and Uncle Joe in northern Minnesota and Wisconsin to put food on our tables. I know how to shoot a gun. I'm willing to take whatever classes or courses or exams or anything I need to do to obtain the proper license. I have no intention of breaking any laws." Evan towered over the Inspector, his hands on his hips.

"His concern is reasonable, Klaus," Aschenbeck said. "He knows a little martial arts. Perhaps we can arrange for him to continue his education in self-defense. Additionally, we both know of excellent security firms which provide bodyguards and other protection for high profile people. It is a matter of common sense, *nicht*?"

"*Prima*. Fine." Leiner whirled to face Evan, a scowl on his face but his eyes sad. "Why is it, Herr Quinn, that Americans always grab for the gun first? Kill the problem to solve it. Killing only creates a worse situation."

Evan met Leiner's eyes but said nothing. The Inspector was right. Violence was easy. It was action, a means to an end. It was power. If the guy's not with you, he's against you. And if you can't beat the guy into submission, kill him. However, Americans weren't alone in this belief.

Another knock on the door. Marco spoke with someone in the hallway. Evan returned to the far end of the table. The shooting had provided him with a perfect natural opportunity to enhance his security with their help. Too bad it didn't work to get a gun.

"All clear," Marco said. "We can leave now."

Fifteen minutes later, Evan sat in the back seat of the unmarked police car, a basic dark river blue four-door sedan. The car drove itself through Vienna's streets. Marco's occasional voice commands corrected for changes in the route. He guessed the windows were bullet-proof glass and the car's chassis reinforced steel. Leiner rode shotgun. Evan was relieved neither cop wanted to talk. He wanted to relax, think about the Mahler Fifth Symphony, the magnificent trumpet solo at the beginning.

"I WANT TO BE A CONDUCTOR!" his ten-year-old voice shouted from memory. His right hand had struggled with his bedroom window's silver lock, prune-purple abrasions encircled his wrist. Outside the window, a black and white cat crouched under a bush of pink peonies at the side of the neighbor's sand-colored Victorian house. His father's icy baritone had said, "How do *you* know? Inside want as much as you like, but always do what you're told. And *never* talk to anyone about our family or the Caines."

Evan looked out the car window to stop the stomach-knotting memory, push it away. They passed the Belvedere Palaces, the Upper Palace visible on a hill overlooking the formal gardens.

"Herr Quinn?"

"I'm fine."

"You decided not to tell them about the audio recording of your father's death?"

"I couldn't play it for them."

"Or for us. We would like very much to hear it."

Leiner still wanted that proof and he wished he had the flash card Dave had plugged into his PDA. "We're not taking the *Autobahn*?"

"Not today."

He appreciated their caution. He slouched back in his seat, comfortable with the familiar maneuverings. When he'd entered the eighth grade in school, four years after Uncle Joe had died, his father had begun his counter surveillance education with how to slip through surveillance shadow fingers. After his release from prison, his father had insisted he have an intense refresher course.

Uncle Joe had taught him music and politics, had opened his life and experience to him. His father had opened nothing to him, only taught him how to survive; there'd been no reason to like him. How well should a son know his father? He had wondered the same thing the night before he departed on tour, when his father had fidgeted on the double bed in his room, chewing his lower lip and scrutinizing how he rolled underwear and socks into tight balls.

"You're doing it all wrong!" his father had said. "Tuck the whole sock ball in and pull the top of one over it."

He packed as he wanted in silence. His father combed his graying blonde hair back from his lined forehead. He'd aged, lost muscle mass and his shoulders sagged forward.

"So you want to do it *your* way. Right. You're a big, famous conductor now. Going on a European tour. But you haven't lived. You know nothing about life."

Evan said nothing.

"It's important they believe they're in control. When you're in Europe—"

"I'm not running any errands for you."

"Errands?" His father laughed his hoarse, coughing laugh. "You don't know what you're talking about. If it weren't for me, you'd be nothing. You have no judgment, no spine. A sniveling little boy," his father sneered at him. "You'll find out in Europe just how much I've done for you."

"You chose to stay when we could have left. Uncle Joe knew what he was doing. He made his choice."

His father's eyes narrowed to electric blue slits that flashed anger. "I told him to shut up. You keep your opinions to yourself, boy. Never let anyone know what you're really thinking or feeling."

"Blah, blah, blah. I've heard this all before. You were the smart one, you've told me often enough. You hated Joe, didn't you?"

His father's hand came out of nowhere, hitting him across the face then backhanding him on the rebound, again and again, until Evan punched him in the jaw followed by a punch to the stomach. His father dropped to the floor with a loud whumpf.

"That's your answer to everything, isn't it? Beat it up. Beat me up. That's the last time you hit me, Father."

"You hit your father! What kind of a son beats his father?" His father gasped and whimpered. "You must honor thy father."

"Now you know how Mom and I felt," he said, massaging his right hand.

His father had glared at him as he had swayed to his feet and shuffled out of the room.

His mother would not have wanted him to hit his father. Evan watched green Austrian fields blur by outside the car window, his throat tightening. Violence was the only language his father had known and understood.

The cultural smuggling. That must have been what his father had alluded to that last evening. What he'd find out in Europe. He respected the risk his father had taken, but he was glad his father was dead.

When the Austrian cops released him, he'd need money to rent an apartment, buy scores, buy everything for living his new life in Vienna. He'd claim the trust fund Caine had left him, finish his part of the deal he'd made, and get on with his life.

Chapter 6

On hands and knees, Evan crawled across the dining room floor to a window in his father's house. He fingered aside a white voile curtain. Outside, black tree branches veined a mother-of-pearl sky. Columns of black smoke rose among skyscrapers to the north and smudged the clouds. To the suburban west, a bomb exploded in a flash of fire, smoke and debris. Minneapolis was under attack.

Instantly he stood in the living room by the sofa where his mother lay, her eyes closed, her black hair fanned over a beige velvet pillow. She wore a long white lace gown, the collar high and frilled. But his mother had loved tropical colors, sensual materials and flamenco styles, not like these clothes.

"Mom, wake up," he whispered.

Wind gusted through the room, vibrating curtains, lamp shades, and rattling the windows. A six-foot tall woman approached him. A red veil fluttered in her black lace gloved hand in front of the bodice of her floor-length, low-cut black dress. Black lace cascaded over her winter wheat-colored hair. Her red lips parted in a toothless smile. Her sapphire eyes nailed him to the floor, his body numbed, immobilized. Her facial features swam into focus and he saw his father's face.

In one twitching hand, she held a spider. Downy black

fur covered its bulbous body. Its shiny, spindly legs lifted and stretched out. She dropped the spider onto his stomach. His pulse rammed adrenalin through his trembling body. He felt its legs prick his skin and he screamed himself awake.

He sat straight up in bed, throwing off the sheet, and in a panic examined his bare chest, arms, and his legs in the light of the nightstand lamp. A spider could hide anywhere. He searched the bed. A wave of nausea sent his vision spinning and started a low waspy buzz in his ears. A light knock on his bedroom door. A hot breeze billowed the window curtains.

Klaus Leiner came in. He smoothed his moustache, a tentative gesture, and his gray eyes had darkened in concern.

"*Was ist los*, Herr Quinn?"

"I thought a spider was on me."

"You have a fear for spiders?"

Evan frowned at the Inspector. "A lot of people do. I have this nightmare about one big, black spider on me. When I wake up, I can still feel it. What time is it?"

"After midnight. Come, Herr Quinn. I will make you something to calm your nerves and help you to sleep."

Evan, wearing only boxer shorts, followed Leiner to the safe house's kitchen. Johann had mopped the floor earlier so the air held the sharp tang of lemon disinfectant. A Bach solo cello suite played low from one of the radios Aschenbeck had brought them. Next to it on the counter stood Leiner's black police radio. Evan sat down at the table. Despite the muggy night Leiner wore jeans. He had not removed his shoulder holster or the gun in it. He went to the refrigerator, took out a carton of milk.

"Is it always this hot during the summer in Austria?" Evan asked.

"Yes, now for many years." Leiner pulled a pot from a cabinet under the kitchen counter.

"Reminds me of Minnesota – the extreme weather."

Leiner poured milk into the pot on the stove. "*Ja*, we could have a severe winter this year. The environmental scientists are most concerned that despite efforts to remove it, the carbon dioxide levels in the atmosphere have not decreased. America and China need to do more."

"Your family must miss you."

The cop stared down at the milk and sighed. "*Ja*, my daughter Laura loves classical music, and she is especially concerned about you."

"That's kind of her. You have other children?"

Leiner stirred the milk as it heated. "Laura is fifteen and my serious one, my intellectual who loves the ballet, Marc Chagall, the music of Bach, Greek mythology, and the books of Virginia Woolf. Her younger sister, Anna, who is twelve, has succumbed to boy madness already. She drives her mother to distraction begging for make-up, to change the color of her hair, and to tattoo her body in strange places." Leiner, his eyes wide, pulled on his moustache.

"The teen years are tough on everyone. At least that's what I've observed with musician friends." He looked up at a ceiling corner surveillance camera. "Your daughters give you the female perspective on life."

"Would you like children, Herr Quinn?"

Evan smiled through his irritation with the question. "Musicians are my family, Inspector. Some are like children, but most are like siblings or parents. The way my life goes, a wife and children are not a good idea."

"Other conductors have done it."

"Do you like being a father?"

"I love it." Leiner set a mug from a wall cabinet on the counter and spooned honey into it. "*Ja*, children challenge you, they make you feel from day one as if you have no idea what you're doing. But they are life. They are unique individuals who have intelligence, heart, soul, and purpose. I feel honored to know my daughters because of their good hearts. I am in awe that I have been a part of their creation." Leiner poured steaming milk into the mug and set the pot off to one side on the stove. He stirred the milk and honey. "I have immense respect for their intelligence."

Leiner sounded real, with genuine emotion, not like the Nepper propaganda from the Medical Council and Population Control to encourage people to have kids who will grow up to be workers and make money for the Neppers. "Well, Inspector, I've been feeling like an ignorant child since I arrived in Europe. I have a lot to learn about the customs and culture. But I'm glad I'm here."

Leiner set the steaming mug in front of him. "This drink has always calmed my daughters when they have problems sleeping."

"Thanks." Evan took a sip. The honey gave the warm milk a welcome sweetness that tasted good. "Anything new with the American-Chinese talks?"

Leiner settled into the chair next to him. "They continue to talk. That is the good news. They talk for eight months without progress, however."

"I didn't know China had investments in America or that they had decided to cash them all in."

"China is America's largest creditor. Japan is the only other country with so much invested in America. However, America enjoys a close alliance with Japan."

Evan took another sip of his milk. "But China is part of the global economy, right? Why would they want to risk hurting their own economy by hurting America's?"

Leiner went to the refrigerator and took out a bottle of raspberry juice. "The Russians thought China's move to sell was perhaps the first move in a larger strategy of expansion. The reason the Russians came to the European Union with their concerns. The EU agreed any economic destabilization would hurt everyone. They proposed broad-based talks with America in order to resolve China's economic concerns. China could choose the location."

"Vienna," Evan said.

"They seek to contain China."

"The American media didn't report on that situation at all," Evan said. He, like most Americans, had had no reliable source of information about the world outside America's borders, only what the Neppers had wanted everyone to know. He had learned during his tour they had lied, created an illusion of global power and influence for the country in order to maintain internal power and control. "I don't understand how I fit into that situation."

Leiner nodded. "You are not a part of that situation in even the smallest way. Please understand, Herr Quinn, the Right Path terrorists who tried to kill you yesterday would have tried to kill *any* high profile American to achieve their goal. They chose the first one available."

"How reassuring. But what about the other—"

"*Achtung! Rot Sieben!*" A male voice crackled from the black police radio on the kitchen counter.

Leiner jumped up, killed the light. "Stay here, Herr Quinn."

In deep darkness, Evan heard him leave the kitchen, the front door open, Leiner's and Johann's whispers as they turned off the other lights in the cottage. The Bach cello suite continued low on the radio. Evan had understood the words "Attention! Red Seven!" but not their meaning. What was wrong? Footsteps entered the kitchen from the front room at the same time the front door closed again.

A narrow flashlight beam settled on his face. "Not to worry, Evan," Johann's whisper came out of the dark behind the light. "We will quickly discover the reason for this code alert."

"You'll stay with me?" Evan whispered back, his voice hoarse.

"I stay with you. You are safe here. Not to worry." The flashlight moved to the counter. Johann turned off the radio and the flashlight. "We wait now for the all clear."

Footsteps walked to the back door. Evan dared not move or make any sound. Sitting in the complete darkness reminded him of hiding behind the furnace, his mother's arms around him, listening to her ragged, frightened breathing.

Gunshots sounded inside his ears so loud he knew they were inside the kitchen.

"Johann! Gunshots!"

"*Ruhe,* Evan. No gunshots," the cop whispered.

Evan's stomach cramped. He slid off his chair and under the table where he sat on the floor. The pulse in his ears drowned out any other sound. He concentrated on his breathing, commanded it to slow. He waited what seemed like hours. The more time that passed without anything bad happening, he thought, the better. He breathed in, and out, deep, and long. The front door opened. Footsteps approached the kitchen. The light flicked on. He saw a pair of legs wearing jeans stop by the table.

"*Wo ist Herr Quinn?*" Leiner said.

"*Ich weiss—*"

"I'm here," Evan said, his voice cracking. "I heard gunshots."

Leiner squatted, peering at Evan under the table. "You heard gunshots?" Leiner frowned. "No gunshots. All is well, Herr Quinn. You can come out now. A false alarm, yes?"

He crawled out and allowed Leiner to help him to his feet.

"You are trembling, Herr Quinn. Please, sit down. What can we do for you?"

"Tell me what that was about!" He jerked a chair away from the table. Johann and Leiner, in his peripheral view, exchanged a surprised look.

"*Prima.* Fine." Leiner picked up his half full bottle of raspberry juice. "The last two nights, a car drove down the access road and parked. You slept through the other alerts, Herr Quinn. We hung a heavy chain at the access road entrance with a warning sign: private property, no trespassing. But the car appeared again tonight." He sighed, took a swallow of juice.

"How old were they?" Johann said, grinning.

"Nineteen." Leiner nodded. "From Neusiedl. Sweethearts in search of a place where they could be alone together."

"Oh, for shit's sake!" Evan sat down. A couple of teenagers had tripped the alarm. What was wrong with them? Couldn't they read the sign?

Johann, slipping his handgun in his shoulder holster, left. Leiner settled into the chair next to Evan.

"Herr Quinn, this spider nightmare tonight, have you had it before?"

"Yeah, sure. What does that have to do with anything?"

"Tell me about it."

Evan looked around the spotless old kitchen, shivering. "I hate spiders, that's all. In the nightmare a big black spider lands on me and I can't move like I'm paralyzed."

"Paralyzed. Powerless. Like you were also powerless during the alert." Leiner drank more juice.

Evan shrugged. "I didn't know what was happening."

"And you heard gunshots. From the press conference yesterday afternoon?"

The gunshots had sounded real. "I don't know. I heard them."

Leiner sighed. "I am not a psychologist, Herr Quinn, but I suspect that you suffer from Post-Traumatic Stress Disorder, a result of psychological trauma. The shooting yesterday, for example. I have seen this often in traumatized people, including Americans I have debriefed."

"I'm not crazy."

"No, you are not. It is your memory, Herr Quinn, your mind reliving the event. A coping mechanism. If you have experienced other psychological trauma in the past – in prison or in childhood – that has not been treated and resolved, the PTSD symptoms will continue to appear until the trauma is resolved and this can magnify the effects of recent trauma. PTSD can affect your body, your perceptions, everything. You are no longer in America. You are safe. Please let me call a psychologist to talk to you."

"There's nothing wrong with me, Inspector." Evan drank off the milk, now cold. "You're seeing a problem where none exists. I appreciate your concern, but please, just stick to your job."

Leiner frowned. "I am doing my job, Herr Quinn."

"I'm going to bed. Thanks for the warm milk." Evan left the kitchen table and entered the front room. On the sofa, Johann looked up from an old paperback book.

"Good night, Johann. Thanks again for your protection."

"*Bitte sehr*, Evan." Johann smiled and returned to his reading.

In his dark bedroom, Evan leaned back against the closed door. He couldn't catch his breath. PTSD. Was a head doctor exam the first step to claiming he's incompetent and crazy as in America? From there, it was only a short walk to locking him up. Or deportation. He couldn't let that happen. He couldn't fail now. He leaned forward and breathed.

He switched on the nightstand lamp and crawled back into bed, pulling the sheet up to his chin. He saw his life, his music, his dream of freedom, everything he'd worked for and sacrificed for, all balanced on the razor's edge of Leiner's perception of him. He must somehow convince Leiner that he was sane, strong, and healthy. He rolled over onto his left side.

Leiner walked through the night darkness to the surveillance shed. The American showed definite signs of unresolved psychological trauma: memory flashbacks or hallucinations of trauma – the gunshots – nightmares, short temper, trembling and sweating, a paranoia about personal safety. He wondered if Quinn also experienced the additional symptoms of insomnia, panic attacks or the depersonalized sensation of someone else occupying the body. He doubted Quinn would tell him.

Over the years, he'd seen the signs in policemen, accident victims, victims of domestic violence or childhood abuse. He'd learned from police psychologists that the Americans accepted psychological trauma as a real, treatable condition only in soldiers who had experienced combat and people who'd survived natural disasters. They dealt with all other cases as scams or fantasies, and "re-educated" the victims in prison psych wards. He understood Quinn's fear of psychologists.

What would happen if Quinn received no treatment for his psychological distress? He had no idea. He couldn't help Quinn get treatment unless he could somehow convince Quinn that it was safe here to talk with a psychologist.

He entered the shed. The three young technicians' faces

popped up. As he closed the door, he said in German, "Peter, any more responses to our inquiry?"

A bespectacled blonde man, his hair pulled back in a ponytail, grabbed a palm-sized computer at his station in front of the internal surveillance monitors. He played his fingertips across its screen. "We have heard from the Russians tonight. I planned to give you a report in the morning and—"

"Now, Peter." Leiner's eyes rested on the monitor of Evan's bedroom. The nightstand light was on. The American lay curled in a fetal position in bed.

"Yes, Inspector. The Russians' response was the same as all the European Union intelligence agencies. No one has heard any chatter about an American spy arriving in Europe. No one has heard anything unusual about Evan Quinn, only concern for him or curiosity about where he'd conduct next. And we have received four confirmations of the details of his biography. What they *have* heard involving America concerns the talks, Inspector."

"Tell me."

"The Chinese have been talking about the arrival of Vice Chairman Jiang Xu in Vienna to attend the talks."

"What?" Leiner stared at Quinn on the monitor, now flat on his back, eyes open. "The source?"

"Traffic between the Chinese Embassy and Beijing. The Russians told us."

"*Verdammt,*" Leiner breathed. The Chinese Security Chief had said nothing about the Vice Chairman visiting Vienna. What were they doing? He had told the Chinese Security Chief often that communication was crucial to effective security. The Vice Chairman would need a special detail. And the Americans? Would their Vice President now attend the talks?

Whatever the political power plays involved, Vice Chairman Jiang Xu in Europe offered a convenient target for the Right Path. If anything happened to him, the Chinese would retaliate. If it happened in Vienna, they'd attack Austria. He must alert Hanna Celine at the Bundespolizei, and call the Chinese Security Chief in the morning for an update.

Movement on the monitor caught his eye: Quinn left his bed, picked up the score to Mahler's Fifth Symphony. Despite the new development with the Chinese-American talks, Leiner could not close Quinn's file. Quinn now sat in bed, reading the Mahler score, raising and dropping his right hand, conducting the orchestra he must hear in his mind.

"Stay in contact with the other agencies, Peter. I want to know immediately about any chatter concerning either Evan Quinn or Jiang Xu."

Chapter 7

Evan tapped his fingers in a rapid staccato on the chair's arms. In the polished wood chair next to him, Leiner fingered his moustache, his gray eyes distant. Beige lacy curtains swirled out on the breeze from open casement windows in Dieter Aschenbeck's outer office. The smell of grilled sausage from a sausage stand somewhere up the street drifted into the room. Evan's eyes wandered over the opposite wall bookshelves filled with identical maroon leather-bound volumes.

"How are you feeling, Herr Quinn?" Leiner said, unbuttoning his wheat-colored suit jacket.

"Like a cat trying to bury *Scheisse* in a marble floor."

"Frustrated?"

Evan stopped his finger-tapping. "I'm just me, Inspector. Evan Quinn, musician and conductor. For the last two weeks, you have questioned me. I've shown you who I am, what's important to me. But I still get the feeling that you don't believe me. How does an honest person convince someone of the reality of his life, of his identity, if that someone wants it to be something else?" Evan leveled his gaze on Leiner's surprised face. "I'm not stupid, Inspector."

"I know," Leiner said.

"Do you think I'm insane too?"

"No. Why do you—?"

"You seemed to think I was the other night. You wanted me to talk to a head doctor."

"Herr Quinn. Post-Traumatic Stress is not insanity." Leiner turned in his chair to face him. "We often, as standard procedure, offer the services of a doctor for medical conditions or a psychologist if the person we're interviewing shows signs of psychological distress, as you have." Leiner's serious eyes held his. "Psychological services in Austria are not the same as in America. I need you to believe that."

"I don't need a head doctor, Inspector. I need you to believe *that*." Evan looked away, allowing himself a brief satisfied smile. He'd planned this confrontation for the last three days. "And why wouldn't I have some 'psychological distress,' huh? I've left behind forever the only life I've known. I'm in a foreign country where everything is strange. I don't know the customs, the culture. I don't know my future. I've gotten the distinct impression that Europeans look down on Americans. And then terrorists shoot at me at my press conference. Oh, and there's this cop who's been hounding me with relentless debriefing sessions for the last two weeks. He's suspicious and unwelcoming. What do you expect?"

Leiner sighed, settled back in his chair. "Your description pains me, Herr Quinn."

"Yeah? It's different through my eyes, isn't it? You might keep that in mind in the future." Evan began his staccato tapping again. "I need music and work, not a head doctor."

Leiner smoothed his moustache. "I have often wondered what it is like to conduct an orchestra."

"Home," Evan said with a slow grin. His fingers relaxed.

"I'm standing in the middle of this incredible sound with the musicians. There's nothing else in the world. I'm inside the music. Inside my heart. I'm home, but part of something larger than myself."

The double doors to Aschenbeck's office swung open. "*Guten Tag*, Maestro. Klaus. I apologize for the delay." Aschenbeck, buttoned up in a tailored navy-blue suit, smiled a sphinx's smile.

"Evan! *Finally* we're allowed to talk with you." A gangly, bald man, Evan's height, in a gray bureaucratic suit approached him from Aschenbeck's desk and extended his hand. "I'm Larry Morgan, the Cultural Attaché at the Embassy." Morgan nodded to the man next to him. "My Deputy, Bernie Brown."

Evan backed away from the Americans. Morgan smelled of sour grapefruit and his brown eyes were vacant, something he'd seen often in Neppers. He recognized Brown from his press conference. The guy still needed a shave, still smiled with smug self-assurance, and wore the same ivory suit on his lean six-foot frame. Other than his attitude and his sense of fashion, he realized, everything about Brown's appearance was average, the kind of guy who could melt into a crowd and disappear.

He ignored Brown's and Morgan's outstretched hands and sank down on a maroon leather wing-backed chair that faced away from the office's sunny windows and flanked the fireplace. Brown chose the wing-backed chair opposite Evan. Morgan and the two Austrians settled on the leather sofa facing the fireplace. The office reminded Evan more of a clubby inner sanctum than a government office.

"We're very concerned about you, Evan," Morgan said. He leaned forward, relaxed, hands clasped between his knees. "This business of thwarting our attempts to see you – to hold you and deny you the right to contact us – a serious breach of international friendship."

"No one held me against my will and I didn't want to contact or see you," Evan said, forcing himself to remain calm. Morgan's pompous tone needled him.

"We insisted on a private meeting, but Mr. Aschenbeck has informed us that he and Mr. Leiner will stay."

"At my request," Evan said. He met Brown's green eyes with a defiant look.

"If that's the way you want it. What happened, Evan? What was the problem? Why didn't you come to us? Was it the Arts Council es—?"

"Brown attended my press conference. Didn't he tell you?" Evan said, his eyes fixed on Brown. Out of the corner of his right eye, he saw Leiner's jaw stiffen, and next to him, Morgan's scowl. "Guess he's not doing his job. I defected of my own free will. I choose to live here in Austria, pursue my music in freedom. That's final. I won't change my mind."

"You are a highly talented conductor, Evan, a valuable contributor to American culture and society," Morgan said, changing his tone to patient and soothing as if speaking to an upset child. "But I can't believe the lies you've told at the press conference about your father. Have you lost your mind? We want to help you. You can still come home and put all of this nonsense behind you. The Arts Council will support you in every way as they always have. You're still a

Party member, still an American citizen until the day you die. We'll provide—"

"The Arts Council will support me?" Evan said smearing sarcasm all over the words. "They care only about money, not people, not music."

Morgan shook his head, sad and resigned. "You need to stop spreading the false and hurtful story that your father is dead. Randall is very much alive. No one would ever hurt him. ISS has not arrested him. We have evidence of it to show you."

Brown retrieved a large ivory envelope from Aschenbeck's desk behind them and pulled a stack of color eight-inch by ten-inch photographs out of it. He offered them to Evan who swatted them away. Leiner accepted the photos. Evan's awareness of the two Americans' positions, eyes, hands, and breathing heightened to a vigilant clarity.

"As you can see, the photos have time and date stamps," Morgan said.

"*Ja*, during the last two weeks," Leiner said.

"We'll release them to the media after this meeting." Morgan smiled at Evan.

Brown held up a flash card storage drive.

Morgan nodded. "Bernie has video of an interview Randall Quinn gave last week on our live TV news show *Twenty-four Hours*."

Aschenbeck opened the mahogany cabinet next to the fireplace. The cabinet held a forty-nine-inch LCD monitor attached to a keyboard, and other electronics unfamiliar to Evan. The lawyer inserted the flash card into the side of the keyboard.

Morgan walked over. "We bookmarked a relevant section, but you're welcome to watch the entire interview."

Evan stood on the other side of Aschenbeck to keep the Austrians between him and the Americans. Leiner handed him the photos which he took without a glance at them.

"My father would never consent to a television interview," he said. "Especially on *Twenty-four Hours*. He'd refuse to participate in a scripted interview."

Randall Quinn's sallow face, framed by graying blonde hair, appeared on the monitor. He stared into the camera, electric blue eyes flashing. Seeing the image gave Evan a jolt. The man physically resembled his father but didn't have his bulldog demeanor nor his hunched shoulders. The camera pulled back to reveal a woman interviewer. Evan recognized her as one of the reporters for the news show but couldn't recall her name. They sat in a book-lined room with warm wood paneling, not a room Evan recognized. Randall began talking, a high baritone raspy like sandpaper on wood, not his normal voice. Not his father's voice.

"I know my son. Evan is a musician. He loves music. He doesn't care about politics."

The woman said, "You believe that he was kidnapped in Vienna?"

"No other explanation. He wouldn't do this to me of his own free will."

"Do what to you, Randall?"

Randall's eyes teared up as the camera moved in for a close up. He said, "Abandon me."

He'd seen enough. Evan rushed to the cabinet and yanked the card out of the keyboard. "That's not my father. Definitely not his voice. And if you were to do a retinal scan or check DNA, you'd find an unrelated actor."

Brown laughed. "If it walks like a duck, quacks like a duck, then—"

Morgan said, "Randall had a cold and scratchy throat when he did this interview."

"You've used actors before. It's easy to photo-shop pictures, change date and time stamps with the right software." Evan slammed the photos into Brown's chest and returned to his chair. Brown's voice betrayed his origins: the South Bronx. He imagined Brown had led his own Vigiciv gang and forged connections with the ISS, which would have positioned him well for foreign service or CIA employment. He remembered the South Bronx people he'd met while working as a garbage collector during his years at Juilliard. He'd liked the cops, the beauticians, secretaries, shop owners, laborers, all trying to make a good, safe life for themselves. They were real people, friendly, unpretentious, hard-working, and tenacious in their loyalties to each other. Brown was an anomaly.

"Actors." Morgan sank down on the sofa. "Evan, I don't understand this delusion of yours at all. It's not reality. It's not you. How could you possibly think Randall was dead?"

Evan stared at Morgan. He knew his father was dead. Dave had played the audio recording of his murder three times for him. He was certain Dave had thought it would hurt him to hear it, but he was relieved. Washington would have sent the Embassy the same information. They knew he was dead. They were attacking his credibility and at the same time implementing plausible denial. He'd seen it before. He noticed that Leiner frowned, his gray eyes dark and cold. Brown leaned against the mantel, a smug smile on his face.

"In London, my AC escorts played—"

"It's the money in London," Brown said. "That's it, Larry. There's millions of dollars in Randall's trust fund."

Angry cold calm seeped into his mind. He shot up to his feet.

"Where are you going, Herr Quinn?" Leiner's tenor voice cut through the air. The cop stared at him, his eyes wide, questioning.

"This is a waste of time, Inspector. I'm sorry, Herr Aschenbeck. This meeting is over."

"Did you defect for the money, Evan?" Morgan said, his tone a sneer.

He'd love to beat Morgan's face to a bloody pulp. Evan sneered back, "I never knew about it until a week ago. Unlike you Neppers, my life does not revolve around money and its acquisition. There's more to life than money. I defected for music. And Morgan, don't bother sending anyone after me. You won't get any return on that investment."

"Evan," Morgan said, his baritone descending into iciness as he raised his gangly body up from the sofa. "We don't 'send anyone after' people. You've made your choice to stay here. Fine. I see now that you've decided of your own free will. And you're free to do as you choose. We won't try to interfere in any way with your life. But you need to accept that your father is alive. He's safe. And I have an obligation to our Austrian friends to expose your dishonesty and questionable mental state."

"Your smear campaign against me won't succeed, Morgan." Evan smiled at the American. What was the phrase his mother had loved so much? If looks could kill. At this moment, Morgan's eyes shot a hundred bullets into Evan.

"You know, Larry," Brown said, sidling up close to Evan who didn't move. "He can't claim the money unless he can prove his father is dead. So, he needs an official death certificate from us, right?" Brown grinned at him.

Evan whispered in his ear, "No matter how thoroughly you research your object, Brown, you'll never know him. You'll always miss something."

The grin faded from Brown's face confirming Evan's suspicion. Brown was CIA.

"That's right, Bernie," Morgan said, buttoning his suit jacket. "And since Randall is alive, we certainly cannot produce one."

Brown whispered in Evan's ear, "You lose." He stepped around Evan and followed Morgan to the door. Aschenbeck escorted the two American Embassy officials out.

Evan massaged his temples. A headache throbbed over his eyes. "Well, now you have some idea, Inspector, what it's like to deal with the NEP." He found the Austrian by the window. "What are you looking at?"

"I am waiting for them to exit the building." Leiner pointed to a shiny black car parked on the street below, a chauffeur leaning against it. "You sounded angry, Herr Quinn, talking with them." Leiner glanced sideways at him.

Evan shrugged. "I'd love to be a fly on the back window of that car. Where's the Embassy, anyway?"

"Boltzmanngasse in the Ninth District. Are you planning to accept their offer?"

Evan smiled. "Not on your life, Inspector. I wanted to know so I can avoid it."

Aschenbeck burst into the room. "*Ja*, Klaus, what we expected, *nicht*? Grand theater."

Morgan and Brown emerged from the building and walked over to the car as the chauffeur opened the back door.

"They made a convincing case," Leiner said, studying the street scene. "The photographs, the video."

"How interesting that they mentioned Randall Quinn's trust fund but not the trust Joseph Caine left to Evan," Aschenbeck said, nodding to Evan as he sat down on the sofa. "We have seen photo-shopped photographs before, Klaus. Our experts will check them. And we have seen them use actors before, *nicht*? They must control the flow of information wherever they can."

"That audio recording you heard in London, Herr Quinn. If you had it, we could check it for tampering."

"Yeah, I know. I wish I had it, but I'm convinced it was genuine. I bet the Arts Council would love to get their hands on my father's trust fund. All that profit just sitting there," Evan said, returning to his chair. Yeah, and he was their only obstacle to it. They'd want both trust funds.

Leiner sighed and turned away from the window. "You look pale, Herr Quinn. Are you ill?"

"Headache."

"I have medication, Evan." Aschenbeck went over to his desk.

"Brown works for the CIA," Evan said as Leiner claimed the same chair Brown had occupied, scooping up the photos he'd left there. "I'm sure of it."

"They are both CIA," Aschenbeck said, bringing a pill bottle and a box of orange juice, a straw poking out of the top, to Evan. "Two pills, Maestro. Morgan has been at the Embassy here for almost five years. Brown for almost three. I had not met Brown until today."

"He's a street punk," Evan said after swallowing the pills with a gulp of juice. "From the South Bronx."

"Ah," Leiner said, his cool gray eyes on Evan. "Where you collected garbage."

Evan nodded. So far, the two Austrians were unreadable. People believed what they wanted but could easily be distracted to believe something else. What if the audio recording of his father's death had been faked? That's what Leiner believed. He knew that as surely as he knew his father was dead. What did Leiner believe he was? He realized the Austrian cop hadn't said.

"Here's what we know," Evan said to re-direct his thoughts. "The Americans will release the photos and video to the media to discredit me. They most likely want the trust fund money for themselves; therefore, they'll continue their story that my father is alive until they figure out how to grab the trust fund when they announce his death. I'm certain my father wouldn't want the NEP to have that money, to benefit financially from his death. They showed no interest in Caine's trust fund, but I believe they want that money, too."

Aschenbeck said, "Have you finished your statement?"

"Yeah." Evan grinned. "I just need to add my take on this meeting. I'll for sure mention their obsession with the trust funds. If anything bad happens to me, the Americans would be the prime suspects."

"You are safe in Vienna, Evan," Aschenbeck said in a voice of conviction.

Leiner shuffled through the photographs. "If these are genuine, Herr Quinn, they substantiate your claim about the surveillance on your father. The photos show him not only at home, but in many different locations, at a distance or close up with a zoom lens, and he does not appear aware of the photographer." Leiner held up a photo of Randall talking with the neighborhood convenience store owner outside of the store, a folded newspaper tucked under his arm. Neither Randall nor the store owner looked toward the camera.

A thought occurred to Evan and he punched the arms of his leather chair. "Here's something," he said. "Why didn't Morgan offer to call my father, right here and now, to prove that he was alive? You could have set up a call, right? Maybe even a video call?" He looked to Aschenbeck, who nodded. "But they didn't. They couldn't do anything spontaneous. Because my father is dead."

"*Ja, ja,*" Leiner said, sliding the photographs back into the ivory envelope.

"Morgan was specific about leaving you alone, as he should have been," Aschenbeck said. "I see no reason, Evan, for you to remain any longer at the Neusiedl safe house."

"I can't believe Quinn's kid is here." Morgan growled the words.

Bernie glanced at his boss, sitting to his right on the back seat, his gaze focused outside the window of the car as it glided through Vienna's quiet Sunday streets.

"Privacy, Bernie."

He pressed a button on his arm rest. A bullet-proof tinted Plexiglas divider slid up from the back of the front seat to the ceiling. He settled back, exhaling. He'd never seen his boss so full of hate.

"He's not in Vienna for any good reason." Morgan punched his right fist into the palm of his other hand. "Contact Langley. He's either with us or against us. Find out. He has a chip, right?"

"His file described the original chip was inserted behind his left ear when he was twelve. A replacement chip, one of the newer organic models, was inserted in 2044 after his arrest."

"Yeah, find out what his frequency is and track the little shit."

"Understood."

"Stay on him, Bernie. If he's against us, it'll be my pleasure to sign his termination order."

"Larry, what if he's genuine? Wouldn't a recruitment—?"

"There's not a genuine molecule in Quinn's body." Morgan's face had flushed lobster red and a vein rose in relief along the temple facing Bernie. "Langley has always warned us about their defectors, haven't they? Well, have we heard from them about this one?"

"We've been over this, Larry. No, Langley didn't notify us." He studied Morgan. Now that he'd met Evan Quinn, he doubted he was a spook, despite his whispered, "No matter how thoroughly you research your object…." He could have picked up the jargon from any number of places, including spy novels and the Underground. He'd bet on the Underground.

"You see? Rattle those cages in Washington. Check with all the intel agencies, civilian and military." Morgan shifted away from him, signaling the end of their discussion.

Bernie kept his voice soft, non-confrontational. "What's going on, Larry? You really hate this guy."

"I hate his father," Morgan said. "The Underground. They bombed the Mall of America, remember that? It killed my brother, his whole family, visiting from South Carolina and shopping for Christmas. Randall Quinn organized it, I'm sure of it. He's not a poet or a novelist or any kind of a writer. He's a terrorist. His son's no better, no matter what the Arts Council says about the two of them not being close or not working together."

Bernie looked out the window as their car turned into the Embassy's rear drive. He'd study the complete Quinn files, prepare himself. Uncle Danny would expect no less.

Chapter 8

The marble staircase, each wide step worn smooth in the center by years of scuffing feet, circled up the right side of the foyer. A frosted-glass enclosed elevator rose up through the middle of its spiral. Cool and shadowy, the foyer smelled of wet stone.

His garment bag slung over his shoulder, Evan climbed behind Klaus Leiner. Their feet scratched the marble like the sound of matches being struck one after another. On the second floor, they stopped at a polished wood door. Leiner pressed the convex white button above a slender silver bar on which was etched in English: Four Seasons Pension, Sieglinda Herbst, Manager. A minute passed before the door opened. A petite woman in her seventies squinted up at them.

"Inspector. Please come in," she said in English and nodded to Evan. He had expected her to speak German. She must have recognized him. Recognition outside the concert hall made him nervous and uncomfortable. It reminded him of surveillance. He preferred anonymity.

Inside, they deposited his luggage on the floor in front of a black registration desk. Shoulder-high shelves filled with books behind glass formed a partition between the desk and the pension's dining area. Evan smelled the aromas of fried potatoes and beef and heard muffled voices at the back of the dining room.

"How are you today, Frau Herbst?" Leiner said in a pleasant tone as he slipped Evan's passport across the counter.

"My knees ache. My arthritis. The terrible humidity today." She opened the passport. "Ah, you honor me, Inspector." She turned to the computer monitor and tapped it several times. Her English, Evan realized, possessed a British accent similar to Leiner's.

"Mr. Quinn," she said. "Have you a bank card?"

Leiner responded. "Not yet, Frau Herbst." He slid a plastic card to her. "Charge the Interior Ministry card for three nights, Frau Herbst. Herr Quinn will give you his bank card to charge when he has funds in his account."

Evan watched her insert the card into the monitor's keyboard. No cash, all computerized. So different from all-cash transactions in America if you wanted to stay out of debt to the NEP.

She gave Evan the receipt and held out her right hand to him. "Welcome, Mr. Quinn. We serve breakfast between seven and nine in our dining room. We offer Continental or American style included in the price of your room." She pointed to a door across the narrow foyer. "The bath and toilet are there with another door on the opposite side for our guests' convenience. We maintain a schedule for the bath so no one has long to wait. Please let me know when you would like yours." A smile flitted across her face, deepening the wrinkles around her brown eyes.

"Is there a phone in my room?"

"Naturally, Mr. Quinn. Local calls are free. For long distance or foreign calls, I will give you a code to dial before the number to charge your room until you have your bank card." She withdrew a set of heavy metal keys from the top right desk drawer. "Please come with me now."

He and Leiner collected his luggage and followed her through the dining room to a hallway on the far-left side that was just wide enough to allow two people to pass without touching. White lace curtains fluttered in the cool breeze from the open windows on their left overlooking the street below. He heard the swish of tires on wet pavement and the faint patter of rain.

Frau Herbst unlocked a door halfway down the hall. Evan's new temporary home smelled of pine with a bleach tang. Comfortable yet austere, the white room contained a single bed, an old hard plastic blue desk phone on the night-stand, and unadorned walls. Two casement windows, framed by white lace curtains, offered a view of a courtyard below. An oblong mirror hung above a sink and a heated towel rack opposite the bed. Leiner opened the maple armoire to hang up Evan's garment bag.

"Your keys." She held up three keys on a steel hoop key ring. "This is the room key." She pointed to a plain brass key. "This key opens the pension's front door." A large shiny silver key with an ornate top that resembled a Celtic knot. "And this key is for the street door." A heavy, tarnished silver key. "Please do not lose them. Is there anything else?"

"The room is perfect for my needs, Frau Herbst, thank you," Evan said, giving her one of his brightest public per-sona smiles. "I need the telephone code."

She nodded and left them, closing the door with firm precision behind her.

"Keys? That's surprisingly low tech, Inspector. I like it."

"And surprisingly effective security. No computer to hack into, no electrical power to interrupt, no card to copy. Few people now know the fine art of picking a lock. The building has surveillance cameras in the main stairway and above the entrances. You are quite safe here, Herr Quinn." Leiner opened the windows. "We assembled recommendations for security firms, martial arts schools and a list of available flats Marco found on the Internet." He removed a thick envelope from his black raincoat's inner pocket. "Most flats in Vienna will have excellent security systems, Herr Quinn. You may not need to contact any of the security firms."

"Thanks. That's great." He hadn't expected Leiner to follow up on his security concerns. So, the Austrian cop continued to do what he said he'd do, trying to build his trust. Evan opened the envelope and the folded papers. A business card fell to the floor. He picked it up. "Who's Lothar Waage? Oh, I see. A psychologist."

"Lothar Waage specializes in psychological trauma and has years of experience helping people heal from it. I am concerned about you, Herr Quinn. If the nightmares continue, or you have insomnia, or disturbing memories again like hearing the gunshots, or you have panic for no reason, or perhaps need someone to help you through your adjustment to your new life, please call Dr. Waage."

"There's nothing wrong with me," Evan said, pocketing the card.

"Marco and Johann recommend the Fischer School of

Martial Arts." Leiner walked over to the door. "And I recommend the First District flat on Stubenbastei, not far from here. It's close to the Musikverein, the Opera, shopping, *und so weiter.*"

"Stubenbastei," Evan said, holding out his hand to Leiner. "Thank you and Marco and Johann for your protection the last couple of weeks. And the guys in the surveillance shed. Don't take it personally but I hope I won't need to spend that kind of time with you again."

Leiner shook his hand with a firm, warm grip and smiled. "I look forward to your next concerts with the Vienna Philharmonic. We are available to you, Herr Quinn, if you should need us." He started out of the room, but stopped, looking back at Evan around the door. "Please remember your appointment with Dieter tomorrow morning."

"Right. The Government Center, nine o'clock."

Leiner nodded and closed the door. Evan sighed with relief. Finally! He thought the cop would never leave. And he'd bet a thousand dollars that Leiner's Stubenbastei apartment had been programmed for audio and visual surveillance so he could cross that one off the list right now. Leiner had never said that he believed him or that he'd been cleared of all suspicion. He'd been told to expect police suspicion for months.

Evan went out to the hallway windows, pulled aside the white curtain. A fine rain drizzled out of the charcoal gray clouds. A storm two nights earlier had broken the heat wave and brought cool and wet relief. A floral garden of bright umbrellas bobbed on the street below. The lights from shop windows leaked golden pools onto the sidewalk. Only eleven in the morning and as dark as dusk.

Klaus Leiner emerged from the pension building and dashed to his dark river blue sedan parked two hundred feet up the street, his black raincoat flaring out around him like bat's wings. He paused after opening the car door, surveyed the activity on the street. Evan followed his gaze to a woman with dark brown curly shoulder-length hair wearing an ivory belted raincoat who hovered in the doorway of a liquor store across the street. Leiner got into his car. The taillights blinked red. The car edged into traffic.

Frau Herbst sat at the registration desk taking a reservation on the telephone when he passed on his way out. He needed to buy some basic supplies and an umbrella at Steffl, a department store on Kärntnerstrasse the Philharmonic musicians had described to him. They said it had anything he'd need at reasonable prices. He smiled at her as he picked up a map from the pile on the counter and headed for the front door.

"Your keys?" she called after him.

He held them up for her to see. Frau Herbst, his new fussy grandmother. Leiner had chosen this pension, so she worked for him.

Outside in front of the building, he paused to study the map. As he found Kärntnerstrasse on it, he wondered if certain sections of Vienna were forbidden to him because of his economic status like in America. He didn't want to make any mistakes that might get him arrested now that he was on his own.

But not alone. The woman in the ivory belted raincoat

opened her royal blue umbrella in the liquor store entrance and headed up the street. Was she part of a tag team? Evan checked around for other surveillance shadows. He saw people with cell phones held to their ears or with headsets or silver and blue ovals above their ears, browsing shop windows or hurrying along the sidewalk and then a man in jeans and a black raincoat with his back to the street. The man stood in the entrance to a Café Konditorei, hands in pockets, attention on the pastries displayed in the window. A possible shadow, but the man entered the café. Evan tucked his map into his navy-blue sport jacket pocket, turned up his jacket collar and strolled in the same direction as Raincoat Woman. Her royal blue umbrella popped out among the black, red, yellow, and white umbrellas on the street.

The mist cooled his face. After a block, he crossed to the Café Danforth on the corner of Strobelgasse. Colorful paper flags on either side of its door advertised ice cream and pastries; in a front window, a blackboard listed the day's specials including baked chicken. Very old fashioned, he thought. Like Vienna, or at least a part of Vienna, a city adept at blending the historical with the contemporary. He made a mental note to eat at the café for supper. He turned down Strobelgasse and five minutes later emerged into a massive square with an imposing cathedral in its center. He'd never seen a church as large as this one. He headed to the left, walking past the cathedral, information kiosks and people intent on their destinations, some talking loudly into the air – into invisible cell phones. He heard French, German, English, Russian and Japanese.

Kärntnerstrasse appeared ahead to his left. He remembered Vienna Philharmonic musicians had described this street as Vienna's Fifth Avenue, a curvy pedestrian mall like Nicollet Mall in Minneapolis. Anyone could shop in its stores. They lined both sides of the street and dazzled him. He doubted he'd ever get used to the abundance available here to anyone. In America, the workers' stores sold what the Neppers wanted available to workers which everyone knew was not the same that was available to the rich in their stores. The black market flourished by selling used items discarded by the rich.

Evan paused at an information kiosk, watching the monitor which ran through the day's news headlines in German: two American states, Georgia and Florida, had announced their secession from Washington, joining the northwest, Rocky Mountain and southwest states; and the British Prime Minister had invited Randall Quinn to London. That made him laugh. Would the Neppers send an actor playing Randall or decline the invitation?

Evan glanced past the kiosk as he moved on. Raincoat Woman matched his pace across the street, browsing the window displays. At regular intervals in the middle of the avenue metal slatted benches encircled pebbly stone containers that held slender poplar trees and red flowers. Vendors sold food, souvenirs, and bouquets from carts under red and white striped umbrellas. Vienna amazed him with its blending of the old and the new everywhere, especially in unexpected places.

He stopped to examine the display of an entertainment store. Over his shoulder in the window reflection, Vigiciv Harold leered at him from the stream of passersby. He pivoted.

Harold was nowhere in sight among the people on the busy street. Turning back to the window, he stared at the display without seeing it. The Americans must have hired a guy who resembled Harold as a teenager to terrorize him. So much for Morgan's claim they sent no one after people. Evan shook his head as if to clear it and walked on.

Steffl's orange, black and white vertical sign rose above an orange awning on his left. Near the entrance, a long-haired young man sold handcrafted hemp goods laid out on the sidewalk. A pastel green placard nearby read "GAIA" in dark brown letters. Evan watched the young man hawk "All natural, biodegradable, inexpensive fibers," showing customers shirts, pants, belts, jackets, and bags.

Inside Steffl, men, women, and children wearing poplin raincoats or vinyl slickers crowded the aisles. The voices and movement and colors among the tables and shelves of merchandise created a bazaar-like atmosphere. Evan found the umbrellas within minutes.

After buying the umbrella, he encountered a salesclerk in the electronics section who greeted him with "Maestro." The salesclerk explained that most apartments already had complete, built-in electronics and computer systems. He needed to rent his apartment first to assess his electronics needs. He asked about the cell phones on sale. The salesclerk advised him to go to a phone store to set up an account first after he'd rented his apartment.

He lingered in the electronics department, thinking that he needed to do everything himself now – no Housing Council to assign him a place to live and set up utilities and telephone, no Arts Council to assign him a job, no Medical

Council to assign him a doctor and so on. He examined the computers, their pencil-thin clear monitors like panes of glass above the tables. A display at the next table looked like sports watches but turned out to be wearable computers. He watched another customer touch one monitor to bring up a menu and choose options with the touch of a fingertip on the screen. Another customer tested a voice control computer. As with its architecture, Vienna's stores offered a mixture of the old and the cutting edge – giving customers an abundance of choices, as respectful to the old as the new.

In America, he could not have bought (if he'd had the money) a new basic personal home computer, usually a laptop instead of a desktop configuration, without first applying for permission from the IT Council. The Neppers controlled everything about computers and Internet access. Office computers, like his computer at Orchestra Hall in Minneapolis, contained blocking chips to prevent the worker from going boldly where the Neppers didn't want him to go, that is, surfing the Internet. His access had been for e-mail and music-related business only. Evan had learned fast in London how to deal with the computers in his hotel rooms. Technology failed to excite him, however. High tech offered too many possibilities for surveillance and tracking, especially cell phones. He'd never carried one in America.

As he left the store carrying an orange and white Steffl shopping bag, he spotted a man on a bench in the middle of the street. The man wore jeans and a black raincoat and held a real newspaper in front of his face. Strange for someone to sit in a misty rain reading a newspaper. His memory flashed on the man standing with his back to the street in the Café

Konditorei entrance. Raincoat Woman hovered by a news-agent shop across the street. She appeared unconcerned. The man dropped the newspaper on the bench and stood, a smug grin on his unshaven face: Bernard Brown.

Evan headed up Kärntnerstrasse at a brisk pace, ready to run if Brown came after him. He turned into the next street on his right, checking back with a quick glance. Brown was nowhere in sight but Raincoat Woman had followed him. Time to lose her, too, he thought, so he'd arrive at Judenplatz without any surveillance.

Oblivious to the dripping mist, the buildings or the people who stared at him, he ran down the street and into a small plaza where he turned left, past two streets until he reached Schulerstrasse, where he veered left and stopped halfway up the block next to an information kiosk. His legs were a little stiff. He needed to return to his run every morning. He glanced back. No Brown or Raincoat Woman. Good.

He set down the shopping bag and pulled out his map to hide a sudden blush of embarrassment. He hadn't han-dled that surveillance slip well. He'd run without thinking, without knowing his route, without exercising the proper vigilance his father had taught him. A young couple under one giant umbrella came out of the street he'd just left, their heads close together in conversation. He heard French when they passed him without a glance.

He picked up his bag and started to move away from the kiosk. At the same moment, a hand tapped his arm from behind. He whirled around to look down into an old man's smudged, rain-moistened face. A beggar. The old man's eyes were teary and a sore on his sagging lower lip oozed a yellowish fluid.

"*Feuer?*" the old man rasped. His dirty, outstretched palm held a single matchbox.

"*Nein,*" Evan said in an aggressive voice and walked away. His heart thumped hard in his chest. The old man had appeared from nowhere and startled him. He had allowed his attention to slip. His father's voice sneered in his ear, "Stupid, stupid, stupid."

The main square, Stephansplatz, was straight ahead. To ensure that no one followed him, Evan plotted a route on the map around the square and on narrow streets away from the crowded shopping area. Empty streets exposed surveillance shadows.

Twenty minutes later, he came to an intersection of narrow streets deep in old Vienna. Between two gray nineteenth-century buildings on his left, antique clocks and watches glittered and chimed under a spotlight in a display window. Round, slippery cobblestones paved the street flanked by old yellow buildings. He passed a bakery, a café, a bookstore, and a compact lime beetle-like car parked half on the ribbon of concrete sidewalk and half off. He sensed that he was in one of the oldest sections of the city where the narrow streets pretzeled.

He strolled along the street's curve and straight into a modest square, deserted in the misty rain. The blue and white street sign read "Judenplatz." A massive rectangular monument in a light-colored stone occupied the middle of the square. The air smelled of pressed grapes and oily dirt.

At the far corner, Evan spotted a café sign on a cream yellow building: Café Chicago.

Two days before he'd left Minneapolis for his European tour, he'd received an encrypted e-mail at Orchestra Hall: "Café Chicago, Judenplatz, First District, Vienna." He'd memorized it and deleted the e-mail. Now he faced the place where he would learn how to fulfill his side of the deal and then be free of the NEP and America. He felt out of his depth. What would they expect of him? He was a musician, not a Nepper operative. He bristled at taking orders from them. He thought for himself. Apprehension fluttered in his stomach. He feared the Americans had more experience than he did at manipulation. He'd had enough of them.

As he turned to leave, an orchestra began playing. The music came from an open third floor window in a white building to his right, past a restaurant with a dining court in front. A wine store occupied the white building's ground floor. The music drew Evan closer. He listened to the familiar rich sound of the strings, the heroic horns, the insistent timpani of the first movement of Brahms' First Symphony.

He strolled into the side street and leaned against the building's wall, listening to the sorrow and yearning in the music. In his memory, he saw the first violins of the Chicago State Symphony Orchestra, their eyes on him, and the timpanist, his lips moving as he counted measures. During rehearsals in Chicago, he'd learned that the AC's Deputy Secretary in Washington loved Brahms' music and had personally approved his program. Conducting on the podium, feeling the sound in his body, and controlling the musicians, Evan had felt powerful. He could not live without music. He could leave now, refuse to play their game, return to the pension, and never have contact with Americans again. He was free to do what he wanted, free of them. Or was that the thinking of a naïve neophyte?

"I WANT TO BE A CONDUCTOR!" his ten-year-old voice shouted out from his memory. His mind's eye blinked through the images: his childhood bedroom, his hand on the silver window lock, the black and white cat under the peony bush by the neighbor's Victorian house. His stomach knotted and he tried to push the memory away.

"Inside, want as much as you like. But outside always do what you're told," his father's baritone sucked him back. "How can you run away, abandon Joe's music and break our hearts?"

He'd hated his father long before the day of that memory. The Brahms pressed into his ears, his mind. His father had been a violent and manipulative man, never a father to him as Uncle Joe had been. He looked up at the window, hummed with the violins. His father wanted him to be and to do exactly what he told him to be and do. Like the Neppers. Evan felt angry blood rush into his face, burning it. He'd left on tour knowing what he wanted for his life and his future. He shook his head once. He didn't need the memories anymore. He needed to remain true to Uncle Joe, to the music, to his dream of freedom. But he needed also to ensure that the Neppers were *permanently* out of his life.

A motor scooter buzzed into the square. Evan jumped, startled. The scooter's driver wore goggles, a pink scarf over his face and a black leather jacket. Evan watched him speed out of the square. The Brahms continued to play from above.

Evan glanced around the square, the slick cobblestones, the gray overcast sky, the misty air, until his eyes rested on the Café Chicago. He had done what he was told. It had saved his life in '44 after the ISS had arrested him. He'd made the secret deal.

Another voice came through his memory, a bass that spoke with confidence and precision. "Congratulations, Evan. You've done far better than expected with your training. You're a shadow warrior now. Your code name: Perceval. As long as you work for us, you'll be as free as you want to be."

Evan nodded to himself. That evening two years ago, he'd guessed from his deference that the General who had supervised his training reported to the Civilian who'd given him his code name, but he hadn't recognized the man. From his custom-tailored black suit and red silk tie, Evan knew the Civilian belonged to the Nepper elite, most likely in the federal government, maybe even the White House. He understood they were top secret and highly classified, covert, and independent of all government agencies. But the Civilian never clarified his position, revealed his name or anything else about himself.

"When the time comes," the Civilian had said. "You'll go to Europe, Evan, and get your assignment there after your defection." The Civilian had chuckled, his pale blue eyes wide. "Exactly what you want. And that's the beauty of your cover. You'll be a genuine defector."

Complete the assignment and that's it. Finished. Then he'd be free to follow his heart and music. No more Americans. His feet moved toward the Café Chicago, that bass voice in his mind's ear: "You are a true son of America."

Chapter 9

A bell rang over the door when Evan entered Café Chicago. Two elderly men played chess at a table to his right. They glanced up but returned to their game. The aroma of sautéed onions permeated the air. Ivory curtains and cascading green plants hung at the tall windows. By the side door, a well-stocked newspaper and magazine rack flanked a cabinet containing games, virtual reality headsets, and tablet and notebook computers.

"*Guten Tag*," a hefty, blonde middle-aged waitress said in a sweet soprano. She balanced a plate of food in the crook of one elbow while holding an additional plate in each hand. Her frilly white apron over a plain black dress with white collar and cuffs reminded Evan of the formality of service in Europe. American restaurants, cafés, and diners open to his economic class preferred self-serve and casual except when paying the bill.

"*Guten Tag*," Evan said.

She headed for a table to the right of a square cream-colored column at the center of the café. All the booths around this column contained computer screens. At one, two businessmen watched a finance broadcast while they ate, earbuds visible in their ears. A short, wiry, white-haired man stepped from the kitchen in the rear, beyond the pastry counter, his eyes on Evan. He wore a short-sleeved white shirt open at the neck and a long white apron over dark green pants. A cook. The man disappeared back into the kitchen.

Evan skirted the front tables. At one, a pair of women ate sandwiches; at another, two men and two women in suits talked about buying ad space in the London *Times* online; at a third, a man with two children finished off ice cream sundaes. The café's customers appeared to be benign, unthreatening to him. Evan passed the central column. He chose a table in the back corner near an ancient black wall telephone. He wondered if the phone worked anymore. After he sat down, he had a clear view of both doors and his back was to the wall. Perfect. No one could sneak up on him. He set his Steffl bag on the floor by the wall. The waitress appeared at the corner of the pastry display to his right, her eyes searching the room. She spotted him and approached his table.

"*Möchten Sie eine Speisekarte?*"

"*Ja, bitte.*" Yes, he would like a menu. He was hungry.

The white-haired guy came around the pastry display. He stopped the waitress, said something to her and nodded toward Evan. He held a folded newspaper in one hand, and no longer wore the apron. The waitress moved on, and the white-haired guy walked with a smooth, spry gait to Evan's table.

"What's too hot and humid for cherry blossoms?" the white-haired guy said, his blue eyes intent on Evan.

"Washington in July," Evan responded, his voice lower than the white-haired guy's. He hadn't expected a *cook*, someone *old*.

"Woodrow Lewis, call me Woody." The white-haired guy

gave Evan's hand a strong shake. "I own the Café Chicago. Welcome to Vienna, Perceval. You're late. I thought the Austrians had caught you." He sat down with a sigh opposite Evan and laid the newspaper between them on the table.

Evan lowered his voice and leaned forward. "Aren't you concerned about someone hearing you?"

Woody giggled. "Not in here. You're a virgin, aren't you?"

"The cops were suspicious about the two years in prison I wasn't conducting. I concentrated on my goal, my music. I worked too hard for my ticket to freedom to lose it to them. You can tell the bosses in Washington that the months of training me while in prison haven't been lost to Viennese cops, OK?"

The bell rang over the front door. A blonde man in a brown suit entered and the waitress greeted him. He chose a newspaper from the rack and, his attention on its front page, sat at the first table he came to across the room. It faced Evan. Blonde Man seemed too focused on the newspaper. People looked around a place when they first entered, even a familiar place. Evan frowned.

"I love virgins," Woody said.

Evan's eyes snapped back to Woody's face. "What's that supposed to mean?"

"All rough around the edges and tight."

Now Evan placed the man's flat American accent. Woody was from Chicago. "Can we get on with it, please?" He glanced at Blonde Man who was giving the waitress his order.

Woody giggled again, a pleasant trilling sound. "It's good that you're so paranoid. You need it. You need to make your cover so solid no one would ever dream that you're not a musician and conductor."

"I – *am* – a musician and conductor. My cover is solid. I know I'll need to be careful. What's with the Embassy? I know he's dead, they know he's dead, but Larry Morgan insisted my father was alive. He mentioned my father's trust fund in London."

Woody had nodded as he spoke, still smiling like a child, a reflection of pure enjoyment. "You're a fluke. First time an orchestra conductor has agreed to do this work. I doubt it'll happen again. I heard that you showed extraordinary talent during your training. Knocked everyone over in shock about it." His amusement melted away. "So. You're a ghost warrior, in the shadows by executive order. You don't exist as Perceval. Only as the conductor, Evan Quinn. But if you're caught doing Perceval business, no one in Washington will know Evan Quinn, either. They'll disavow you."

"I won't get caught." Evan shifted on his chair. His stomach knotted tight. Getting caught, being exposed, would mean the end of his music career. He couldn't bear that.

"Our bosses have made a major investment in you. So, you need to make certain you maintain your cover, OK? Don't get complacent just because it's the so-called real you." Woody glanced around the room, nodded to one of the elderly chess players. "As for Morgan, he's a *pissoir*. Don't worry about him. They need to show Randall alive, first to discredit you because that's their game, and second to avoid the world's outrage, the bad PR, his death will create for them."

"Bernard Brown tailed me earlier. They must have my GPS frequency. I need to get rid of the chip."

"Hmmmmm…." The lines around Woody's frown deepened into weariness. "Good point. I'm surprised they didn't remove it before you left Minneapolis but maybe that would have been a problem. Here, it's not." He pulled a paper napkin from the freestanding chrome dispenser on the table. "Did you lose Brown?"

"Yeah, visually. But he's probably tracking my frequency. I think the Austrians are on me, too." Evan sighed. "I'll need to do surveillance detection runs every time I go out."

"No." Woody slid the napkin across the table to him. "If you do surveillance detection, Brown or the Austrians will spot that behavior and your cover will be blown. You need to act like a conductor who's just moved to Vienna. Be careful, but like a civilian. Lose your surveillance, but like a civilian. After what happened at your press conference, they will expect some paranoia." Woody tapped the napkin. "I'll give him a call. He's performed this kind of removal under the table for me before and he's trustworthy. Go to that address in the Eighth District tomorrow evening at eight o'clock. The procedure takes about fifteen minutes."

Evan read the napkin. In boxy handwriting, Woody had written "Dr. Maas, Langegasse 45/10" in black ink from the pen he now laid on the table. "How much?" Evan said. He still had his per diem euros from the tour.

"Don't pay more than one hundred fifty euros. Do you have it?" Evan nodded. "Where are you staying?"

"The Four Seasons Pension on the Wollzeile. Leiner gave me a list of apartments that are available to rent. I thought I'd check them out in the next few days."

"Klaus Leiner?" Woody's eyes had turned a serious darker

blue. "He's smart, Evan. He's caught operatives no one else even suspected. He'll be on you for months."

"Yeah, I figured as much." Evan noticed the waitress approach with a tray. "I didn't order yet."

Woody's mirth returned. "Lunch is on me, Evan. You'll begin with a *Griessnockerl* soup."

"*Bitte sehr*," the waitress said as she set a bowl of steaming soup in front of Evan. Two oblong white semolina dumplings floated in the clear broth. The soup smelled delicious.

"You had surveillance and surveillance detection in your training?"

Woody questioning his training in such a delicate tone made Evan wary. He slurped a spoonful of hot broth as he considered his reply. "I had basic surveillance training. Officially. My instructor said counter surveillance wasn't on my schedule, but I talked him into teaching me on the sly. It didn't make sense to have one and not the other."

His instructor during training hadn't taught him any counter surveillance. He'd learned counter surveillance from his father. Now he knew he wasn't supposed to know counter surveillance. Why hadn't they given him a complete course of training?

"Your code name," Woody said, amused. "You know who Perceval was?"

"A knight of King Arthur's Round Table," Evan said.

"He was a Grail knight, one of three who saw the Holy Grail." Woody giggled. "But he didn't know what he'd seen because he'd been taught not to ask the importance of something he didn't understand. He was blind to it, ignorant."

Evan shrugged, returned to his soup. "I ask questions. I've completed the quest for my freedom."

Woody shifted in his seat, his eyes watching Evan's spoon dip again into the soup. "Most Americans come here to eat American food, and I'm proud of our menu. But my wife is Austrian," Woody said. "She cooks the best Austrian and Hungarian dishes in Vienna, if I may say so. As our welcome to you, we serve you this soup and Wiener Schnitzel with a mixed vegetable salad. *In Ordnung?*" Woody smiled, his tone and expression now paternal.

"Yes," Evan said as he sliced a dumpling. "Thanks. My compliments to Frau Lewis for this delicious soup. You know, I need to find a reference book that will help me with Austrian culture and customs."

"Let me see." He opened the newspaper on the table. "Check the bookstore ads in here. But don't get yourself in a lather about Austrian culture and customs. If the natives see you're trying, they'll help you. They're good people. And the customs aren't so different."

"An English-language newspaper?" Evan said, ripping a slice of bread in half.

"The American expat newspaper, *The Village Spectator*," Woody said. "Subscribe to it. I'll put coded messages into it for you, if necessary." He folded the newspaper back to one page. His left index finger tapped a large photograph of a Chinese official standing by a limousine with other Chinese men. "Your assignment. Vice Chairman Jiang Xu. He needs to join his ancestors in the afterlife. According to my sources, he's coming to Vienna to attend the Chinese-American talks at the Hofburg. We haven't nailed down a date yet. Could be any day. The Chinese delegation is staying at the Parkhotel Schönbrunn." He slid the newspaper over to Evan.

They wanted him to kill someone?

Beyond Woody's head, Evan observed the Blonde Man pay the waitress. He looked at Evan, met his eyes, but showed no recognition. He returned his newspaper to the rack and left by the side door. Blonde Man hadn't paid attention to anyone else in the café except him. Evan's eyes returned to Woody. "I don't think we should meet here often," he said.

Woody nodded. "You spotted someone."

"Maybe. He's gone now."

Woody giggled. "I love your paranoia, Evan. It's so healthy. Here," he said, sliding a sleek black cell phone over to Evan. "It's clean. The number's under a corporate account I established. Anyone asks, I gave it to you as a welcome gift to help until you get settled. Use it to contact me until December thirty-first when the number expires. Use the name Georg when you call, in case anyone picks up the frequency."

"Were you DIA, Woody, or CIA?"

Woody laughed, his mouth wide open, head back. He laughed for a full minute, then, shaking his head, said, "I taught American Studies at the University of Vienna for thirty-five years while my wife ran this café. I came to Vienna to study and I stayed."

Evan looked away, feeling as if Woody had slapped his face. The waitress appeared with her tray and removed his empty soup bowl.

Woody continued. "Bernie Brown is CIA, so he may try to contact you. If they run a check, and they will, and you are clean and not with any government agency, which you will be, they may try to recruit you."

Now it was Evan's turn to laugh. "Not in a million years."

The waitress brought his Wiener Schnitzel with a salad of lettuce, potatoes, onion, green beans and tomatoes. "*Möchten Sie etwas zum trinken, mein Herr?*" she said.

"*Ein Bier*, Marta," Woody said.

"*Kein Bier*," Evan said. "*Danke. Ein Glas Apfelsaft, bitte.*" The waitress nodded and left. "Thanks, Woody, but I don't drink alcohol."

"None at all?" Woody's blue eyes widened in surprise.

"I saw what it did to my mother." He cut a thin slice of the breaded veal. "Do I give you my order?" He felt, suddenly, as if he were saying lines in a gangster movie. They wanted him to kill another human being.

"Your order?" Woody, his eyes on Evan's food, looked puzzled for a moment. "Oh, yes, of course." He pulled another paper napkin from the dispenser. "Write it on this. I can never remember details about guns."

"I'll also need a duplicate passport, alternate passports, and ID documents, per operating procedure. I want two for now: one Canadian, one Swiss. How long?"

Woody giggled, smoothed back his wispy white hair with one hand. "My forger can work miracles on the computer. But, he's out of town on holiday. You'll have to wait. In the meantime, figure out what physical appearance and identity you want for each alternate. You're lucky EU customs and border agents don't scan retinas yet but it's coming."

Evan frowned. "I need alternate IDs as part of my escape routes, Woody. How long is your guy on vacation?"

"You'll have your escape routes, if that becomes necessary. Write your order." Woody, serious again, nodded to the blank napkin on the table.

Something was off track here. They had taught him to expect his handler to provide what he needed, including alternate documents and escape routes away from the operation location. No hesitation, no delay. But he was stuck with this old guy. And they wanted him to kill a human being. Evan picked up the pen. "When he gets back, I want to talk to your forger myself. OK? I need orphans. Do you know what that means?"

"Untraceable. I work with solid, reliable suppliers with the utmost discretion. You'll have them by the end of the week."

Evan handed him the list on the napkin. "You'll destroy that?"

The mirth returned to Woody's face. "I'm still here, aren't I?"

Evan felt the blush burn his face. "I don't want to get caught."

Woody pocketed the napkin. "You'll be fine, Evan. Relax. Be yourself. That's the way you won't get caught. Leiner's smart. He'll spot any tradecraft so don't use it unless you must. And don't worry about Brown's Mickey Mouse games." He stood up. "Call me if you need anything. You're welcome here any time. Enjoy your lunch, Evan."

"Thanks, Woody." He shook his hand. Woody ambled off toward the kitchen. As Evan glanced around the room, he realized he had not believed that he'd make it this far. He didn't know who the bosses in Washington were who'd made the investment in him, only that they were shadows, top secret, hidden. They wanted him to assassinate the Chinese Vice Chairman. A human being. He'd never shot a human being. It didn't seem real. There was time – time for something to happen to relieve him of this assignment forever so he wouldn't have to complete it. Maybe the Uighurs would get to the Chinese Vice Chairman first.

The tender Wiener Schnitzel tasted better and sweeter than any meat he'd eaten in America. He sipped apple juice. He'd need to stay on Woody, make certain he did his job. No one could ever find out about Perceval. No one could ever truly know him. Paranoia was self-preservation.

"Ellie's diversion succeeded completely," the soft-spoken Blonde Man said, leaning back in his chair in front of Klaus's old and scuffed walnut desk. His precise German pronunciation reminded Klaus that he'd worked as a speech therapist before joining the police. "He never spotted the rest of us."

"Bernard Brown stood in the Café Konditorei doorway. Did you see him, Freddy?" He tapped the record button on his desk computer to insure it recorded them, feeling pleased with the day's work on Evan Quinn.

Freddy nodded. "Martin picked him up. Brown followed Quinn to Steffl's and sat outside on a bench opposite the front entrance, reading a newspaper."

"Not very subtle." He looked up as Marco appeared in

his office doorway. "Come in, Marco. You haven't missed much."

"He's an easy tail?" Marco said, sliding into the chair next to Freddy.

Freddy nodded. "Quinn's a civilian, unsophisticated in surveillance. It's an easy job."

"And Brown?" Klaus said, tapping a pen on his desk.

"Bernard Brown tailed him, too?" Marco sat up straight with interest. "Are the Americans going to make a mistake?"

"We shall see," Klaus said. "Freddy?" He nodded to the former speech therapist.

"*Ja*, Brown dropped Quinn in front of Steffl's. We staggered surveillance. Brown returned to the Embassy. Quinn went to the Café Chicago in Judenplatz."

"Hungry for American food already," Marco said, laughing. "How did he find out about it?"

Klaus shrugged. "Perhaps the Philharmonic musicians. Frau Herbst would have called me if he'd asked her for anything American."

Freddy continued. "I entered Café Chicago and observed Quinn talking with the owner, Woodrow Lewis."

"They know each other?" Marco said.

Freddy shook his head, no. "Lewis was sitting at Quinn's table when I came in. Quinn's a famous American conductor. The owner of the café wanted to welcome him. My impression from their behavior. I saw Lewis give Quinn a newspaper. It looked like *The Village Spectator*, that newspaper Americans here have published for, how long, Inspector?"

"Twenty-five years, I believe. It's quite popular with the University students. Herr Lewis taught American Studies there for years." Klaus leaned forward. "Freddy, did you hear any of their conversation?"

"I didn't have the proper electronics and I couldn't get close enough." Freddy shook his head in disappointment. "I saw Quinn look at me several times, not at anyone else in the café. So, I didn't stay long."

"Kristofer picked him up?" Marco said. Klaus looked at the sergeant, feeling a surge of confidence in his choice of him to lead the surveillance operation.

"*Ja*, Kristofer. Quinn walked all over the First District after he left the café. He stopped in a Tabak Trafik and bought a streetcar fare card. He stopped in an English language bookstore but bought nothing. Then he strolled on the Ring Boulevard from the University to the Wollzeile."

Marco frowned. "Was he checking for surveillance? It sounds like it." Marco looked at Klaus. "Brown made him nervous?"

"Brown would make anyone nervous. He'd enjoy it, too," Klaus said. "Morgan told him at their meeting that they would leave him alone. Quinn encountered Brown at Steffl. Now he's paranoid. However, it cannot be coincidence that Herr Brown was following him today." Klaus got up, walked over to one of two windows in his modest office and a row of begonias on the sill. He tested the soil in one pot with a fingertip. Dry. Laura would scold him. "Marco, tell your team: one tails Brown if he shows up. You handled it correctly today, Freddy."

Marco nodded. "Café Chicago?"

Klaus frowned, testing the soil of the three other begonias and finding them all dry. He could never remember to water them. "We know Lewis. He's not a subject of interest. Our primary subject, Marco, is Quinn. Freddy, who's on him now?"

"Kristofer. If Quinn leaves the pension, Gianni will take over. Frau Herbst has reported Quinn's in his room, making telephone calls. She said he has called Peter Windsor and Nigel Fox in London, and Vassily Bartyakov here."

Bartyakov? How did Quinn know that Russian? Klaus pinched a dead leaf off a begonia. He hadn't talked with Bartyakov in perhaps two years. Well, they were both musicians.

"Good," he said, glancing at his two cops. "You will have a quiet night. Quinn meets with Dieter Aschenbeck in the morning. After that meeting?" He looked at Marco who nodded. "Thank you for your fine work today."

Klaus watched Marco and Freddy leave before he sat down at his desk again. He stared at his overflowing in-basket without seeing it. Nothing. Nothing Evan Quinn had done today clued him to the American's mission here. Brown's interest, however, could mean one of three things: either the Americans wanted to make contact with their new spy, or they wanted to recruit Quinn for the CIA, or they planned to kill him.

Chapter 10

The laser crossed Evan's eye with a breath of sensation and bright pinpoint of light. The retina scan for his new ID card. He leaned forward on the high stool, his chin resting on the cushioned platform, his forehead pressed against a cushioned holder.

"This contract that arrived yesterday from Nigel Fox," Dieter Aschenbeck's reedy voice said behind him. "Does this mean that he now manages your business?"

The robot technician in a white lab coat thanked him and Evan sat back. Her thick, shiny black hair framed her delicate face and matched her eyes. He smiled and she smiled back but turned away to her computer. He'd never seen such a life-like robot.

He nodded to Aschenbeck. "Once I've signed the contract, and he's signed it, we're in business. I'm excited, Dieter. He told me the Amsterdam Concertgebouw may want to hire me for their American Music Festival."

"Excellent," Aschenbeck said, tapping Evan's arm. "Fingerprinting and DNA now. I could refer you to a lawyer, if you would like."

"Why would I need a lawyer?" Evan dug his hands into his jeans pockets. As soon as he'd blurted out the question, he felt uneasy. Exposing his ignorance could hurt him.

As the Interior Ministry lawyer spoke, he directed Evan out of the dark gray, modern scanning room and into the old clubby oak-paneled hallway with gleaming parquet floor then to a door on their right. "I understand, Evan, that the Arts Council prevented you from learning how to protect your best interests, professionally and personally. Or perhaps contract law as we know it here no longer exists in America." The Austrian gave him a sympathetic smile. "When you have business that involves money or a contract, which is most business, it is essential for a lawyer to review all the documents before you sign anything. Additionally, individuals have other legal business in their lives; for example, if they buy a house or draw up their Last Will and Testament or establish a trust as Mr. Redfield did for you with Caine's publisher."

The Arts Council had never arranged legal counsel for him in any situation. Aschenbeck had been the first lawyer with whom he'd worked. He disliked the complexities and complications of European life and that he must do everything himself. If business concerns occupied his time, he wasn't working on his music which was his life. In America, the Arts Council had taken care of everything to ensure a profitable bottom line, and as a result, also insured that he concentrated all his time on music. He hadn't been free to choose the music he studied or conducted but the AC freed him from business tasks and concerns.

In London six weeks ago, he'd learned from the orchestra musicians about artist managers and the need for representation. He believed Nigel would take care of everything for him as the Arts Council had. According to Aschenbeck, he also needed a lawyer to review contracts. How many more people must he hire, how much more must he do for himself that took him away from music, how much more didn't he know that might put him at a disadvantage and make him vulnerable?

They entered a laboratory with long tables and equipment that reminded Evan of chemistry lab in high school. Subdued lighting threw shadows around the tables. The air held the faint sharpness of mustard.

"Fingerprints and DNA for Herr Quinn. ID number 378Q999," Aschenbeck said to a short lab technician who appeared no older than twenty.

Evan scrutinized the lab tech. He'd drawn his long brown hair into a thick pony tail down his back. Was he a robot also or human? Not all lab techs were robots. He would not have known one way or the other if Aschenbeck hadn't warned him before they met the first lab tech, the woman robot.

"You are a new resident in our fine country, *nicht wahr*, Maestro?" the lab tech said with a sweet smile. "Has Austria given you asylum?"

Evan nodded. "Herr Aschenbeck told me this morning. Political asylum and a resident visa."

"Congratulations. Sit here, please." The lab tech indicated a clear, hard plastic chair by one of the long lab tables. He tapped the desktop computer's wafer-thin clear monitor on the table, bringing up file Number 378Q999. He opened a scanner next to the computer. "You will please place your hand open and flat within the outline and press down gently but firmly."

The outline appeared on the scanner screen for the left

hand. Evan pressed his left hand onto it. He saw the hand print reproduced in his file on the monitor.

The Austrian system made criminal activity nearly impossible, similar to the Federal Identification Cards required for everyone in America, created in response to increased terrorism. His Federal ID card contained fingerprint, DNA, a photograph and other personal information, but no one here had asked for it. The Austrians possessed his retina scan, and his finger and palm prints for identification, his DNA, and photographs. At least the Austrians weren't tagging him with a tracking chip as the Neppers had.

His DNA. Uncle Joe had told him that the NEP's nationwide campaign to register all American citizens by their DNA was perceived by opposing political parties, the ACLU, civil rights activists, and states as illegal, a violation of constitutional rights and the beginning of oppression. The Rocky Mountain States had seceded, sparking the insurgency. The NEP succeeded, however, in registering everyone. They arrested the opposition and destroyed the ACLU. Now the Austrians possessed his DNA for a far different purpose than the NEP had in mind. He was a conductor, a civilian, and needed the bank and ID cards to live his new life. He'd need to avoid leaving his DNA when working as Perceval.

Aschenbeck led him to a lounge and left to collect Evan's cards. The black and cobalt blue room resembled VIP lounges he'd waited in at European airports and train stations, but without the food and drinks and people. Three fresh bouquets of summer flowers scented the air. He walked over to a window, noticing the double-thick glass. Bulletproof. Bullets. He'd forgotten to list ammunition on his order to Woody.

That was stupid. Maybe his handler would include it anyway. The International Wal-Mart store would sell latex gloves to protect against leaving fingerprints and DNA. He'd need to locate a theatrical costume store for wigs and makeup. He couldn't make a permanent change to his appearance because of his conducting career so he would rely on soft disguises.

The window faced a gray stone 19th century building across the street, identical to the one he was in. The poignant *Adagietto* movement of Mahler's Fifth Symphony floated into his mind, soothing him, and he began singing it soft and low to himself. He closed his eyes, feeling the sunshine from the window on his face, and visualized the score, the harp's line above the violins, violas, cellos, and basses. He sang the first violin part and his right hand beat Mahler's time *sehr langsam*.

"Maestro," Aschenbeck said in a quiet voice behind him.

"Oh, sorry," Evan said. "I'm working on the Mahler Five for the Philharmonic concerts in September."

"No need to apologize, Evan. You have much work to do, so let us finish here."

Aschenbeck held out two hard plastic cards to Evan. "The black one is your Identification card. You understand, Evan, about the decision to place you on six-month probation?"

Evan nodded, clenching and releasing his teeth. He'd been told to expect this obstacle. "I'm fine with it," Evan said hiding his irritation by flashing one of his bright public persona smiles and taking the cards.

Aschenbeck nodded. "The blue card is your bank card for your main account. Use this to pay for everything. Please keep the emergency telephone numbers for each of these cards in a safe place, Evan. You will need them if you lose either of the cards." Aschenbeck smiled, nodded once. He pulled a card from his suit jacket pocket. "My business card. Please contact me if you need anything, Evan."

Evan put the cards with the business card in his wallet. "Peter Windsor?"

"Done. Phone him to follow up, especially to confirm the money transfer which you can check at the bank's website." Aschenbeck handed him another business card. "I would trust Christian Bach with my life, and I cannot say that about all lawyers. I believe he can protect your best interests. He has worked for other musicians."

Evan pocketed the card. "Thanks, Dieter. You have the list of doctors?"

Aschenbeck pulled a folded paper from inside his suit jacket. "You have indicated that you plan to live in Vienna. Remember to receive a vaccination against the tick-borne encephalitis. Any of the doctors on the list can give it to you, as well as provide any other medical service, as necessary. They all speak English."

Evan scanned the paper, relieved to find Dr. Maas on the list. He'd request the vaccination this evening from the good doctor after he removed the tracking chip. Evan turned to leave.

"Maestro, before you go." The lawyer pulled a palm-sized, neon blue cell phone from his suit pocket and handed it to Evan. "A small welcome gift."

"Thank you, Dieter. From you and the Ministry?"

"From me and Klaus. You will need to stop by any telephone store to activate the account and confirm your home address when you have a flat. I set it up for you."

Klaus Leiner, Evan thought with a mental chill. Directional surveillance or listening bugs. He assumed the cell phone capable of both. "Good thing I'll be looking at apartments today. I really need a home address." Evan laughed. He examined the phone, its keypad and display. "I thought cell phones in Europe had camera and video capabilities."

"No longer, Evan. Those functions were abused, horribly abused. By malicious people and criminals, by spies, by pedophiles and stalkers – we learned that, like guns, the negative uses overwhelmed the positive. No cell phones now have those capabilities. They are illegal."

"People before technology." He slipped the neon blue phone into his jacket pocket. "I've noticed that's a priority in Europe."

Dieter nodded. "Human life is more important than technology."

Evan held out his right hand to Dieter. "Thank you again for everything, Dieter. Your help has been invaluable to me." He spoke the truth.

"My wife and I wish only the best for you in your new life, Maestro."

A half hour later, Bartyakov waited for him in front of the Staatsoper portico.

"Vassily! Sorry I'm late. I had to stop at my lawyer's office to drop off a contract."

"Maestro, good morning!" The Russian piano student hopped from one foot to the other, grinning. "You here. You really here. Greta and I so excited you call last night."

"It's great to see you, man." Evan grasped the Russian's hand, feeling a tightening in his chest. Despite his compact wrestler's body, the Russian's resemblance to Uncle Joe was eerie. Had Bartyakov ever looked in the mirror and seen Joseph Caine's intense blue eyes and wolf-like face looking at him from his own face? Evan wanted to trust their connection above and beyond simply trusting a fellow musician.

Bartyakov's round blue eyes sparkled. "Beautiful day to hunt apartments. You bring list from cops?" Evan handed over the list. "OK. Four apartments close to us here. One in First District on Stubenbastei, two in Third District and one in Ninth. We can see apartments in outer districts another day, OK? You call to set up viewing?"

"I have to call first?" All these procedures. No calls in America. The Housing Council just told him where to live.

"No problem, Maestro. I have cell phone. We call them now."

"Forget the Stubenbastei place. The cops pushed it. And call me Evan. Maestro is for work."

"Evan, me Vasia." Vasia dialed the first number. "We look at Stubenbastei last, if you find nothing." Vasia nodded, his eyes knowing.

Vasia persuaded each apartment's rental agent to meet them that afternoon, emphasizing the importance of finding a world-famous conductor somewhere to live in Vienna as soon as possible. Fame conquered all. It made Evan uneasy, like waiting for the other shoe to drop.

They ate lunch at the Café Landtmann on the Ring Boulevard. Vasia claimed a table for them outside to enjoy the sunshine and fresh air.

"And we watch girls," Vasia giggled.

"What would your girlfriend think?" Evan sipped his

mineral water, gazing out at the steady flow of bicycles, motor scooters, the occasional car and pedestrians on the wide boulevard, punctuated by a red and white rumbling streetcar.

"Greta watch boys." Vasia giggled again. "You have girl-friend in America?"

Evan shook his head no. Attachments offered the ISS dangerous opportunities for control.

"So you free for love," Vasia said and lifted his beer in a toast. "To freedom!"

Evan frowned. "Everything is so different here." He leaned back and squinted up at the sun.

"Everything is adventure here." Vasia leaned forward and grinned at him.

"But I feel stupid, Vasia. The Arts Council took care of almost everything for me in America. I feel like I've lost all my experience, everything I know."

"No one expect you to know everything, Evan." Vasia heaved a dramatic sigh. "You have lifetime of experience but for America. Here, new way of life to learn, that's all. You smart, you can do it."

Evan laughed, shaking his head. "You sound like my high school basketball coach. So tell me, do you know how to cook and clean and wash clothes? I don't. There's always been a housekeeper in my life to take care of all my domestic needs."

"Beautiful young housekeeper?"

"Vasia." He gave the Russian a stern frown. Apparently, Bartyakov had yet to learn that women were more often than not the flies in the honey of life. Women always left. "All middle-aged. The last one was my father's age and complained about her arthritis all the time. She was a good cook, though, and creative about finding good meat."

"We saw your press conference. The Right Path terrorists have been already charged with attempted murder. Soon they have trial."

"Well, that's good news. Are they in jail?" The last thing he needed was two terrorists on the street who'd like to kill him.

"*Da,* in prison. How are Americans? You meet with them?"

"Yeah. They're a pain in the ass."

Bartyakov snorted. "Entire workforce of eyes and ears paid to follow objects because of certain subjects. They will follow you because of your father. These people have nothing better to do with their lives." Bartyakov snorted again.

Evan's ears burned. He'd heard a similar comment from the surveillance instructor. "I'm surprised you know such things, Vasia."

"Oh, believe me, I can teach you things to protect you. Russians gave me extreme hard time three years ago. Guy at Russian Embassy told me I was object he was going to follow because of subject of my unknown loyalties. I am loyal, but after their treatment, I lost all loyalty for Russia. Now I have residence visa for Austria and I apply for citizenship."

"When did they stop, Vasia?" His mind raced. Appearing to learn surveillance detection techniques (that he knew already) from a Russian piano student in front of the Austrians would only reinforce his cover. He couldn't believe his luck.

"They never stop. See man there?" Vasia nodded toward a pasty blonde man who hovered in front of the City Hall across the street. "He Russian. He follow me before. I don't care. The police and everyone at University know about them. If something happen…." Bartyakov exhaled as if blowing dust away.

"The police? The Viennese police?"

"Of course, Viennese police. I am registered. You must register also, Evan, after you move to apartment. So, I call them and report Russians. If Americans harass you, call police and tell them. But first," Vasia leaned in, his voice lowered to a conspiratorial whisper, "I teach you how to lose them."

They lost the pasty blonde Russian after ducking into the Minoriten Church and out a side door, around the back and through a skinny street. Evan had marked a possible shadow – a dark-haired guy with a moustache – but said nothing to Vasia about him. They cut through Volksgarten Park, and Vasia led him into the Ninth District behind the University to the first apartment on the afternoon's schedule.

Neither of them liked the old building, the dank smell in the hallway, or the few windows in the Ninth District apartment. The next one was in a working-class neighborhood south of Schwarzenberg Platz that Vasia deemed inappropriate for a famous conductor. In America, his economic status would have made him just barely eligible for that neighborhood. The last one on the cops' list for the day was on the Landstrasse Hauptstrasse across from Stadtpark and the Hilton Hotel. The apartment occupied the front half of the top floor of the building which the owner had renovated twenty years earlier. Vasia fell in love with its spacious rooms filled with windows, gleaming wood floors, its large kitchen, and the master bedroom in the rear, away from the noisy boulevard.

While the Russian discussed the financial details with the rental agent, Evan looked out the gigantic front window surrounded by casements. Trees rustled on either side. Traffic whisked by below. He smelled lemon with an edge of bleach. Evan wanted a quieter neighborhood and few distractions. Like White Oaks in Minneapolis or the Brooklyn neighborhood where he had lived during his Juilliard years. He sighed, his eyes resting on the Hilton Hotel across the street. He'd relaxed with Vasia. He felt safe with him. He liked the Russian. He'd be a solid source of information on how to live in Vienna, among other things.

"Evan, what you think? Perfect, yes?"

Evan nodded. "I'm tired, Vasia. You finished here?"

"Look. City Air Terminal at Hilton Hotel across street. Excellent for touring. Better for environment not to buy car."

He pointed at the electronics wall. "Do all apartments have the electronics built in like this?"

Vasia walked over to the wall. "Old apartments no. But you can renovate."

"Security?"

"Top of line. All apartments now have security system. Some excellent, some only basic. You want top of line, Evan."

"The computer controls the security?"

"Separate computer with separate power source. Very, very important, Evan. Security system must have separate computer, separate power source."

"Right." Evan examined the electronic components in the wall. "Did you do any hunting in Russia, Vasia?"

"Of course. I hunt now. You hunt also in America?"

Evan nodded. "When I was a kid, with my father, Joe and Paul Caine. I haven't hunted for years because of the weird situation with the insurgency, but I'd like to get back into it now. The cops won't approve a gun license for me here in Austria yet. I'm on probation for six months. I'd like to check out hunting in other countries."

"Romania! We hunt bear in Romania, wild boar, wolf, rabbit, anything." The Russian's eyes had lit up and he punched one fist into the palm of his other hand, dancing from one foot to the other like a boxer. "Unbelievable! No one else I know here want to hunt. I want to hunt bear and wolf this October. You want to come with me, Evan?"

"Sounds good. But I need to check my schedule and find a way to buy a gun. Maybe in Romania?" His sniper instructor had told him to keep back-up guns. Hunting provided the perfect cover for a gun collection.

"No problem. I buy gun for you. I have license for hunting rifle." The Russian slapped his shoulder. "We celebrate now. I know perfect place."

"Oh, sorry, Vasia. I already have plans. We're not far from my pension, though."

Evan left Vasia at the Café Konditorei across from the Four Seasons and returned to the pension. A twenty-something blonde man sat at the registration desk. Evan hadn't seen him before but noted a family resemblance to Frau Herbst. He nodded to the man in greeting.

Back in his room, he took out the neon blue cell phone

Aschenbeck had given him and turned it over. He slid the back cover off, popped the battery out. He examined the phone's hard drive and other parts. He saw nothing unusual, but still believed the phone was bugged, the surveillance protocols programmed into the hard drive. He set it on the upper shelf in the armoire, thinking that he'd have to activate it. The Austrians would expect it. He grabbed the black cell phone from the armoire shelf and dropped it into his jacket pocket.

What was Quinn doing? Bernie thought as the blinking green dot on his cell phone's display moved. The GPS tracking chip was no substitute for the behavioral clues he'd see with visual surveillance.

Bernie sat on a street bench near Schottentor. He'd watched Quinn's GPS dot travel around the Ring from the Four Seasons Pension as he'd walked from his office at the American Embassy. He hadn't arrived at Schottentor in time to see Quinn cross to Alserstrasse where Quinn's dot blinked now, heading for the general hospital. Fascinated, he got up to walk to Quinn's location.

According to his file, Quinn liked to run, but went on his runs in the mornings. Maybe the Maestro had gone out for an evening walk. He checked his watch: 7:45 p.m. What was Quinn doing? He knew that Quinn didn't know Vienna, knew no one in the city except the people he'd met at the

Philharmonic. Maybe a musician who lived near the hospital had invited Quinn to visit.

About twenty minutes later, Bernie turned down Langegasse. Quinn had not gone to the hospital, so his theory of Quinn visiting a musician showed more promise. He opened his cell phone again to check Quinn's position. The dot had stopped and the address had appeared at the bottom of the screen: Langegasse 45.

The day before he'd marked an Austrian surveillance team on Quinn. Now, as he ambled down the street, he noted a young couple talking in front of a building next to a park. They each surveyed the street. Farther along, a person sat in a canary yellow car alone but Bernie couldn't see if the person was male or female. At any rate, for a Viennese to sit in a car alone on the street for a long time was unusual behavior.

He passed Number 45, glancing at the plaque next to the door. The building held offices and the only name he'd been able to read was a public relations firm. He jogged across the street to take up a position in the park. As he turned to sit down on a bench facing the street, the canary yellow car left. The couple remained up the street. At this time of year, the sun set after nine o'clock giving him good light for another hour. He slipped out his phone and checked the display. Quinn's dot remained at Number 45. He pretended to dial and talk on the phone.

Half an hour later, Quinn emerged from Number 45, studying the street and the park. Bernie smiled. Quinn was paranoid about surveillance. Good. He knew neither Quinn nor the Austrians would recognize him because of his old codger disguise. Bernie opened his phone to pretend to dial. Quinn's dot had disappeared from the display. He frowned.

As Quinn walked up the street past the talking couple, Bernie dialed his man at Embassy technical support services.

"There's nothing wrong with the equipment, Bernie. He's gone."

"Explanation?"

"He removed the chip."

"Why isn't it showing up at the location where he removed it?"

"It's no longer functioning. Deactivated and destroyed."

"Terrific. You can cross Quinn off your duty roster." Bernie slapped the phone shut. Yeah, if he were Quinn, he'd want to get rid of that tracking chip as soon as possible now that he could.

The conversing couple strolled after Quinn toward Alserstrasse. Bernie walked over to Langegasse 45, up the steps to the slate of doorbells. He wanted to know, for future reference for himself, who'd done the removal job for Quinn.

Chapter 11

Evan walked toward the Kunsthistorisches Museum, the large art history museum. He felt the weight of history all around in the mix of architecture from different centuries contrasted with contemporary buildings, the abundance of computerized kiosks that resembled stainless steel bullets, the ubiquitous cell phone in all its forms, people wearing computers on their wrists or pinned to lapels or attached to eye glasses, sleek stainless-steel streetcars and older red and white ones, and the press of walking people. Few cars. Public transport ruled this city of environmentalists, he thought.

Evan observed the people around him, how they moved, where their eyes looked and memorized faces. He'd spotted an old guy the evening before in the park across from Dr. Maas' office, and expected to see him again, although he hadn't been certain the old guy was a shadow. The surgery to remove the tracking chip behind his left ear had been a success, which blinded the Americans, increasing the chance of closer surveillance by them.

At the streetcar stop, older tourists dressed in shorts or skirts and sandals for the steamy weather waited with a group of chattering Italian teens tapping their wrist computers to message friends or twitching to music from ear-buds, and Viennese holding shopping bags or briefcases. The smell of oil from the tracks permeated the air. Evan slipped in among the older tourists, smiling, wishing he didn't stick out so much in his jeans, light blue Oxford shirt and sport jacket. He carried a dark blue knapsack, his guide book and city map which he now pretended to study as he made note of the people who arrived after him. Only one caught his attention: an attractive woman with shoulder length, dark brown curly hair. A mental tug with the flash of memory – royal blue umbrella open in the rain– signaled familiarity.

An older red and white streetcar rolled up to the stop, electric wires sparking, its bell ringing, the number "58" flashing white in a black circle on top of the front car. Evan moved with the tourists. The curly-haired woman followed the group of teens, but other people hung back, waiting for a different streetcar. Evan boarded at the front with the tour-ists, waiting as each inserted a ticket into the computerized ticket machine. Curly Hair boarded in the back with the teens, scanned her fare card at the ticket machine and chose a window seat at the back. A melodious female voice on the public address system announced in German that the doors were about to close. He took a window seat.

Half an hour later, they turned left and proceeded down a gentle hill to a stop. Spread out in front of them stood a massive Baroque palace in the favored ochre yellow of the period. The PA system's female voice announced "Schloss Schönbrunn."

Evan disembarked with the older tourists. He glanced back. Curly Hair had gotten off also. With one hand, she combed her hair back from her face. Something flashed in her ear. She was a shadow. He needed to flush her, find out if there were others. He followed the tourists across the street to the palace's main gate flanked by columns topped by statues of imperial eagles, wings spread. He stared for a long moment at the expanse of the palace, the elegance of its symmetry and lines. What does an ordinary conductor do when he's seen someone following him and he doesn't want to be followed?

Instead of entering the palace grounds, he strolled to the right along the street, out in the open, alone, the palace's black metal fence on his left, grass and shrubs a buffer to the street on his right. Almost to the corner, he abruptly reversed direction. He walked straight for Curly Hair following him. She had nowhere to hide. Far behind her, a lone man broke into a run. A surveillance tag team. As Evan strode up to Curly Hair, she froze. He gave her his bright public persona smile.

"*Das macht mir nichts aus,*" he said as Lone Man ran up to them. Evan continued in German, "It doesn't matter to me if you are with the police or the Americans. I don't need this – this harassment. Are you with the police?" Curly Hair nodded. Lone Man avoided Evan's eyes. "Has a threat been made against my life? Why do you follow me? I see your ear bugs and you look exactly like the ISS agents who follow, arrest, and disappear people. Show me your identification." They pulled out their Viennese police IDs.

"Maestro," Curly Hair said and continued in German, "We have been assigned to follow you, nothing more."

"It is not necessary to tell him anything," Lone Man said to her.

"I'm certain it's not," Evan replied with a smile. He took

out his black cell phone and Dieter Aschenbeck's business card from his wallet. He spoke as he dialed the Austrian's number. "I plan to walk around this neighborhood, check out the sights, spend some time at the palace. Then I plan to visit a martial arts school that Marco and Johann recommended to me. Do you know Marco and Johann? If you both would like to accompany me, I have no objections. Otherwise," and now he switched to English, "get lost." He heard Aschenbeck's reedy voice on the phone. "Herr Aschenbeck? Dieter, it's Evan Quinn. Did you know that I'm being harassed by the Viennese police? I'm talking right now to a pair of them."

Lone Man threw up his arms in helpless surrender and pivoted away.

Dieter said in Evan's ear, "I apologize, Evan. Please let me talk with them."

He handed the phone to Curly Hair and stepped away to give her some privacy, although it probably didn't matter. As she spoke with Dieter, he watched Lone Man walk back toward the palace's main entrance.

Curly Hair closed the phone and said in English, "No more surveillance, Maestro. I am sorry if we disturbed or upset you." She returned his black cell phone.

"Apology accepted. I remember you from the other day. You stood in the entrance to the liquor store across from the Four Seasons Pension."

Her cheeks colored a gentle pink. "You have a good memory. But Maestro, please, be careful, yes? Any problems with anyone, call us. We will come *sofort*." She walked away. Lone Man waited for her by the palace's main entrance.

Successful surveillance detection. He hoped Dieter would

order Inspector Leiner to stop shadowing him. As he turned left at the corner, he glanced back. No sign of the two cops. Or Brown for that matter. He was alone.

The Chinese delegation, according to *The Village Spectator*, stayed at the Parkhotel Schönbrunn near the palace. The Austrians planned a state reception for the Vice Chairman at Schönbrunn Palace the evening after his arrival, but no date had been announced. Evan strolled on the palace side of the street past the pastel yellow hotel. It originally had served as the emperor's guest house during the time of the Hapsburgs, matched the larger palace in style, and was surrounded by a park. He opened his guide book to continue his masquerade of exploring tourist while he cased the hotel and surrounding area.

A Chinese security detail flanked the front entrance, the four men standing as straight and still as the double pillars under the half moon balcony. Viennese cops in river blue uniforms patrolled the front sidewalk, checked cars that stopped, helped hotel guests out of them, and waved a security wand over their luggage as porters waited. The police allowed no one to park in front of the hotel.

Evan looked up at the roof where two men in street clothes hovered at each corner. The sharp slope of the adjacent roofs made them inaccessible. He checked the buildings on his side of the street. Their red tile roofs also sloped at a forty-five-degree angle. According to his guidebook, the Baroque ochre yellow building directly opposite the hotel had been a vacation pavilion for Empress Maria Theresa's foreign ministers and today served as a post office. A bell clanged as a streetcar passed. Evan observed the moderate bicycle and motor scooter traffic for a minute, thinking.

Of all the hotels in Vienna, the Chinese had chosen this impossible one. Where could he create a sniper nest? No place that he could see. Possibly the post office if he could enter undetected and set up behind one of the upper windows. But what about escape routes?

Evan ambled down the street studying the guidebook map. In the post office building, the map noted a police station. He couldn't believe his terrible luck. Unless no one would think to secure the post office building because it housed a police station.

He continued past a church, consulting his guide book. Through the black metal railings on his left, he glimpsed green lawn, topiary bushes, broad tree-lined gravel walkways and buildings farther into the palace's grounds. The formal gardens continued well beyond the buildings and even farther down the street. Evan saw no gate ahead. He pivoted. More bad luck. Not enough gates. The cops could block the gates and trap him in the palace gardens, cut off from the street, transportation and escape.

He entered the palace grounds by the Hietzing Gate, one of the six gates according to his guide book. He took the left gravel pathway behind the post office. An older couple strolling arm in arm passed him, and he noticed a family a hundred feet ahead. No one paid any attention to him. He studied a possible rear entrance in the post office building before moving onto a narrow path to the right leading away from it. His stomach felt queasy. No place for his sniper nest.

During his training, he'd learned that public figures were

best assassinated by rifle from a distance. This method offered invisibility, multiple escape routes, and circumvented security. Failure to find a secure sniper nest would force him to operate closer to the target, use a handgun or a knife. The Chinese bodyguards would stop him. No time to implement poison or arrange a "natural causes" death. He thought of creating an explosive device but he wouldn't know where to plant it in the palace for the reception. Or a roadside bomb detonated by remote control. No. How could he plant a bomb *unnoticed* either on the street leading to the palace's main entrance or somewhere within the courtyard? Another problem: he'd ordered guns from Woody, not C4 and electronics. He detested bombs anyway. Too sloppy and imprecise. The collateral damage was unacceptable. No, he preferred the objective and impersonal method: two shots to the head from a distance, a clean kill.

Evan had killed rabbits, gophers, squirrels, grouse, and deer but never a real human. They had used dummies during the training which had seemed more like an intellectual exercise than something real. He remembered his first lesson: beginners always, always use a sniper rifle from a distance. The more experienced the assassin, the closer he could operate to the target. His training had focused exclusively on guns. He'd felt comfortable on the firing range because of his hunting experience. Every day, he'd approached the training as an intellectual game, like playing pretend soldiers as a kid. It still didn't feel real to him. Perceval must remain separate from Evan the musician and conductor. Perceval, America, his father. He'd escaped forever the last two. The ends truly justified the means. After he completed this Chinese assignment, Perceval could disappear forever, too.

He glanced at his watch and decided to return another day to investigate the rest of the gardens and the palace itself. He'd need to check the neighborhood at night also to test if he could penetrate the grounds unseen. Perhaps he could use the foliage behind the palace's fence railings for his sniper nest or an upper floor window in the palace.

He rode the Number 58 streetcar as far as Westbahnhof. North of the train station on Löhrgasse, he passed a mixture of small shops and offices, and gray or sand-colored old apartment buildings before he found the Fischer School of Martial Arts in a charcoal gray nineteenth century building. The school's owner, an older Japanese man with laughing eyes named Okada, expected him. Marco had called him. Evan toured the school's spacious rooms, observed a structured class, and discussed the classes and his options with Okada, who suggested proficiency tests to begin and private lessons to work around his conducting schedule. He was welcome to practice whenever he wished during the hours the school was open.

When he left, Evan found Bernard Brown on the street in front, leaning against a taxi by the curb while the driver read a newspaper behind the wheel. "Good idea, Maestro, signing up for martial arts classes. I'm glad to see you doing it. This is a good school, too. I work out here on a regular basis myself." The American kicked a black nylon gym bag at his feet.

Brown's South Bronx accent made Evan smile in spite of his dislike for the guy. "Morgan promised not to send anyone after me. What are you doing here?" Evan slung his knapsack over his shoulder.

"Extending an invitation for lunch at a great café that serves the best American food in the city. Lip-smacking cheeseburgers with all the fixings." Brown opened the door of the taxi. "I think you've heard of it. Café Chicago?"

"Yeah, the Philharmonic musicians told me about it. I'm not interested in your invitation." Evan turned up the street. His pulse pounded in his ears.

"Oh, man. My Uncle Danny would be so disappointed to hear what a snob you are, Quinn," Brown called after him. "He loved classical music, especially Caine's witty, defiant music."

"Good for him," Evan said over his shoulder. "Leave me alone, Brown." He heard the cab door slam. He walked, taking deep breaths to kill the urge to run.

The cab pulled up next to him. Brown leaned out the open passenger window. "I gotta tell you, Maestro. I am really glad to see you learning martial arts, thinking in terms of self defense. Everyone needs to know how to defend himself." Brown flashed his cocky grin and gave him a thumbs up as the cab sped away.

When the cab turned at the next intersection, Evan bent forward and massaged his side as if working out a muscle stitch, his breathing ragged from adrenalin coursing through his body. He glanced around the quiet street.

A white van approached from his left about a block away. Blackened windows. A street cleaner van. He bolted down the street, passing the intersection where Brown's cab had turned. On the next block, he hid behind a parked car and peeked over it. The white street cleaner van appeared to wobble as if it moved under water as it approached. Evan glanced toward the train station. If he could reach the subway station near the train station, the van couldn't follow him there and snatch him. Before sprinting, he checked the street. The white van had disappeared.

He jogged up to the cross street and checked all around. The van was nowhere in sight. Evan shook his head, massaged his chest to calm his breathing and his racing heart. He closed his eyes, opened them. The streets' landscape remained the same. How could the Americans operate street cleaner vans here? He had no doubt, however, that if the Americans wanted to snatch him, they would whenever they felt like it. Brown must have initiated this terrorizing tactic against him.

"No matter how frightened you feel," Joseph Caine's soothing tenor voice said to him from memory, "never show your fear. Never give them the satisfaction." Uncle Joe's craggy, wolf-like face framed by wild blonde hair appeared in his mind. His brilliant blue eyes. He'd never give Brown the satisfaction.

The U6 subway took him north, then a Number 41 streetcar took him into the Eighteenth District to see an available apartment on Sternwartestrasse or "star waiting street." He loved the street's name. He'd called the landlady, Freda Kirsch, the evening before. He got off the streetcar as Frau Kirsch had instructed at Türkenschanzplatz, a circular plaza next to a lush green park where he could hear the clear high voices of children playing. He followed a gentle slope past the park to Sternwartestrasse.

Dignified houses loomed up on the left and right behind stone walls or five-foot tall hedges pruned to form impenetrable green barriers. Magnificent old oak, maple and beech trees stood in the expansive front yards and lined the street. Upscale and secluded, this neighborhood made Evan nervous. He checked around for police but he was alone. Vasia would tell him to relax. The transfer of Caine's trust fund money into his bank account had raised his economic status. He now belonged in this neighborhood.

He stopped at a six-foot high gate of black round steel bars. Behind it, a gravel driveway curved up and split right toward a pine green building and left toward a three-story brick house, green ivy creeping over half of it. Gothic oriel windows projected out from the house's upper floors. A six-foot gray stone wall hid the front yard from the street. Evan pressed a red button three times by a sign that warned "*Vorsicht Bitte!*" on the gate's left stone column.

A barking golden retriever bounded out from behind the brick house and down to the gate. Seconds later, a tall woman dressed in gardening clothes and removing thick gloves appeared from the same place. She had an air of experience and wisdom, an earthy plainness, her smile radiant.

"*Guten Tag,*" Evan said. "*Ich bin* Evan Quinn."

"Yes, of course," she said, her alto voice warm, her English British. "I am Freda Kirsch. A pleasure to meet you, Maestro." She pressed a pebbly square on the right stone column and the gate swung open with an electronic hum.

"The pleasure is mine, Frau Kirsch."

She shook his hand, her grip firm. "Sasha, my golden

retriever. She's quite friendly but manages ferocity when necessary."

"Hello, Sasha." Evan squatted and rubbed Sasha's ears. She licked his hand, her tail wagging. "I love dogs, Frau Kirsch."

"Good. You're welcome to have pets, if you'd like. I have no objections."

"My job makes it hard. I'm not home much. I don't think it's fair to a pet to leave it alone all the time." He smiled at her. "Are you British, Frau Kirsch?"

"Austrian. I grew up in this house. Come, the flat is over here." She waved to the pine green building on their right. "I studied in England and lived in London for several years before returning here to teach English. My husband was English of German descent. He made certain that I spoke his language well."

"And does he teach also?" He matched her pace.

"He was killed five years ago serving on a peacekeeping mission for the United Nations in Nigeria."

"I'm sorry for your loss." Sasha pranced next to him, licked his hand.

Frau Kirsch nodded. "After his death I returned to Vienna, to my home here. My father decided to move to a retirement community in the country, so he gave the house to me. Here we are."

"*Hier ist* Freda," she said into a speaker on a black and silver security panel to the left of the door near the back of the pine green building. He heard the door lock click.

"How is the security set up, Frau Kirsch? Is the computer separate? The power?"

She opened the door for him. "Of course. I have top of the line security at both the main house and here. You will have two computers: a house computer for the flat and the security computer." She led the way up the stairs illuminated by a plain round ceiling light. "Your security system is separate from the house's. Your power source is also separate." At the top, she leaned toward another security panel to the right of the door. "*Hier ist* Freda." The door swung open. "I can help you program it if you've not had experience with this type of system. You can use retina scan, voice recognition, or fingerprint access, or any combination."

They entered a square foyer with a small closet to the left and an oval window facing the back yard. Through an open door to the right, Evan entered a brilliant whiteness: white walls and ceiling, white carpet, and bright sunlight from the windows that spanned the front and back walls. Floral and fresh-cut grass scents wafted in through the open double casement windows. The room's high ceiling, its airiness and clean white appealed to him. He imagined a four-foot black grand piano by the front windows.

"You can program your house computer for either voice or keyboard control, Maestro. At the moment, it controls the ceiling fans and lights, windows, and kitchen appliances. You can program it to control more or less. The same is true for the security computer, of course."

"Please call me Evan." He entered the kitchen, Frau Kirsch close behind. White cupboards dominated the wall over the stove, the counter and stainless-steel sink. A stainless-steel refrigerator hummed in the corner past the bay windows. Pearl gray shades covered the windows' top half. Evan glanced out the window at the dense leaves and branches of a maple tree before turning to examine the videophone on the wall by the door to the front room.

"A land line." He smiled with relief. A land line was far more secure from eavesdropping than his cell phones.

She nodded. "The prior tenant was a lawyer and required separate and secure transmission of documents. Low-tech is by far more secure now than the Internet. The fax function is below the video monitor."

Evan headed through an open door into a smaller room with windows in two white perpendicular walls. Immediately to his left was a walk-in closet.

"Please let me show you something."

Frau Kirsch entered the closet and said, "Light." The ceiling light came on. She knelt at the back wall, her right index finger tracing a large square, its lines faint. "The law-yer often brought important papers home. He installed this hidden compartment." She pressed an upper corner and the square swung open.

"Clever," Evan said. He squatted next to her and peered into the empty space about two-feet wide and a foot deep. Maybe large enough for a disassembled rifle.

"You can use it for your important papers, your passport for example."

He backed out as she closed the compartment door. Next to the closet, another open door led to a white bathroom with aqua and white tiles on the floor and walls. The bathtub included a shower. He smelled disinfectant. Sunlight bright-ened the room from a large oval window over the tub. He returned to the adjacent room. His bedroom. He liked all the windows that looked out on a broad green lawn, maple trees, evergreen, and oak trees, while lilacs and dwarf conifers formed the yard's perimeter. Sasha lay snoozing on the grass. Red blossoming trees among a profusion of flowers grew in a garden behind the brick house. A flagstone path wound through the garden to a trellised arch where an old-fashioned swing hung like the swings he'd sometimes seen on front porches in Minneapolis.

"When is it available?" he asked.

"Immediately. Have you a bank card?'

He pulled out his wallet. "What's the neighborhood like?"

"Quiet. Quite safe, actually. We have many families, and we're close to parks and the Vienna Woods, as well as shopping and restaurants."

He handed her his bank card. "I like solitude for my work. When my conducting schedule kicks in, I'll travel a lot."

"At the moment, I'm on summer break from school and home most of the day. If there's anything I can do to help you, Evan, please let me know. I'll process your card on my computer at the house and print out the receipt. I'll debit a security deposit of eight hundred euros and the first month's rent of the same amount." She moved into the front room. "You will need to register with the police in this district. I will go with you. The process goes faster if the landlord is present also. Have you an ID card? The police will change the address on it also."

Evan accompanied her outside where Sasha ambushed them. Frau Kirsch went into her house. Evan chased Sasha around the back yard, found a stick and threw it for her to fetch. Sasha jumped up, planting her forepaws on his chest, holding the stick in her mouth, eager and ready. Evan laughed. She was a wonderful dog. He liked everything here. His new home. Out of the corner of his eye, he noticed Frau Kirsch standing in a ground floor window, phone receiver to her ear. Confirming my account, he thought, throwing the stick and racing Sasha for it.

"*Danke*, Frau Kirsch," Klaus said into the phone wedged between his jaw and shoulder as he wrote notes. He continued in German, "As we discussed, please provide me with a daily report. If you notice anything unusual or threatening, contact us immediately. *Auf wiederhören*." He dropped the receiver into the cradle on his desk.

"Not the Stubenbastei apartment?" Marco said, seated in front of his desk.

He gave Marco a rueful smile. "You're surprised? After he confronted Ellie and Anders this morning? Install the surveillance devices before he moves in."

Marco nodded. "Aschenbeck?"

"*Na, ja*." Klaus sat back with a sigh. "The Ministry has ordered no more human surveillance on Quinn unless we can provide them with evidence that it is necessary. He cut off the money for it. We have money for the electronic surveillance."

"But Frau Kirsch?"

Klaus smiled, adjusted his tie, the slate blue tie Anna had

given him for his birthday. "She is happy to do her duty as an Austrian citizen *gratis*. What else?"

Marco consulted a computer notebook on his lap. "Nothing from our allies on chatter. Nothing about an American spy. And the only unexpected action was Quinn's doctor visit."

Klaus raised his eyebrows as Marco continued. "We talked with the doctor. Dr. Maas. He told us that Herr Quinn had made an appointment with him for an encephalitis vaccination. Dieter Aschenbeck referred him. Dieter confirmed this. Bernard Brown from the American Embassy has been keeping an eye on Quinn."

"Has Quinn made contact with Brown?"

"Today, Brown initiated but Quinn seemed to rebuff him," Marco said. "After Brown left, we observed strange behavior. Quinn ran up the street, hid behind a car. Then he came out, looked all around, shook his head and went to the U-Bahn station. We came back here as you ordered."

Klaus frowned. "What spooked him?"

"We saw nothing, Inspector. It was a quiet street."

Was the American hallucinating? It sounded like it. He'd call him, check up on him. Klaus nodded to Marco to continue.

"What about the Russian teaching Quinn how to lose surveillance, Inspector? Vassily Bartyakov. His lesson for Quinn yesterday hurt Ellie and Anders today – hurt the operation."

Klaus smoothed his moustache without feeling it. Bartyakov was a musician, a piano student. He wanted to become friends with a conductor who could help his career perhaps. Bartyakov offered him another opportunity, another pair of eyes and ears. "I'll talk to Bartyakov. He knows me. I think I can persuade him to watch Quinn for us. Keep an eye on his behavior. We need to step back now, watch and wait. Allow them to relax."

A staccato knock drew his eyes to his office door. Hanna Celine of the Federal Police, the Bundespolizei, smiled as she entered.

"How was your meeting this morning, Hanna?" Klaus said in greeting. He nodded to Marco who slipped out of the office.

"How can we persuade the Chinese delegation that it is *not* a good idea to continue changing hotels every three weeks?" Celine's voice betrayed frustration as well as annoyance. "Has Chou provided a security rationale to you?"

Klaus smiled. Chou Zemin, the head of the Chinese delegation's security detail, had indeed provided a rationale to him. "He said it was what the delegation wanted. That was reason enough for him."

Celine sighed, hugged her briefcase. "I tried, Klaus. They were obstinate this morning. Vice Chairman Jiang Xu's plan to visit makes me nervous."

He opened a desk drawer, took out a pad of paper. "*Ja,* me too. Chou's silence about when Jiang Xu will arrive makes me even more nervous. We need to develop a security plan for him but Chou isn't helping."

She sat in the chair Marco had vacated. "Perhaps Chou doesn't know anything yet. The Chinese seem to prefer not to admit ignorance about anything. I've heard the Americans are as frustrated as we are."

"I've heard the same." Klaus wrote on the pad. "Let's

discuss our options for the Vice Chairman's visit. All scenarios."

Celine shivered. "If anything should happen to Jiang Xu, it could start a war."

Chapter 12

"The order arrived," Evan said into the black cell phone he now called his Georg phone. A heavy cardboard box longer than a violin case and at least twenty inches deep stood open before him on the pension bed. Out of it he lifted a four-inch square jewelry box. "You sent me jewelry?"

Woody Lewis' chuckle filled his ear. "Open it."

Evan resisted the urge to verbally punch down his handler's amusement. He flipped off the box's lid. Inside he found a half-inch by half-inch silver square the thickness of a fingernail in a clear plastic holder. "OK, I'm looking at—"

"Stick it to the back of your watch, Georg, or your wallet or your skin. It'll vibrate if you are within one hundred yards of any kind of surveillance device, video or audio."

"Clever. Thanks." Woody chuckled again in his ear. He lifted a black 9mm handgun secured and protected in bubble wrap out of the box. "Has your forger returned from vacation?"

"Not yet. I'll let you know."

"I'm surprised you don't have a back-up."

Five seconds of silence. Evan heard a faint hissing on the cell phone.

Woody giggled. "Right now, he's not necessary."

Evan unpacked five boxes of ammunition. "I need those

ID documents. Thanks for the ammunition. I need something else."

"Shoot."

"I need more information about the state reception. Especially where in the palace." He heard Woody's breathing, an assessment, in his pause.

"I'll see what I can find out. Is there a problem?"

"No. I'm checking news outlets also."

"Good. If you need anything else, let me know. Take it easy."

Evan tossed the cell phone onto the bed. He unwrapped the 9mm and checked it over. A Ceska Zbrojovka or CZ. No identifying numbers, an orphan weapon. During his training in America, he'd used 9mms for target practice, as well as rifles and machine guns. His training had emphasized repetition – disassemble, clean, assemble, shoot fast and accurate, faster, fastest, until he'd transformed into an automatic weapon firing a gun. His marksmanship had improved to top scores. But he'd never liked the smell of cordite, never liked guns.

Guns had not changed significantly in decades. The basic truth about any gun was, is, and always will be that it's the brutal and powerful delivery system for bullets designed to damage, destroy, and kill targets whether property, animal or human. Guns served no other purpose. To believe anything else was pure delusion.

His father and Uncle Joe had taught him to respect guns, to treat his hunting rifle as a tool for obtaining food, not for killing people. His trainers had objectified targets, never called them human or gave them names. His queasiness as he thought this warned him that he needed to objectify the Chinese Vice Chairman, dehumanize him. He was a target, no more. The 9mm fit his hand perfectly. During his training, he'd been surprised how much he'd enjoyed the power he'd felt with a gun in his hand. He still felt the power.

From the box, he lifted out another black CZ 9mm identical to the first, five more boxes of ammunition and a black metal case almost the size of the cardboard box. Nestled inside it was a disassembled black Ruger .308 sniper rifle. He started to lift it out of its protective foam casing but a firm, staccato knock on his door stopped him. He closed the metal case, returned the two handguns to the cardboard box and went to the door.

Frau Herbst waited outside in the narrow hallway. "Mr. Quinn, my nephew has told me that you will leave us tomorrow." She smiled up at him, tucking a wisp of white hair back into a wave at her right temple.

"I've rented an apartment and I move in tomorrow. I've enjoyed my stay here and your fine service. Thank you."

She inclined her head in thanks. "You received that heavy box?" She tried to peer past him into his room. He didn't move, blocking her view.

"Yes, thanks. A friend sent me supplies for my work," he said, recognizing it as both a lie and a truth. He glanced at his watch. "A friend will pick me up soon for a concert this evening. I'll be out late tonight."

"The building's front door is locked after nine o'clock, Mr. Quinn. Remember to press the button to turn on the light in the foyer."

"The button?"

"White and round, raised out from the wall. The foyer light button is by the door on the left. For the stairs, one is on the wall of each landing." She smiled. "Americans never know about this lighting system in the older buildings in Vienna. In newer buildings, the lights turn on automatically when someone enters."

"Good to know, Frau Herbst, thank you."

She hovered as if she wanted to tell him something else. She coughed.

"I need to change clothes for the concert, Frau Herbst. I'll see you at breakfast? Before I leave?"

She nodded, waved her hand to him in farewell and ambled down the hall. He closed the door with a relieved sigh. She'd wanted to know about the package. Had she told Leiner about it yet or had she decided to try to find out more about it first? While shopping earlier that day for the Amsterdam gig, he'd activated the neon blue cell phone from Leiner and Aschenbeck at a telephone store. He had chosen the opening to Mozart's Fortieth Symphony for its ring tone.

Now, he pulled the Mozart cell phone from his pocket and waved Woody's surveillance detector over it. No vibration. He circled the room holding out the device which remained motionless. No bugs in his pension room. He peeled the surveillance detector off its plastic holder and applied it to the back of his watch. He still believed that Leiner had somehow bugged the Mozart cell phone. In a couple weeks, he'd lose it. People lost cell phones all the time. But for the moment, he'd use it, especially if he could use it to torment Leiner.

Two hours later, Greta laughed as she parked her lime green Geister, a compact car that reminded Evan of a bug-eyed blowfish but with more subtle fins. "Vasia has a deep well of information," she said, "that you don't realize you want to know until he tells you something. He sponges up knowledge. He also devours good food and vodka." She pressed the ignition button on the steering wheel column with her index finger. In response, it turned off and released the hard drive access card from below the steering wheel. "Vasia moves next week into his new apartment. We will have a party the week after. Will you come, Maestro?"

"Love to." Evan slid out of the Geister and looked around at the gray, five-story nineteenth-century buildings on the quiet street. Blue, purple, silver and red motor scooters but no white vans. The evening was warm, the sky clear with a balmy breeze from the east. Greta's heels clicked on the dusty pavement.

They dodged motor scooter and bike traffic to reach the modest park in front of the Palais Schwarzenberg, a cream yellow Baroque palace whose dozens of windows reflected the evening's brassy sun. An enormous geyser fountain splashed to their left. Clusters of people milled around in the park or strolled up the crescent drive to the palace's front entrance.

Greta said, "The violinist, Lisl Schatzmann, is a Swiss citizen, so the Swiss Embassy in this palace hosts her recital this evening. This palace has a wonderful musical history, often used in the past for recitals and chamber concerts but not so much now."

Inside he trailed two steps behind Greta, his eyes taking in the people in the entry hall. Older women, decorated with diamonds and stiff coiffures, greeted each other. Four intense students paged through oversized music scores. Couples drifted through the doorway. They passed two young men conversing in French. An Indian couple glided past, her sari a shimmering parrot green satin. Perfume and an aged mustiness scented the air. No sign of Brown's smug, unshaven face in the crowd.

They entered a Baroque ballroom converted to a concert hall for the evening. Oil paintings in heavy gold frames jampacked the walls. Plump, grinning infants in pastoral murals frolicked across the ceiling. Gold straight-backed wood chairs stood in rows facing a black grand piano on a raised platform that served as the stage. People seeking seats bustled around them. Greta chose their seats on the center aisle.

As he sank down on his chair, Greta leaned in toward his right ear. "I am so very nervous for Vasia," she whispered and handed him a program booklet.

"He's a pro. He'll do fine," he whispered back. He squeezed her hand.

Voices faded away to a hush of anticipation as the hall darkened, leaving the stage in a pool of white light. A door opened to the left. A petite, blonde woman in her mid-twenties strode in, her violin tucked under one arm. Polite applause rippled through the air. Vasia entered a second later, wearing a white dinner jacket and scarlet bow tie. Evan grinned. A scarlet instead of the conventional white or black tie opened up the evening to all emotional colors and possibilities.

He checked his program. The first work on the all-Brahms recital was the Scherzo from the FAE Sonata, followed by the Violin Sonata No. 1, Op. 78. After the pause, the Second and Third Violin Sonatas. Although Evan had studied each of them when they had each enjoyed Arts Council favor, however briefly at different times, he'd performed only the Op. 78. Joseph Caine had told him once, an offhand comment a long time ago, that Brahms' music was about memory, emotional memory. Whenever Evan thought of Brahms, he thought of earthy rich, resonant textures of the sound of longing for the unattainable. Vasia and Lisl completed their tuning. She nodded for them to begin.

Lisl's precise, fluid bowing, her wrist control and her white arm moving before her shimmering sapphire gown commanded Evan's attention as he listened. She played well. The Brahms sang through the air. Greta sighed next to him and shifted on her chair. Vasia's accompaniment revealed experience and sensitivity. Applause erupted in the hall after the Scherzo's final chord. Vasia and Lisl bowed and disappeared out the door. Programs rustled. People wormed in their chairs. Voices whispered. Latecomers sought the few open seats.

"She is good, yes?" Greta said, leaning in to him, their arms touching.

"Yeah. Vasia's excellent. They're a special team."

Enthusiastic applause greeted Vasia and Lisl when they returned to the stage for Brahms' First Violin Sonata. Evan stretched his legs out under the chair in front of him and folded his arms across his chest. He relaxed into the sonata's poignant melody, opening to it. His breathing rose and fell with its phrasing. Lisl's bowing wove the sound into his consciousness, sliding away everything else. His shoulders dropped as his neck muscles released tension. The music enveloped him into its world and carried him into memory. He felt safe cuddled in his mother's protective arms.

She had laughed low and throaty in the shadows behind the furnace. Her sultry wine breath had rushed past his ears. He snuggled in closer to her. Above them, the storm of crashing furniture and his father's raging rant continued. During ominous silences upstairs, they breathed together and listened to each other's hearts. He had found the hiding place behind the furnace in the cellar, his and his mother's secret place. When they hid there, she whispered to him in German, sometimes telling him Till Eulenspiegel stories. At other times, she had said things in German he hadn't understood and now couldn't remember.

He lived in a German-speaking city, a musical city, in a German-speaking country surrounding him, holding him in its arms safe away from America. The violin's voice lingered in the air, commingling with his mother's in his mind. He leaned back, gazed up at the ceiling and a mural of cherubs that melted into a new moon night sky glittering with stars.

A year after his mother's death, their last summer up north at their cabin, he had paddled their canoe out to the center of the lake at midnight for the first time on a new moon night. The air was calm. Wisps of ghost fog had risen from the glassine water near shore. He switched off his flashlight, shook water off the paddle and stowed it. He slid down in the canoe until he lay on his back, unable to see anything but the velvety black dome above. For over an hour he had drifted, cradled by the canoe, mesmerized by the immense sky, disconnected completely from solid ground. He had floated up among the glittering stars, and had wondered if this was how it had felt to float safe in his mother's womb.

In front of him now, Vasia and Lisl moved together,

breathed together, shared a fleeting smile. Vasia threw back his head, his blonde curls flying, a flash of gold at his ear. When Evan closed his eyes, Vasia's playing resurrected Uncle Joe at the piano.

Uncle Joe had defined music as the poetry of sound, the expression of emotional realities through sound, and therefore, the most subversive and covert of art forms. He loved Uncle Joe's music for its reflection of the love in his heart, the defense of freedom and being human. Music told stories through the sound of human emotion in space and time, there one moment, gone the next, with only the sound's story lingering in the mind's ear. Uncle Joe's music told Uncle Joe's story, a story close to Evan's heart. Performance methods evolved, interpretations or a musician's mood changed. Musicians created the sound, repeated it, but never the same way twice. The music endured in notation on paper. Uncle Joe's music endured because of Mr. Redfield, Randall Quinn, and the people in the world who demanded to hear it. Music conveyed the nuances of feeling like the human voice in conversation, here now a conversation imagined by Brahms between violin and piano on which they eavesdropped.

During the final movement, Evan visualized the printed score, traced the progression of notes on the page, the harmonic relationships, to prevent his mind from wandering. A fading phrase into a dying breath ended the sonata. Vasia rocketed off the piano bench, grabbed the violinist's hand, and bowed with her to the audience's warm applause. Evan shouted, "Bravo!"

"That was brilliant," he said to Greta.

She nodded. "They play together like one person."

Evan gathered himself and stood. "I'm impressed with Vasia."

"Would you like to see him now?" She rose in one graceful movement that reminded Evan of a dancer.

"I'll see him later. I need to stretch my legs. These wood chairs are like sitting on stone."

He leaned back, stretching, his eyes scanning the painted ceiling. In one mural, rosy children surrounded a virile old man, clad only in a white loin cloth, his long white hair and beard wind-swept. Evan frowned at the image. What a dirty old man leering at those innocent children.

"Religion inspired much art in the past," Greta said, gazing also at the ceiling. "The paintings in this hall illustrate stories from the **Bible**." She checked her watch. "Another fifteen minutes for the pause. I'll meet you here?"

Evan nodded and Greta slipped through the crowd toward a side corridor. He meandered toward the front doors. People watched him, whispering to each other, but no sign of Brown.

"Maestro Quinn!" The screeched exclamation attracted the attention of everyone in the entry hall.

"Maestro Quinn!" A short woman, a sphere of flesh in pink brocade, grabbed his arm. Her gray-streaked blonde hair curled back from her jowly face. He couldn't begin to guess her age, although she was beyond youth. "Your Vienna Philharmonic concerts were wonderful," she breathed as she pressed her body against him.

Evan cringed back but assumed his public persona smile. She was after all a member of his concert audience. He lifted her hand off his arm and said, "Thank you."

"Maestro." She stretched the word out by rolling the "r."

"Allow me please to introduce myself. I am Antonia Himmler."

"Frau Himmler." He glanced around for an escape. Women like Frau Himmler of all ages appeared in the Green Room after concerts. They wanted something from him that he didn't have or wanted simply to possess him. This much he understood.

She grasped his right hand in one sweaty palm and squeezed it in a pumping rhythm. "The Caine symphony was so beautiful, so intense." She slid closer, her eyes ravenous. "You are the greatest conductor in the world!"

He groaned at her exaggeration. "Frau Himmler—"

"You must come to my home for dinner tomorrow."

"Dinner?" He pulled his hand from her grasp.

"Hey, Evan. Sorry I'm late." The South Bronx accent cut through the murmuring around them. He turned to his left and his eyes locked onto Brown's laughing green eyes in his unshaven face. Brown gave Frau Himmler a smug smile and said, "You can't have him, you know. For dinner or anything else. He's a very busy guy. I bet you have a daughter, huh?"

Frau Himmler blushed red as her rouge. "Americans are so rude."

Brown bowed to her. "My lady, we aim to please. However, the French really have elevated rudeness to an art form, far above anyone else. Now, please excuse us."

Evan allowed Brown to guide him through the palace's front doors and out into the park. He felt gratitude for Brown's rescue, but resented the American's presence here.

"Groupies," Brown said, releasing Evan's elbow. "They're

more prevalent here than in America." He smoothed the jacket of his ivory linen suit.

Evan glared at him. At the same time, he filed away in his mind Brown's contempt for "groupies," the term for Frau Himmler and her ilk.

"Great concert. My Uncle Danny would love it. He loved Brahms. I'm a country western guy act—"

"Get lost, Brown." Evan pivoted but Brown stepped in front of him with a grin.

"See that fountain over there? The Hochstrahlbrunnen." Brown pointed to the tall geyser-like fountain illuminated in rainbow colors in the dusky evening light. "After World War Two, the Allies occupied Austria."

"Brown."

"Wait, just listen, Maestro. I'm trying to share with you a little history of the place. As part of the deal for the Soviets to leave, the Austrians agreed to erect a statue to the great and wonderful Soviet Red Army soldier to honor the Soviets' liberation of their country." Brown laughed, a wheezing from his throat. "Check out where the Austrians placed the Soviet soldier."

Evan sighed, playing along. "Behind the fountain."

"*Ge-nau*, exactly. When the fountain is on, which is most of the time, you can't see the statue from the front, only the back and the statue's backside!" Brown's wheezing broke into a high-pitched giggle. "Those rascal Austrians. I guess they showed – hey, look at that gorgeous piece of ass." Brown nodded toward the palace entrance.

Evan turned in time to see a cascade of chestnut brown

hair over the back of a mauve dress that ended at shapely knees. A gold chain belt encircled her slender waist.

"Oh, too bad you missed her. The famous, award-winning actress, Sofia Karalis."

"What part of 'get lost' don't you get?" Evan heard the chimes that signaled the end of intermission in five minutes. He headed for the palace.

"We have to talk," Brown said behind him.

"No, we don't," Evan said over his shoulder. Greta peered out the front door, looking for him.

Brown grabbed his arm, stopping him. "Listen, man. When someone approaches you, how do you know what that person's motivations are? You can't really assume anything, can you? You know the game. We have to talk."

Evan heard the chimes again. "What game? Go to hell and stay there." He shook Brown's hand off and left him standing on the crescent drive. Evan waved to Greta.

Brown had ruined the second half of the recital for Evan. That South Bronx voice repeated in his ears, "We have to talk," blotting out the music. What did he want? Oh, yeah, Woody had warned that Brown might try to recruit him for the CIA. Evan smiled in spite of himself. Greta smiled at him and suddenly Brahms' music burst into his thoughts. He listened to Lisl and Vasia until Brown's voice broke through again, knotting his stomach. Woody had said no one knew about him, that he'd come up clean in any check. But what if Brown's interest aimed not for a recruitment but for killing him? An accidental death? Or get close to him to execute a "natural causes" death? He breathed back into the Brahms to escape his thoughts.

After Lisl and Vasia had played two encores, neither of which Evan recognized, he and Greta raced to the corridor that led to the artists' dressing rooms. A long line of excited and chatty people already waited. Evan glanced around: no Brown. Greta scurried ahead to stand with Vasia, but Evan remained in line for his turn to congratulate them.

Lisl Schatzmann's eyes widened when he stepped in front of her and extended his hand. "Ms. Schatzmann, I loved it. Congratulations," he said with genuine warmth. "Tonight, the Brahms sonatas were transcendent. May I ask about your encores? I didn't—"

"Yes, thank you, Maestro," she said, her face radiant. "The first was a Scherzo by the Hungarian composer Gerhard Novosti. He is perhaps sixty years old now, continues to compose, and lives in Budapest. The second was composed by a friend of mine, a student at the Hochschule für Musik, named Sean Taylor. He calls it '*eines Lied für Geige.*' He has composed three songs for violin."

"Evan!" Vasia's voice boomed in the hallway. The people in line behind Evan laughed with an edge of giddiness.

He moved the three feet to Vasia, where Greta stood to his right. He recognized the mauve dress and gold chain belt on the woman next to her. She spoke with a Maori man close by and a woman in pastel blue. He gave Vasia a big, warm hug, patting his back.

"Evan, I would like to introduce you first to Sofia Karalis, excellent good friend and best cook of Greek food outside of Greece." Vasia bowed to the woman in the mauve dress.

"A pleasure," Evan said as he shook her warm, dry hand.

As he met her hazel green eyes he felt as if his stomach had flipped over.

"I loved your Paris concert, Maestro." Her smoky alto voice surprised him, unusual for a woman's voice.

"Thank you…thank you."

"Sofia promotes her latest movie," Vasia said. "You must tell us about it at dinner," he said to her. "And may I introduce Owen te Kumara, composer from New Zealand. And his wife, Lucia, also pianist."

Evan shook the hands of the Maori man next to Sofia, and the woman next to him. "A pleasure to meet you both. I've wanted to meet more composers in Europe, and Lisl Schatzmann has just told me of two more."

"Ah, Gerhard Novosti, yes," Owen said, his smile brilliant against his walnut brown skin and thick black hair. "I've met him. I'm sure he'd welcome hearing from you, Maestro."

"Please, everyone, call me Evan." He smiled around at them. "Maestro is for work, thanks." Owen te Kumara, Gerhard Novosti. If orchestra musicians were his family, composers were his bosses. Without them writing music, he'd have nothing to conduct.

Vasia draped his arm around Evan's shoulders. "Here's plan," he said. "Owen, Lucia and Sofia go to Chinese restaurant we know in Third District and we meet them when I finish here. You come, too." Vasia slapped his shoulder and turned to greet a fan with Lisl.

Sofia smiled at him. Butterflies fluttered in his stomach. He couldn't show his fear to anyone, especially not her, or let anyone know what he really felt. He smiled back, his eyes on her smooth skin, her Patrician nose slightly off center as if broken years ago and poorly set. He couldn't think of a thing to say and he felt a tension in his body as if ready to flee a threat. He slipped on his public persona, aware also of the familiar physical sensation of peering out of his eyes as if he occupied someone else's body.

"You hear story of dogs and Mahler Fifth Symphony?"

"Vasia." Greta rolled her eyes to the Chinese lanterns overhead.

"What dogs?" Evan wanted another of Vasia's wild stories. He loved them, and he wanted to hear Sofia's sweet laugh again.

He returned to his delicious beef Chow Mein. He glanced around at the smattering of diners in the room, the red Chinese lanterns that provided subdued light, and the red beaded curtains that separated their dining room from another. He had chosen a chair that faced the front door area, his back to the wall, but he hadn't spotted any possible surveillance shadows.

Vasia shoveled stir-fried noodles, vegetables, and shrimp into his mouth with his chopsticks. Owen wagged a finger at him. "I've heard that story, you crazy Russian. It's not funny. You know Evan's not like that conductor."

"What dogs?" Evan said. "The Mahler Five isn't scored for dogs."

Vasia and Owen laughed. The women exchanged smiling glances with each other. He'd made them laugh and smile. His sense of occupying someone else's body receded.

Sofia Karalis sat opposite him at the large round table covered with a red tablecloth. Greta and Vasia had told him on the drive to the restaurant that Sofia had begun acting at fifteen, and she worked in both film and theater. She was Greta's best friend. He stole another look at her now. She glowed, an unattainable goddess.

"You see, conductor – maybe Romanian, maybe German or Polish, I don't know—"

"He was Russian, Vasia," Owen said.

"Is this the dog story?" Sofia asked, her tone mischievous.

"—but *big* personality." Vasia giggled. "When he young, he is fresh, nice conductor. When he is old, no one like him. No one respect him because he dictator. He never talk or listen to musicians. But public love him, always give him loud standing ovations, etc., etc."

"How many vodkas have you had, Vasia?" Sofia asked.

Greta sighed in exasperation. "You know Evan isn't like that conductor."

"I'm conducting the Mahler Five with the Vienna Philharmonic in September," Evan said. He wanted to hear the story now because everyone thought it might offend him.

"Lucia, there's a concert we cannot miss." Owen pulled his wife to him and kissed her. She blushed rose pink.

"Lucia, where do you work?" Evan asked, and smiled at her to ease her embarrassment. "You're a pianist?"

She nodded. When she spoke, her *pianissimo* soprano voice carried a lilting Italian accent. "I teach music in a public school, young children, and I have also private piano students."

"Where did you grow up in Italy?" he said.

"Firenze, Florence. I lived all my life in Florence until I come to Vienna to study piano at the Hochschule."

Out of the corner of his eye, Evan saw Vasia finish his noodles. "I want to see Florence," Evan said. "I'd love to see Michaelangelo's work."

"If you like sculpture," she said with more confidence. "The 'David' is in The Academy with unfinished sculptures so you can see how he worked with the marble."

"So, conductor," Vasia said, placing both hands on the table to either side of his empty plate as if to push off into the air. "He conduct Mahler Fifth Symphony. Concert open with Mozart *Jeunehomme* Piano Concerto. Young pianist, no experience – a boy! Conductor scream at him in rehearsal. Pianist cried and threw out after rehearsal. Terrible. Orchestra musicians not happy."

"Threw up, Vasia, not threw out," Evan said as the others giggled. He'd never met any stupid orchestra musicians. Earning their respect was essential. They could tell in the first five to ten minutes of the first rehearsal if he knew what he was doing. Conducting an orchestra required intense preparation, respectful and delicate persuasion at times, a firm hand, a spirit of collaboration, and the ability to inspire the musicians to play a composer's score. Dictators made enemies, not music. He watched Vasia swallow another shot of vodka.

"OK," Vasia said. "Threw up. *Spaciba* – thank you. Orchestra hate conductor, but first performance beautiful.

Pianist played *brilliante*. Conductor say bad things to him after concert. Jealous, you know." Vasia shrugged. "Pianist threw up again. Everyone in orchestra know this."

"Where was this, Vasia?" Evan caught Sofia smiling at him. The heat of a blush spread up from his neck. He could not meet her eyes. The others, giggling and laughing, had settled back in their seats to listen. Evan ate another mouthful of Chow Mein.

"Somewhere in Europe. Not important. Critics give conductor excellent review. Pianist not so excellent review. Musicians angry. So, some musicians realize idea to visit circus. They hire dog trainer to bring dogs to next concert. So, at concert, after pause, trainer and dogs sit behind brass section." Vasia giggled as Owen shook his head with a moan. "First movement begin with dramatic trumpet solo. Funeral march. Conductor wave...." Vasia wind-milled his arms. "Conductor has no beat. He waved stick everywhere. Trumpet begin solo. After two bars, one dog howl. AAOOOUUUU! Two more bars, another dog howl, and then all dogs howl with music. But as you say, Evan, Mahler not write howling dogs in score."

"Maybe Mahler should have included dogs," Lucia said, wiping laugh tears from her face with a red cloth napkin.

"He must have stopped," Evan said, his stomach clenching in a spasm of fear. Only two things worried him about performing: the possibility of walking onstage with an open fly zipper, or a memory lapse. Musician sabotage should never happen, but dictators deserved a defiant response in rehearsal, not in concert.

"How can he stop?" Vasia said. Lucia giggled, her hand

over her mouth, as Owen shook his head. "Conductor in rage. Nothing he can do. Public *love* dogs! After first movement, audience cheer. But critics know dogs not in score, so they slammed up conductor in reviews for adding dogs."

"You made it up, Vasia," Evan said. Greta and Sofia nodded in agreement.

"True story! I hear at Hochschule. Owen hear it also."

"OK, what happened to this tyrannical conductor, huh?" Evan sipped his ice water.

"Some say he emigrate to America."

Evan guffawed, an explosive release of air, raspy sound and water droplets. "That's rich. Why would anyone want to emigrate to America?" From the surprise on their faces, he knew he'd blundered somehow. He bowed his head, feeling intense discomfort, to hide from their eyes. Someone sighed.

"The New Economic Party," Owen said, his tone sarcastic. "Of course they rewrote history. They're in power. I'd like to know what they teach about the past."

"People wanted to live in America before the New Economic Party, Evan," Greta said, her voice quiet. He looked up at her gentle smile, those penetrating ebony eyes. "America was where a person could live a better life before they closed the borders. It's not your fault. Owen's right. You wouldn't have known because the NEP controls education."

"Before the NEP, America was country of promise for everyone to do anything," Vasia said.

"Isn't it true in human history that power ebbs and flows?" Sofia said, her smoky alto voice drawing his eyes to her. To his surprise, he saw kindness in her face, not derision or disgust. "And America's time as a superpower, as an imperial power, is finished. The New Economic Party and their policies insure it."

"The NEP will find some way to protect America's position." Owen sipped his wine. "They still possess nuclear weapons."

"No one is so stupid to use nuclear weapon," Vasia said. "To drop nuclear bomb on someone same as dropping nuclear bomb on yourself. And you know, everyone work very, very hard to prevent terrorists buying or stealing nuclear weapons."

"Oh, my nightmare," Lucia said. "An idiot terrorist who believes he'll become a martyr and go to Heaven by murdering people in Vienna with a nuclear bomb. Murder is murder. They will go to hell for their honey and virgins."

"They brainwashed, those terrorists who believe in that martyrdom. They programmed to believe they fight for God so they will murder," Vasia said, throwing back another shot of vodka. "America same. Many people over many centuries believe same idea."

"They believe what they believe," Sofia said, turning her wine glass slowly on the table. "We believe what we believe. It is a problem of thinking, of belief. I believe God had more interesting things in mind for humans than for them to kill themselves all the time."

Evan realized the moment of his embarrassment had passed. The only consequences of his ignorance this time had been simply not knowing. He gazed at Sofia from the side. In America, he had dated in high school but after high school had avoided romance, attachments that might turn against him, report him to the ISS for money or revenge. Sofia's presence drew him to her at the same time he felt afraid, repelled.

His cell phone played the opening to Mozart's Fortieth Symphony with startling clarity. He dug it out of his sport jacket pocket, flipped it open. "Hello?" He watched Sofia drop her eyes to her plate, pick up her chopsticks to eat more of her chicken stir fry.

"Herr Quinn, Klaus Leiner calling," Leiner's soothing tenor said in his ear. "I have been trying to reach you for several days."

"Sorry, Inspector. I activated your gift only this morning after I completed more pressing tasks." Evan felt a hand on his arm, Vasia's. The Russian mouthed something to him that he didn't understand. He shook his head. "It's late, Inspector. I'm out with friends at a post-concert soiree. What's on your mind?" He glanced around the dining room again for shadows but no one looked in his direction.

"I wanted only to check on you, to ask how you are doing, if the cell phone works well for you. I understand I have called at a bad time."

"Everything's fine. The phone works fine. Thanks. Are you going to check on me often?" Vasia mouthed something again as the others looked on with concern. "Your surveillance team yesterday assured me that there'd be no more surveillance." Vasia froze, his eyebrows shooting up and blue eyes widening.

Leiner grunted at the other end of the line. "Yes, Herr Quinn, I would like to check on you now and then. As a friend. I am interested that you find a place to live, that your life in Vienna goes well. I want you to know that you can call me at any time, if necessary. Dieter entered his phone number and mine into your cell phone's memory."

"As a friend? Really, Inspector? I'll believe you when you believe me. Please tell Marco and Johann I've signed up for classes at the Fischer School. And I've found a place to live in the Eighteenth District. I'm surprised you don't know that already."

"I removed the surveillance, Herr Quinn. I'm certain Marco and Johann—"

"Listen, my friends are waiting for me, so I need to go, Inspector." Evan flipped the phone closed, growling in frustration. "Friend? I don't think so," he said. Leiner had confirmed though that the cops no longer shadowed him, unless that's what Leiner wanted him to believe.

"Who, Evan? Who call you?" Vasia said. "I know only one Inspector who—"

"Klaus Leiner with the police. He held me in custody for almost three weeks after my defection. To debrief me because they thought I was working for the Americans. Like a spy or something."

"Ridiculous," Owen said.

"I know Inspector Leiner," Vasia said. The Russian looked him straight in the eyes. "When Russians harass me three years ago, I call police to report them. Inspector Leiner interviewed me. He advised how to protect myself and he check up with me with phone calls."

Evan looked around at the five concerned faces. He didn't want to talk about Leiner with these people. He couldn't. Sofia studied her chopsticks moving food around on her plate. He said, "I wouldn't work for the NEP for anything." No one would ever know he had agreed to do one job for them in exchange for his freedom. And his father. "What they did to the Caines, to my family...." His voice faded away.

"You said, I believe, that you'd rented an apartment?" Owen said.

Chapter 13

"Have you any furniture, Evan?" Freda Kirsch gave him a worried look. She appeared cool and fresh in white shorts and a yellow tank top. He liked that she wore no make-up. She said, "I mean, you must have something to sleep on."

They stood in his new apartment's sunny white front room with his luggage, bag of music scores from Doblinger's, bags of new clothes and the large cardboard box at his feet. He'd been so eager to escape Leiner's eyes at the pension, he hadn't thought about furniture. He slipped off his navy-blue sport jacket. Only nine-thirty in the morning and already hot.

"Not a big deal, Freda," he said. "I've slept on the bare ground many times in my life, camping with my family and the Caines, so I won't have any problem sleeping on the floor for a few days."

"I have a futon I'll loan you and sheets for it." She shook her head, her expression open amazement. "Until you've bought your own bed and sheets. Shall I show you how to program the security system?"

His kind new landlady instructed him on the finer points of his security system. Through the open windows, he heard Sasha barking in the back yard and smelled the flowers in Freda's garden, their scent carried by a light breeze on the hothouse humid air. After he'd programmed his security system for his access and hers, he followed her over to the main house for the futon.

"I had expected more of a snob, to tell the truth," she said on the way back to his apartment. Sasha pranced around them.

"A snob?" He laughed, almost dropping his end of the folded futon. "I'd never want to be someone who doesn't care about people. That's the NEP and wealthy elite in America. They're snobs. I was a member of the poverty class in America. Having money now is a strange experience for me."

"Well, I'll tell you, then, be careful. People exist in this world who will try to separate you from your money. Scammers and con artists with investment schemes and sob stories. Never give out your personal information to strangers in person, over the phone or on the Internet and keep your cash to yourself."

Her concern surprised him. She was kind. To him. "Thank you, Freda. Thank you for helping me." He felt a buzzing tingle of energy course through his body.

They'd reached the door at the back of the garage. Evan pressed his right middle fingertip on the fingerprint scanner as he leaned into the security panel's speaker and said, "*Der schattige Affe.*" The lock released. They carried the futon up the stairs where Evan repeated the access procedure. Before they carried the futon into his new bedroom, Sasha on their heels, Evan keyed in his code on the security panel inside. The blinking red lights changed to steady green.

"Sasha, you shouldn't be in here," Freda said, frowning at the golden retriever in his bedroom.

"It's OK, Freda. Sasha's welcome anytime."

"I wouldn't want her bothering you when you're working."

"She won't. If I want to work, I'll put her out. You don't mind, do you?" He accepted the sheets and pillow from her and began to dress the futon.

"I must warn you, she has her neuroses."

Evan chuckled. He'd never heard of a neurotic dog before. "I guess I really need to learn how to cook." He smoothed the top sheet and tucked in the bottom of it.

"Cooking is like chemistry. That's how my husband thought of it. If you have any questions, I'd be pleased to help."

A suspicion fingered his thoughts. Was she trying to get close to him? Or was she only offering help like a good neighbor? He decided to accept the latter. "There," he said, dropping the pillow on the bed. "That's fine for now. Oh, towels."

"I have hundreds of towels. I'm certain I can spare a dozen for a month or two. I'll also bring over the manual for the electronics wall and home computer. Do you read German?"

"Yes," he said as they strolled out to the front room. Sasha trotted to the door.

Freda looked around, her arms crossed over her chest. Sweat darkened her blonde hair around her face. "I hope you'll be happy here, Evan."

He smiled at her desire to please. "I am."

"Well, Sasha, shall we leave our new tenant to unpack his things?" Sasha barked, whipping back and forth in front of the door. "If you need anything?"

"I'll call. Thank you." He saw her and Sasha out and re-set the security panel by the door.

Now a security sweep. He strode around the apartment, holding out his left arm wearing his watch, waiting for Woody's bug-finder to vibrate against his skin. Nothing. He opened the box of guns. The two CZ 9mm handguns, wrapped in bubble wrap, went into the refrigerator freezer compartment. Frozen food would block the guns from view. He stowed the Ruger in the lower cabinet by the back windows in the front room. He pushed it to the back. He slid the empty cardboard box in front of it and closed the cabinet door. Imperfect hiding places but good enough until he figured out something else.

He carried his luggage and bags of clothes back to the bedroom to unpack, but there were no clothes hangers in the closet. He kicked the wall in frustration, paced around the room, angry that he had nothing, angry he must do everything himself now and angry at himself for not waiting a week in order to shop first for necessities before moving. He was stupid. He changed clothes and left for the First District.

Forty-five minutes later, Evan sat at a white marble-topped booth table under a tall window at the back of the elegant Café Danforth. The café's interior reminded him of pictures of nineteenth century Vienna: golden rooms lit by glittering chandeliers populated by men in top hats and knee-length suit jackets and women dressed in high-necked gowns with bustles. The murmuring voices of a dozen other diners closer to the front filled the café. Evan faced the entrance, his back to the rear wall, confident he'd see anyone enter the café before they spotted him.

A Viennese family of six wearing Sunday finery hurried past outside the window. The smells of baked chicken, sautéed onions and coffee hung in the café's air-conditioned air. The espresso machine hissed and dishes clacked in the kitchen. Evan shifted on the booth seat's uneven springs, slipping on its light green leather upholstery. Vasia would arrive in an hour. He searched the newspapers he'd grabbed when he'd come in for any news about the Chinese Vice Chairman's arrival and the reception at Schönbrunn Palace.

The one article he found reviewed the political-economic situation, the importance of the Chinese-American talks for world peace and only mentioned the Chinese Vice Chairman's intent to visit Vienna. An ominous tone permeated the article. China led a coalition of Asian countries called the Asia-Pacific Coalition, or APCO. Japan led a second alliance, the Pacific Alliance. China and Japan continued their historical rivalry for power in Asia.

In the last six months, a flurry of diplomatic activities had erupted as countries positioned themselves for future economic benefit from the talks. China and APCO courted the insurgents in the western half of America and South American countries on the Pacific. The European Union and Russia, as well as the Atlantic half of South America, Mexico and the southern half of Africa had allied with Washington. The Pacific Alliance, which included the Philippines, Taiwan, South Korea, the Pacific Island nations, Australia and New Zealand, like Canada, had declared neutrality. Japan, however, the writer suspected, continued its close alliance with America and he questioned Japan's absence from the Chinese-American talks.

The acquisition of money or the protection of it motivated everyone, Evan thought. America had become a target for acquisition. America would defend herself by any means necessary. Evan felt relief that he'd escaped to Vienna.

The blonde waitress, a pretty gamine with freckles wearing the traditional black dress with white collar, cuffs and apron, brought his lunch. As he ate, he thought how little he knew about China, its culture and government. He had no desire to learn more, either. He'd met superb Chinese musicians during his tour, kind and gentle people who revered authority. He'd also met superb Japanese musicians. All had loved music as much as he, and that's all he cared about. Music motivated him, the making of music, not money.

He forked a chunk of juicy baked chicken, piling potato and tender sweet green beans on top of it and sliding it all into his mouth. This Sunday dinner in Vienna tasted better, fresher, and more flavorful compared to any Sunday dinner he'd eaten in Minneapolis.

An old man with a cane shambled past his window. A white cloud of hair floated around his head. At the corner, almost out of Evan's vision, the old man paused to wipe his face with a handkerchief. Under the blazing July sun, he appeared shrunken, small, inconsequential, an ant on the sidewalk of life, oblivious to the giant foot above him.

"Hey, Maestro."

Evan whirled to his right where Brown stood wearing his usual smug smile. "Now is not the time, Brown."

The American slid onto the booth seat opposite him, signaled with a wave for the waitress. "I know, it's never a good time for you, is it, hon? Food good here?"

The pretty blonde waitress arrived. Brown ordered, in precise German without any trace of his American accent, a *mélange* coffee with a slice of *Topfentorte*. After she left, Brown sighed back in his seat. "You know, Quinn, you and I aren't that different. I mean, besides the fact we're both Americans in a foreign country. I studied acting in college. Planned to work in theater and movies. Did a lot of Shakespeare, Masterson and O'Neill before they banned him, and even a couple student films for friends. I've got a great ear for languages, accents. I consider myself an artist."

"Yeah, right. An artist. I'm sure your acting experience serves you well in your current position." Evan skewered a bite of chicken with his fork.

Brown squinted out the window, chewing on his lower lip for ten seconds before speaking. "Yeah, my acting skills have helped me in my job. You're right. But you need to know, Evan, that I'm not acting now. I won't ever act with you. By the way, my boss, Larry Morgan, detests you and your father."

"No surprise there." Evan ate another mouthful of chicken and potato.

"Morgan won't last forever. He's angling for a job in Beijing, God knows why. I'm thinking, would you be interested in working for us?"

Evan choked on his food, coughed and coughed until Brown slapped him three times on the back. When he could breathe and swallow again, he said, "You must be out of your mind. Why would I want to work for the Americans? The CIA? No way."

Brown nodded, unfazed. "That's what I thought you'd

say, but I had to ask. You know the game." The waitress arrived with his coffee on a dainty silver tray with a side glass of water and his lemon cake. Brown winked at her and she blushed. He watched her walk away.

"Nice legs," he said and grinned at Evan. "You know, I wouldn't mind owning a café. It's a solid investment here. What do you think? We could be partners." He stirred two lumps of sugar into his coffee.

Evan said nothing. Brown had accepted his rejection of the recruitment attempt too easily. And a direct question? He'd believed recruitments proceeded like slow, careful seductions, not direct invitations.

"How about a music café? Maybe like the places in Nashville where songwriters perform their songs to try to break into the business."

"This isn't Nashville." He had no idea what game Brown played. "I'm not interested, Brown. Waste of money and I really don't have—"

"You've claimed Caine's trust fund from his music publisher, right? If you haven't, get a move on, man. It's yours, you know." Brown sipped his coffee, sliced a bite from the cake with a dessert fork and ate it.

Evan tore a roll apart and sopped up the tasty chicken juices and butter. He wanted Brown to leave, but Brown needed to do his job. Ferreting out the nature of Brown's game might help him.

"Evan, have you been following the American-Chinese talks?" Brown shook his head. "I hate the Chinese. They act so courteous and smiley when they're playing power games and maneuvering for dominance. You know, everyone got upset with America, accusing us of imperialism, blah, blah, blah, when we weren't imperialists. Americans just wanted everyone happy and free, so we didn't have to worry about somebody dropping the bomb on us. But the Chinese? They don't know the meaning of—of—"

"Get to the point." Evan waved the other half of the roll in the air. "I couldn't care less about the Chinese."

"Me neither. Now they insist our delegation stay in their hotel and hold the talks in the hotel instead of at the Hofburg. But they change hotels every two to three weeks. They insist on it for 'security reasons.' They're playing a power game, manipulating the venues, forcing everyone to dance their dance. It must drive the Austrians crazy, but, God bless 'em, they haven't said a word."

"Brown."

Brown wagged his head, his muddy brown hair swishing across his polo shirt collar. "OK. The point. My Uncle Danny loved classical music, especially Caine's." Brown grinned, lifted his coffee cup in a toast. "To my Uncle Danny." He drained the cup, set it on the tray and leaned forward, lowering his voice. "You better be a musician, a conductor. You better be genuine. If I find out you're here to do some mischief for some agency in America that has lied about not knowing you—"

"You're checking me out?"

"Of course. We check out all defectors we don't know about before they defect. Morgan's so pissed, he's ready to pop a vein. So you better be legit, or you'll answer to me for betraying my Uncle Danny."

Betraying his Uncle Danny? Evan nodded, his eyes focused

beyond Brown, convinced this guy was nuts. But Brown had just threatened him, and despite its mildness, it was still a threat. Only two tables of diners remained, and a booth of four in front. The pretty blonde waitress accepted payment from a pair of older women near the door. As they rose to leave, Vasia Bartyakov burst through the front door, glancing around. His wrestler's body bobbed as he walked toward him, a huge grin on his face.

"OK, Brown." Evan leaned close to Brown's face as Brown leaned over the table. "No agency has lied about me because I am not with any agency. I'm genuine. I'm a musician and conductor. I hope Morgan pops a vein. Now get lost. If I see you following me, Brown, I'll call Inspector Leiner and turn the matter over to the Viennese police."

"Evan! So sorry I late," Vasia said, looking at Brown with wide-eyed curiosity. "Who's this?"

"A friend," Brown said, sliding out of the booth. "I'll be in touch, Maestro." Brown grinned and left.

"Not a friend," Evan said, as Vasia took the seat opposite him. "He's from the American Embassy, Vasia. I know you can connect the dots."

Vasia frowned, turning to watch Brown pay the pretty blonde waitress. "Maybe call Inspector Leiner."

"No, no. It's fine. What's going on?"

Vasia pushed Brown's half-finished cake and coffee tray out of the way. "I rehearse with soprano this morning. Margareta Baum. She invite me to lunch with her parents. It's first rehearsal and I think maybe a good idea to stay."

"Is she a good cook or a better soprano?" Evan gazed out the window, relaxing into Vasia's boyish voice, and massaged his tense stomach muscles. A young mother strolled past on the street across from the café pushing a baby carriage. A boy, perhaps five years old, straggled along behind her, grasping the skirt of her peach sundress.

"Better soprano, but food OK. Her parents nice people but talk and talk. So I am late. So sorry, Maestro." The waitress appeared at Vasia's side, her eyebrows raised. Vasia shook his head and said, "*Nichts, danke.*" Evan ordered a hot tea and the waitress cleared the table before she left.

"So, Maestro. How you like Sofia? What you think of Sofia?"

Evan sighed. "I know where you're going with this, Vasia. She's a lovely woman. I hope we can be friends. I don't want any complicated attachments right now. That's all."

Vasia groaned. "All humans complicated. She like you."

"Drop it, please." He glared at the Russian who, after studying Evan's face for half a minute, shrugged.

"You move today, Evan?"

He nodded. "This morning. I have nothing, Vasia. Not even clothes hangers. My landlady has loaned me a futon and sheets and towels, but I need to shop. Where can I get some good deals?"

Vasia giggled, the sound high and silvery. "Good deals? Why? You have money to buy best of everything."

"I don't *need* the best of everything. I need good stuff at reasonable prices. No rip-offs. Right?" He heard the impatience in his voice and took a deep breath to relax. Vasia wasn't Brown. He pulled a wad of euros from his jeans pocket and handed it to Vasia. "For the hunting rifle. My per diem cash from the tour. Is it enough?"

Vasia unfolded the money and riffled through the bills. "Maybe too much."

"Use whatever's left to buy extra ammunition for both of us. You'll keep the rifle for me until I get my license?"

"No problem."

"We can hunt in Romania this fall?"

Vasia nodded. "I check but I think no problem. Romanians have more relaxed regulations because hunting big business for them." He slid out of the booth and stood, stuffing the cash into his jeans pocket. He glanced toward the door, frowning. "Greta wait at my new apartment. We clean, make repairs. I talk to Greta about best places for shopping. No rip-offs." He leaned down to Evan. "Tell Inspector Leiner about American Embassy guy."

Evan dug in his jeans pocket and pulled out the Mozart cell phone. "OK, Vasia. But Brown's just an annoying mosquito buzzing around hoping to find some food."

Vasia laughed, rueful. "Siberian mosquitoes like small birds, Evan. Their bite painful."

"Brown's from the Bronx, not Siberia."

"OK. I call you later in week after I move and I have rifle. You come to my party?" The Russian was backing away.

"I'll be there." Evan flipped open the cell phone. Vasia grinned and jogged out of the café. Evan closed the phone and set it on the table. He'd cut Brown some slack. He'd call Leiner if it became necessary. But for now, something about the American, something in his friendliness, gave him the feeling Brown might be harmless. The risk: anyone who made a point of saying he's not acting probably was.

Klaus wished he was with Eva, Laura, and Anna at their favorite Neusiedl Lake resort to swim and sail, and escape the city's heat, but the Chinese and the informal surveillance on Evan Quinn had made it a working weekend. Now, he sat on a Stadtpark bench, sweating in the bright July sunshine, annoyed with Bartyakov for his relaxed view of time and appointments.

A draft of cold Pilsner would taste especially good right now. He stood up to take off his light gray suit jacket. In his peripheral vision, he could see to his left a cluster of chess tables and engrossed players, to his right the empty path leading to the duck pond. Klaus sat down, laying the suit jacket on the bench next to him.

Bartyakov had been easy to recruit for his surveillance on Evan Quinn when he'd called him two days earlier. He'd pointed out to the Russian that he'd already done a good job of teaching Quinn how to lose surveillance. The Russian had thanked him in a sheepish tone. Quinn was his friend. They were fellow musicians. Bartyakov's experience three years earlier, harassed and threatened by Russians, insured that he'd understand the possibilities and want to protect Quinn, which was true. So Bartyakov had agreed to help him without further discussion.

An ice cream vendor with a neon green and white shade umbrella over his cart approached from the direction of the Kursalon, the park's elegant pavilion and café where Viennese had spent their summer Sunday afternoons for decades, gossiping and listening to Strauss waltzes and marches played by a band. He waved the vendor over to buy a small cone of vanilla gelato. The perfect summer food.

Vassily Bartyakov emerged from the grove of trees to Klaus's right. The Russian's appearance hadn't changed. If anything, he'd gained weight. Bartyakov had mentioned an Austrian girlfriend who worked at Österreich Eins, his favorite classical music radio station. The Russian rushed past the ice cream vendor, a frown closing his usually open face.

"*Guten Tag*, Herr Bartyakov," Klaus said when the Russian stopped in front of him. "*Wie geht's Ihnen heute?*"

"Inspector," Bartyakov said, catching his breath, and he continued in German. "Has Maestro called you? I think something wrong. At Café Danforth when I meet Evan a man from American Embassy is there with him. Evan said man not friend and called him Brown."

"Herr Bartyakov, please sit down, calm yourself," Klaus said in German, pleased the Russian had chosen that language rather than English for their conversation. The Russian sat next to him on the bench, Klaus' suit jacket between them. "Now, please tell me, did you hear what Herr Brown said to Herr Quinn?"

Bartyakov shook his head vigorously, no. "Evan talking to him when I stop at table in café. Evan said," here the Russian switched to English, "If I see you following me, Brown, I'll call Inspector Leiner and turn the matter over to the Viennese police." Back to German, "That's all I heard."

Klaus nodded. Vanilla gelato dripped on his hand. He finished the ice cream while Herr Bartyakov waited. He knew that Bernard Brown was following Evan Quinn, but not why. The Russian had now told him that Quinn wanted Brown to turn his attention elsewhere, not on him. Or, Quinn had seen Bartyakov approach and chosen to hide his alliance with Brown.

"Tell me, Herr Bartyakov," he said, crunching on the last of his gelato cone. "Did Herr Quinn see you enter the café? Was he watching you approach his table?"

The Russian nodded. "I see his eyes on me."

He wiped his hands on his white handkerchief. Likely that Quinn had covered himself when he saw Bartyakov. "Anything yesterday?"

The Russian shook his head, no. "I see no one bother Evan or follow him at violin recital and our dinner. But your phone call anger him. He said you believe he is spy. I try to tell him—"

"*Prima.*" Klaus gathered his suit jacket and stood up.

Bartyakov shot to his feet. "Inspector, Evan call you about Brown?"

Klaus shook his head, no. No call. Another sign perhaps that Quinn and Brown were working together, but not concrete evidence. "Herr Bartyakov, you've done him a favor by telling me. Will you see him tomorrow?"

The Russian sighed. "I move tomorrow or next day. Landlord tell me today. After that, I shop with Evan. He need everything for new apartment."

Klaus shook his hand. "Anything unusual, call me, yes? Good luck with your move. And thank you."

The Russian jogged back the way he'd come as Klaus shrugged into his suit jacket. He headed toward the Kursalon, where he'd parked his car, reaching into his inner suit jacket pocket to turn off the voice-activated digital recorder that had recorded their talk.

Chapter 14

The faintest hint of light breathed into the day from the east. A breeze exhaled the scent of Freda's roses through the open windows. In the light from the forty-nine-inch LCD television embedded in his electronics wall, Evan drank cold water as he watched the BBC morning news on television.

The anchorman's crisp delivery matched his tailored dark gray suit. "In the latest fighting in the American insurgency, according to the USA News Service, American insurgents with support from the dissident Underground in that country attacked and bombed Chicago's O'Hare International Airport yesterday, damaging three terminals, four runways and injuring hundreds of travelers and airport workers. The airport has closed and all flight arrivals have been re-routed. This is the deepest insurgents have attacked in Washington's territory since the state of North Dakota joined the insurgency five years ago and insurgents bombed the Mall of America in Minnesota. Yesterday's attack was well planned and executed. No insurgents were captured. Washington has denounced the attack on civilians but will not discuss its current strategy or its response. The insurgents' goal is to restore true democracy in America. They claim the Washington government is a dictatorship that has suspended the Constitution. The insurgency is now in its thirtieth year."

Evan finished off the water. "No insurgents were captured" meant government soldiers had killed all of them, not that they had escaped. He turned for the kitchen.

"Now to Chinese Vice Chairman Jiang Xu's expected visit to Vienna," the anchorman said.

Evan froze, his eyes locked on his television.

"No date for the Vice Chairman's visit has been confirmed yet but the Austrians have announced they will welcome him with a formal state reception at Schönbrunn Palace," the BBC anchorman said, "for his first visit to Vienna. The Austrians have released few details in deference to security concerns. Many state receptions in the past lit up the Great Gallery in Schönbrunn Palace with banquets and balls and included concerts in the palatial gardens." The BBC anchorman announced a special report on the Chinese-American talks' progress and the impact the Vice Chairman's visit could have on them.

"*Fernseher abstellan*," Evan said and the television flicked off.

No specifics. "In deference to security concerns." Evan kicked the air, his foot snapping back with precision. He needed specific information, like the date of Jiang Xu's arrival. He wanted to finish with this job.

"Not yet," Woody had said when he'd called him two days ago. Woody hadn't heard from his contacts. Woody's forger was still out of town. Why was Woody stonewalling him?

"I need alternate ID to get a room at the Parkhotel Schönbrunn."

"Bad idea, Georg. What's your escape route?"

"Ever heard of operational disguise, Woody? And your bug-finder doesn't work. I see surveillance cameras in stores but your bug-finder doesn't vibrate."

Woody giggled. He had explained in a paternal tone that the device was calibrated to detect frequencies most often used in covert surveillance, not those used in overt surveillance such as store cameras.

Evan's fist punched an imaginary face and he swirled down into a defensive crouch. A slow burn of suspicion heated his memory of that phone call. What was Woody hiding behind his amusement and reluctant cooperation?

He went into the kitchen, stuck his head under cold water from the faucet and then drank another glass. He had the feeling Woody was trying to sabotage him. He must play defense. On his way out, he grabbed his ID card just in case.

The breeze swayed the full maple, elm, oak, and beech trees on Sternwartestrasse. At dawn, he expected few people on the streets or in the parks. He preferred solitary runs. Exiting Freda's driveway, he turned up the hill, setting a brisk comfortable pace in order to continue prepping his muscles.

Past Türkenschanz Park he turned left. A car passed. He called to mind a medium fast two-part invention for keyboard by Johann Sebastian Bach, the tempo for his run this morning. He hummed snatches of it, noting the length and angle of his stride, the slight complementary twist of his upper body and the solid feel of the sidewalk under his feet. The humidity level had increased, thickening the air. The sun peeked over the eastern horizon on its climb through the rose, mauve and gray-blue sky.

No surveillance had shadowed him since the week before,

and no Brown, either, not even at the Fischer School of Martial Arts the day before when he met Okada for his skill assessment. Evan ran northwest. He'd studied his city map the night before to have a general idea where to run. If he continued on his present route, he would arrive eventually at the Vienna Woods, a crescent park around the outer suburbs from the Danube River north down to the southwest. He changed course.

Twenty minutes later, after winding through quiet residential streets, he found what he wanted: Pötzleinsdorfer Park. He jogged onto a pebbly dirt path that curved east through a grove of mature beeches and maples that reminded him of a wooded area not far from his father's Minneapolis house. He and Paul Caine had cut through it walking to and from school.

In those woods, he had believed that if he ran fast enough, he could lift off the ground and fly. The last day of fourth grade. Skinny Paul had raced ahead of him through the woods. Harold and his Vigiciv gang chased them. Evan was terrified, breathless, bramble thorns sticking to his jeans as he ran. He longed to soar on the updrafts, ride an air current far up in the sky away from Harold, and everything, and hide inside the clouds.

Now Evan sprinted on the path through the woods of Pötzleinsdorfer Park. He pushed himself to fly. A sharp pain knifed through his right side, knocking the breath out of his lungs. He halted by a bench at the edge of the woods, and bent over to breathe through the muscle spasm and massage his right side. He was alone. He had always felt safer alone.

Squirrels chirred in the trees behind him. Birds sang.

Leaves rustled in the breeze. He straightened about six inches, feeling the pain shoot up his side. He looked around at the bucolic landscape. He wasn't a woodsman despite his father's and Uncle Joe's attempts to awaken a love for hunting, fishing, and wilderness exploration in him. They had taught him, though, strategies for survival that he'd used during his Perceval training. He had always felt more comfortable in a forest of skyscrapers, and he preferred city culture and urban anonymity.

A green field rolled out to a wooded area in front of him. An idea made him straighten further. The woods. He smiled to himself. A secluded location for target practice. They'd instructed him to join a gun club or hunting club, but he couldn't do that yet because of his probation. The Ruger had a night scope and silencer. He could come here early morning or late at night and practice without anyone knowing. A farther location wasn't an option. Rental car agencies required too much information and GPS positioners tracked every car.

He sat down on the bench, massaged his right side. He'd rest until the muscle stitch disappeared. Stupid to push himself when he hadn't run in almost a month. Slow, take it slow and build. He must be ready for anything. He scrutinized the field, woods and paths, half expecting Brown or a Uighur terrorist to appear.

"Well, hey, look who's here. The heretic poet's kid," Harold said, his voice like dried corn stalks brushing together. Evan spun around. Harold and his gang of three emerged from the trees.

Evan shot off the bench. He bolted across the field to the

woods on the far side. He glanced over his shoulder. Harold and his gang had vanished. He was alone again. How did Brown know about Harold? How had he found another teen Harold to send after him? How had this Harold found him? The past popped up without invitation, sending seismic shocks through his consciousness.

He stopped, kneading the muscle stitch, allowing the image of the small sun-dappled clearing to slide into his mind. Paul had escaped that last day of fourth grade, but hadn't returned with help. Harold and his boys had tied Evan to a tree and piled kindling at his feet to burn him "like they burned witches and heretics." Disjointed images flashed into his mind, his movie trailer of that experience. Bushy wood ferns. The hot sun's blinding light through the branches above. Harold's black scarf draped over his head. Harold's face inches away. Harold's lips kissing his and Harold's hot breath tasting of mustard and hot dogs.

Bent over at the field's edge in Pötzleinsdorfer Park, Evan felt his testicles contract with the physical memory of Harold's fondling hand. A wave of nausea rose up from his stomach. He felt dirty. Filthy dirty shit. His mind resembled a haunted house more than a modern mansion resplendent with the music he loved. He forced the memory, as he had memories for years, far back in his mind's dark closet. How did Brown know about Harold? Brown reached into his past in order to weaken him, control him. No more. Now he knew Brown's game.

Focus on the present, live and breathe in the moment. He was in Vienna, Austria, free from Minneapolis and the past. The muscle stitch was gone. He took deep breaths and jogged at an easy, steady pace to a Bach solo violin partita in his mind. On the other side of the park, he veered down Pötzleinsdorferstrasse. He passed houses, apartment buildings, more shops, a post office, police station, and cafés exuding the aroma of fresh brewed coffee with servers setting up sidewalk tables for early morning customers. A goldenrod yellow streetcar clanged past. He had returned to the present and the urban civilization he loved.

Fifteen minutes later, he approached Freda's driveway gate. He checked around: quiet residential street, a neighbor leaving for work. As he pressed his right middle fingertip on the scanner, he spoke into the security panel on the left stone column: "*Der schattige Affe.*" The gate swung open. Sasha bounded from behind the house to greet him. She trotted with him to his door. Out of the corner of his eye, he glimpsed Freda moving away from an upstairs window in her house.

"Sit, Sasha." Happy with his attention, she bumped against his sweaty legs and tried to lick his hand. "Sit, girl." She whined. "You can't come in today, girl." To distract her, he pretended to throw a stick into the back yard. She ran after it, but he figured that trick wouldn't work again for a while.

Inside his apartment, he reset his security panel and headed for the bathroom. He stripped and stepped into the shower, soaping and scrubbing over and over again to wash away Harold's filth.

After two hours' score study of Barber's *Adagio for Strings*, he went to a café near Türkenschanz Platz where he ordered the Austrian version of a big American breakfast: fried eggs, fried potatoes, toast with Swiss cheese and sliced ham and coffee. The waiter and café owner recognized him, welcomed him with delight, which mystified him. They didn't know him, only who he was. The oddity of fame. On the positive side, people wanted to help him and he appreciated that. The owner recommended a local graphic artist for his scheduling wall calendar.

Streetcars in Vienna provided an efficient but leisurely method of travel from place to place. Today Evan wanted to travel faster to complete the Perceval business faster to return faster to score study for the Amsterdam gig. He rode the Number 41 streetcar to the Währinger Gurtel, a broad, traffic-laden boulevard like the Ring Boulevard that encircled the city farther out. He switched to the subway to the Twelfth District. Vienna's subway was clean, brightly lit and comfortable with no rabble-rousing riders. At least none on his rides. And no gang graffiti. The Viennese clearly worked as hard to maintain their subway in perfect order as they did their buses, streetcars, and trains.

At Schönbrunn Palace, he prowled the neighborhood again. Nothing had changed at the Parkhotel Schönbrunn. He decided that security occupied the front top floor rooms and the Chinese delegation the top rear rooms. That's where he'd place them. He considered stealing a room card and slipping into a front room, but decided to case the palace's interior first. A sniper nest there gave him more distance, more time to escape.

He returned to the palace's main entrance. The cashier in the ticket office called him "Maestro" with a broad smile and asked if he wanted an English-language tour and guidebook. He nodded. People recognizing him created a liability for the Perceval business. They'd remember him. He made a mental note to search the city directory on the Internet for a costume shop.

As he slid his bankcard across the counter to the cashier, he said, "I heard on the news this morning about a big state reception here. Will the palace and gardens close?"

She swiped his card in her computer register. "Yes, we will close at noon the day of the reception."

"Including the gardens?" he said, accepting back his bankcard.

She nodded. "We reopen as usual the next day."

"The news report said the reception would be in the Great Gallery. Is that room on the tour?"

She frowned, her eyes suspicious. "Yes, of course. But the reception's date and location are not yet known. What news report was it?"

She was a dead-end. "The BBC, I think," he said. "Would it be a paid holiday for you?" He gave her one of his bright public persona smiles.

She laughed, handing him his tour ticket and guidebook. "Unfortunately, no."

He would need to enter the palace before noon the day of the reception. He should find the room for his sniper nest and plot his escape routes during the next week. The English-language tour began in half an hour so he opened the guidebook. He paced as he studied the palace's floor plan, specifically areas closed to the public: storage, offices, the upper floors and staircases he might use on the side of the palace closest to the hotel. Where could he make his sniper's nest?

He hated the uncertainty of this business, the waiting. He wished the Chinese Vice Chairman would just come to Vienna. This Chinese guy's whims prevented him from completing his assignment. This Chinese guy prevented him from fulfilling the contract, prevented him from getting rid of the Americans.

"Ladies and Gentlemen," a young blonde woman said in accented English. She wore a summer skirt in white and a lime linen blazer. "My name is Serena. I am your guide for your tour today through the magnificent Schloss Schön-brunn, the summer palace of the Hapsburgs."

Evan joined the group.

Who left all the paper? Bernie rubbed his jaw with both hands as he stared at his cluttered office desk. Why throw reports on his desk instead of in the in-basket or slide them into his mailbox at the Embassy's mail center? Computers hadn't eliminated paper from offices. Not now, not ever. When he pulled out his swivel desk chair, he found a hill of classified envelopes piled on it. He needed an assistant. He turned on his computer, brushed the envelopes to the floor and plopped into the chair.

Larry Morgan's assistant, Maddy, smiled in his office doorway. "The boss is looking for you. Where were you this morning? He said you're late with a report." She rolled her eyes.

Bernie had liked Maddy immediately when he met her his first day in Vienna to serve as Deputy Chief of Station. He knew she loved her job, loved her husband and two kids, and protected the people she respected. She was now protecting him.

"Any news about his transfer?" he said. She shook her head. "If he asks again, I tailed Evan Quinn this morning, bored out of my mind."

She grinned. "You got it."

"And I want to put in a request for an assistant just like you."

"You, flirt," she laughed as she left.

Bernie logged on to the Internet to check his e-mail. He opened a note from his wife, short and sweet: *Bernie, the divorce papers are in the pouch.* She'd made her decision. He filed her note in the "Needs Action" folder. He read e-mails from his two daughters. Christine at ten wrote about equestrian camp and asked him when he'd come home again. Could he attend her dressage in August? Seven-year-old Jennifer wanted a kitten. He wrote replies, each signed with two lines of hugs and kisses. They'd be fine with his soon-to-be ex-wife.

He opened the file marked "Quinn Inquiry." He'd received responses from Langley and State the previous week. Quinn's behavior confirmed what they'd told him: he was genuine. Not on their payroll. He considered printing them out as his report to Morgan.

"Bernie." Morgan's voice startled him. "Maddy says you were following Quinn all morning."

He faced his tall, gangly boss standing two feet inside the doorway. His bald pate shone in the ceiling fluorescent light. "Yeah. He was seeing the sights. He didn't mark me. I wore one of my disguises."

Morgan's lopsided smile tilted his features into a demonic grin. "What did Langley say?"

"I was just going over the responses to print out for you. Quinn's not CIA. Also not with State Department Intel."

"Check all the military branches."

"Quinn never served in the military."

"Doesn't matter. You know the Pentagon lusts for our territory. I bet Quinn's DIA. Keep on him. If he's not with us, he's against us." Morgan pivoted and strode from the office.

Bernie sighed. He doubted Evan Quinn worked for the DIA or any military intelligence, or anything other than as a symphony orchestra conductor who had the misfortune of having a father hated by Larry Morgan. He began composing a note to his buddy Jack Marshall at the Pentagon.

Chapter 15

This morning, his fourteenth on his own in Vienna, he had explored Grinzing directly north of his apartment. The suburban village center had reminded him of the downtown area of Wayzata or Excelsior, two affluent suburbs west of Minneapolis, but without the armed guards on every corner and the limos with tinted bullet-proof windows driving through town. He had realized that he no longer feared arrest for straying into an area above his economic status.

Now, he sprinted across Sieveringerstrasse on his way to Währing where he lived, and stopped near a Tabak Trafik, a tobacco-newsagent shop. A young businessman talked on a cell phone nearby. Motor scooters and bug-like Geisters scurried down the street toward the inner city. Evan headed downhill.

Music had ruled his days, in one form or another. A particular joy came from Robert Waldstein, the Vienna Philharmonic's congenial concertmaster, who had introduced Evan to a master violin maker. The master showed Evan his inventory and provided him with a loaner fiddle until his new violin was ready. As he'd played Bach on the loaner fiddle in the violin maker's studio, his chin cupped in the smooth chin rest, his nose inhaling the faint scent of rosin, his ears attuned to the violin's vibrations and sound, he exhaled, calm and content at last.

Waldstein had taken him to the depths of the Augustinerkeller, a wine cellar in the First District, where they met six orchestra musicians for lunch. Their exuberant welcome, their laughter and stories, their jokes and their abiding goodwill had buoyed him through the following days of furnishing his new apartment. The musicians had helped him with the furniture and called him with invitations, and he had talked with Robert about putting together a string quartet. He loved being back in the musician family in a more settled way.

As he approached a busy intersection now, he glanced behind him. A block away, a jogging man with wheat-blonde hair slowed then turned right into a cross street. During his turn, the man looked at him. Evan saw his face clearly – Harold Smith. An *adult* Harold Smith. Evan turned and ran back up the street. By the time he reached the cross street, Harold was gone. Vanished. Just like his teen version with his Vigiciv gang. Evan bent to catch his breath. How could Harold, the adult Harold, be in Vienna? Following *him?* Harold's father had told his father on that audio recording that Harold was in the military and fighting against the insurgency. No, it couldn't have been Harold. Evan shook his head as if to clear it and straightened, hands on his hips. The man had reminded him of Harold, had resembled him. Yeah, that had to be it.

Evan jogged back to the busy intersection where he spotted a familiar corner, turned into the street and continued his run listening to Copland's *Appalachian Spring* in his mind.

Copland's dancing rhythms lifted his mood. Better Copland than letting his paranoia run away with him. The program for the Amsterdam gig in five days – Barber's *Adagio for Strings,* the Copland and Caine's Fifth Symphony – was almost ready.

The traffic on Krottenbachstrasse stopped him. He jogged in place until a lull allowed him to cross. Over train tracks and after a right turn he expected Peter-Jordan Strasse, but found Chimanistrasse. Lost. He headed downhill again. He'd passed three large houses on his right when a familiar blonde-haired man with a moustache appeared in his peripheral vision on his left. He ducked down behind a parked car.

Inspector Klaus Leiner faced a gleaming black sedan in a driveway across the street. He talked on a cell phone. A willowy auburn-haired woman, dressed in jeans and a white sleeveless tunic, shot out of the house's front door. Two teenaged girls followed her, one tall and slender with thick auburn hair like the woman's, the other a chunky blonde, and both dressed in white short-sleeved blouses and floral skirts. Behind them loped two dogs, one a shaggy black and white dog the size of a small pony, and the other a Springer spaniel. The scene reminded Evan of family values commercials on American TV. So this was Leiner's family and this was his home on Chimanistrasse.

Leiner closed his cell phone and opened one of the sedan's back doors. The blonde girl danced around him, giggling, poking his sides and jumping out of his reach before she climbed in. Anna, the younger daughter. The tall one must be Laura, the lover of ballet and Bach. She glided to the front passenger door, a princess, carrying her knapsack rather than wearing it on her back. The woman handed the Inspector his bulging leather briefcase. They kissed. Not the sweet farewell peck on the cheek of a long-married couple, but a deep kiss on the mouth. Leiner caressed her jawline with the back of his hand. They kissed again. Thumping and shouting erupted from the car. The adolescent beasts protested for attention.

Leiner slid into the car. His wife waved as he backed out of the driveway. Evan ducked out of sight again as Leiner paused for five seconds then drove toward the inner city. Leiner's wife entered the house with the spaniel. The shaggy dog sniffed around flowering bushes close to the house.

Three stories high, painted forest green with ivory trim and a well-tended lawn, Leiner's house appeared upper middle class and perfect in every detail, unlike what he'd have imagined for a cop. In America, local cops occupied the upper levels of the working class and lived in dense neighborhoods of overcrowded apartment buildings and bungalows, and he'd expected the same for Austrian cops. This neighborhood reminded him of his father's in Minneapolis when he was a kid. He walked about ten feet down the sidewalk. From this new angle he could see the Leiners' spacious back yard and a flower garden and a mint green gazebo covered on one side with blue morning glory flowers.

Evan continued down the street, his head bowed, hoping he had not sparked someone's interest by lingering too long. He increased his pace to a slow jog. No one shadowed him this morning. No one knew where he was. A smile crept across Evan's face. He now knew where Leiner lived, but the cop didn't know that he knew. Evan felt a jolt of energy.

Whether or not it mattered, he felt that he had an advantage now over the cop.

Seven minutes later, he raced Sasha to his apartment's outer door. Freda kneeled in the garden behind the garage.

"Morning, Freda," he called as Sasha barked. "You're up early this morning."

"I love the early morning sun. How was your run?"

He strolled over to her as Sasha trotted toward the house. "Pretty good. Not as humid today. What a beautiful vegetable garden. And the roses by the house, too. They're huge, gorgeous and wonderfully fragrant."

She blushed under the wide brimmed yellow canvas hat protecting her head. "Thank you, Evan. I love gardening. Had you a garden in Minneapolis?"

He squatted next to her, reached out to a weed and pulled it. "Yeah, I miss it. We grew all our vegetables and herbs. The housekeeper canned the surplus at harvest so we'd have vegetables during the winter. I really loved digging potatoes." He pulled another weed.

"You're welcome to pick what you'd like when they're ready. Would you like a garden of your own here?" She yanked on a stubborn weed.

"Well, I'd love a small one, sure. Let's see what my schedule is like. I may not be around enough to tend it." He straightened. "I could help you with yours, though. Thanks for the offer to share your bounty."

She smiled. "Shopping again today?"

He headed for his outer door. "I've finished with that for a while, *Gott sei Dank*. Score study this morning, a Krav

Maga lesson before lunch and visiting a musician this afternoon. Have a good day, Freda."

Inside, he drank two large tumbler glasses of water in the kitchen and started the brewing cycle on his wall coffeemaker. In the shower, he sang the Quaker hymn theme from Copland's *Appalachian Spring* at the top of his voice, aware of the open window. Freda, working in the garden below, could hear it. In Minneapolis, he wouldn't have dared sing like that for anyone to hear, even AC-approved music. If you wanted a safe life, you practiced invisibility as much as possible.

Dressed in denim shorts and a T-shirt, Evan stood in the doorway to the front room and said, "Radio Österreich Eins." The radio came on broadcasting a Haydn string quartet. He began making his favorite meal of the day. He had observed Beth, their housekeeper, cook breakfast for him for the past two years, which had given him the confidence to cook his own now. As he sipped a mug of steaming black coffee, he cooked two strips of bacon in a ten-inch skillet on the stove. While the bacon drained on paper towel, he hummed along with the Haydn on the radio and scrambled eggs in the same skillet.

He ate sitting at his small oak kitchen table facing the wall-sized calendar he'd bought the week before. A local graphic artist had created the template for the calendar in a day. She had printed five years as he'd requested, each year with its own color and two-foot by four-foot panel. Two years, 2048 and '49, hung between the windows and videophone. The other three hung on the wall and bedroom door opposite the windows. For the rest of 2048, in his favorite color royal blue, he'd filled in four weeks for conducting gigs:

Amsterdam this month, Vienna Philharmonic in September, the Oslo Philharmonic late September and Madrid in early December.

After breakfast, he practiced the violin for an hour as he'd done nearly every morning since he was four. He ran through scales and exercises and immersed himself in a partita by J.S. Bach. Bach took over his mind, his breathing, took him out of himself, and into a world of order and clarity. Daily practice maintained his playing in top form and provided a bridge into his score study. The life of a musician required constant study and practice. He felt real, alive when he was working on scores or playing music.

His audiences in Minneapolis had loved Aaron Copland's *Appalachian Spring*. He had conducted it once a year. He reviewed the score for an hour, sitting in a wing-backed chair by one of his open front windows, the score on the black music stand, a sharpened pencil as baton in his right hand, both hands moving to the music in his mind.

The videophone warbled in the kitchen. He'd chosen a ring tone entitled "Bird song," a digital approximation of a singing warbler or thrush (he couldn't recall which), gentle and unobtrusive. As he walked into the kitchen, he said, "Hello?"

The monitor flashed on, revealing his elegant, white-haired British manager at his desk, framed concert posters on the wall behind him. "Good morning, Evan. How are you?"

"Great, Nigel. How are you? What's new in my world?"

Nigel chuckled, smoothing a cornflower blue tie over his pale peach shirt. He wasn't wearing his suit jacket which was unusual. "I've got good news for autumn, Evan. Two more orchestras confirmed as a result of American cancellations."

"Excellent. When and where?"

"Bucharest in early October, the week after Oslo. And Helsinki the week of November first. I'm working on St. Petersburg for the following week in November. They all want Caine's music, of course."

"Bucharest in October, that's perfect. I've made plans for a hunting trip in Romania but was waiting on my schedule. Don't book anything for the week after, OK?"

Nigel nodded, pursing his lips as he wrote notes. "I've heard the hunting is quite good in Romania. Edinburgh persists for August, and—"

"Nothing in August, please." Perceval needed an open schedule in August, but he wanted Edinburgh. Frustration sent him to his refrigerator for a bottle of mineral water that he opened with one violent twist of the cap.

Nigel frowned on the monitor. "Evan, what would you have me do?"

He sighed. "I know, I know. Please tell Edinburgh that I'd be honored to conduct a gig with them next year. Try to nail down a date. I don't want anyone to feel I'm avoiding them. And please e-mail me the requested programs for Bucharest and Helsinki."

Nigel nodded. "Good. I've received inquiries and mail for you about Caine from conductors and musicians. Any unpublished music of Caine's you might know about. And they want information about specific works of his."

"There's no unpublished music that Joe left behind. ISS destroyed fragments of a string quartet and a cello concerto when they arrested him. I'm happy to answer any questions, give any interviews, about Caine and his music. Please forward the mail, the phone messages. Anything else?" He drank more mineral water.

"You sound quite happy. How is the new flat?"

"Excellent. I spent some time with Robert Waldstein last week and musicians from the Philharmonic. They're helping me figure out the holes in my repertoire. Have you heard of Vassily Bartyakov? He's a pianist."

Nigel cocked his head to one side. "Someone I need to watch for?"

"I'm thinking of requesting him for the Caine Piano Concerto next year after he graduates. He's a *Mensch*. He and his girlfriend have helped me a lot. He's the one I'll hunt with this fall. How are things in London?"

Nigel looked up from writing notes. "Devilish hot. The air conditioning in our office failed overnight. I'm working on possibilities for you next year in the Far East and Pacific, Buenos Aires perhaps in January. We also need to conference with the website designer for your professional website. I'll call you in two or three days, Evan, sooner if I have something more urgent." Nigel leaned forward, his hand reaching out to his phone.

"OK. Good to talk to you, Nigel. Thanks."

Evan used blue marker to fill in the weeks on his wall calendar for Bucharest and Helsinki, and blocked off the weeks after them for hunting and St. Petersburg. Time to leave for his Krav Maga lesson.

Forty minutes later, he arrived at the Fischer School of

Martial Arts as Brown, dressed for work but his brown hair wet and slicked back, trotted out the front door.

"Hey, Maestro!" Brown shouted in his irritating Bronx accent. "Coming for a lesson or just a workout?" He whipped off his sunglasses.

Evan tried to pass him, but Brown grabbed his arm. "Let go," Evan said in a low, firm voice.

Brown matched Evan's tone. "Seen the news?"

Evan's gaze locked onto Brown's green eyes. "What news?"

"The Chinese invaded Taiwan. Annexed it so fast, nobody had time to react. Didn't I tell you? The Chinese want to rule the world. You can bet this will affect the delicate geopolitical situation. America has defense pacts with all the Pacific Alliance countries, including Taiwan."

Evan stepped back and Brown released his arm. "Why are you telling me this?"

"Have any travel plans in the next few weeks?" Evan nodded as Brown assessed the street's activity. "OK. If it's in Europe, you're safe. But if it's in Asia, if I were you, I'd consider rescheduling. Where is it?"

"Amsterdam."

"*Great* city! Beautiful people, the Dutch. And I've heard they have a great orchestra, but then you'd know more about that than I would. When you're there, check out the jazz cafés. They're amazing. Hey, you know what? We could open a jazz café here together, the café I've found that's for sale. It's been years since—"

"Thanks for the news, Brown." Evan reached for the door handle. "You really need a wife to talk to."

"She and my daughters are living the good life in Manhattan," Brown said, sliding the sunglasses over his eyes as Evan turned and entered the school.

Klaus waited in the middle of Evan Quinn's front room as Freda Kirsch reset the security system. The American had moved in before Marco had installed any surveillance devices. He planned to install two devices himself today unless Frau Kirsch would not leave him alone long enough.

A black leather recliner faced the television in the electronics wall, and a matching wing-backed chair stood near one of the open windows, a black music stand in front of it. Black and white, stark colors for interior decoration. He checked the score on the music stand: Aaron Copland's *Appalachian Spring*.

"Inspector," Frau Kirsch said behind him and continued in German. "He's not had time to—"

"He's bought music scores," Klaus said, walking over to the bookshelves to the right of the kitchen doorway. He picked music scores at random, fanned their pages, returned them to the shelf and after one, he pressed a listening transmitter to the bottom of the shelf above. "Herr Quinn is rich now, Frau Kirsch. Why hasn't he bought more for his apartment? For himself?"

"He told me to have money is strange, almost incomprehensible to him." Frau Kirsch shrugged, a gesture of helplessness. "I think he dislikes shopping."

Scowling, Klaus spotted the neon blue cell phone on a

shelf to the left of the doorway, and a black cell phone next to it. Two cell phones? He picked up the black phone. Empty directory. He took out a palm-sized computer, opened a file on it marked "Quinn" and entered the phone number that popped up on the black phone's display for last number called. He chose "trace" from the computer's menu and entered the phone number.

"He wants his own garden, Inspector. He has had no visitors."

"Where is it, Frau Kirsch?" He pocketed the computer and returned the black cell phone to the shelf above the neon blue phone.

"The bedroom closet."

Klaus noticed the huge blank calendar panels on the left kitchen wall and bedroom door. He glanced around. His eyes rested on the two calendars with writing on them next to the videophone. Quinn's conducting schedule.

In the bedroom, Frau Kirsch opened the closet door and said, "Light." Klaus stepped in, running his hand along the clothes hung on the left. Quinn had bought more clothes, but not another tuxedo yet. A pile of clothes lay on the floor to his right in front of a wall of drawers. Quinn needed a laundry hamper.

"Straight ahead, in the back wall down by the floor," Frau Kirsch said behind him.

He'd wanted to search Quinn's apartment the week before, but Marco had convinced him to wait, give the American time to settle in, acquire incriminating evidence. He kneeled at the back wall, running his fingertips over it until he felt the outline of the door.

"Press the upper right corner," Frau Kirsch said.

The door sprang open and he pulled it wide, revealing the empty compartment.

"You showed it to him?"

"Yes, Inspector. I told him about the lawyer who installed it and that he could also store important papers here."

Klaus closed the door and stood, wiping his hands of dust. "Any other secret places?" Frau Kirsch shook her head.

Quinn's unmade bed yielded nothing. The American needed an armoire. He found another pile of clothes under one window and nothing else in the bedroom. The same for the bathroom where Quinn had left towels draped over the shower curtain rod and on the floor. The disarray reminded him of his bachelor days.

In the kitchen, Klaus opened the drawers and cabinets. One cabinet contained food, another glasses and disposable plates. He noted the dirty skillet, glasses, and mug in the sink. Food filled the refrigerator. Quinn had stocked his freezer well. Klaus pulled out four frozen meals. "He cooks for himself?"

"He told me he doesn't know how to cook but he wants to learn." Freda watched from the bedroom doorway.

The computer in his pocket beeped. He returned the frozen meals, closed the freezer. "Café Chicago" appeared on the computer's display. Why had Quinn called Woody Lewis? Why a second cell phone? None of the American spies he'd caught in the past had known Lewis. He'd ask Marco to check the black cell phone's account and order a surveillance program for it.

Frau Kirsch returned to the front room. Klaus joined

her, picked up the neon blue phone in which an Interior Ministry's computer technician had loaded a prototype of an experimental surveillance program to trace and record calls and provide information on Quinn's location when he carried it, independent of it being on or near cell phone towers, which was of no use today.

"Frau Kirsch, please check the wall cabinets."

As she opened the cabinet doors, he accessed the neon blue phone's directory and scrolled through the names and numbers: Bartyakov, Owen te Kumara, names he recognized as Vienna Philharmonic musicians, Nigel Fox, his name, Dieter's name, Robert Waldstein, Greta Fasching, and... *Sofia Karalis*? Klaus laughed in surprise and looked at Frau Kirsch. She kneeled in front of the last cabinet by the back window.

"Let me know, Frau Kirsch, if Sofia Karalis visits Herr Quinn," he said with a smile. He thought of how much his two daughters would love to meet the actress.

"He knows Sofia Karalis?" Frau Kirsch sat back on her heels, eyes wide.

"*Ja, ja.*" Klaus replaced the neon blue cell phone on a shelf by itself. All those names but no Woody Lewis on that phone, only the black one. "Find anything, Frau Kirsch?"

She shook her head, no. "A violin in the first cabinet. Empty boxes here." She closed the last cabinet door and rose to her feet. "He saves empty boxes. He told me he was poor in America."

"One moment, Frau Kirsch." Klaus returned to the kitchen and, with the quick nimbleness that comes with experience, installed an electronic surveillance device in the videophone's receiver. He would hear for himself if Sofia Karalis, or anyone else, called or visited Evan Quinn.

Evan stood in the sun at the seven-foot tall, round information kiosk between a flower vendor and a bratwurst stand at the corner of Landstrasse Hauptstrasse and the Ring Boulevard. The eye-level computer monitor flashed images of tanks in the streets of Taipei, Chinese soldiers patrolling the streets, and the Chinese Vice Chairman Jiang Xu in Beijing announcing to the world press that China welcomed home Taiwan after a century of misguided wandering, translated on the screen in German subtitles. Brown's news about Taiwan had been true. Would America suspend the talks in Vienna? No, he guessed that the EU, Russia, and America would yell long and loud, condemning China's aggression, but they'd want to negotiate rather than attack China and its nuclear arsenal.

Motor scooters and the occasional car whizzed by on the boulevard, and the air smelled of dust and oil. The flower vendor exhibited fresh summer flowers in white buckets arranged in rows on shelves in a white cart. On impulse, Evan bought a bouquet of blue iris to give to the Russian. His heart raced at the sight of a woman with a cascade of chestnut brown hair and shapely legs waiting for the light at the corner. Sofia? Her head turned left revealing another woman's profile, not Sofia's. He crossed the Landstrasse

Hauptstrasse behind her. She hurried past Vasia's apartment building.

Following the Russian's instructions, Evan slid his ID card into the slot by the security keypad to the right of the building's heavy glass and chrome doors. He pressed the button by Vasia's name and squinted in the sun up at the security camera angled above the doors to the left.

"Evan! Welcome to my new home." Vasia's voice, sounding tinny, burst out of the security speaker.

The security slot spit out Evan's ID card. He caught it as a raw buzzing signaled the doors had unlocked. He entered the building's foyer. Brass mailboxes adorned the wall to the right. The ornate baroque glass elevator required Evan to insert his ID card in order to operate it.

The Russian pianist waited for him in his open doorway. "Evan! How are you? What in bag?" Vasia pointed to Evan's pale blue gym bag.

"I had a martial arts lesson before lunch."

"You eat already? I have food. You like smoked salmon?" Vasia ushered him into his spacious foyer with its three interior doors.

Evan handed him the bouquet of blue iris. "Congratulations on your new apartment, Vasia."

"Oh, we love flowers! Thank you, Maestro." The Russian disappeared through the door on the left. Evan trailed after him into the mocha, turquoise and silver kitchen, warmed by the Russian's exuberance.

"Greta at work?" Evan sat on one of four stools at the high black granite counter, the kitchen's central island.

"Yes, but she come here after work. You stay for dinner?

We can play some music, drink some vodka." Vasia filled an elegant fluted green vase with water.

"You know I don't drink, Vasia."

"You can start today." The Russian giggled. He arranged the iris in the vase.

Evan shook his head, surveying the four-burner stove and double oven, stainless steel refrigerator, abundant counter space on either side of a double sink. "You cook a lot?"

"Greta cook more. I cook Russian food, of course. When you have house-welcome party, Evan?"

He grimaced. "I don't give parties, Vasia."

The Russian shrugged. "Come on."

The tour began in the living room where Evan recognized Greta's stylish influence: plush maroon sofa and chairs, cherry tables, fin de siècle lamps, a Persian carpet and framed photography on the walls. As he set the vase of irises on the four-foot black Bösendorfer grand piano near the front windows, Vasia said, "We unpack all boxes before party Saturday night. You still come to party? Bring violin. We play music all night."

"I plan on it," Evan said, following Vasia through the archway into the dining room where packed cardboard boxes surrounded an oval cherry table that could seat eight comfortably. Doors led to the kitchen and a hallway they now entered. Vasia opened one door after another, showing Evan a guest bedroom, the master bedroom, and the marble and gold bathroom off of it.

"For you I buy hunting rifle like mine." The Russian pulled a gleaming walnut gun case down from a closet shelf and set it on the rumpled queen-sized four-poster bed. "But it has better, more advanced scope. You can shoot with absolute accuracy up to one mile." Evan heard the front door slam. Greta's voice followed. "Vasia, *bist du da?*"

"*Ja, Liebchen! Ich bin mit* Evan *im Schlafzimmer.*" Vasia giggled as he assembled the hunting rifle.

"Vasia, you'll drive her crazy," Evan said, but he smiled at Vasia's giggling which reminded him of Paul Caine's infectious high trills.

"Ah, here you are," Greta said from the doorway. "Evan, he shows you the messy bedroom, not the living room?" She gave him a light kiss on the cheek. "Will you stay for dinner?"

"Yes, he stay," Vasia said, giggling again.

"What mischief, Vasia?" Her gaze settled on the assembled gun in Vasia's hands.

"Vasia bought me a rifle for our hunting trip in Romania." He accepted the rifle from the Russian.

"Ah. Bears." She pulled a pink tank top and jeans from an armoire next to the door. "You must tell me more at dinner. I am hungry for chicken curry. What do you think? Or lemon chicken?"

Vasia embraced her from behind, nuzzling her neck. "I always hungry for chicken curry."

She pushed him away and headed for the bathroom. "I know you, Vasia. You have mischief in your eyes."

Vasia's silvery giggle filled the bedroom as Greta closed the bathroom door. "Stay for dinner, Evan. Greta excellent cook. We call Sofia."

Evan sighted the hunting rifle out the bedroom window framed by filmy aquamarine curtains. "No, Vasia. Don't bother Sofia." He targeted a roof chimney, adjusted the setting. "I think all the bells and whistles on this gun might be lost on me."

Vasia gave him a puckish sideways look. "Sofia visit all the time. No bother, Maestro." He grinned at Evan's scowl.

"I said *no*."

The smile faded from Vasia's face. He shrugged. "OK. You really hunt with Joseph Caine?"

"Yeah, when I was a kid. He loved nature, loved to hike and hunt. He said it cleansed his soul." The rifle was a perfect back-up weapon. The Russian had paid cash for it and the license was in his name. At least until the Russian transferred it to him in six months.

"Clean soul for him to compose music."

"Yeah. He and my father liked to get away from the city and the ISS. Looking back, I'm amazed the ISS let them do it." Evan disassembled the rifle, returning the parts to the case. "You'll keep this for me?"

"One hundred percent. When we hunt in Romania?"

"I have a gig in Bucharest the first week of October. How about the week after that?"

"Yes! Now I play Caine Piano Sonata for you, OK?"

Evan closed the gun case. "I want to hear you play, Vasia."

Chapter 16

As he climbed his front stairs, Evan hummed the playful theme to the last movement of Caine's Piano Concerto No. 1, Op. 22, dedicated to him by Uncle Joe. Caine sang again under Vasia's fingers and transported Evan back to the Caines' living room, Uncle Joe at the piano facing him, his intense blue eyes on him, his long blonde hair swishing across his shoulders. He had played the violin part on his violin feeling Uncle Joe's love for him in the music. The intimacy of knowing Uncle Joe in music intertwined with Vasia and his performance.

Uncle Joe would have loved Vasia playing his music. The Russian's powerful technique, the strength and independence of his fingers that produced clarity of sound, combined with his musical imagination and his understanding of the concerto's unusual structure, tempos and themes, had given Caine a new voice. Evan loved it. He soared inside the music.

"You must come to my recital, Evan! At Palais Pallavacini August twenty-nine," Vasia had said as he'd jumped up from the piano bench.

"That'll depend on the program," Evan said, his tone challenging, and he winked at Greta. He relaxed with them – his mind, his body – as if he'd never lived in America.

"Excellent program." Vasia rested his hands on his hips.

"J.S. Bach Partita No. 6, Caine Piano Sonata No. 7 and Beethoven Op. 110. Let's eat."

Evan wanted to perform the Caine Piano Concerto with Vasia, definitely, but he had said nothing. He wanted Nigel to book a gig for them first.

For once, he felt no need to review and analyze every moment of the evening to insure he'd neither said nor done something stupid. Now he was home after a long day. He felt vibration against his skin under his watch. His house computer had turned on the three lamps in the living room. The ceiling fan circled overhead, laboring to create a breeze in the heavy air. He reset the security system. The vibration under his watch persisted. As a reflex, he tapped the entry record button which usually told him no one else had entered his apartment. This time, Freda Kirsch's name appeared on the screen with time of entry early afternoon.

He realized the vibration against his wrist was Woody's bug finder. Freda had bugged his apartment? No, not Freda. But maybe she'd let someone in to bug his apartment.

He scrutinized the front room, frozen in place. Someone had moved the Mozart cell phone to a different shelf away from the Georg phone. Evan went to the wall cabinet by the back window, opened it, and pulled out the empty cardboard box. The Ruger case remained in the back shadow, the invisible tape he'd wound around it undisturbed. He pushed it farther back.

Outside the kitchen windows, the shadowy maples had taken on a furry quality in the late dusk. Evan opened the freezer, took out two stacks of frozen meals to check the two CZ 9mm handguns in thick bubble wrap in the back.

Neither had been disturbed. He checked the bedroom, the closet, and the bathroom. Nothing out of place.

"*Fernseher* BBC," he ordered his house computer. The television flicked on to BBC news. Evan picked up the Mozart cell phone. Had someone used it, or perhaps checked the directory? But why? The last number called was Vasia's the night before.

"Outraged reaction to China's invasion and annexation of Taiwan has poured into the United Nations today. America, the European Union, Russia, the Africa Federation, and the Pacific Alliance have condemned China's aggression and called for sanctions. The UN Security Council has called an emergency session." The BBC's anchor read with an even tone and dispassionate face, looking into the camera. Her pert nose twitched. "The European Union has suggested a suspension of the Chinese-American talks in Vienna, but the Americans have insisted they continue. Chinese troops patrol Taipei and all roads in Taiwan, enforcing a strict curfew. Beijing has released a statement that Taiwan is a province of China, not an independent country, and warned not to interfere with China's internal affairs. All calls to Taiwan's president's office and the government's information office have been referred to Beijing."

The Mozart cell phone played the opening of Mozart's Fortieth Symphony. "*Fernseher abstellan*," Evan said. The BBC had now confirmed what Brown had told him earlier in the day which made Brown a reliable source. At least about the Chinese.

"Hello?"

"Herr Quinn, Klaus Leiner calling. How are you?" Leiner's tenor voice sounded gentle in Evan's ear.

"Fine, Inspector. How are you and your family?" The image of Anna poking Leiner in their driveway that morning popped into Evan's mind. He knew where Leiner lived and the cop didn't know it. Evan smiled. His digital watch clicked to the next minute, nine-twenty-two, and the vibration under it continued.

"We are all quite well, thank you. They ask about you. Especially Laura."

"That's kind of her. Tell her I'm up to my ears in score study. I leave on Sunday for a gig in Amsterdam." No matter how friendly he sounded, Evan reminded himself, the Austrian cop was on duty, checking up at a time he might catch his suspect off guard.

"The Concertgebouw's American Music Festival?"

"Yeah. Will you notify the Amsterdam police I'm there and request surveillance on me?"

Leiner sighed. "I see no need, Herr Quinn."

He hadn't expected that answer. "Now you believe I'm not a spy or what?" Evan moved the cell phone to his other ear.

"I believe...Herr Quinn, have you moved yet? I believe you said you had found a flat in—"

"Yeah, I've moved. The security system is excellent." The cop hadn't answered his question. He closed his eyes and visualized Freda giving Leiner a tour of his apartment. The image clicked. "But you already knew that."

"*Bitte*? I don't know where—"

"You expect me to believe that? Come on, Inspector. I

had to register with the police in this district. They'd tell you my address so you could search my apartment when I'm not here."

The only sound in his ear was a faint crackling. The Austrian cop's hesitation confirmed his suspicion: Freda had shown him his apartment today. The Austrian cop had bugged it. Where were the cops listening to him? In a van on the street like in America?

Leiner sighed, resigned. "I know your address, Herr Quinn. But you are—"

"Paranoid? I have every reason to be paranoid, Inspector. Remember Neusiedl? The surveillance after you turned me loose? Now, I don't mind you calling me as a friend, but not as a cop who thinks I'm a spy."

"I am always a cop, Herr Quinn, and will continue to be concerned about you." Leiner's tone remained even, controlled. "All defectors have a six-month probation."

He'd answered his question. The Austrian cop had six months to prove he was a spy. "You're concerned. For my best interests or yours? Does that mean you'll bug my apartment like the Americans did?"

Leiner laughed, a dry, rasping sound in Evan's ear. "Relax, Herr Quinn. I'm happy you have a conducting job in Amsterdam and you have moved into your new flat. Perhaps someday we might meet for a social lunch and I will bring Laura to meet you."

Evan sat up in the recliner, slapping down the foot rest. The idea of lunch with Leiner cramped his stomach. "We'll see, Inspector. After September, I expect to be on the road most of the time. By the way, do you play a musical instrument?"

"I played the trumpet in school and sang in the choir. I left the trumpet in school, but I continue to sing in church."

Evan grinned into the phone. "The trumpet. Perfect. Got to go, Inspector. Have a nice evening."

"Enjoy Amsterdam."

Evan flipped the phone closed and returned it to the shelf next to the Georg phone. Even if Leiner checked the black phone's account and questioned him about it, Woody's suggested explanation that it was a gift from him would cover it. After all, Leiner and Aschenbeck had given him the Mozart phone.

He searched his apartment using the intensity of the bug finder's vibrations to locate the bugs – one stuck under a shelf over music scores in the bookshelves to the right of the kitchen doorway, and another in the landline phone's receiver. He left them in place. It made sense they'd bug his apartment. He'd forced Leiner to stop the visual surveillance. He'd wait. Perhaps the bugs offered an opportunity he hadn't yet met, and better that Leiner did not know he'd found them.

Leiner had played the trumpet. Evan considered the entire brass section in any new orchestra as his most challenging and harshest critics. They will test a new conductor mercilessly, examine every movement, decision, and word under their collective microscope to see if he's worth leading them. Once he'd earned their confidence and respect, however, they would play their hearts out for him and give him their unwavering loyalty and support. Ah, the brass and their unrelenting scrutiny. Leiner, exactly.

He sank into the recliner facing the TV to watch a movie on "American Cinema Classics," the channel he'd discovered late one evening when insomnia had kept him awake. It broadcasted American movies from the last century, most of them he'd never heard of. The voice-over announcer introduced a classic American western from 1990 with German subtitles. The music drew him into the story that began in the Civil War and followed a Union lieutenant to the frontier west where he befriended a wolf and joined a group of Lakota people. Evan drifted off to sleep.

Hours later he screamed himself awake, sitting bolt upright. The recliner slapped his back. The movie channel now showed a comedy about a dentist and a hit man from what he heard as he stripped off all his clothes and examined every inch of his naked body for spiders.

That nightmare again. The image of the twitching Spider Woman filled his mind. He bent over to quell the nausea.

"*Fernseher abstellan.*" The TV clicked off. He stepped into his boxer shorts. To take his mind off the nightmare, he thought about China's invasion of Taiwan. Apparently, Vice Chairman Jiang Xu had supervised the invasion. The aftermath would keep him in Beijing for a while. What if the Chinese Vice Chairman never came to Vienna? Would he have to travel to Beijing to complete the Perceval business? He reached for the Georg cell phone on the shelf. Darkness outside his open windows stopped him. He'd have to wait until morning to call Woody, and outdoors, away from Leiner's bugs.

"*Schlaf gut,*" he said to his house computer. The living room lamps clicked off. In his bedroom, he lay down on his bed, only a mattress and box spring made up with plain white cotton sheets. He turned off the light.

Shadows flitted across the ceiling and melted into the corners. He could smell Freda's roses and hear a swooshing sound outside in the backyard – Sasha. He thought of the first time he'd played Bach's Goldberg Variations straight through, the elegant and delicate lines of the aria, how each variation changed the aria's personality. Closing his eyes, he concentrated on each note, first the right hand, then the left. He had used the Goldberg Variations often as his sleeping pill, not because it bored him, but because it was so comforting and sublime. Other music also worked, such as Haydn string quartets that he'd played with the Hartleben Quartet or the German Lieder his mother had sung to him. These were his lullabies.

On this night, however, nothing worked. For an hour, he tossed and turned, feeling like an electric current hissed through his veins. Finally, he went into the bathroom and washed. He dressed in running shorts, chose fresh white socks and grabbed his running shoes, and worked through his warm-up stretches and exercises in his silent front room. He left his apartment for his daily run as dawn broke in the east.

His route took him past Türkenschanz Park and north to Pötzleinsdorfer Park. He saw no one else. He ran hard and circled back down to Türkenschanz Park which he jogged through for the first time. A thick line of trees formed the perimeter and provided shade for a children's play area with slide, jungle gym, swings, and sand boxes, and farther along a cluster of chess tables. A symphony of birdsong accompanied him. He decided to run over to Chimanistrasse and spy on Leiner.

Ten minutes later, Evan crouched in the eighteen-inch-wide dirt pathway between a garage and a row of lilacs on his left. He breathed deeply, calming his heart rate after his last sprint. His face and chest dripped sweat. No breeze stirred the hot air.

Across the street, nothing moved inside or outside Leiner's house. Unlike Freda's house, Leiner's had no walls, fences, hedges, or barriers of any kind to protect it. Sloppy of the Inspector. Anyone could gain access. He had a clear shot. His rifle had a silencer, no one would hear a thing. He glanced around, considering escape routes. He could slip back behind the garage to the next yard and street or simply jog away, perhaps wearing a suitable light disguise. A wave of guilt rose and doused his thoughts like a tsunami through his mind. Leiner had helped him, treated him with respect despite his suspicion.

The traditional double-hung windows in Leiner's house reminded him of his father's house. His ten-year-old hand had reached for the silver lock at the top of the first tier of his bedroom window. "Inside, want as much as you like, but always do as you're told." His father's baritone voice spoke from behind him on his bed. Now Evan looked back expecting to see him crouched behind him.

Barking erupted across the street. On its hind legs, the Leiners' black and white shaggy dog leaned up one of the oak trees, harassing something in the branches above.

"And *never* talk to anyone about our family or the Caines," his father had growled.

After Uncle Joe's arrest, Evan had wanted to run away to Canada. He had planned to sleep in the woods and avoid the main freeways, as he'd heard Uncle Joe instruct people the Underground smuggled out of the country. But his father had caught him at his bedroom window clutching the white pillowcase bulging with clothes and everything he'd thought he'd need.

He felt a hand grasp his shoulder, pull him backward. Evan shivered, glanced around to insure he was alone and shrugged off the physical memory. He had tried to escape and failed. His father had caught him in his bedroom. The past was in the past and done and meant nothing now. He had escaped to Austria, to freedom, and his father was dead.

Blinds rose at a second-floor window in Leiner's house. Leiner's wife, dressed for running and her auburn hair pulled back into a pony tail, came out the front door with the Springer spaniel on a leash. The shaggy dog bounded over to her at the same moment Evan heard scuffing inside the garage.

He crabbed back and pressed his body against the wall. Footsteps crossed to the front of the garage inside. The garage's front door rumbled open. Evan held his breath. A whirring sound began and moved out of the garage. A car door slammed. The car started, backed out of the garage, paused for the driver to close the garage door via remote or the car's computer, and proceeded out into the peaceful street.

Breathing fast, Evan scooted forward and peeked around the wall's edge. The car disappeared down the street. Leiner's wife had left also. The whirring sound continued. Evan leaned forward for a clear view of the house's front lawn. His mouth dropped open in surprise.

A square orange machine, about twelve inches wide and six inches tall, traversed the front lawn, cutting the grass in straight rows, and turning when it reached the concrete driveway. Evan had never seen anything like it before.

Someone would come out to put away the lawn mower. He checked around the empty street. No one in the windows of Leiner's house. Jogging out to the street, he headed for home.

After a shower and a hearty breakfast, Evan went downstairs to his entry door where the bug finder no longer vibrated and called Woody Lewis on the Georg phone.

"Georg," Woody said.

"Yeah. The events in Taiwan this week."

"Our friend is busy."

"Will I need to travel to Beijing to complete my business with him?" Evan opened the door and peeked out at Freda's quiet, dark house.

The old American's faintly mocking giggle filled Evan's ear. "Have you ever heard the saying, 'If you build it, they will come'?"

"No." He was certain Woody had moments of insanity.

"The Chinese-American talks are here. That's what's built. Our friend will come. Here."

"Oooooo-kaaaay." Evan closed the door. "But wouldn't it be faster if I went there?"

"Chill, Georg. They will wait for the upheaval over Taiwan to subside. They wanted to make a point, which they did. When our friend comes to Vienna, he will arrive in a much stronger position than before."

"What was their point?"

"Their point, Georg, is that no one can stop them. They are the world's sole superpower."

"OK. I leave for a gig in Amsterdam on Sunday."

Woody giggled again. "Enjoy yourself. This will blow over in a few weeks. I'll stick my neck out and predict our friend will visit in August. In the meantime, continue establishing your cover so it's solid. We'll talk later."

His tone gave Evan the feeling he'd irritated Woody. He was relieved, however, that he could concentrate on score study free of the need to explain a trip to Beijing to Nigel or anyone else.

Mahler's Fifth Symphony frightened and fascinated him. The symphony was well over an hour in duration, filled with tricky passages and tempo changes guaranteed to challenge the confidence of any conductor. The Vienna Philharmonic musicians had told him they'd performed it many times. He had never heard the symphony, so for him, it was as if the composer had completed the score last month and handed it to him to prepare for performance.

As he read the music, sitting in his black leather wingbacked chair by the front window, the score open on the music stand in front of him, he heard in his mind the sound the black notes represented, knowing that what he imagined only approximated the reality. Something else existed, too, behind the notes, between the notes, encasing the notes, just beyond his imagination's grasp. Mahler spoke in a musical language foreign to him. He picked up a notepad from the floor and scribbled a note to himself to research Mahler's life and time.

Break it down. The most efficient way to dig into the music was to study small sections at a time. He decided to focus on the symphony's second movement entitled "*Stürmisch bewegt, mit grösster Vehemenz.*" He read through it twice, played the string parts on his loaner fiddle. Next, he paced the room, singing the parts, score in left hand, conducting with his right and stamping one bare foot for emphasis on the composer's direction: "*Nicht schleppen. Nicht eilen. Wuchtig.*" So many specific instructions in the score, far more than he'd ever seen in other scores. Mahler must have been a control freak, obsessed with how musicians would play his music in the future. Evan penciled in his own comments, notes for dynamics, tempo and bowing to check in rehearsal.

Late morning, Evan left for the Fischer School. His Krav Maga lesson went well. Okada's assistant bowed low with a smiling nod, ending it. The workout felt good. He wanted his body to perform like a machine in superb working condition, able to hit an object with precision and speed whether by hand or foot. He wanted strength and control. He didn't enjoy the martial arts but his lessons at the Fischer School helped maintain his body in good physical shape for both Perceval and conducting.

Evan passed two buskers playing a cello and guitar in front of Westbahnhof and dropped money into their instrument cases, pausing to ask them about their solo experience. He walked northeast on Mariahilferstrasse and stopped at a deli where he ate lunch observing the street scene. The crowded street provided camouflage for surveillance. He decided on a brief surveillance detection run to lose any shadows on his tail.

Rather than using the crowds of shoppers in Generali Centre or the Virgin Megastore as his cover to disappear, he crossed the street and went to the Mariahilfer Church, a Baroque church with two towers. No one followed him inside. He waited ten minutes in a back pew before leaving. He crossed a street and stopped to scrutinize the street in a store window's reflection. Satisfied with the unexceptional activity – no eyes on him – he proceeded to his destination on Zollergasse.

The costume store's size surprised him as well as the number of customers he found inside. Six salesclerks answered questions and rang up sales. Evan found the wig section away from the clothing sections. He sought the perfect long, chestnut brown wig, curly or straight. Blonde wouldn't work. His black beard stubble and eyebrows would betray him. A short auburn wig reminded him of a Juilliard friend's hair. He tried it on. A woman with long, fluffy, bright pink hair watched him from the next aisle. She smiled. The frames of her horn-rimmed glasses glittered with cheap rhinestones and she wore a shapeless powder blue sundress.

"That looks fabulous on you," she said in a smoky alto voice.

"Sofia?"

She laughed, nodding. He snatched the wig off his head. What was his cover story for being here? Beyond Sofia, a white-haired man with scraggly beard, glasses and a cane watched them from the clown section.

"Why take the wig off? Evan, it looked fabulous on you

and changed your appearance. Perfect," Sofia said, walking around the display. "It's brilliant."

"What are you doing here, Sofia?" He held up the auburn wig between them as if it could ward her off. Attachments created opportunities for someone to exploit you, betray you and destroy you. Even in her radical disguise, she was beautiful.

"I love costumes! Sometimes I need something specific for a character I am playing. Sometimes I need a disguise so that I am anonymous." She smiled up at him. "A light disguise works best, I have found. It is cheaper, less work. Often, I wear only eyeglasses and pull my hair back. No one recognizes me."

"I don't have enough hair to pull back," he said, his tongue tripping over the words.

"But you are so smart to want disguise. For anonymity when you shop or go to a movie or a concert, to live a normal life, yes?"

"I don't like people recognizing me all the time."

The old white-haired man hobbled to the make-up section within hearing distance. He wore a blue seersucker suit that hung too loose from his shoulders. Evan met his eyes. His green eyes. The old man smiled, Brown's smug smile.

"Exactly," Sofia said. "An occupational hazard for a performer. People see me on stage or in movies and they think they know me." Her voice sounded bitter. "They make me something I am not and treat me like that in public."

His eyes on Brown, Evan said, "I know what you mean. No one bothered me in America. But a disguise is an act of desperation, a betrayal somehow of myself."

"Disguise protects your true self." Her voice was low and comforting. "If you would like, I will help you. I recommend more than one disguise to alternate them. Always changing decreases the chance anyone will learn your disguises and make it impossible to use them."

Sofia helped him with the wig. Shopping with her provided him with an excellent cover for owning disguises. He eyed Brown in the make-up section. The American winked, mouthing something incomprehensible. Evan glared at him. He preferred Brown not see what he bought, not know what disguise he created. On the other hand, he now knew Brown's old man disguise, probably one of many. Brown saluted him with two fingers touching his forehead, pivoted lithely and left.

"You see how the change of color and style alters your appearance?" Sofia said, holding up a mirror, her tone triumphant.

"He was buying *wigs*?" Morgan said, thwacking a curled-up report against his thigh. "Damn! Is he a fag? That would explain a lot, like why he's not married. Has he ever dated anyone?"

Bernie, his feet resting on top of his messy desk and eating his favorite black cherry yoghurt, laughed, spattering yoghurt over the papers on his desk. "No way, Larry. He's so straight it scares him. He was with a woman today. I'd say he was totally in to her."

Morgan stepped closer. Bernie knew what was coming. "By the way, Larry, no one wants to claim him."

"Impossible. What about DIA?"

"Especially not them. I think he's genuine and ripe for picking."

"Recruit the son of that bastard who killed—? Ask Langley about a possible ISS or NSC connection. He was arrested, right? Maybe they put the screws on him."

"His father was a drag on his career, Larry. He wanted to get as far away from him as he could. He defected."

"Who informed on Randall Quinn? ISS will know. It had to be someone close to Quinn. He's here for a reason, Bernie. If he's not with us, he needs termination. That's my order. Nothing fancy or expensive. A fatal accident would be fun, or blow him up." Morgan turned to leave.

"What about Washington?"

"Washington has approved whatever I want to do about Evan Quinn."

"OK, Larry. I'll stay on him. I'll even check with MI6. They always seem to know what we're doing when we don't."

Morgan left. Bernie clicked on the "create" button for e-mail. Now he'd request ISS's complete files on the Caines, Randall Quinn and Evan Quinn.

Chapter 17

"*Mon Dieu*, you do not resemble your father." The words puffed from the French woman's mauve lips with a breathy coyness as she stepped closer.

Evan's eyes searched Vasia's crowded living room for an escape. The flickering light from dozens of candles placed at different heights created shadows that danced in the corners and crevices, played across the animated faces of the house-warming guests. Ice clinked in glasses. Someone laughed over the wave of voices. Someone else played a beer hall song on the piano.

"You have magnificent black hair! So thick." Her mani-cured fingers smoothed a lock back from his face. He caught a whiff of her spicy perfume. "Mmmm, so soft and fine," she breathed, her fingers tickling the sensitive skin behind his left ear.

He brushed her hand off, shifting away from her. The guests milled around them, a typical movement of people at parties seeking conversation or a more advantageous pos-ition to watch other people. Near the bookshelves to the right of the dining room archway, Vasia was kissing a young Asian man full on the mouth. Shocked, Evan looked away, gave an idiotic smile to a clutch of four people on his right who, interested, returned his smile. They'd been watching him like everyone else from the moment he'd arrived. He hated parties, the social performance they demanded. He'd rather be home working on the Mahler. He looked down at his empty glass.

"I think I'll get more mineral water," he said to the French woman. "Would you like something?"

"Oh, *oui*," she said, pressing her body against his hip. "I would like you." She slid her hand under his black linen sport jacket and began to unbutton his white shirt.

"No," he snapped, plucking her hand from his chest. "I mean, another drink?" He wanted to punch this woman to make her stop, but he resisted with a step back from her. Like prickly burrs, she clung to him.

"Evan!" Vasia squeezed around a group singing along with the beer hall piano. When he saw the French woman, her arm around Evan, the Russian grinned and said, "Chantal. Kitten. Wolfgang wants you."

"Pah, Wolfi!" Her hand caressed Evan's back and squeezed his rump before she moved over to Vasia and slipped her arm through his. "Vasia, you hear about my new movie?"

"Of course. You big movie star. Go to Wolfgang. Maybe important."

"*Oui*, I am a star above Sofia Karalis." She pouted up at Evan. "Wolfi never leaves me alone." She swayed away from them, the crowd parting for her like a wind of bad breath.

Vasia giggled. "Chantal not woman for you. Especially when she drink vodka. Wolfgang, her husband, big movie director. Sofia worked with him in Africa." He took a sip from his iced vodka. "Many beautiful women here tonight. Don't be shy. You bring violin?"

"Yeah, I stashed it by the piano. Where's Owen? Have they arrived?"

Vasia lifted his drink in a salute to Owen, whose face rose above a group in the dining room. "There! They arrive with Sofia ten minutes ago."

As Evan pushed into the chattering crowd, Vasia shouted, "I make galactic bar in kitchen!"

Evan reached Owen as the surrounding guests shifted again. Owen extended his hand and leaned in to Evan. "I have something for you."

They threaded their way to the kitchen and Vasia's galactic bar on the center island. Evan relaxed in the kitchen's spaciousness, its air tangy with the scent of squeezed lemons and limes. They were alone.

Owen handed him a music score. "My English horn concerto. I hoped you might look at it."

"I'd love to. Thanks."

"Before Greta met Vasia," Owen said, picking up a bottle and splashing a finger of vodka into a glass, "you wouldn't have seen a bar like this at one of her parties. Vasia does love his vodka."

Evan lifted a bottle of ginger-flavored mineral water from among its brethren on the massive refrigerator's bottom shelf, thinking of Vasia kissing the Asian man. "Among other things," he said.

Owen's high-pitched laugh pierced the air. "Struth! That's true enough. He possesses quite a zest for life's experiences."

Leaning back against the counter, Evan opened the score. "Your music, Owen. Vasia mentioned, I think, that you'd been influenced by Joseph Caine." Evan scanned the concerto's first page. The English horn sang over a timpani ostinato.

"Ah. Somewhat. I grew up listening to his music. I am in awe of the way he layered rhythms and melody, set them against each other to create powerful sonic emotion. My Maori and Pacific heritage have also influenced me, especially the rhythms. I'm writing a piano sonata for Vasia right now that draws on Malaysian music I discovered a couple years ago."

As he sipped his mineral water and skimmed the concerto score, Evan discussed the music with Owen, the successes and failures with public performances, and recording it. He made a mental note to buy the recording. He liked Owen, and the concerto.

Greta found them. Tonight she resembled an Egyptian queen in ornate filigree leaves of gold jewelry. She shepherded them out of the kitchen to mingle with the rest of the guests. Evan left Owen's score with his violin by the piano. As he turned toward the dining room, Vasia grabbed his arm.

"I want to show you something," he said, his tone conspiratorial.

Vasia guided Evan through to the kitchen where he opened an unobtrusive door. He pulled Evan into a long, narrow room. On the left stood another steel refrigerator, a twin to the one in the kitchen, and a freezer. On the right were shelves and shelves of canned and boxed food.

"Agent showed me this room first day. But agent not know about *this*." Vasia opened a door at the end of the pantry painted to blend in with the wall. "You see, Evan? Secret stairs!"

Evan peered at the steep wooden stairway, not more than two or three feet wide, and up into darkness. "What's up there? An attic?"

"I hear stories about secret passages under streets, tunnels, hidden rooms, secret escape doors, etc., etc. You know, from World War Two when Germans run over Austria. Hiding places but also passages for moving around city in secret, like for partisan fighters. But I never hear about anything like this." Vasia climbed the stairs like a monkey into the darkness above.

Evan heard the metal snap of a lock opening and hinges creaking. He climbed the stairs to an open door and scrunched through it. When he straightened next to Vasia, he saw they were on the building's roof.

"Fantastic, Vasia. Are you the only apartment with access?"

"See hut there?" Vasia pointed to a metal structure like the one they'd emerged from. "Maybe more secret stairs."

"You really think the stairway is from World War Two? It looks more recent." Evan turned in a slow circle, taking in the multi-colored lights of the First District at twilight, the clear, starry sky above. Evan smelled wine on the warm northwest breeze. Would they ever see rain and cool weather again?

"Greta wants small vegetable garden over there. I want trees. I miss Russian forests. We see other roofs in city with gardens and trees like Hundertwasser Haus."

"Is Greta moving in with you?" Evan strolled to the front and looked down at the wide boulevard, the Hilton Hotel across the street, the Stadtpark next to it.

"You know what women all over world say. *Wait and see.* Also she wants garden on roof."

Evan nodded. "What's next door?"

Vasia gave the building to their left a dismissive wave. "U-Bahn station and state bus station. All possible methods of transportation surround me!" The Russian grinned, a sly, impish curl to his mouth. "Bring Sofia here to roof, you can be alone with her."

"Let it go, Vasia." He drew his index finger like a knife across his throat.

"You only guy I know not want to talk about women. Maybe you like men. OK. We find you good man."

"I'm not gay, Vasia. You need to respect what I say. Let it go."

Vasia shrugged. "I respect you, Maestro." He pushed the hut's door open. "I need light up here. I think I break lock." He wiggled the lock. The metal sounded loose, insubstantial.

Evan joined him. "Nobody else comes up here, do they? I mean, you could leave it until you replace the lock. And what about the pantry door? You could install a lock there, too, and insulate the door for winter weather."

Vasia grinned over his shoulder and said, "Sofia woman for you, Maestro." He ducked through the door as Evan's slap hit the metal.

Greta met them in the kitchen. "So, Evan, you've seen our roof patio. I've shown it already to perhaps twenty people tonight." She gave Vasia a shove. "Owen has organized some music. He wants you now for the Shostakovich Piano Quintet."

"Evan, come to living room for Shostakovich." Vasia

started for the door, past a group of older guests who greeted him with a boisterous "Va—see—ya!"

Evan smiled at Greta. "Any place I can eat in relative peace?"

"Try the guest bedroom." She spotted someone beyond Evan and waved to her. "Join us soon, Evan. Everyone wants to hear you play."

Evan found the buffet in the dining room and filled a plate with food. In the hallway, he eased past four young Asian men arguing in German about China's recent invasion of Taiwan, and into the guest room. Sofia and four strangers lounged on a black sectional sofa and turquoise floor pillows.

"Evan, please join us." Sofia gestured to a space next to her on the sofa. Her hazel green eyes welcomed him.

"You've got yourself a mountain of food, mate," said a bearded man with curly brown hair who sat on a floor pillow. "There's drinks in the mini fridge over there in the corner."

"Everything looked delicious," Evan said as he sank down next to Sofia on the plush sofa. "Tough to choose." Energy radiated from her. Their arms brushed.

The four strangers' agreeable laughter blended with the chamber music coming from the living room. He flashed them one of his public persona smiles. The stranger was back – the sensation of someone else in his body looking out his eyes.

"Please allow me to introduce everyone," Sofia said. But before she could start, they each introduced themselves: Freddy Markovich, an actor; Hans Fischl, a writer; Andrea Churchill, a British journalist; and Lothar Waage.

Lothar Waage. The name sounded familiar but he couldn't

place it. Evan said, "A pleasure to meet you all. But no musicians here?"

"Music lovers, Maestro! Especially Joseph Caine's delicious music."

"The Fifth Symphony. Wow. It made me feel like I was on a journey through a war-torn country. Caine must have been clairvoyant about the Insurgency. Did he talk about it?"

Evan smiled at Fischl. "He was a leader in the Underground resistance, and helped my father with smuggling people out of the country. His music, I think, reflects his experience, his feelings about America and what it had become."

Andrea Churchill, shifting her heft on the floor pillow, said, "I hear a great deal of keening sorrow in his music, his symphonic music, I mean. Especially in the woodwinds."

Evan nodded. "But that sorrow transforms into a defiant triumph."

"Exactly," Sofia said with conviction. "His music, like Dmitri Shostakovich's for Russians in Russia, speaks the truth about life in America."

Lothar Waage leaned forward to look past Sofia. "What do you hear in his music, Maestro?"

Evan sighed. "Please, call me Evan. I'm not working right now." He popped a cherry tomato into his mouth and spoke around it. "I hear all that you've said, it's true. I think the comparison to Shostakovich is probably right on, but I haven't heard much Shostakovich. His music was banned in America."

"Vasia talks about the piano concerto, Evan. It was dedicated to you, yes? But I thought you played the violin?" Sofia nodded to him, then motioned to Freddy to get her a drink from the fridge.

"Uncle Joe was a pianist. He told me, he could have written a violin concerto or a sonata or partita for me – and actually, he did end up writing a violin sonata for me. But for the concerto, he wanted me to *conduct* it. He believed in my dream to conduct. When I listen to the concerto, I feel his love for me." He'd never said that out loud before. He looked around at their solemn faces, the tears in Sofia's eyes.

"Mate, you just put a whole new dimension on to listening to Caine's music. Love."

Andrea heaved a sigh. "Unbelievable that they arrested him. They banned his music. Your father was his friend, right?'

He nodded in agreement as he chewed a spoonful of potato salad with a piece of ham.

"From your press conference, Evan, it sounds like they're doing the same thing to him."

Evan swallowed. "They've done it already. They'll announce it when they're ready, but I'm sure he's dead. As I said at my press conference." He met Andrea's eyes.

"But you are here, mate. Caine and Quinn live through you."

"Yeah, thanks. The way I look at it, artists are like weeds. No matter how diligent the gardener, weeds will always pop up."

They laughed. He relaxed a little, eating more potato salad. The stranger inside began to loosen his grip.

"In the garden of life, artists are the most precious flowers, the treasured roses, the rare orchids," Freddy said, his glass lifted and his left hand over his heart.

Hans slapped Freddy's thigh. "You are not on stage tonight, *Liebchen*."

"We see American society as violent to itself and others, which has only worsened with the NEP," Lothar said.

Evan nodded as he swallowed another spoonful of salad. "It's violent. For the NEP it's a means to an end. For the insurgency, it's a means to an end. Uncle Joe told me once that America has a violent past, and its leaders have justified continuing violence with that past."

"You also witnessed violence, Evan?" Sofia frowned.

"Of course. I experienced violence, also. It's just a part of life."

Sofia furrowed her forehead into a deeper frown. "Has it not been known and accepted for decades that violence causes psychological trauma which if left untreated can cause more violence?"

Psychological trauma. Sofia's smoky voice speaking those two words melted into Inspector Leiner's tenor speaking the same words. Evan wanted to change the subject but his mind went blank – just when he needed it. He crunched down on a raw broccoli floret.

"Maybe people are addicted to violence," Freddy said. "They want it in movies and digigames to have control over it and that's why they can't let it go."

"Desire for control and power," Hans said. "To have power over people and territory and to feel powerful. Highly pleasurable for the powerless and insecure."

"What happened to America? I sometimes think your

addiction theory, Freddy, has created a self-destructive society in America," Lothar said, his smooth tenor voice penetrating. Lothar's presence, self-confidence, made Evan uncomfortable, like hearing the ISS arrive outside and there's no escape.

"The NEP appealed to nationalistic feelings and the fear of terrorism, the fear of economic collapse," Andrea said, sounding like a high school teacher. "They presented themselves as the reasonable problem-solvers America needed, the economic party for the future, the one that would stand up to the terrorists, protect the country and the people. Violence was always the elephant in the room."

"If the NEP delivered on its promises, what are Americans afraid of now, Evan?" Lothar asked, his brown eyes resting on Evan. "What were you afraid of that gave you the courage to defect?"

Evan shrugged. "Yeah, how ironic. Fear giving me courage. I think Americans fear everything they feared before, plus now they fear the NEP and ISS. They fear each other because no one knows who's a snitch for the ISS and who isn't."

"Because of their power," Hans said. "The NEP defines the Underground as terrorists and the secessionist states fighting for freedom and democracy as insurgents and terrorists. American elections are a joke now."

Andrea was shaking her head back and forth. "America fought a war of independence against the British crown, and yet they have created a ruling wealthy class that is their new royalty. You see, the Islamic terrorists succeeded. They made Americans so afraid, all they wanted was security, and they would sacrifice everything for it. The NEP saw their opportunity. Now, the wealthy NEP members use their money to sustain their power, and they use their power to control everything."

Lothar nodded. "In reality, the only person one can truly control is oneself. The only way to control another person, or a country, is through—"

"Violence," Sofia said. "I saw this in Africa while working on Wolfgang's movie."

"To have power, to feel powerful, is highly pleasurable," Hans said.

"A vicious cycle, isn't it, Lothar?" Andrea said, hefting her plump body up to her knees to crawl over to the mini-refrigerator. "Like 'an eye for an eye.'"

"But where did it start? With government?" Sofia said.

"No, with individuals. Untreated psychological trauma creates a sense of powerlessness," Lothar said, sipping red wine. "That powerlessness motivates the need for control and to use violence to establish control. In the family, parents would use violence against their children to control them: physical violence or emotional, psychological or sexual violence. They use the fear of violence or the fear of abandonment for control as well. The children grow up feeling powerless, worthless, with a need to control their environment for security. They crave power."

Evan felt lightheaded. His father's rages. His mother's depression. He'd lost any sense of being in his body.

"American psychologists," Lothar continued, "back in the early twenties tried to stop the NEP. They tried to educate people about psychological trauma, its causes and treatment, and to help people, empower them. This would be a threat to the NEP's power and control. So, the NEP destroyed their careers or they disappeared. The NEP reversed the education. For example, the NEP pronounced childhood abuse, especially sexual abuse, a cliché and not a cause of psychological trauma, not *real*, only a product of an over-active imagination that produced false memories. Eventually, the NEP controlled psychologists and the mental health of the people. This is nothing new. Also the Communists did it. Psychology and therapists need to be separate and independent from government. As we have them here."

The Psych Council subsidiary of the Medical Council. Waage was right about the NEP control. He hadn't heard about head doctors trying to stop the NEP, though. "Never let anyone know what you're really thinking and feeling," Uncle Joe whispered in his mind.

"For millennia, fear has motivated human behavior and interaction. Not only of the environment or others, but also fear of the inner self. Each person must confront his fear and its sources before he can become powerful in himself and not need power over others," Lothar said lifting his wine glass. "To seek power over others destroys human connection."

"I experienced terrible psychological trauma when I was in Africa," Sofia said, her voice sad. "We were captured by the rebels, all the actors, Wolfgang, the movie crew. They tortured and raped three of our crew in front of us. They beat all of us. I lived in constant fear for my life. The rebels had complete control over us. The desire for power and control excludes love, compassion, and kindness for people but not hatred or rage or terror or the addiction to violence. It's everywhere."

"As long as people seek power, are addicted to power, there can be no real freedom," Lothar said.

Evan stared at Sofia in surprise. She had been captured, beaten. She admitted her fear, her weakness, to everyone. He looked around at the others, expecting someone to tell her it was the past so get over it or it's not important so forget it.

"*That's* how you met Lothar!" Freddy said.

"*Ja*, Lothar helped me through the healing process," Sofia said.

"Are you a doctor?" Evan leaned forward to see Lothar past Sofia.

"A clinical psychologist."

A bone chill shuddered through Evan. He wanted to run from the room. Now he remembered. Leiner had given him Waage's business card. "A head doctor."

Lothar's eyes met Evan's. "We know the NEP has used psychiatrists and psychologists to—"

"Torture." Evan fisted his hands, ready to defend himself.

"Torture causes psychological trauma, Evan. Psychotherapy is different here, respectful and dedicated to healing."

Time to leave. Evan set his empty plate down on the floor.

"American society now, as any in its position, refuses to admit that violence causes psychological trauma because it's afraid of losing the power violence gives it," Lothar said. "They perceive the admission as weakness. Individuals deny it for the same reason. They refuse to consider that their power addiction is as toxic as any poison. It's not external power over others they need. They need to heal from the trauma in order to know their internal power."

"Evan?" Vasia said from the doorway. The sight of the Russian's grinning face brought Evan relief. "Play for us now, yes?"

"With pleasure. Please, excuse me," he said as he hurried after Vasia. Music expressed his soul and empowered him. He knew himself in music. He wasn't crazy. Waage was a head doctor, a threat to his music and his life.

In the living room, it was standing room only. Evan picked his way to the piano and his loaner violin, aware of eyes on him, the halted conversations, and the surge of anticipation in the room. As he tuned the loaner violin, the conversation in the guest room faded away. The Stranger faded away also. He breathed deeply. Sofia now leaned against the electronics wall near Greta whose arms encircled Vasia. The others had scattered around the crowded room. Lothar Waage had chosen a seat on the floor in front of Evan. He finished the tuning and without introduction played the Allemande of Bach's first partita, the music's dance of trilling and dipping punctuated by chords. He descended into the music, his refuge from the confusions of existence.

After the Bach and a Scherzo composed for him by Caine, after the Beethoven "Ghost" trio with Vasia and a cellist friend of his from the Hochschule, and Vasia's performance of Mussorgsky's "Pictures at an Exhibition;" after promising to call Vasia as soon as he'd returned from Amsterdam and kissing Greta good-night, Evan exited the apartment building on Landstrasse Hauptstrasse, the boulevard so boisterous during the day almost deserted in the middle of the night. No streetcars approached. He headed for the Ring Boulevard stop two blocks away. The walk would do him good.

The music at the end had saved the party for him. The Russian pianist's talent had shone once again and impressed him. A gust of wind rustled a newspaper abandoned in the gutter. Lothar Waage's voice spoke with the wind: "Their power addiction is as toxic as any poison." He passed the entrance to Stadtpark. Sofia. He was certain he'd acted like an idiot in front of her. Sofia. Two cars sped past. Ahead, the silhouettes of maple and linden trees lined the Ring Boulevard. Streetlamps cast pools of light on the sidewalks that glinted off the steel tracks in the street.

The slatted bench under the trees looked hard and uninviting. He set the violin case down on it, Owen's concerto score on top of the case. He paced a circle around the bench, a vigilant eye on his surroundings. Sofia. In the past he had never acted on his attraction to a woman because the ISS would have used that woman against him or used him against her. "Do this for us, we leave your lover alone," the ISS demanded. The last Minneapolis orchestra musician who'd related those exact words to him had been a shy, brilliant bass player who'd had the misfortune of falling in love. The ISS pressured the bassist to inform on him. The bassist asked Evan to fire him so he would not be in a position to inform on him. They'd worked out an arrangement: Evan told the bassist what to tell the ISS. Their secret. Maybe his defection had eliminated the pressure on that bassist and he'd be free. At least for a while.

A double streetcar approached from his left. A blue light shone on top of the front red and white car, the last one of the night for that line. No one sprinted out of the shadows to board with him. The older streetcar rumbled around the

Ring to Schottentor where three people disembarked with him. Only one, a businesswoman who carried a briefcase, rode the escalator with him down to Schottentor's underground passage. Muffled thunder from the level below signaled the passing of a subway train.

The peach-tinted fluorescent light softened the marble pillars and concrete platform. He passed darkened shops, a closed sausage stand and shuttered newspaper kiosk. The bright lights and computer monitors on the information kiosk beyond indicated it was open for business. Leaning against one pillar, a man read a newspaper. The briefcase woman paced back and forth five yards away, and farther on, cigarette smoke curled out from another pillar. Evan positioned himself near the newspaper man. Waiting people meant he hadn't missed the blue light Number 41 streetcar.

Through the giant ellipsoidal hole over the streetcar tracks, he studied the towering gothic Votiv Church, illuminated by eerie chartreuse light. Sofia. Sofia was alone also. She was busy and traveled for her work. She had made that comment about fame in the costume store – people thinking they knew her or wanted to make her into something she wasn't. She needed to be careful who she invited into her life. He imagined she'd say the same to him.

Footsteps scraped across the gritty concrete behind him. "Hey, Maestro."

Evan whirled around to Brown's cocky grin.

"Why'd you leave the party so early, Maestro? I expected you'd stay all night." Brown swaggered closer. "Not much fun? Nothing worse than a boring party. Wasn't Sofia Karalis there?"

Evan turned his back on Brown.

"You know, it's a beautiful night," Brown said, sidling around to face him. "Nice night for a walk but not all the way to Sternwartestrasse."

"I'm not walking home." Evan glanced at the other people. No one paid any attention to them.

"You've missed the blue light Number 41, Maestro. About half an hour ago. Now, the subway will take you to Heiligenstadt, if that line's still running. But that's quite a hike home, too."

Evan looked at the smug American in front of him. His brown hair was slicked back from his unshaven face. "I'm not stuck here," Evan said, stepping away from him. If he'd missed the last Number 41, he needed to find a cab.

"You need a cab, Maestro. I got one waiting for you upstairs."

"I don't need a babysitter."

"I know. Just take the cab."

Evan imagined punching Brown's face, blood spurting from his nose.

"Or, we could go to an all-night café I know in the Ninth District and talk about buying a café together. Or go clubbing, if that's your scene."

"Yeah, right," Evan said, sarcastic. "I have a long travel day tomorrow. I need my beauty sleep." He started for the north escalator, but Brown grabbed his arm.

"The cab's not over there, Evan," he said in a low voice. He twisted Evan's arm up his back until Evan gasped in pain. "I'll walk you to the cab."

Their eyes met and held. Brown's green eyes, his unshaven

face, betrayed no emotion. After half a minute, Evan nodded in agreement.

"Good boy." Brown released his arm. "Right this way, Maestro." They strolled to the south escalator. "So, you taking the train to Amsterdam tomorrow or flying?"

"Train."

"It's a great city, Maestro. I haven't visited there in a while. The jazz cafés, the chocolate, the flowers in bloom, the women in bloom. The food. The Genever. The ambiance. *Sehr holländisch.* Hey, a jazz café. That's what we could do *here.*"

"I'm not interested in investing in your café, Brown."

They stepped onto the up escalator. Evan began to feel nervous about whether or not a cab waited on the street above or a white street cleaner van.

"What's the concert program, Maestro? Is it with the Concertgebouw?"

Evan nodded, scrutinizing Brown's face, the curiosity in his eyes. "Barber, Copland, and Caine. I thought you were a country-western kind of guy."

Brown slapped his back. "Yeah, and jazz. I know my Uncle Danny would love to hear you conduct that program with the Concertgebouw. Who was your friend with the pink hair at the costume store, Maestro?"

Evan shivered as they reached the street. "Pink hair?"

"Yeah, pink frou-frou hair, horn-rimmed glasses, a light blue dress. Female, I assumed. Did she pick you up?"

Evan let a giggle build to laughter as he saw the cab waiting at the curb ahead. Its "TAXI" roof light glowed white and its engine was running.

"She picked you up," Brown said. "Who was she, Maestro?"

They stopped by the cab's back door. Evan smiled at Brown for the first time, a smile of genuine amusement for knowing something the CIA agent didn't. "She didn't pick me up, Brown. She helped me create disguises to protect my privacy."

Brown nodded, his eyes serious. "OK. But you need more paranoia, Maestro. There's always someone out there who'll want a piece of you and won't care how he or she gets it. There are also people who'd love to grab an American for ransom and unsavory purposes. You understand?" Brown opened the cab door. "Now, get in."

Evan slid into the cab. The driver glanced back at him.

"Safe trip, Maestro. See you around." Brown closed the door.

Evan set his violin case and the music score on the seat next to him and pulled out his bank card. The driver waved it away and said in German, "Your friend has already paid the fare to Währing. What is the address, Maestro?"

Evan pressed the window control too late. Brown trotted around the corner. He shook his head. Brown was playing a confusing game. The American had sounded almost like he cared about him. Or maybe that was part of the set-up to earn his trust, get close to him, and arrange for his accidental or "natural causes" death. Well, he needed to get home. He gave the driver his address.

Chapter 18

"Watch your step," Juliana Pekelharing said, slowing her pace. She pointed ahead to a dollop of brown dog feces that decorated the cobblestone sidewalk like modern textural art.

Evan chuckled as he sidestepped the dog poop. He adjusted the strap of his leather shoulder bag in which he carried his scores and baton. "Those jewels are everywhere, even in Vondel Park where I run in the mornings. Is Amsterdam going to the dogs, Juliana?"

She smiled and sighed, apologetic. "These dog signs are not the jewels of our city. But in Amsterdam, dogs are prized and indulged like old royalty."

He loved Amsterdam, despite the vigilance required when walking the city's sidewalks. Bicycles and pedestrians outnumbered cars on the bustling street. He inhaled the faintly salty sea breeze that ruffled his hair like playful fingers. The morning sun was a warm hand on his head. White gables swirled and dipped near hoist beams at the apex of each building. At street level, glass doors revealed shops or lobbies; above, on window ledges, boxes overflowed with bright flowers and lace curtains hung in the windows. Amsterdam possessed an air of domesticated self-contentment scented by shrimp. He felt safe in this city.

Work with the Concertgebouw Orchestra had sent his

spirits soaring. He was home again with his musician family. This was his real life, the life of freedom he'd bargained for with the NEP. The life of a musician and conductor. The orchestra had responded beyond his expectation with Barber's *Adagio for Strings* and Copland's *Appalachian Spring*. This morning, they would read through Caine's Fifth Symphony.

Juliana's floral perfume reminded him of Freda's garden. He had liked her warm charm immediately at the train station the previous Sunday. She'd introduced herself as his host for the week, and he'd quickly become dependent on her. She valued silence as much as he – refreshing to meet someone who didn't need to fill up the air with chatter every minute. Each rehearsal morning she'd accompanied him on the walk from his hotel to the concert hall. She fielded all media requests for him, all phone calls, set up interviews and guarded his time as he had requested of her the first day. She left him alone to do his job and to enjoy his time in her city. Her presence created confidence and comfort much like Amsterdam itself.

Her blue eyes squinted up at him against the sun. "Sven, our principal trumpet, mentioned that he and a small group of musicians wanted to invite you out to a jazz café this evening. He wanted to know if you had already plans."

Evan shook his head, no. "I love spending time with the musicians, Juliana."

Juliana motioned him left into a short side street. "How was the string quartet last night?"

"Excellent. Thanks for getting the ticket for me. I heard three pieces of American music I didn't know existed."

"The musicians will appreciate your shirt." She smiled, her expression as clear and sunny as the sky above.

"They better. They gave it to me." His index finger traced the black lines of Joseph Caine's rugged profile and long hair on the peacock blue cotton material. Drawn around Caine's eyes was a crimson mask, and a canary yellow music staff with magenta music notes snaked out from his open mouth. "Dr. Loos gave me the two official festival T-shirts. I wear them when I run in the morning. A little free advertising, right? I'm amazed how many people are in the park around dawn."

"Your concerts are sold out, Evan," Juliana said with pride in her voice.

"I love a full house," he said. "Great audience energy."

At the Concertgebouw's side door on Jan Willem Brouwersstraat, they met two amiable musicians Evan recognized as violists but couldn't remember their names. Inside, he and Juliana went down to the guest conductor's dressing room under the stage where she reminded him before leaving that the stage manager would call for him at the proper time. He'd learned before the first rehearsal to wait for the stage manager after becoming lost in the unfamiliar maze of stairs and elevators connecting the backstage to the stage and upper levels.

The scents of orange and clove suffused the air in his cozy dressing room, furnished in plush white, glass and chrome, and connected to a private room with a small bathroom and shower. He stretched out on the sofa which was too short for him. He felt good, solid. He began his podium prep: five to ten minutes of silent meditation focused on the music and work ahead.

Fifteen minutes later, he descended one of two red-carpeted stairways that led to the bottom level of the terraced stage. Around him, orchestra musicians chatted or practiced, their eyes on their scores. Between the viola and cello sections, he came to two bare wood steps. With a light touch, he stepped without a problem on the first, but the second let out a shrill creak and wiggled under his weight.

A Chinese violist and African cellist grinned on either side of him. The violist said, "Every conductor who knows those steps, including our principal conductor, complains to the stage manager."

Evan chuckled. "Would it help?"

The cellist laughed. "The repair never lasts, as you see."

"Every hall has at least one gremlin. Keeps us on our toes," Evan said in a stage whisper, his eyes darting from one to the other smiling face. "Haunting our fallibility." He laughed and continued down to the podium center stage where a violinist, Lucas, a member of the orchestra committee, greeted him.

As the musicians took their seats, he gazed around the hall, its design similar to a Roman atrium with rounded arches and pillars and off-white walls. Four people occupied seats halfway back from the stage. He recognized Dr. Loos, the Concertgebouw's administrative director and Juliana's boss, with a man and woman, wealthy patrons, perhaps. Three rows in front of Loos, Nigel Fox sat, his piercing eyes fixed on him. He gave his manager a brief wave and received a nod of acknowledgement.

Evan placed his score of Caine's Fifth Symphony and his baton on the podium stand. He draped his black linen sport jacket over the podium's brass back rail. The musicians were in their places. Evan thrust out his chest to them like a comic book hero. Laughter greeted him, a smattering of applause, a field of smiles. A trumpet played a phrase of fanfare. Grinning, Evan raised his hand to quiet them.

"At the risk of sounding crazy, folks," he said, tapping Caine's profile on his shirt. "*He's with us* this morning. Let's read through his symphony, please. Page one." He opened the score, aware of pages flipping on the violinists' stands to his left.

Evan lifted his baton. One hundred pairs of eyes trained on him, instruments held ready, bows poised above strings. For this moment, Evan possessed absolute power. They waited, alert and unwavering, for his downbeat. With an inhaled breath, he brought down his baton. The symphony began. He listened to the sound, the acoustical balance in the hall, and he signaled the musicians with his hands how their sound needed adjustment. His sense of power sloughed away with each measure. The music took control, a tapestry of sound, each spun musical thread essential to the beauty and success of the whole.

During the symphony's first two movements, the musicians played well, followed him well, but he sensed something missing. He made mental notes for specific refinements, and quelled the recurring frustration that the orchestral sound never matched perfectly what he imagined in his inner ear while studying the score.

The violins' keening sound in the third movement pleased

him. He smiled and caught reciprocal smiles from the strings. As in the other movements, minor glitches appeared in the Finale but the only major problem arose in the final pages. The timpanist raced a little ahead of his beat. Evan stopped the orchestra.

"Timpani. Slow down, please. Please give me a deliberate, heavy beat here. Think of a hammer, or goose-stepping soldiers stomping down a street." The timpanist nodded, marked his score. "OK, everyone, Number 130. I'll cue percussion. Thank you."

They repeated the ending more to Evan's satisfaction. He cut them off with a flourish of his baton. "Thank you, timpani, much better. Thank you, everyone. Is there time to go on?"

"A break, Maestro," Lucas, the orchestra committee member, called out.

Most of the musicians filed out, talking or laughing, while a handful remained onstage to practice their parts. The concertmaster asked Evan about the violins' bowing at the beginning of the third movement. Evan reassured him and brought up a trouble spot in the first movement. Evan left, following two musicians down the stage stairs to backstage and the guest conductor's dressing room.

After splashing his face and drinking a glass of cold water in his dressing room's silent bathroom, he returned to the podium refreshed. In the second violin section, long, wavy brown hair cascaded over a woman's face as she bent to talk to a violinist in front of her. Evan stared, his pulse quickening. Sofia's hair. No, too brown and Sofia was in Vienna.

"OK, folks." Evan combed back his hair with his fingers

and flipped the pages of his score back to the beginning of Caine's symphony. Lucas gave him a brisk nod.

"Let's dig into the details," Evan said. "Page one, Number one."

Halfway through work on the first movement, Evan realized the musicians played the notes without Caine's voice. What was he doing wrong? What did they need to connect with Caine? They must walk together a tightrope between objective restraint and emotional immersion. What could he say to help them? He knew Uncle Joe. He stopped the orchestra.

"OK, listen up, please," he said, pulling twice on the tip of his craggy nose. "When Caine wrote this music, he knew Internal Security Services watched him, was building their file on him. ISS could arrest him at any moment. He feared for his wife and son, *not* for himself. His family. But, he was angry and defiant. A*ngry*. Not cold, *hot*. Piano: play heavy." He sang two measures of the piano part. "Strings, play out, *out*. OK? You're playing this music as if your loved ones' lives depended on it. It *is* the last thing you get to say." He looked at the serious faces in each section for a moment and raised his baton.

Joseph Caine's anguished rage resounded through the hall. They worked for another half hour on tempo changes, rhythmical layering, dynamics, and the last four or five pages of the movement which Evan wanted to refine more than he'd done with the Vienna Philharmonic. They also had time to polish the second movement which needed less work. When they finished, the surge of energy he felt in his body confirmed his thoughts. The first two movements were absolutely right.

"Excellent work this morning. Thank you," he said as he applauded them. "See you tomorrow morning for the rest of it."

He remained on the podium, available for questions. The musicians stirred, talked, and drifted out. The timpanist and another percussionist questioned him about the Finale. The principal flutist checked with him about his phrasing in the second movement. When only two or three musicians chatting among themselves lingered on stage, Evan left.

In his dressing room, Juliana and Nigel Fox were laughing about something. Fox, dapper in a crisp light gray double-breasted suit, rose to his feet and greeted him with a warm handshake, deep laugh lines around his green eyes.

"Good to see you, Nigel. How'd it sound?" Evan said, dropping his baton, score, and sport jacket on one of the plush chairs near the sofa. He opened the mini-refrigerator and took out a quarter-liter bottle of mineral water.

"Superb, Evan. I'm looking forward to the Barber and Copland. You seem quite pleased."

"Yeah. I love work. I love this wonderful orchestra." He smiled at Juliana before taking a long drink of mineral water.

She handed him a white envelope. "Sven talked to me. I have made the appropriate changes to your schedule. Please carry your cell phone tonight. If you have problems finding the jazz café, Sven's cell phone number is on your schedule as well as mine."

"Great. Anything else I need to know?" He set the envelope on his sport jacket.

"Please remember the interview this afternoon."

"Right. Four o'clock here and you'll take me to the radio station for the half hour chat about American music today."

"Perfect. Enjoy the rest of the day. If you need anything, please let me know." She headed for the door.

"She's a delight," Fox said after Juliana had left. He glanced around the dressing room, his white-haired head bobbing twice in approval. "They've renovated in here again I see. Are you hungry?"

"Famished. What'd you have in mind?"

"One of my favorite restaurants here," Nigel said. "Do you like seafood, Evan?"

They feasted on calamari salad and swordfish steaks at an out-of-the-way restaurant, talking about Amsterdam, London, and sports. Skipping dessert, he and Nigel sipped smooth but strong coffee at their patio table on the veranda. A large blue and red umbrella shaded them.

"Well, Evan, Manchester and Madrid Real are the teams to watch," Nigel said, nodding.

"I loved the swordfish," Evan said, sitting back with a satisfied moan and squinting at the nearby canal. A wisp of wind tickled his neck. "Thanks, Nigel, for bringing me here."

"You've tried the famous herring?" Nigel said.

"I've seen the street carts. Is it safe?"

"Yes. And quite special." Nigel pulled a plain white envelope from his inner breast pocket. "I've booked five more engagements for you next year, including Sydney, Australia in March, and ten more for 2050. The details are in here." He slid the envelope to Evan. "I had Beatrice print them for you."

"Thanks. Did Buenos Aires confirm?"

Nigel nodded. "Buenos Aires in January and Moscow in June." He lifted his coffee cup. "Your father's London publisher contacted me, Evan." Nigel licked his lips before sipping more coffee. "He told me about Mr. Redfield and the trust fund. Did you know about the smuggling operation?"

"Not a clue." His father's business again. "Uncle Joe left me a trust fund. I've already had the money transferred. I know about my father's but I can't touch it until the Americans provide me with an official death certificate."

Fox frowned. "I see. The Americans won't confirm his death. Did your father or Caine ever mention Mr. Redfield?"

Evan shook his head, picked up his coffee cup. "They shielded me from their Underground activities."

"Your father's publisher asks that you call him. I have his phone number here." Fox handed Evan a pale blue business card. "He's a member of my club. He believes Redfield told his predecessor about your father's plans to leave America."

"Father never planned to leave."

"To your knowledge."

Evan frowned. "My mother and I tried to persuade him to leave. He refused. He had a personal vendetta against the NEP, especially after Uncle Joe's arrest and murder."

Nigel signaled the waiter. "Then he made no arrangements for the fund in the event he couldn't claim it."

His father had been secretive, distrustful of everyone outside of the family and the Caines. It wasn't until he'd asked, two years ago, that his father had told him any details about the Underground and its activities. "All that money sitting there in London and the NEP can't claim it. Pure torture for the NEP. And Randall Quinn got the last word, as always."

"Please call Henley, Evan. They need to hear from you," Nigel said as he paid the waiter. "I have an appointment with a diamond dealer and must leave, but please stay and relax, if you'd like."

"Oh, before I forget, Nigel, could you request the Caine Piano Concerto for my Moscow gig next June? I want Vassily Bartyakov as the piano soloist and he needs to know when I've scheduled the concerto to make his own arrangements."

"I'll let Moscow know. Has he a manager?"

"I don't think so. I'll talk to him. Thanks, Nigel." Evan watched the Englishman stand up and smooth his suit jacket. "Will you attend my rehearsal tomorrow?"

Nigel shook his head, no. "I'll see you at the post-concert reception. Toi-toi, Evan."

He grinned at the old, traditional "toi-toi" for good luck among musicians. The tall, graceful Brit threaded his way around the patio tables and out onto the sidewalk. The waiter came over, but Evan waved him away with a smile. After he finished his coffee, he left.

A quarter mile from the restaurant, Evan strolled onto a bridge that spanned a quiet canal. He slipped the neon blue Mozart cell phone out of his sport jacket pocket as he stopped in the middle of the bridge. Leaning over the waist-high metal grillwork barrier, he looked down at the grayish-blue water, thinking about Leiner's disappointment when the phone's surveillance device no longer registered on his tracking monitors. Evan had copied out the phone's directory on a slip of paper he kept in his wallet, and erased the numbers. He patted the outline of the clean Georg cell phone in his pocket. He turned off the Mozart phone, opened the back and removed the battery. Glancing around to insure no one watched, Evan dropped the Mozart phone and the battery into the canal and walked away.

"*Was ist los*, Marco?" Klaus said into the speaker of his desk phone. Aschenbeck perched on the edge of his cluttered desk, scratching his dark auburn beard. Hot sunshine streamed through the windows, heating the office to stuffiness. A floor fan hummed and blew air at them from a corner.

Marco's frustration growled through the speaker in German. "There are no cell phones in this apartment. I have searched everywhere, even through his clothes and pockets. Frau Kirsch confirmed that Quinn owned two cell phones, a blue one and a black one, that he left on bookshelves in the front room. Neither is there."

"Why take *two* cell phones to Amsterdam?" Klaus said, scowling at Aschenbeck.

"He's a conductor. Who knows?" Marco responded. "However, now I have no phone in which to load and program the surveillance software."

"*Prima*. Return to the office." Klaus punched the disconnect button on his desk phone.

"What have you learned, Klaus, about Evan?" Aschenbeck asked in a thoughtful voice as he slid off the desk to one of the chairs facing Klaus.

"The black cell phone. Marco traced it to a subsidiary account for the Café Chicago. We're watching Woody Lewis. The next time Herr Quinn meets with him, we will have the equipment in place to listen and record them. Frau Kirsch has reported nothing unusual. We know from Herr Quinn's home videophone that he plans to hunt in Romania this fall. I have already notified Bucharest not to issue him a license. I have a source who can find out more about the hunting trip." He left his desk and went over to the three withering Begonias on the window sill. "Bernard Brown continues to show more than the usual interest in Herr Quinn. Somehow I doubt Lewis is involved, but Brown could be Herr Quinn's control. We only need to discover how they communicate with each other, whether the hunting trip is a cover for an operation, how and where Herr Quinn would obtain a hunting rifle, *und so weiter*." Leiner picked up a small cherry red pitcher and watered one of the Begonias.

"Woody Lewis gave Herr Quinn a gift of a cell phone," Aschenbeck said. "We also gave him a phone. They are popular gifts, cell phones." Aschenbeck rose from his seat. "Brown is in Amsterdam. He left last night by train."

"What?" Klaus faced him. "They must have an operation." He reached for his desk phone but Aschenbeck pulled it away.

"What will you tell your Dutch colleagues, Klaus? Perhaps they will have some interest in Brown, but none in Quinn. It's not illegal to meet and talk."

"I would be negligent not to inform my Dutch colleagues of the possibility of—"

"And they will ask for evidence, Klaus. Evidence you do not have."

"We need more time. More human surveillance." Leiner turned back to the window and watered another parched Begonia.

"He's a respected conductor, a productive member of society. You suspect him only because he is American."

"May I remind you, Dieter, most of the American defectors in the last twenty-five years have been spies. Only a handful were genuine defectors and none were in Austria."

"Concentrate your attention, Klaus, on security for the Chinese-American talks instead of chasing a phantom spy."

"Hanna and I have the security issue covered." Leiner set the water pitcher on his desk and sighed, resigned. "To provide you with what you want, I need more time."

"One month," Aschenbeck said, heading for Leiner's office door.

One month. No, as long as it takes. Klaus picked up the water pitcher and returned to the last thirsty Begonia on the window sill.

Chapter 19

Evan waited in semi-darkness with the crusty stage manager who smelled of cigar smoke and juniper. He fingered the gold convex circles in his cuffs. His father had given them to him when the Arts Council appointed him as Assistant Conductor in St. Louis. They'd belonged to Joseph Caine. Evan wore them to every concert he conducted.

No matter what city or what concert hall, it was always the same, these last moments with the stage manager. Over the years they had become an important ritual for Evan. He imagined his entrance on stage, his step up on to the podium, his bow to the audience and turning to the orchestra, the score open on the podium's stand. He visualized the first downbeat, heard the orchestra's response in his mind. He straightened and looked at the stage manager whose hand rested on the door handle.

"Maestro?" the stage manager whispered.

Evan nodded. The door flew open. The burst of stage lights blinded him for a second. Polite applause began in the concert hall. He descended the red-carpeted stairway to the bare wood steps where he skipped down over the one weak, unsteady step near the Chinese violist. His arms open wide to the Concertgebouw musicians acknowledging their partnership, he strode briskly toward the podium, shoulders squared to communicate confidence and authority. The applause continued as he ascended the podium and bowed to the audience.

His father whispered in his inner ear, "Inside, want as much as you like. But always do what you're told." Evan shuddered. As he turned to the orchestra, he fingered Uncle Joe's cufflinks. He'd wanted to be a conductor and to be free, and he'd gotten what he wanted.

He lowered his head, taking a deep breath. He imagined the sound of the first note, the first chord of Samuel Barber's *Adagio for Strings*, held it for a moment in his mind before looking up at his musicians. They waited, attentive, their faces open and expectant, instruments ready. The silence in the hall thickened the air, and in it Evan felt the power of anticipation. Everyone waited on him. He controlled them. With his left fingers, Evan made a trickling tears movement from eyes to chin, then clenched his fist before his face.

He brought down the baton. The strings played, *pianissimo* at first, and the sad melodic line rose and fell, gathering strength and transforming into a knife of grief that sliced the air. He had sat on his father's lap at the piano, his father tapping on the middle C key; his four-year-old fingers playing the C major scale with his father's fingers. Evan glanced around at his musicians, noting their concentration. Barber's voice, warm and full, reigned in the hall.

The Arts Council had approved the *Adagio*, which had begun life as the second movement of a string quartet, for funerals. His mother had hated its tension, its painful dissonance, the keening strings. His father had played a recording of it at her funeral. In a flash of his mind's eye, he saw his mother in her casket, her black hair fanned across the pillow like a black splotch on the white satin lining of the American way of life. Evan wondered if anyone would arrange a funeral for his father. In the same instant, he became aware of the sound of his father's laughter, loud next to him, punctuated by a hissing white noise. His vision blurred. He lost all sense of his body. He felt like a stranger standing next to himself, watching himself, waiting for himself to respond. His heart sounded like a bass drum. A sudden panic gripped him. He realized that his eyes were closed.

When he opened his eyes, he saw the musicians staring at him, their eyes wide in alarm, their instruments down. No one was playing. What had happened? He felt the tingling sensation of the blood draining from his face, his wet face. He'd lost control. He heard the sounds in the hall: someone coughed, pages rustled, a whisper of a voice. He'd had some sort of blackout and he needed to get the music going again. He glanced at the music score in front of him, and used his handkerchief to wipe his face.

With his left hand, he held up fingers to indicate the measure where they'd start playing. He lifted the baton. With the downbeat, the musicians played. He noticed a flutist wipe tears from her face. The sound filled him, grounded him back in the present moment, and he breathed with it. Evan commanded the musicians with his eyes and gestures to sing out the music. The *Adagio* rose to its keening climax, a shrill, angry sound suspended above them, each progressively altered chord a turn of grief's knife in the heart until he severed the sound. It echoed in the hall. Subdued now, resigned and accepting, the music advanced to its peaceful, fade-away resolution. With a tiny circle of the baton's tip, Evan cut off the orchestra.

Silence. Evan faced the musicians, head down and eyes closed, his hands suspended in mid-air, imprinting in memory this particular suspension of time, this last chord of loss, of grief, of pain. When he dropped his hands, it was as if someone had switched on thunder: roaring applause and cheers, and feet stamping the floor.

Light-headed, he took two deep breaths and motioned for the orchestra musicians to stand before he faced the audience. A sea of hands undulated above smiling faces. Evan bowed, dropped his baton on the music stand and jumped off the podium. He shook the concertmaster's hand and waved for the musicians to bow. They refused and tapped their instrument bows on their music stands or applauded. Evan smiled, left hand over his heart, and bowed to them before taking the red stairs to the stage door two at a time.

The stage manager handed him a white towel and gestured him out the door to the conductor's lounge across the hall. Evan wiped sweat from his face and neck. The memories, the loss of physical sensation: the Barber had never affected him like that before. He stood in front of the lounge's windows, looking out at the dusky clear sky tinged with gold. A skittish adrenalin energy left over from the panic tingled his hands and feet. Relax. Breathe. Everything was fine. He paced in front of the large windows. The woodwinds, brass and percussion musicians were joining the strings on stage. Evan shook out his hands, arms, and legs, reassured in feeling his connection to them again. He needed to restrain his emotions.

"Maestro."

"Everybody on stage?"

The stage manager nodded. Evan walked with him back to the stage door. "Time for some cheerful dancing music." He nodded as the stage manager opened the door.

Near deafening applause accompanied his second trip down the red stairs that evening. Grinning with mischief in mind for the Chinese violist, he stomped on the weak step, producing a shriek from the protesting wood that startled the closest musicians in the viola and cello sections. The Chinese violist laughed.

On the podium, Evan bowed to the audience and faced smiling musicians. He realized the memories would enter his mind but he decided how to respond to them. American music would not affect him that way anymore. He brought down the baton to begin the dawn of Copland's musical portrait of Appalachian life.

"Bravo, Maestro Quinn! I loved your program, Caine's powerful music, and the joy in Copland's," a lanky blonde Dutchman in a tux said, pumping Evan's hand. "I hope often we see you leading our orchestra."

"Thank you, sir," Evan said. The man's tux, from the cut and styling, was custom made. He loved its satin paisley vest. Maybe he could find a tailor in Vienna to make him a new white tie and tails for work. No more buying used clothes or off the rack and ordering alterations.

Guests clustered around him in a reception foyer decorated with portraits of past Concertgebouw principal conductors. Waiters threaded through the crowd carrying silver trays of finger food or glasses of champagne. Evan's stomach gurgled in hunger. He smiled at the men and women around him. "I love Amsterdam and your orchestra," he said to them.

He stopped a waiter. "Would it be possible to get something non-alcoholic to drink? Juice?" The waiter nodded.

Juliana had described the reception guests as civic leaders (politicians, he assumed) and patrons of the arts and music. He had never seen so much diamond jewelry in his life. The place sparkled. Even the men wore diamond rings or tie clasps, earrings or bracelets. Perfume and voices filled the air. Orchestra musicians mingled among the guests but none came to rescue him. Security guards surveyed the crowd from the room's periphery. Nigel Fox towered over heads in a corner, a glass of champagne in one hand, gesturing with the other as he talked. He'd chatted with Nigel half an hour ago. The waiter arrived with a glass of mango juice for him.

A head of muddy brown hair not far from Fox caught his eye. Evan leaned left to see the man's face but the man turned away. No, Brown was in Vienna. His paranoia needed an off switch. He was safe from Brown here. He smiled and nodded as the guests around him complimented his performance and the program. Their orchestra musicians deserved all the praise. He was hungry. He wanted to leave. He hated post-concert receptions.

"Maestro Quinn?" A willowy woman touched his elbow. Her straight blonde hair, combed back from her face with a black velvet headband fell to her waist. Her face radiated the freshness of youth not yet intimate with the world's corruptions. "Please sign my program, Maestro Quinn?" she said, her accent Dutch. He'd been saved by a fan. She handed him the program booklet and a pen with a coy smile. She leaned in close and said in a whispery voice, "The Caine symphony was wonderful, Maestro."

Her voice and coyness brought to his mind yellow cabbage butterflies flitting from one milkweed plant to another in a country meadow. "Glad you liked it," he said as he returned the program and pen to her. He smiled his public persona smile. She had given him the opportunity to slip away. "Would you excuse me, please?"

Carrying his champagne glass of mango juice, he weaved through the crowd in the direction of the elevator to the guest conductor's dressing room. He plucked two shrimp puffs from a waiter's tray, popped them into his mouth. Eyes observed him, voices called to him, a woman's satin gloved hand reached out to him. He felt the public press in and he needed to get away. The muddy brown-haired man stood off by himself, examining a portrait. He wore an ivory linen suit like the one Brown had worn the first time Evan had met him in Aschenbeck's office. No, Brown was in Vienna. Evan shook his head as he pressed the elevator call button.

The silence in the empty dressing room was a relief. He changed out of his white dinner jacket and tux pants and into the jeans, white Oxford shirt and black linen sport jacket he'd stowed in the closet that morning before an interview. With meticulous care, he hung up his work clothes and stuck the dress shirt in the drycleaner's bag Juliana had left for him. In the bathroom, he splashed cold water on his face as his stomach rumbled. Maybe Sven or Lucas or some of the other musicians would join him for a late evening dinner.

As he hurried out of the dressing room, he collided with a woman who was waiting in front of the door. They each made apologies and he noticed her English accent, the mass of strawberry blonde curls around her delicate waif-like face. She looked familiar and attractive. Silver shone at her throat and ears. A lavender silk blouse softened the severe lines of her tailored black suit.

"I'm Valerie Peters," she said, offering her hand. "A flutist with the London Symphony. I don't expect you to remember—"

In his mind, he placed her face in the flute section of the London Symphony and it clicked. "No, Valerie, I remember you. I remember your face. How's Misha? And Julian?" He'd dined with Misha, the principal flutist, and Julian, the principal violist, one evening in London. They'd had a lively and fun conversation about rugby and cricket and European movies vs. American, in spite of Richard and Dave, Evan's bored Arts Council escorts, at the neighboring table. The next day Dave had forbidden socializing with musicians for the rest of his tour.

"They're fine, Maestro." Her gray eyes met his. "I'm sure they'd agree with me that we'd love to play Caine with you some time. I loved his Fifth Symphony tonight. Will you return to us soon?"

"My manager has booked at least a week in London next year. Sorry, I can't remember when it—"

"Oh, excellent." She gave him a brilliant smile of even

white teeth. "These receptions. They're always too bloody rich and political for my taste."

He laughed, grateful for the understanding and sympathy in the tone of her soprano voice. "Yeah, I know." He leaned close to her and whispered, "Boring."

"I see you've changed out of your concert togs," she said. "I'm famished. Might I interest you in going out for something to eat?"

"Blow this place?" He raised his hands in mock horror. "But I'm the guest of honor."

"It's been at least an hour, hasn't it?" she said, her smile flirtatious. "And you'll have another reception tomorrow night, right? I know a cozy restaurant that serves the best gnocchi I've ever eaten."

"Italian," Evan said, his mouth watering. "I love Italian food." He cupped her elbow and guided her toward the stairs that led to the side door. "Is it far? I'm really hungry."

"We'll need a taxi."

Outside, Valerie led him to a taxi stand a block from the concert hall as he described his favorite Italian restaurants in New York City, how much he loved fresh parmesan cheese and thick, hearty pasta fagioli. They got into a taxi and Valerie gave the driver an address. Evan noticed the driver's uncertain, questioning look but thought the driver hadn't heard her correctly the first time as she repeated it. The driver entered the information on his dashboard computer and they drove off.

"What are you doing in Amsterdam, Valerie?" Evan said, settled next to her in the back seat.

"I'm on holiday. When I heard you'd conduct at the American Music Festival, of course I had to come over."

"I thought the London Symphony went on tour this summer." He had a warning feeling now, like someone tugging on a thread in the back of his mind, that something wasn't quite right.

"The tour's in August. We're on break now. Where are you living, Maestro?"

"Call me Evan. Work's done for tonight." He smiled as she glanced out the window. "Where are we going?"

"It's a small place tucked away near the harbor."

"Let's invite some of the Concertgebouw musicians to meet us there." Evan pulled out his Georg cell phone. He recalled only Sven's cell phone number, but Sven would corral others to join them.

"I don't know, Evan," Valerie said, checking out the window again. "It's an awfully small restaurant, more like a café, perhaps ten tables." She smiled, her gray eyes steady. "A family-run restaurant which is the reason I love it. We should have invited them before we left, don't you think? Perhaps gone to a larger restaurant?" The corners of her red lips drooped in disappointment.

"Let's see how crowded it is. If there's room, I'll call Sven and have him gather a group together." He slid his cell phone back into his sport jacket pocket. The warning feeling persisted, a tension in his stomach. He looked out the window. The taxi sped through an industrial area. He had no idea where he was, where they were going. Valerie, however, was a musician. He sighed and smiled at her, quashing the nagging feeling. She talked about her performance of Caine's flute sonata when she was a student in Paris and the best Italian restaurant in that city.

Five minutes later, the taxi stopped in front of one of many warehouses on a dark, deserted street. Evan slid out as Valerie paid the driver. The taxi sped off past a sodium streetlight thirty yards away. Evan glanced around, the alarm returning. Another streetlight stood twenty yards in the opposite direction. Valerie walked up to him on the sidewalk.

"Valerie, I don't see a restaurant anywhere around here. What's—?"

"Evan Quinn!"

Evan pivoted. Two men dressed in black cotton pants and tunics emerged from the shadows next to the warehouse. Kaffiyes wrapped around their heads obscured their faces. They stopped about ten feet from him.

"Famous orchestra conductor from rich infidel America," the taller of the two men said. The other wore round eyeglasses. "Now you will serve us."

Evan turned to Valerie. "Are you a musician?"

"My sister," she said with a smirk as she pushed him toward the men.

He resisted, pushing back. "Your sister? But you talked about the Caine—"

"My *twin* sister tells me everything, *Maestro*."

He felt her press the muzzle of a handgun into the small of his back. His anger flared. This woman needed to be taught *not* to screw with him. He focused on observation and assessing the possibilities. They were relaxed, over-confident. They perceived him as only a conductor who wouldn't know how to defend himself. An easy target. Icy calm and clarity spread through his body and mind. He raised his arms up about a foot as if in submission. "Who are you?" he said. "What's this about?"

The tall one laughed, his voice derisive. "We fight Jihad against infidels for justice. We will show America what we—"

"Tell him later, Mohammed. Let's move." Valerie prodded Evan with the gun.

Eyeglasses pulled a black hood from a pocket and stepped up to Evan, facing him. As he raised the hood to slip it over Evan's head, Evan ducked and spun tight and fast away to the left. A gunshot cracked the air. Eyeglasses fell back. Evan continued his spin up behind Valerie, grabbing her neck and head in a vise. He jerked her head in a quick twist. Her neck snapped like a wishbone.

Valerie collapsed, dead, in his arms. Evan lifted and threw her at Mohammed as he aimed a 9mm pistol at him. Her body hit, pushing him back, throwing him off balance and giving Evan the time he needed to move. The gun went off. Evan felt the bullet whip his left sport jacket sleeve. He skirted Mohammed on the ground shoving off Valerie's body. The whites of his eyes flashed at Evan. In the next second, Evan felt the arm chop across the back of his knees, knocking him back and to the ground.

As Mohammed heaved Valerie's body off, her gun clattered across the pavement toward Eyeglasses. Evan rolled after it as Mohammed kicked out at him. Valerie's gun was his only chance of getting out of this mess alive. He grabbed it and turned, aiming up at Mohammed now standing above him, his gun aimed at Evan's face.

Two gunshots. Mohammed twitched, blood trickling

down from the center of his forehead. Evan hadn't fired. He hadn't had time. As Mohammed fell to the ground dead, Evan spun over to face the direction Mohammed had faced.

Bernard Brown crouched in front of a car about twenty yards away, just beyond the streetlight, his gun aimed at Evan. Evan shot at him. Brown scurried around to the car's side, using its metal body as a protective barrier. In one fluid motion, Evan rose to his feet, scooped up Mohammed's gun and sprinted for the warehouse. Once around the corner, he plastered his body against the wall, breathing hard, his mind racing. What was Brown doing here? Had he been sent to kill him and the Arabs had gotten in the way? Or had the Arabs given Brown the perfect opportunity to kill him? Go on the offensive, surprise Brown with an attack from behind.

Evan peered around the corner of the warehouse. Brown still crouched behind the car. The American was shaking his head as if in disbelief. In order to approach Brown from the rear, Evan would need to run behind two warehouses before returning to the street.

"Hey! Maestro!"

Evan frowned. Now what?

"Evan! Come on, man! I'm not going to shoot you. See?" Brown stood and holstered his gun.

Evan took a deep breath. "Throw the gun out on the ground!"

Brown shrugged. He threw his gun out in front of the car. Its clatter on pavement sounded sweet. Brown raised his hands high in the air. He was wearing that ivory linen suit.

"What the *fuck* are you doing here, Brown?" Evan stepped around the corner, a gun in each hand aimed at Brown, but he remained in the warehouse's shadow. "You're supposed to be in Vienna."

"I had some vacation time. I hadn't visited this city for a couple years." Brown grinned. "Loved the concert, Maestro."

"You were at the reception." Evan took two steps out of the shadows. "Did Morgan send you to kill me?"

"No. My Uncle Danny would never forgive me." Brown's voice was firm. He dropped his hands. "I'm here to protect you, stupid."

"Protect me?" Evan aimed Mohammed's gun at Brown's forehead, Valerie's at his chest. "*Protect* me? Like the NEP? Oh, yeah, keep it all American, all in the family. Only we can terrorize him, torture him, no one else. Does Morgan give you bonus pay for the job?"

Brown shook his head. "Morgan's a shithead. From what I've seen tonight, you can defend yourself. That's military training. But you've never been in the military."

Evan had his cover story ready. "The guy told me it was a martial art. He told me the name but I don't remember." He breathed slow and deep to calm himself.

"What guy? Where?" Brown, his eyes on Evan, walked slowly to the three dead bodies. His expression was open, questioning, without suspicion. "That's why you signed up for classes at the Fischer School?"

"Yeah. After the Uighur terrorists at my press conference, I wanted to buy a gun but the cops wouldn't approve it. They suggested bodyguards but I don't like to travel or live that way. They gave me the address of the Fischer School, and I thought I could learn more there."

"What guy? In Minneapolis or New York?" Brown squinted at him.

"A guy showed up in my neighborhood in Minneapolis," Evan said, moving to join Brown. He still held the two guns on the American. His heart raced, adrenalin coursed through his bloodstream. He felt euphoric. His training had worked. He had killed someone. With his bare hands. He could kill Brown. "He asked my father for help in getting to the insurgent states. While my father made the arrangements – it took months – the guy – his name was Mark – taught me some self-defense moves. When I traveled to guest conduct, the AC stuck me in ratty hotels in rundown areas. They refused to pay for better lodging. I wanted to be able to protect myself." He stood over Brown who examined Eyeglasses' pockets.

"Where'd Mark learn the moves?" Brown glanced up at him.

"He said he'd been a Navy Seal."

Brown nodded. "OK. Do me a favor?" He looked up at Evan. "Actually, you look a little pale."

"I've never killed anyone before."

"Why would you? You're a *conductor.* And thank god for it. Not something you'll want to do again, right? You won't develop a taste for the power rush killing can give."

Evan nodded, swallowed. He *loved* the rush, the exhilaration, the power. He looked at Valerie, her body on its side. "She told me she was a flutist with the London Symphony. Her twin sister is the flutist not her. But she was so convincing." He felt in control now, his guns aimed at Brown squatting next to Valerie, going through her pockets. Brown couldn't slip his hands into the pockets of his mind, could never know how much he enjoyed the killing, the power.

"Yeah, well, deception is nothing to these people." Brown went over to Mohammed.

"She called him Mohammed. Those scarves they're wearing. They're Arabs, aren't they?"

Brown shrugged. "No ID, no wallets, no money, nothing. Could be Islamic terrorists of one kind or another. There are so many groups and subgroups now I couldn't begin to guess which one." He stood up. "You OK, Evan?"

"I learned all that stuff from Mark, but I never thought I'd ever have to use it. You know? I mean, I can't believe... is she really dead?" His cover story gave him the power of deception that protected him.

"As a door nail." Brown grabbed Evan's shoulder and squeezed it. "Do me a favor? You can drop the guns now." Their eyes met. "Think about it, Maestro. If I'd wanted to kill you, I could have done it long before tonight."

Evan dropped the two guns by the bodies. Brown acted more like an ally than an enemy. Maybe he had his cover story, his deception, too.

"You'll have an adrenalin crash soon. Way too much nervous energy. And horny." Brown grinned. "I've been there a couple times. If you want a hooker, give me a call. I'm staying at the American Hotel. We'll have a party and put it on my expense account."

"No way!" Evan stepped away from him, shaking off his hand.

Brown chuckled, pulled a cell phone out of his suit jacket pocket and flipped it open. "I'll clean up this mess. Go back to your hotel, and if they have a gym, I'd suggest a hard workout. By the way, Morgan does want you dead. I've been dragging my feet about hiring someone to do it. Morgan put in for a transfer and I'm waiting for that to come through, stalling, telling him we really need to recruit you. Once Morgan's gone, I can forget the order. Want to work for us?" Brown laughed, a dry, papery sound.

Evan shook his head. "Why does Morgan want me dead?"

"He believes your father masterminded the bombing at the Mall of America that killed his brother and his brother's family, so he hates your father and anyone related to him. He wants to avenge his brother's death by killing you."

Evan nodded, looked around. The physical world had never looked so clear and crisp to him before. However, he also knew adrenalin could blur the world, give him tunnel vision. He hadn't seen Brown arrive, hadn't been aware of his environment as much as he should have been.

Morgan was right. His father and the Underground had bombed the Mall of America. His father had told him two years ago when he'd returned from prison. Morgan's motivation was personal and sloppy not professional. Brown was a professional.

Brown dialed his cell phone, spoke with someone in curt phrases. When he flipped the phone closed, he picked up the guns. "So, Maestro, go back to your hotel. It's better if no one else sees you here."

"But these people—"

"I'll take care of them. No one will know, Maestro. Walk in that direction and you'll come to a brighter street where you can catch a bus to Central Station. There's a taxi stand there. Just tell the bus driver you want Central Station."

"Thanks, Brown." Evan headed down the street.

"Call me at the hotel if you need to talk or anything, Evan."

Evan raised his right hand in a wave without turning. He had no intention of calling Brown. He'd learned all he needed to know for now. Valerie Peters and her two terrorists had altered his consciousness. During his training, he'd never believed he could kill another human being. Now he knew he could, and that made Perceval real and dangerous.

Chapter 20

Something was missing in the information they had collected on Quinn, perhaps something so obvious that none of them had noticed it. What was the missing puzzle piece? Klaus had reviewed the file that morning, but nothing had sparked his intuition. Dieter's deadline irritated him. He hadn't imposed a deadline on him before. Of course, they had not investigated before a famous orchestra conductor whose father was an internationally renowned writer and dissident.

Quinn's cell phone had disappeared but Quinn had not. He had conducted both his scheduled concerts (he and Laura had listened to them on internet radio) and returned to Vienna. But there had been that silent moment in the first concert during the Barber *Adagio for Strings* that he especially wanted to ask Quinn about.

On Kärntnerstrasse, Klaus eyed a female mime dressed in a skin tight black and pink tuxedo body suit. He walked at a steady pace, his eyes and ears taking in the swirling street activity, the talking, laughing, cameras clicking, the spider-like headsets curled around heads, pastel diaphanous dresses, children screaming in delight, balloons, techno dance music, the bright red flowers in the pedestrian street's center, the mingled smells of perfume, bratwurst, and coffee. Despite the searing hot sun and high humidity, people filled

Kärntnerstrasse, most of them tourists, Klaus guessed. He'd heard on the news that morning that Austria's tourism revenue had increased this summer and crime had decreased. Good news. People felt safe on the streets of his city.

Vassily Bartyakov, according to Marco and Gianni, enjoyed a mid-morning coffee every Wednesday at a Café Konditorei near the Staatsoper. Perhaps the Russian piano student knew the reason Quinn's cell phone no longer functioned. Bartyakov hadn't reported to him in three weeks. He wanted also to know the reason for that.

He weaved around the people on the sidewalk moving in both directions. He felt thirsty now, hot in his light gray suit and he looked forward to the air-conditioned coolness of the café. He squinted up at the sky, searching for high cirrus clouds that might signal an approaching storm. No clouds, not even wispy cirrus, marred the cornflower blue sky. His thoughts returned to Evan Quinn.

The American conductor had returned from Amsterdam ten days ago. Frau Kirsch had called each day with her report of the activity she'd observed: his daily early morning run, his help in her garden, visits from musicians, his leaving to meet friends or shop (she didn't know which, although he had mentioned a Russian piano student and a composer from New Zealand) but most of the time he worked at home. Quinn had noticed on his security system Frau Kirsch's entry with Marco into his apartment and had asked her about it. She'd covered herself well – she'd brought him more towels. Frau Kirsch believed Quinn worked hard to prepare for his autumn and winter concerts. Marco reported nothing suspicious on Quinn's house computer internet account or on calls on his videophone.

Bernard Brown had returned from Amsterdam the day after Quinn. Why had Brown gone to Amsterdam? For holiday? Or had Brown gone to meet with Quinn away from their eyes and ears? He wished now that he'd gone to Amsterdam himself. They didn't know if the two Americans had had contact there. He was nervous about this gap in their knowledge, the potential that Quinn could have made contact with anyone in Amsterdam, not only Brown.

According to Marco and Johann, the old American, Woody Lewis, attended a regular poker game on Thursday nights in a back room at the Casino Wien, but spent most of his time managing the Café Chicago in Judenplatz. His wife ran the café's kitchen. Lewis' telephone and Internet communications focused on his two adult children, suppliers for the café, several other American friends scattered around Europe, and local Viennese friends. Quinn's black cell phone account listed three calls to the Café Chicago the first two weeks of July then nothing more. Without recordings of those calls, he had nothing.

Klaus stopped in front of the Café Konditorei, gazing at the window displays of delicate layered pastries, cookies, and cakes. Inside the café, a college-aged couple wearing backpacks sipped coffee and fed each other apricot cookies at one of the front marble-topped tables. Behind them, half a dozen people at the counter ordered their sweets to go; two more individuals stood at tables, listening to their personal music or checking the Internet on cell phones as they drank coffee. Vassily Bartyakov read a newspaper – a real one, not on his phone or a tablet computer – at the front far corner table in the sunshine, and sipped a frothy *Schlagobers* coffee that left a faint white moustache on his upper lip.

"*Guten Morgen,* Herr Bartyakov," Klaus said as he approached Bartyakov's table. The Russian started. A boyish smile split his face.

"*Hauptkommisar! Wie geht's Ihnen heute?*" Bartyakov shook his hand.

Klaus switched to English and lowered his voice. "Somewhat concerned about our mutual friend. You haven't called me, Herr Bartyakov."

The Russian shrugged, responding in English. "Nothing to report."

"Have you seen him?"

"Only once since he return from big success in Amsterdam. We shop for piano for his apartment. Store deliver new piano in three weeks. Nobody bother Evan, Inspector. He live quiet life of musician."

Bartyakov's report echoed Frau Kirsch's. The Russian's expression was serious and genuine, his gaze steady. No deception there. Bartyakov was Quinn's friend. He would notice any strange behavior or strangers and would not want anything to happen to Quinn. "Dieter Aschenbeck and I gave him a blue cell phone as a welcome present. I haven't been able to reach him at that cell phone's number."

"He lost blue cell phone in Amsterdam," Bartyakov said, nodding. "Maybe stolen. He told me at least he remember to copy out people and phone numbers in phone's directory. We call him at home phone now."

"That is unfortunate," Klaus said. "I hope he plans to tell

everyone in his directory." An all-too-common occurrence with cell phones. He'd lost two himself. However, Quinn had taken both his cell phones to Amsterdam which could suggest he'd planned to lose the blue one. He smiled at the Russian.

"I lose three cell phones in last two years, you know. Coffee, Inspector? Some Strudel?"

He shook his head. "Has Herr Quinn mentioned plans to hunt in Romania this fall?"

The Russian's head bobbed up and down, his blonde curls bouncing slightly. "Yeah, sure. I tell him about hunting in Romania. We hunt together." Bartyakov's tongue licked his *Schlagobers* moustache.

"Really? Has he already acquired a gun?" Klaus smiled.

Bartyakov shrugged with that special distancing nonchalance characteristic of any Russian dealing with authority. That shrug usually hid a special interest in or knowledge of the subject.

"He is on probation until the end of the year, Herr Bartyakov, and cannot obtain a hunting license anywhere in the European Union. He also cannot obtain a gun license. Unless he thinks he knows a way to circumvent our laws."

"No license, OK. We hunt maybe in spring. I tell him Sunday. We picnic in Vienna Woods."

"What will you tell him?" Klaus frowned.

Bartyakov shrugged again. "I tell him I call for hunting license and Romanians said no. Simple." Bartyakov glanced at his watch. "I have rehearsal with soprano. Margareta Baum. I accompany her in recital in three weeks."

"A good job?" Klaus asked. He knew the Russian had a

flourishing business accompanying other music students for their recitals.

"Excellent. But after graduation, I must find solo work, you know? It's not my idea I always accompanist." Bartyakov extended his hand again. "I call you if anything happen, Inspector. But no one bother Evan. He work hard now preparing programs to conduct. *Auf wiedersehen.*"

"*Auf wiedersehen*, Herr Bartyakov." He had the feeling the Russian hadn't told him everything, but the hunting trip had been Bartykov's idea, not Quinn's. The hunting trip was not a covert operation for an American spy. Klaus sighed and headed for the counter to order an iced coffee to go.

Gustav Mahler's Fifth Symphony told a story. Each person who listened to the symphony might hear a different story depending upon that person's thoughts and emotions at the time and his past experience. Someone might hear the story of a tragic death transformed into ecstatic revenge and victory. Someone else might hear a call to arms, fierce battles, and the triumphant end of a war. Another might hear the end of a love affair, loss, confusion, and wild despair, followed by the jubilant discovery of another love. They were all correct. That was the transcendent personal in the universal connection of music. In his research, Evan had found that Mahler had described his symphony as a new beginning which implied the end of something. Reading the score, Evan heard the story of his own defection, an act that marked the end of one life and the start of a new one in a foreign land, working toward his complete freedom and success as a conductor.

The symphony's score lay open before him on the music stand by the front window. He had gone through each movement several times, thinking how to deal with the tricky tempo changes, singing passages, playing sections on his violin, and marking potential problem spots in the score. He wrestled with the friction between what Mahler had heard in his mind and written on the page, and what he heard in his mind and would recreate in concert. He strove always to conduct the composer's score, the composer's music. He wanted his first performance of this symphony to be such pure Mahler that conductor Evan Quinn disappeared.

The light had faded in the room. Thunder rumbled in the distance, barely audible. A slap of wind whipped the trees outside his open windows. He hoped a storm would clear the soupy, muggy air that had plagued Vienna for the last month. A Caine "Summer Wind" storm followed by a week of light, steady rain and cooler weather would bring relief, although the forecast had predicted only a fifty-percent chance of rain.

The Vienna Philharmonic gig was six weeks away, plenty of time to finish his preparation, including the Sibelius Violin Concerto for the concert's first half. He loved this concerto and looked forward to working with the young Finn the Philharmonic had invited to play it. He also prepared for his October and November gigs, studying scores new to him by Caine, Shostakovich, and Stravinsky, and reviewing familiar scores by Beethoven, Mozart, Dvořák, and Rachmaninoff.

He hadn't programmed the Barber *Adagio for Strings* again. The Barber had done something in the first concert that caused him to black out or something, he still wasn't sure what had happened. While in Amsterdam, he needed to move forward from it rather than think about it so that the concert the next evening would go on without a hitch. The Barber had been fine for the second concert. Memory lapses happened, which is what the Concertgebouw musicians assumed had occurred to him. Now, Evan didn't think it had been a memory lapse but something else triggered by his memories that had been brought up by the music.

At least Amsterdam had been more of a success for Perceval. He'd been threatened, his training had taken over and he hadn't been afraid which surprised him. He'd been angry that night, angry at Valerie Peters, angry at himself for trusting her, and he'd used his anger for the energy and clarity he'd needed to defend and protect himself. They hadn't taught him that in training, but he would always remember it. He understood, however, that uncontrolled emotions could destroy focus, just as in conducting. Control was essential. They hadn't told him to expect powerful feelings afterward, either. Only Brown had mentioned the power rush, adrenalin crash, the horniness. His training had been incomplete. He was proud of his convincing act of the upset and horrified conductor. Brown never suspected how much he'd enjoyed that power rush. Brown never suspected that he could have easily killed him. His cover remained intact.

Sasha's barking in the back yard brought him back to the present. He glanced out the window at the overcast sky. As much as he hoped for rain, he wanted it to hold off until after his target practice. Since his return, he'd carried the Ruger in its case to Pötzleinsdorfer Park three times at night and used the night vision scope and silencer. He'd shot squirrels and birds, tree trunks, branches and leaves. Since Amsterdam, he wanted to practice shooting, wanted to work out regularly at the Fischer School of Martial Arts, wanted to sustain the power he had felt that night near the Dutch city's harbor. He wanted Perceval in top shape, always ready for anything.

"*Fernseher* BBC," he said to his house computer as he headed for the kitchen. As he made his dinner, he listened to the news summary on TV: an earthquake had hit Ethiopia with a magnitude of 8.1 on the Richter scale and humanitarian relief rushed to the area; a terrorist bombing in Sydney, Australia, had killed one hundred and wounded hundreds more, al-Qaeda claimed responsibility; the summer Olympic games would open in Berlin August fourteenth despite international tensions and increased terrorist activity; Taipei had announced the process for the reintegration of Taiwan into China; and the International Space Station reported the successful completion, in partnership with the Chinese Space Station, of the first phase of construction on the dry dock for space ships.

Evan poured his steaming hot dinner from the microwave bag onto his plate and carried everything into the front room. For the evening, he watched two classic American movies he'd never seen: **Serpico** and **Indiana Jones and the Last Crusade**. He understood why the NEP had banned each of them with their themes of individual initiative and challenging authority. He loved Indiana Jones.

Close to midnight, Evan changed into black jeans and a

black long-sleeved T-shirt. He pulled the Ruger case from its hiding place in the wall cabinet by the back window. "*Licht abstellan*," he commanded his house computer. He left his apartment in darkness, in stealth, and walked on the soundless grass next to Freda's gravel driveway. Freda's house was dark. No sign of Sasha, either.

He avoided the pools of light cast by the streetlamps, moving through the shadows closer to the sleeping houses he passed. He gazed up at the loamy night sky, the clouds ripe for rain. The air smelled of freshly mown grass and the hint of flowers over dankness, the smell of humidity. The wind had died down, never a good sign before a thunderstorm. Tonight, he had planned a new route to the park to avoid attention and detection. He turned up a slight incline, passing an open café with customers talking and singing old Vienna songs at the sidewalk tables. He checked them in his peripheral vision. No one showed any interest in him. No one stood as he passed.

Twenty minutes later, he squatted in darkness behind a broad oak tree deep in the park, assembling and loading the sniper rifle. Lightning flickered in the sky above. He had maybe half an hour before he'd have to race the storm home. He studied the target line of trees on the other side of an expanse of green grass. The nearest street and light in any direction was out of sight and hearing. He wanted to test the Ruger without the silencer.

He positioned himself behind the oak and aimed at the tree line, the night vision scope giving him a clear view of specific trees, branches, even leaves. A pair of eyes flashed above a branch. An owl. He braced himself, targeted and fired. The owl fell. The gunshot blended with grumbling thunder, closer now. He scoped for another target. Greenish lightning, tinged violet and red, bled through the black sky. A gust of wind jostled him from the side. He checked the northwest sky where a layering of storm clouds in shades of white, gray, and black in an anvil configuration over the Vienna Woods bore down on him.

Another sound penetrated the wind and rumbling thunder. He listened. The up and down repetition of a siren's musical fourth interval. Confident the siren would pass by the park, he braced himself against the oak and aimed again at the line of trees. Through the night vision scope, he spotted movement in the branches to the right of the owl's tree. He braced himself again and fired at the shadow. Something dropped to the ground.

The siren wailed closer. The trees creaked and moaned in a sudden mauling wind gust. The storm had moved fast. The siren moved faster. To his surprise, a police car with flashing blue and white lights and high intensity headlights careened onto a pedestrian path across the meadow to his right. Another silent police car with lights flashing appeared to his left.

He dropped to the ground, disassembled the rifle in seconds as he'd trained to do, and closed the case. A human shadow sprinted out from his target line of trees toward the police cars. The image of the lighted café came into his mind, the customers at the sidewalk tables. He hadn't marked anyone following him. He hadn't done a surveillance detection run. He hadn't plotted an escape route. He hadn't thought it necessary. Sloppy and stupid. Possibly a life-threatening mistake. Stay calm. Think. An escape route out of the park, now.

The police cars stopped on the grass fifty yards away and the doors opened. Cops slid out using the car doors as protective barriers.

He sensed the strike before his brain registered the brilliant jagged thread of lightning snake out of the sky to a tree six or seven yards behind him. The air buzzed and the tree exploded into white-hot light, sparks and yellow flame. Simultaneous thunder cracked, the sound of granite splitting.

Use it. Move. Evan scurried away behind the oak, dodging sparks, pushing against the bushes with the Ruger case to create a path. He paused for a second to check back. The wind shook the branches and bushes back and forth. Shouts and beams of light danced toward the oak. He pushed clear of the bushes and sprinted through a dense grove of trees. Lightning pulsed through roiling clouds, thunder pounded, the wind tore at the trees.

He ran as fast as he could buffeted by the wind until he reached the park's north edge. A river blue police car crawled past under a streetlamp fifty yards away, its lights flashing but its siren silent. Something hard hit his shoulder. He looked back but saw no one among the trees behind him. He looked up. A hailstone stung his cheek. A moment later, the clouds poured buckets of hail pebbles onto the earth, obscuring the green grass. Hail was not a good sign. He needed to find shelter. Lightning strobed now, the constant growl and roar of thunder its accompaniment. Ferocious wind whipped the giant raindrops into horizontal knives. Evan squatted under an old oak tree, knowing the risk of another lightning strike but its branches the only shelter available. The police car on the street blocked his route home.

He had to hide the Ruger someplace. If he met anyone, the rifle would incriminate him. Without it, he could talk his way out. He was a famous American orchestra conductor out for a late-night stroll and caught in the storm. He shivered. The wind had turned cold. Perceval needed to hide the rifle and go home.

Deep in the grove of trees at the park's edge, he searched for a suitable hiding place, ignoring the gusty, soaking rain. Distant shouts. He shifted to the right and his foot sank in mud. His footprints in the mud provided his pursuers with his path. He jogged on his toes in circles, obliterating the footprints. Still on his toes, he leaped through bushes on his right to a grove of mixed evergreen and deciduous trees where evergreen needles, grass and dead leaves covered the ground. Only light rain came through the thick ceiling of branches. Evan heard more shouts, closer. Straight ahead, he spotted a mature maple tree in a lightning flash. Across the grove opposite the maple, he wiped the mud off his shoes.

Shouting erupted yards away where he'd squatted by the oak. Too close. If he could hide in the maple tree…he wedged the Ruger case on a lower branch and swung himself up. The last time he'd climbed a tree he'd been twelve or thirteen years old. He reached down for the case, secured it on another branch farther up. He climbed with slow care so as not to lose his grip in the darkness.

Two uniformed policemen with flashlights entered the grove as Evan reached dense, full branches that hid him from view. They followed his footprints to where he'd cleaned off his shoes, searched the ground for more footprints. In slow motion, he pulled the Ruger case up from the branch below. Thunder roared overhead. A vicious wind gust wrenched the top of the tree. He embraced the trunk with the Ruger case between it and his torso.

The two cops persevered in their search for footprints. Minutes passed. They finally each straightened and shook their heads in defeat. One cop called someone on his shoulder-mounted radio. They left the grove. Safe above ground in the tree, sheltered by the full branches, Evan checked his digital watch, wiping rain from his face with his other hand. He would give the cops an hour.

The wind began to subside, but the rain continued, blurring the cloud-to-cloud lightning above. A lousy night. He had screwed up. If the cops caught Perceval, he could kiss his musician's life good-bye. From now on, protecting Perceval was critical to his life as a musician. He could not be caught. Any time he engaged in Perceval business, he needed to *think like* Perceval, not Evan Quinn. Now he understood that Perceval also needed to protect and insure the survival of Evan Quinn, conductor. The one was but the shadow of the other.

He sat in the maple's upper branches, thinking, oblivious to the rain diminishing and the thunder hiccuping in the distance. When he checked his watch again, almost two hours had passed. He listened. Water dripped from the branches around him. Think like Perceval. The cops would patrol the park's perimeter, waiting for him to come out. He wedged the Ruger case between two upper branches and the trunk and climbed down. The Ruger would stay hidden there until the situation cooled off and he could retrieve it.

The rain had soaked his clothes and his feet squished in his running shoes. Shivering in the cool air, he emerged from the park near the oak tree facing the street. No police car waited on Pötzleinsdorferstrasse. He checked around. Water dripped from trees, melting white hail covered the grass but he heard no voices or shouts. He saw no one in the area.

Surprised, he sprinted to the street and jogged at an easy pace past dark houses and apartment buildings, shops, and cafés, to Türkenschanz Platz. The small plaza was deserted, no sign of police. From the plaza, he jogged home.

His house computer had closed all the windows. The air conditioning hummed. "*Schlaf gut*," he said to the computer which flicked off the front room lights. As he walked through to the bathroom, he stripped off his wet clothes. He hung them over the side of the tub, splashed warm water on his face and fell onto his bed. His last thought before the blissful darkness of sleep: he'd been lucky. The police hadn't thought like Perceval. But he couldn't practice shooting anymore in that park.

A warbling bird woke him. Sunlight streamed through his bedroom windows. The house computer had turned off the air conditioner, opened the windows and turned on the ceiling fans. The videophone warbled again in the kitchen. With a groan, he forced himself up, pulling a white bed sheet over his nakedness. He approached the warbling videophone with "Hello?"

The monitor flashed on the concerned face of Klaus Leiner, who sat behind a cluttered desk in a modest office, beige filing cabinets behind him. His steady gray eyes locked on Evan. "Good morning, Herr Quinn. I apologize if I have woken you."

"Apology accepted, Inspector. I slept like a rock last night. Felt great."

"You did not hear the storm?"

"We got a storm?" Evan pulled a chair away from the oak kitchen table and sat down facing the phone. "About time."

"Herr Quinn, I thought you ran early every morning." Leiner smoothed his dark blonde moustache once and picked up a coffee mug from the desk.

"Yeah, I usually run early." He ruffled his hair. "I needed the sleep this morning. What's on your mind?" Evan pulled the sheet up around his shoulders.

Leiner nodded, his eyes narrowing. "I am calling to warn you about a dangerous situation in Pötzleinsdorfer Park. Someone has been using the park for target practice, shooting squirrels, birds, and other wildlife. We almost caught this person last night but he escaped in the storm. You live close to the park, Herr Quinn. If you have used it for your runs, please consider a different route for a few weeks."

"Sure, thanks for the warning." Evan nodded, yawning in order to suppress a smile. "You have any leads?"

"Several. My colleagues in your district are checking them today." Leiner's eyes looked beyond the camera and he reached toward his phone. "Stay away from the park, Herr Quinn."

Several leads. His stomach cramped, expecting the door-bell to ring and the police at his door. No. They could not possibly suspect him. He was just a conductor, after all, an American immigrant on probation and not a gun owner. Perceval smiled.

Chapter 21

"Here! Evan, pass it here!" Sofia ran down through the summer meadow toward the goal of branches stuck in two one-liter bottles positioned seven feet apart. Evan feigned a move to the right. Greta copied him.

"No, you!" Greta said as he veered left.

"Go, go, go!" Evan passed the soccer ball to Sofia. He sprinted ahead to defend her right from Vasia. Greta cut in from the left to steal the ball. Sofia swerved the ball back behind Greta. Vasia whirled around to a defensive position in front of the goal.

As Greta came at her again, Sofia feinted left and passed the ball to Evan. He stopped within twenty feet of the goal, his foot on the ball, facing Vasia.

"You never make goal, Evan. Never in million years." Vasia rushed him. Greta ran in to guard the goal.

Evan tapped the ball to Sofia who sent the ball soaring inches beyond Greta's outstretched hands and between the bottle goals.

"Nooooooo!" Greta threw her arms up in despair to the blazing sun in the milky blue sky.

"Game point," Evan said. "Best two out of three?"

"We need break," Vasia said, wiping sweat from his face with the bottom of his white tank T-shirt.

"Next time, women versus men," Greta said. Sofia slid her arm around Greta's waist with a smile and a nod.

Vasia shrugged. "Not fair match. Women better than men."

The two women laughed. Vasia gave Evan's arm a playful punch and waved him toward the picnic oasis they'd created earlier in a circle of beech and maple trees at the edge of the meadow. "I need drink," the Russian said.

"*Ach, Mausl,* we must leave soon," Greta called after them. She walked over by the goal to a pink towel on the dried green grass. Sofia picked blue and yellow wildflowers a few feet away.

"Vasia, does Greta have to work every Sunday?"

"Never on Sunday. But she help another producer today. He travel to funeral in Munich."

Vasia flopped down on the pale green cotton blanket Greta had brought. Evan collapsed next to him and wiped down with another pink towel. The shade from the trees felt good. Despite the storm the previous week, the weather had continued hot and sultry. At least today a light wind cooled them. Evan watched the two women, talking as they collected flowers and the soccer ball.

"Now they talk about us. We talk about them," Vasia said, giggling. "Everybody need love, Evan." He bumped Evan's upper arm with a cold bottle of mineral water. "You and Sofia good team." He swiveled and yelled, "*Dushenka,* water?"

Evan snorted. Vasia's obsession with women was the second most predictable thing about him. At least the first was music.

"*Ja, Mausl*," Greta called back, waving.

"Stop it," Evan said, opening the bottle with a violent twist.

"What? Stop what?" Vasia gave him an impish look but his eyes were contrite.

Evan squeezed the bottle in his hand, thinking if it were Vasia's throat, he could end the Russian's obsession with his love life. "It's none of your business, Vasia."

Vasia grinned. "OK." He leaned on one elbow, swigged from his mineral water bottle, his eyes on Greta picking up the goal bottles. "I am absolute lucky man, Maestro. Lucky to live in Vienna, to do what I love and to find Greta. I not understand before the importance of balance. You know? To balance parts of life, like with mind, body, heart, and soul."

Evan thought of balancing the sound of an orchestra. If one section played *fortissimo* when it wasn't supposed to, it could throw off the music, sour it. He needed to find a balance between Perceval and the conductor. He preferred the latter, but craved the power and control of the former.

Sofia laughed at something Greta had said. Maybe about him. She wore her long froth of curly chestnut brown hair in a pony tail halfway up the back of her head leaving her face and neck naked and vulnerable. Her hazel green eyes sparkled like lake waves catching sunlight. He wanted to slide his fingertips under her yellow tank top and across her smooth skin, hold her slender waist in his two hands. What would Sofia think of Perceval?

"Evan!"

"What?"

"You not listening to me," Vasia said, nodding toward Sofia and Greta.

"You're right. What did you say?"

"I call Romanian National Travel to arrange our hunting trip, OK? We must postpone now."

"Why?" Evan frowned at the Russian.

"You are in probation until January for all European Union including Romania. No hunting or gun license. We can hunt bear and wolf next year."

Evan sighed. "Too bad. I've got that gig in Bucharest in October. It would have been perfect." Sofia and Greta strode up the hill together, each carrying a nosegay.

"You hear from Moscow? Maybe we can make week together after Moscow."

"Oh. Ye-ah. Nigel called late last night. Moscow approved my request for the soloist for the Caine Piano Concerto. You've got the gig."

Vasia rocketed off the blanket, leaping into the air with a whoop. "*Da, da, da!*" Vasia shouted, dancing a jig around Evan on the blanket.

"What's happened?" Greta said as she and Sofia reached them.

Vasia grabbed her, swung her into the air sending the goal bottles and flowers flying. She squealed in surprise. Sofia stepped back, laughing. Evan had never seen such exuberance, such complete and uncensored and spontaneous emotion from anyone, not even Joseph Caine. This response alarmed him at the same time he found it irresistible. Vasia was fearless.

"It's just a concert, Vasia," Evan said. "Probably the first of many, but it's still just a concert."

"I play Caine concerto with Evan! I go to Moscow! I play Caine with Evan!"

"That's wonderful!" Sofia said, smiling at Evan. She dropped the soccer ball on the blanket.

"Put me down, *Liebchen*!" Greta pummeled Vasia's shoulders. He set her on her feet but enveloped her in a hug.

"I play Caine concerto with American conductor who know Joseph Caine, who learn from him. In Moscow where all my family can come to listen. Best possible concert. Thank you for opportunity, Maestro."

"I'll check my schedule to see if the week after is open for our hunting trip." He got up from the blanket.

"You are still planning the hunting trip?" Greta said. Vasia puppy kissed her face. "Enough, Vasia. We must collect our things and go or I'll be late for work."

Evan gathered trash in a biodegradable bag. Vasia and the women packed up Greta's basket, and raided Sofia's cooler for ice to rub on the backs of their necks. They headed downhill through the meadow to the pedestrian path that led back to the parking lot a half mile away. Greta and Vasia, swinging the picnic basket between them, sauntered ahead. Sofia walked next to him, so close that her presence blocked everything else from his mind. Their bare arms brushed once. This was the fourth time he'd seen her, and they hadn't really talked alone.

Sofia smiled up at him. "A perfect day, *nicht*?"

He nodded. Her smile for him and only him in this

moment sent a rippling thrill through his body. He wanted to say something witty and intelligent to impress her.

"Nature is essential for the soul," she said, her smoky alto voice soft. "Essential for the inner music in life." Her eyes met his and darted ahead. "When I was a little girl, my father taught me that nature nourished the soul, that being in nature is being in the true church of the spirit."

"My mother believed," Evan began and stopped. Sofia's eyes rested on him, black eyebrows raised. He caught her scent, a spicy perfume that conjured a memory of his mother baking apples. "Well, what she told me she believed," he said. "She told me not to listen to the ministers or the priests because we didn't need them to be one with the universe. With God, I suppose she meant, but she never used that word. She said that the divine creative energy existed in every individual and every animal, object and plant. The relationship with God existed inside from birth. The clergy was not as necessary for a person's spiritual growth and relationship with God as the clergy wanted people to believe. Uncle Joe said the same thing."

Sofia nodded. "Humans created religion to celebrate and try to understand the world, themselves, and the divine. Like all human creations, it is not perfect." She looked up at the sky, eyes squinting in the sunlight. "I feel nature everywhere and in my body. My body is the home of my soul, my consciousness, my direct connection with the divine creative energy, as your mother said."

"You turtles!" Vasia wagged his finger at them. "Too slow."

They had reached the pedestrian path where Vasia and Greta waited for them.

"I must leave for my job," Greta said. "Evan—"

"I'll drive Evan home, if that's in order with him," Sofia said, smiling.

"Sure," he said. More time with her, her eyes, her voice, and alone. He threw their garbage bag into the concrete trash receptacle by the path. "You guys go ahead. I'll talk to you tomorrow, Vasia."

Greta kissed Evan on the cheek and Vasia hugged him. He'd never been comfortable with male hugs, not even as a child. Aware of Vasia's body, his hands on his back, his own body's stiffness and discomfort, Evan stepped away.

Vasia grinned. "Let's go, Greta. We leave Evan and Sofia alone now." The Russian grasped Greta's hand and pulled her along the path.

"I love movies," Evan said, "How many movies have you done?" He wanted Sofia's eyes on him not on Vasia's glee in leaving the two of them alone together.

Sofia laughed, the sound low and sweet. Her fingertips brushed his arm for a second to invite him to stroll with her. "I have worked in fifteen movies. A gallery of diverse characters." She laughed again.

He felt that her voice pulled him into the warmth of her.

"I have played a woman obsessed with revenge in a psychological suspense script, the villain, which I loved. I want to play a villain again. Villains are the most interesting characters. I have played a detective in a mystery, a princess in an historical drama, a peasant in a war movie, and I can't remember the others." She took a mock dramatic breath.

He was surprised she loved villains. "**The Distance Between Two Points**," he said.

"*Ja*, of course! How can I forget? I love your father's writing, his poetry, and I felt honored to work in the movie of that novel. I own all his books published in London. I read them in English, the original language, although they have been translated into German and many other languages."

He nodded, his eyes on the path ahead. She spoke with ease and confidence, her English musical with a lilt and faint German accent. He felt inadequate to her ease and confidence. They approached the turn that led back to the parking lot.

"Have you read your father's books?"

"No." He avoided her eyes, afraid of her disapproval. "He gave me Caine's music to read instead."

"You must miss him."

"Everyone makes such a big deal about Randall Quinn. Believe me, he wasn't a big deal. Far from it. And he's dead. End of story." He fisted his hands.

They rounded the turn in silence. He estimated another quarter mile to walk to the parking lot, too far and yet too short a distance.

"I am so sorry, Evan. I did not mean to hurt or offend you."

"You prefer to work in movies or in the theater?"

"You prefer not to talk about your father?"

"Joseph Caine was more a father to me as well as a mentor." He peeked at her in his peripheral vision.

She swung the cooler back and forth, her head bowed. "I have an extra copy of **The Distance Between Two Points**. I thought to give it to you, send it by e-mail, but if you prefer not…."

"No, no, I'd love it. Thank you." He swallowed hard, his mouth dry. He felt like he walked through a swamp, pulling against sucking mud. "I'd love to see your work."

But she rewarded him with a smiling glance. "I love the theater. To answer your question. I prefer to work on the stage. To me it offers the best challenge, you know, to work before an audience where there exists no opportunity for a second chance each performance."

"Like conducting," he said. "You only get one chance to do it right." And like life. And Sofia. And he was mucking this up but good.

"Yes, live performance. The same whether theater or concert."

"Is your next job a movie or a play?"

"A movie. In October. On location near Siena, Italy. Next month I will prepare with costume fittings, hair, make-up, rehearsals."

"You don't sound very excited."

"*Ja*, well, the script is good. The director is good. I miss the theater. The tour last spring gave me incredible satisfaction and joy."

"What play?" She was still talking to him. He felt on firmer ground and relaxed.

"**King Lear** by William Shakespeare. Do you know it?"

He listened to her describe her first professional experiences and her love for playacting as a child growing up in Zurich. He felt hyper-aware of her voice, her smile, her presence next to him, on edge and ready to run. They had walked halfway across the parking lot when a familiar voice pierced the air.

"Get the heretic's bastard!"

Evan spun around, his stomach a sharp knot. Across the parking lot strutted Harold and his Vigiciv gang, dressed in their uniform of black jeans, red T-shirts, and black and red striped vests.

"What is it, Evan?"

Sofia's voice jolted him. Hadn't she heard Harold? He shook his head as Harold and his gang approached. "You see those guys in red and black?"

After a moment, she said, "No. I see a family with two crying children."

His stomach clutched into another spasm. She faced the same direction as he, her expression a concentrated frown. When he looked back at the parking lot, he saw a thirtyish man holding an open blue and white beach umbrella over a woman and two children. The children wailed and begged to stay longer. No Harold and no Vigiciv gang.

His head expanded, threatened to drift on the breeze like a balloon and burst. The sensation disoriented him, encased him in a bubble of shimmering air. He looked down at his lean body, clothed in pale blue denim shorts and the peacock blue Caine T-shirt. He saw but couldn't feel his body.

"Evan?"

Sofia's hand grasped his right arm but he didn't feel it. She moved him to the side of the parking lot.

He had thought Brown had sent actors who resembled Harold and his Vigiciv gang to terrorize him. If they were actors, real people, Sofia would have seen them. She hadn't. She'd described the family in the parking lot and he'd seen them also. Harold and his Vigiciv gang weren't real. He had been seeing things all along.

She couldn't know. Sofia couldn't know that he was seeing things. Evan placed his left hand on his solar plexus and pressed. He felt it.

She pulled him into the shade near a silvery green Geister car and rubbed his upper back. He felt her hands, felt his feet, felt his lungs expanding with air and emptying.

"You are so pale, Evan. Are you ill?" she said, her voice full of concern.

"I...I think...too much sun," he rasped. His mouth was parched, his throat like sandpaper. "I'm really thirsty."

"*Ja*, too much sun is dangerous. None of us wore hats today. *Scheisse.*" She pulled an ice-cold mineral water bottle from the cooler and opened it for him. "Take a long drink. We remain here in the shade until you feel better. You want to sit?"

The cold liquid sliding down his esophagus shivered his body. Between drinks he breathed slow, deep breaths, as he breathed before going on stage, and visualized the length of his body until he felt the uneven, grassy ground under his feet. He scooped ice out of the cooler and held it against the back of his neck.

"Better?" Sofia said, her hand on his back. Her touch comforted him.

"Better, thanks. I was really thirsty." He surveyed the parking lot. The young family had left. A group of six teenagers wearing earbuds danced and whirled toward the entrance. At the opposite end, a group of ten or twelve people entered the parking lot from the large coffeehouse. A man with brown hair broke away from them. Bernard Brown.

"Let's go, Sofia," Evan said. "Where's your car?" He tossed the ice. Rivulets of cold water skittered down his back and chest. He hadn't seen Brown since Amsterdam. He had no reason to talk to the guy now, not with Sofia.

"This Geister," she said, pointing to the silvery green car. Like Greta's car, it reminded Evan of a bug-eyed blowfish. She unlocked the doors with a flick of the ignition card. "We can stop at my apartment, Evan, to send you the movie, yes?"

"Sounds fine." He opened the front passenger door, glancing across the parking lot. Brown gave him a big smile and a wave. Evan folded his body into the car.

The Geister's air conditioning cooled him during their quiet twenty-five-minute drive. He felt much better out of the sun. Like Juliana in Amsterdam, Sofia appreciated companionable silence that gave him time to think.

Why had he seen Harold and his Vigiciv gang? And more than once. They weren't real. Ghosts from his past. People had their ghosts that haunted them, their shadows, their sob stories. Some people whined about them, refused to get on with life and played the victim. They expected the world to give them what they wanted as compensation for their suffering. A free ride. Well, he wasn't a whiner. He wasn't a victim. No one need know about his shadows. They might think he'd lost his mind, have him committed, and he'd lose his music, everything he'd worked so hard for his entire life.

Sofia lived in the Eighth District, a ten-minute walk west of Schottentor. Her well-maintained apartment building, nineteenth century or older, stood on a narrow, winding street, an urban canyon, with similar six- and seven-story buildings of charcoal gray and dun. They crossed to her building's street door and into a wide entryway that smelled of damp stone. Straight ahead, sunshine filled an open atrium court-yard. She turned into a hall on the right, before the court-yard, and he followed her to the second door on the left.

The high ceilings in Sofia's apartment created an airy spaciousness in contrast to the homey clutter of the furnish-ings. A kimono hung on one wall in the living room. Fringed drapes framed the tall double casement windows. Hundreds of books, along with African wood sculpture, Matryushka dolls, a geode and other souvenirs from her travels crammed the bookshelves. A Persian rug covered the floor. Sofia ges-tured toward the sofa upholstered in a maroon, green and gold paisley velvet.

"Please be comfortable in my home, Evan. A pot of tea perhaps? Or something cold to drink?" She hefted the cooler against her hip.

"Cold, thanks."

She disappeared down a hallway. Her living room had no electronics wall. The bookshelves caught his eye. Oversized art books occupied two shelves near the ceiling, and below them two shelves of history books, including **A People's History of the United States** by Howard Zinn, and next to it **The New Economic Party and the Destruction of Democracy** by Adam Burns. The next shelf contained his father's books. He pulled out **The Brandy of the Damned**, his father's memoir of Joseph Caine. He remem-bered when his father had finished it in 2027, but his father hadn't let him read it.

As he opened the well-worn hardcover, Sofia carried in a tray with two tall tumbler glasses of ice and a pitcher of bubbling raspberry red liquid. "*Himbeersaft*," she said. "Sweet but refreshing." She set the tray on the coffee table, pushing aside magazines, a cell phone, and a tablet computer to make room for it. "What are you reading?"

Evan showed her the book's cover. "Uncle Joe called music the brandy of the damned."

"Interesting. Your father does not mention that." She picked up the tablet computer and asked, "What is your e-mail address, Evan?"

He gave it to her, and watched as her long, slender fingers picked out the movie file, attached it to the e-mail and clicked to send it.

"Thanks, Sofia." Evan returned the book to the shelf. "My father always wanted everyone to believe he was *the* authority on Uncle Joe but he wasn't."

"I understand." She smiled. "Your father had a brother, yes? Did you know him?"

His eyes moved to her bare, smooth skin above the tank top's scooped neckline. "Uncle Russell. He was a journalist in Boston. I met him once when I was five. He was killed during the First Purification." His fingertips touched her shoulder. Her skin felt warm, silken.

"I have an older brother, an older sister and many, many cousins. Was your family large?"

She hadn't flinched or moved away when he'd touched her. "Just the three of us in Minneapolis. My father's aunt lived in a Chicago nursing home. Everyone else died during the First Purification."

"How monstrous, those 'purifications.' You would have every reason, yes? To hate the NEP, the people who hurt you and your family."

"I don't hate them. I don't think about them."

She caressed his left cheek and on tiptoe kissed him lightly on the mouth. Her lips felt soft and tasted of raspberry. He slid his arms around her and kissed her. She responded, surprising him.

"Come with me," she whispered in his ear. She kissed his neck and released him. She slid her hand into his and led him into the hallway. He kissed her again and again, and she moved him step by kiss by step by kiss down the hallway to her bedroom. On the right, a wall of windows looked out on a garden. Straight ahead stood a broad bed canopied with white chiffon draped down around each corner post. Her hands caressed his back under his T-shirt. He held her face between his hands. He had held Valerie Peters' head between his hands. He kissed Sofia, her neck, her shoulders, and Valerie Peters left his mind.

Sofia laughed, low and throaty, her eyes wide as she gave him a gentle push back onto the bed. Falling back bothered him, but her body on top of his, her lips kissing his face, distracted him. He liked being kissed in this way and his mouth sought hers. Her hands slid his T-shirt up to expose his chest. She moved down his body.

He closed his eyes, his fingers curling her hair. An image pressed in behind his eyelids: the ceiling of his childhood bedroom with its field of stars and moons and planets that his mother had pasted there when he was a toddler. Sofia's hands opened his shorts. A hot flash of nausea spread up from his stomach. Her mouth kissed his abdomen. Another image clicked into place: the top of his father's head moving over his naked ten-year-old abdomen.

"*NOOOOO!*" He yanked his father's head away from his body and punched him hard. He threw his father onto the floor, and after a hard kick to his kidneys, ran out of the bedroom, holding up his shorts.

At the front door, he fumbled with the three locks, his hands shaking. He sobbed once, bent over to contain the hot nausea rising into the back of his throat.

"Evan, wait! Stay. Please. Talk to me."

He heard her voice, but couldn't face her. He had only the deadbolt to unlock.

"Evan, tell me what happened. Why did you hit me?"

"Leave me alone." His trembling fingers flipped the deadbolt and he depressed the door handle. She said he'd hit her? He hadn't hit her.

"Evan, please let me call Lothar Waage."

Her hands grasped his arm, his back. He opened the door and jerked away without looking at her. "Don't follow me," he said.

"I will call you."

He jogged out to the entryway as his father's clear, icy baritone replaced Sofia's voice: "I know you, boy. Without me, you're nothing. I'm the only one who knows you, always knows what you think, what you feel." He zipped up and secured his shorts as the connections came fast, the ending of that memory of his bedroom when he was ten, what his father had done to him, why Sofia's touch had triggered nausea and fear.

He was scum, worse than shit, worse than a plague, not worth shit. Not good enough for Sofia. Damaged beyond repair.

"Don't tell anyone our secret," his father had whispered, his face inches from his. "Not *anyone*. I know you. You're a good boy. You never tell. But if you do, I'll kill you."

You never tell. How many times hadn't he told? Of course, no one would have believed him. Everyone loved his father. No one would have believed. But he believed it. He felt the memory's sensations on his skin, in his body, tasted it in his mouth. He saw it in his mind. His father took what he wanted without thinking of others. He had known this all his life.

His body couldn't distinguish past from present. Sofia had done what his father had done but his father had done much more. He understood now why he'd been so careful to stay away from women in the past. It wasn't safe. Would Sofia tell? Maybe Greta. What could she say? Sofia didn't know.

His father couldn't hurt him anymore. His father was dead. He was no longer a powerless little boy trapped in an unbearable place of his father's creation. He was an adult now, and free, and...his father may be dead but he *still* interfered with his life. The anger flared, flushing his face with heat. He was strong now. His anger strengthened him.

Evan headed for the building's main door. Using the bottom of his Caine T-shirt he wiped his sweaty face. Why hadn't he remembered the rest of that memory before? How many memories had he hidden from himself? It had not been only his father's rages and beatings. Is that how memory worked? In selective pieces? Why hadn't he deleted them, forgotten them forever? Were they imprinted on his brain like "eat your vegetables," "don't play with matches" or "don't get into cars with strangers?" Would they always jump out at him from the darkness without warning to mug him? He needed to find how to stop them, defend himself.

He opened the main door, squinting in the sunlight. His father had done what he wanted with no regard for anyone else. He had remembered that always. The NEP operated much the same way. The anger simmered inside him. His anger made him strong, powerful.

He left the entryway, blinking in the bright sunshine. His breathing had calmed, the nausea had disappeared.

"Need a ride, Maestro?"

Brown's South Bronx voice startled him. Across the street, Brown leaned against a pale-yellow mailbox on the corner. He wasn't smiling and his arms were crossed over his chest. He wore a pink polo shirt and khaki pants. His brown hair shone in the sun. He looked so *normal*.

"Leave me alone." Evan rounded the corner onto Alster-strasse and set a brisk pace toward Schottentor. He heard running footsteps.

"Wait, Evan!"

Brown's hand grabbed his arm. He pivoted fast, boxed Brown's ears and threw him against the sand-colored corner building. He pinned Brown with his left arm across his chest and pulled back his right fist to beat in the American's face.

"Stop, man! Think about it!"

Their faces inches apart, Evan's eyes bored into Brown's. "They arrested the wrong guy. They should've arrested my father. They should've murdered *him*, not Caine."

Brown's expression softened. "Your dad was a piece of work. Caine should've lived."

Evan nodded. He'd said too much, blurted it out. He'd not give Brown anything else to use against him. He still was unsure if he could trust the guy.

"You're OK, Evan. You're safe. I want to help you. Give you a ride home if you need it. OK? Just chill, relax. OK?"

Brown's breath smelled of peppermint. Evan released him, stepped back with a deep gasp for breath. "I prefer public transportation."

"Wanna talk about it?" Brown followed him.

"Fuck off." The anger subsided again to a simmer. Business as usual.

"My college roommate used to say it was better to be pissed off than pissed on."

Evan turned to Brown. "As your roommate, he must have been pissed off most of the time."

Brown groaned. "At least you haven't lost your sense of humor. What happened with Karalis to make you so pissed off, Maestro?"

"Nothing."

"That'll do it." Brown grinned.

Evan realized what he'd said. "No, not that, not Sofia. Look, thanks for your help in Amsterdam, OK? That doesn't mean we're close buddies now." He resumed walking. Brown matched his stride.

"The café I found here is still for sale."

"Yeah? And how are the Chinese?" Evan enjoyed the sarcasm in his tone.

"Playing power games. I hope to hell these talks will stop them because they want to take over the world. I hate 'em."

Evan laughed. The laughter released pent-up tension, relaxed his stomach, his shoulders. The anger dissolved away. "Have you ever heard that saying, Brown, 'You can't live with 'em, can't live without 'em'?"

"Sure, but that's about women, not the Chinese."

"Yeah, but if the Chinese behaved, you wouldn't have anyone to complain about."

Brown cackled and stopped Evan with his hand on Evan's arm. "So, OK. You don't want my scintillating company. And I was going to invite you out to dinner, show you that café that would be such a great investment. See ya around, Maestro." Brown slapped his back once and headed up the sidewalk away from Schottentor.

Evan watched him, thinking that he liked Brown about as much as he disliked him.

Chapter 22

The list of subject lines and senders filled his office computer screen and continued on and on and on as Bernie scrolled down. He hadn't checked e-mail, TMs, or VMs since the previous Friday, only two days. About one third of the mail related to his diplomatic cover as Assistant Cultural Attaché at the Embassy. Another half, encrypted, concerned his work as the CIA Deputy Station Chief. The rest was from family and friends. Larry Morgan, Cultural Attaché and CIA Station Chief, delegated most of the CIA work to him while he took the lighter, less incriminating cultural tasks. Would Morgan's transfer ever come through?

Bernie opened an e-mail from his wife. She wrote news about her retired parents, projects for her public relations job, their daughters' preparation for school. She suggested he schedule his next home leave for Thanksgiving through the day after Christmas. No mention of the signed divorce papers he'd sent her. He sat back, chewing on his lower lip, unsure what to tell her.

"Clean up your office, Bernie." Morgan stood in the doorway, cradling a stack of files against his hip.

"Stop working me so hard, Larry, and I might."

"The Chinese are jerking us around again." Morgan

thumped into a metal and canvas sling back chair in front of Brown's cluttered desk.

"Yeah, I heard." Bernie laced his fingers together behind his head and put his feet up on his desk. Morgan hadn't noticed the sling back chair that he'd stolen from his office. His boss was usually more attentive and territorial. "No surprise there. So, what's new?"

"Transfer came through."

"Really?" Finally, he'd have the place to himself. "Where?"

"They pulled Harris from Beijing. They want me there."

Bernie laughed, a hearty rumbling of genuine amusement. "They must have heard how much you love the Chinese."

"Yeah? They like the way I've handled the situation with the talks here. *You* should've let those Arabs kill Quinn in Amsterdam."

Bernie met his boss' eyes. "And I told you before – have some terrorist group benefit? I don't think so."

Bernie had his friends in Washington, especially at the Pentagon. They'd alerted him to Morgan's exaggerated reports, always making himself look the hero. He knew that Langley had known nothing about Morgan's termination order on Evan Quinn but Morgan didn't know he knew. When Langley had found out about it, they hadn't rescinded the order. Nobody in Washington had claimed Quinn, and they didn't care if he died, either, confirmed by Jack Marshall on the E-Ring in the Pentagon.

Morgan snorted in disgust. "The Arab terrorists could have had him for all I care. Serve Quinn right." He dumped his files on top of the clutter on Bernie's desk. "Quinn's your problem now. Those are my actives. Keep a leash on our friend Sergei at the Russian Embassy. He really likes the hookers on Annagasse. I fly to Washington tomorrow morning for a week's home leave."

"Will Peggy go with you to Beijing?"

"Why would I want my wife with me?" Morgan unfolded his tall, gangly body and stood up. "She wouldn't want to go either. I can't say I'm sorry to miss the reception tomorrow night."

Bernie dropped his feet off his desk and poked at the pile of files. "Anything in here need my immediate attention?"

"Only Sergei. And clean up your office. I don't know who they'll send to replace me. Try to make a good impression for a change."

Bernie grinned at Morgan's departing back. With Morgan's transfer came his promotion to acting Chief of Station until Morgan's replacement arrived. He glanced at his watch. Evan Quinn usually worked out at the Fischer School around lunch. He needed to talk to him.

His wife's e-mail remained open on his computer screen. If not for the photograph he carried in his wallet, he wouldn't be able to remember her face. They'd waited too long to have children after he'd been assigned abroad. He barely knew his daughters and he regretted it, but they were well provided for and would have a good life. His oldest brother, a cop in Brooklyn, would keep an eye on them. He imagined Uncle Danny would be proud of him, proud of his plan.

His videophone warbled. Evan swung himself out of bed and pulled on the pale blue denim shorts he'd worn the day before. A cool breeze from the open kitchen windows ruffled papers and faxes on one end of his kitchen table. He greeted the videophone on the wall. The monitor clicked on to Klaus Leiner in the same office he'd called from before, sitting at a desk stacked with files, a computer to his left.

"Good morning, Herr Quinn. How are you?"

"Half asleep, Inspector," Evan said, yawning. Leiner's pleasant British-inflected English and his soft tenor voice were the cop's most effective tools for his interrogations, Evan reminded himself.

"No run this morning?"

"I'll run later. What's on your mind?"

Leiner shifted in his chair, smoothed his blonde hair. "Would you like to join me for lunch today? I promised Laura I would ask you about Amsterdam. We listened to the internet radio broadcasts of your concerts there."

Evan opened the refrigerator, took out a bottle and poured apricot juice into a clean glass from the counter. Leiner's steady gray eyes followed him. He didn't think he could decline the invitation. He was on probation.

"Sure, Inspector. I'd love to hear what you thought of the concerts. Will Laura join us? I'd love to meet her." He took a sip of his apricot juice.

"Unfortunately, Laura cannot join us today. Herr Quinn, this is the second time I've tried to call your cell phone and have received an out of service message. Does it need repair?"

His Georg cell phone worked fine. Then he remembered. The Mozart cell phone that he'd ditched in an Amsterdam canal. "Sorry, Inspector. I should have called and let you know. I took it to Amsterdam and either lost it or someone stole it. If you're getting an out of service message, that means no one's using it, right?"

Leiner's eyes were like lasers on him. "Correct. I am sorry to hear that you lost it. Dieter and I would like to replace it for you."

Evan lifted his juice in a toast to the screen. "Not necessary, but thanks." He thought of the cop's bugs in the videophone and the bookcase. Maybe time to kill them now.

Leiner nodded. "I shall pick you up, Herr Quinn, at twelve-thirty. I know an excellent restaurant in Grinzing I haven't visited in months."

"See you then, Inspector."

The screen went black. Evan exhaled. He'd rather spend his day on score study than lunch with Leiner. The cop's invitation also cancelled his regular work out at the Fischer School.

He listened to a Beethoven string quartet on Österreich Eins as he made breakfast. Japan and the Pacific Alliance challenging China's invasion of Taiwan had dominated the news the night before. The American western secessionist states would hold democratic elections to elect a bicameral legislature that would establish sovereignty and write a constitution. Another interesting news item last night: Amsterdam police had discovered the decomposing bodies of two unidentified Arab men and a Caucasian woman in an abandoned warehouse near the harbor in Amsterdam. Dutch authorities reported that evidence found at the scene suggested a murder-suicide. Valerie Peters and her two Arab terrorists. Thank you, Brown.

Evan set his plate of scrambled eggs, sausage and sautéed fresh tomatoes on the kitchen table and sat down to eat. Nothing about the Chinese-American talks on the news last night. Woody had predicted the Vice Chairman would show up in August. Today was August tenth. Waiting for the Chinese Vice Chairman pissed him off. He smiled, remembering Brown's college roommate's preference for pissed off, not pissed on.

He ate a bite of egg and tomato, savoring the flavors. Freda had left a bag of fresh vegetables from her garden by his door with an envelope full of recipes, including one for an Italian pasta sauce with eggplant that he planned to cook tomorrow with fresh tomatoes and eggplant from her garden. Cooking relaxed him more than he'd thought it would.

After a shower and a couple hours' score study of Stravinsky's *The Rite of Spring,* Evan waited by the driveway gate for Inspector Leiner. The scorching sun beat down on his head. He smelled Freda's roses on the breeze. Neither she nor Sasha had been around when he'd left his apartment.

Leiner's shiny black four-door sedan glided into the driveway entrance and stopped. The front passenger door swung open.

"Hey, Inspector," Evan said, sliding onto the maroon leather seat. Immediately he felt a vibration against his skin under his digital watch. Woody's bug detector detected a surveillance device within one hundred yards.

"How are you, Herr Quinn?" Leiner headed the car up Sternwartestrasse's gentle hill. "Awake?" Leiner smiled.

"Definitely, Inspector," Evan said, his eyes straight ahead. Was the bug on Leiner or in the car?

Leiner glanced at him, his face as unreadable as a rock. "In Neusiedl, you mentioned a manager you wanted to contact. Have you contacted him?"

They chatted amiably about Evan's score study and conducting schedule, the programs for the autumn gigs and how he decided what he wanted to conduct, usually with suggestions from an orchestra's staff. Leiner appeared interested in his life – like a friend. However, this cop was not his friend which was too bad. Leiner loved classical music. He was intelligent, a family man who lived in his neighborhood, a congenial man, but his occupation threatened Evan, threatened Perceval. If his life were different...but he could not imagine Leiner ever letting go of his suspicions.

At the *Heuriger* restaurant, Evan followed Leiner and a waiter through a full dining area with subdued lighting, polished wood paneling and intimate booths as well as tables on the floor. Mounted stag and boar heads hung on the walls, interspersed with paintings and lacquered grape vines. Diners glanced up as they passed and returned to their conversations and meals. An occasional outburst of laughter broke the clubby atmosphere. The scent of wine mixed with the smells of mustard, baking bread and roast beef. The waiter led them to a table under a trellis by a large oak tree in the back. No other diners occupied tables in this garden area. Woody's device continued to vibrate. Leiner was wired.

Leiner ordered for both of them, one eyebrow raised to Evan who nodded his approval.

"You know, Inspector, it's not always a good thing to be recognized."

"What do you mean?"

"People have expectations. They see me as a famous American conductor and they either want to invite me to dinner to meet their daughter or kill me."

"Kill you?" Leiner frowned. "Who has tried to kill you, Herr Quinn?"

A young woman wearing a dirndl served them their drinks from a round silver tray.

"The Uighur terrorists. You know Bernard Brown, that guy at the meeting in Dieter's office? I've run into him at the Fischer School. He's told me all kinds of terrorists have an interest in kidnapping or killing me."

"Herr Brown cautioned you about terrorists?" Leiner's eyebrows rose as he sipped his white wine. "I had not thought the Americans would have concern for your safety. What is Herr Brown's interest?"

"Oh, I think he just wanted to scare me. But people recognize me, watch me, approach me for autographs or to talk. After Brown's warning, I like the attention even less. I'd prefer anonymity. A Russian pianist I know introduced me to Sofia Karalis, the actress. She taught me about disguises."

"Disguises." Leiner sat back, his jaw slack.

"Yeah, nothing radical. With a little disguise, I can attend concerts, shop, whatever and no one recognizes me. I've regained my anonymity. I feel safer, you know? I like running in Pötzleinsdorfer Park. Have the police caught that target shooter yet?"

Leiner frowned. "Not yet. The police patrol the park and

have it under surveillance, but I would suggest running elsewhere for the next few weeks."

"The cops think the guy will return? It's been all over the news." The melodious ring of his Georg cell phone interrupted him. Leiner reached into his navy-blue suit jacket pocket and pulled out his silent cell phone. "It's mine," Evan said, pulling out the sleek black ringing phone and flipping it open. "Probably Nigel. Hello?"

"Georg," Woody Lewis' spry voice said in his ear. "Our friend arrives tonight. The party's tomorrow evening."

Evan grinned at Leiner, who raised his wine glass to drink. "Finally!" Evan said. "Have they suggested a program?"

"Ah. You're not alone. They're at the Inter-Continental."

"OK. I'll see what I can do. Talk to you later." Evan shut the phone, as Leiner's phone rang, playing the waltz from Tchaikovsky's *Sleeping Beauty*.

"Laura chose the ring tone," the Austrian said as he opened the phone. "Leiner," he said into it.

The Chinese Vice Chairman arrived tonight. Perceval needed the Ruger. With the cops all over Pötzleinsdorfer Park, Evan needed a way to retrieve the Ruger without being seen or caught. A problem. He wasn't sure where the Inter-Continental Hotel was, either.

Leiner stared at the Georg phone on the table. He responded in German into his phone that he would return to his office later. He shook his head as he dropped the phone into his suit jacket pocket. "Cell phones are the ultimate distraction. The ultimate social offense. They are a true hazard, also, in cars. I wish they hadn't been invented."

Evan sipped his mineral water. "Have you ever noticed

how everyone in a group will reach for their phones when one rings?" Leiner stared until Evan laughed. They laughed together. Evan slipped his Georg phone back into his pocket as he continued, "The Russian pianist I know told me about all the electronic gadgets I could buy now. I couldn't believe all the stuff. At least in Europe, the choices exist to be high tech or low, old fashioned or modern. I really like that. There is some value to the old ways, like the keys at the Four Seasons Pension. I decided on a cell phone but no Internet account for it, no games, no scheduling computers, no more gadgets. One cell phone and my house computer and videophone. I don't need anything else. But it's interesting how some people must distract themselves all the time, how they prefer noise over silence, machines over *Menschen*."

The waiter served their food. Evan ordered more mineral water.

Leiner sliced his grilled pork cutlet. "Herr Quinn, we understand Bernard Brown visited Amsterdam the same week as you. The two of you met?"

"Brown?" Evan cut a bite of his grilled venison. "No, I didn't see him."

Leiner ate a forkful of pork and potato. His silence made Evan think he should say more.

"I can't see Brown at a symphony concert. He's mentioned an Uncle Danny who loved classical music. But not Brown's type of music. Maybe country western or old rock and roll, not classical."

"You have said he has an interest in you, Herr Quinn."

Evan skewered a bite of fresh cucumber from his mixed salad. "All I know is he likes to harass me. You'll have to ask him, I guess. In Amsterdam, I was busy with rehears-als, attending concerts in the American Music Festival, and hanging out with the musicians." He crunched the cucum-ber. "But you know, Brown asked me once outside the Fischer School if I would be interested in a job at the CIA." To see Leiner's head snap up gave him a moment of satisfaction. "I told him no. Absolutely not. I have no interest in them or any other American agency, not now, not ever."

Leiner's eyes narrowed for a split second. "Have you met Woody Lewis?"

Evan laughed. "Oh, yeah. The Café Chicago. Several Vienna Philharmonic musicians told me about it. Lewis—" He caught himself. He'd almost said that Lewis had given him the Georg cell phone. "He's a real character. You know him, Inspector?"

Leiner nodded, his steady gray eyes studying Evan. "You talk often with him, Herr Quinn?"

"No, actually not often enough." He kept his tone light even as fear flipped his stomach. Had the cop made the con-nection somehow between him and Woody? Was the call to Leiner right after Woody's about a trace on Woody's call? He cut another piece of venison and piled mushroom rice pilaf on it as he spoke. "He really makes me laugh. I should stop by the café for a meal. I haven't eaten there since—" He looked up as if seeking the answer in the trellis overhead. "Yeah, I think it was the day you left me at the pension. Have you eaten at his café?"

"*Ja*, for the cheeseburgers. Anna loves them." Leiner sipped his wine, his head at a slight angle, his expression thoughtful. "The radio announcer did not explain the silence in the Barber *Adagio for Strings* during your first Amsterdam concert. I wondered what that was about, Herr Quinn?"

"Oh." Evan felt the heat rising from his neck. "I had a memory lapse, Inspector. It can happen." He had avoided talking about it, even with the Concertgebouw musicians. He'd had memory lapses before, and that hadn't been a memory lapse. It'd been more like some kind of black out. He'd pushed it far back in the farthest closet in his mind.

"Have you had that spider nightmare again?"

Evan's laugh rasped over his dry throat. "I'm fine, Inspector. No problems at all."

For the next hour, Leiner plied Evan with questions about the American Music Festival in Amsterdam and shared his experiences traveling with his family in northern Italy earlier in the year. The Austrian failed to admit to his fishing expedition over their lunch. The cop had nothing on him, although his questions about Woody and the Amsterdam concert made him nervous. Would Leiner put human surveillance on him again?

After the cop dropped him at his apartment, Evan changed to a T-shirt and shorts, and gave himself a light disguise of eyeglasses and a moustache, styling his thick black hair straight back from his face with a dab of hair mousse. He checked the address of the Inter-Continental on the internet. He picked up his wallet and Georg phone from the kitchen table on his way out.

The trip into the First District took approximately twenty minutes. A computerized feminine voice announced the stops along the way, and at each one, the streetcar screeched to a halt, the automated doors flapped open, and passengers disembarked. Evan scrutinized the people who boarded at each stop, plotting out in his mind a short surveillance detection to run when he reached the Ring Boulevard.

At Schottentor, Evan transferred to a Ring Boulevard streetcar. He spotted no one suspicious during the transfer. In fact, no one appeared to take notice of him at all which was totally opposite his usual experience. The light disguise worked. Evan got off at the north end of Stadtpark, diagonally across from Dr. Karl Lueger Platz. Motor scooters, bikes, and pedestrians made up the street traffic at this time of the afternoon. He memorized faces as he made his way south along the tree-lined Ring Boulevard. He doubted he'd see any of them again, but he needed to be careful. Be on the defensive. Evan continued up the middle of the shaded sidewalk, the park on his left and the wide boulevard on his right. People came out of the park and others entered it. No one gave him even a glance.

The activity around the Inter-Continental Hotel alarmed him. He circled it twice before pausing across from the main entrance. From his past experience at the Parkhotel Schönbrunn, he'd expected extra and visible security but this hotel had none, only the normal arrivals and departures of guests. He flipped open his Georg cell phone but his finger froze over the speed dial for Woody. If Woody's phone was bugged, it'd be wiser to talk to him in person. But he didn't have time to walk to the Café Chicago on the other side of the First District. He'd have to take the chance. He pressed speed dial.

"Our friends aren't at the hotel you mentioned," he said after Woody answered.

"I'll check it."

"As soon as possible. We have to find them."

Woody's dry chuckle filled Evan's ear. "You are such a virgin. Relax."

"I need another toy."

"What?"

"I had to hide it, so…."

Woody's chuckle turned into a giggle. "Why?"

"I can't join a club yet and I needed to practice."

Ten seconds of silence. "You're the one," Woody said and inhaled with a slight wheeze. "I'll see what I can do, but a rush order like this? Maybe not enough time. Think about retrieving your toy."

The disconnecting click in his ear sounded like a pistol cocking. Four laughing young girls came out of the hotel. He checked around. A familiar man stood military straight diagonally across from him. Evan's heart pounded. Was he real or a ghost? The man jogged across the street, sauntered up to him. Up close, there was no mistaking the wheat-blonde hair, ice-blue eyes and arrogant demeanor. Evan tensed.

"Hey, Evan, ol' buddy. Remember me? Harold. You look shocked. I like your minimal disguise." Harold's raspy voice still sounded like dried corn husks rustling in the wind.

"Not long enough." Evan took a step back from him. "What are you doing here?"

"Let's walk." Harold slipped his arm through Evan's and guided him toward the park.

Evan was *not* going for a walk with this guy in a park. He knew what Harold liked to do in wooded areas. He stopped. "You can tell me whatever the message is here. I haven't got the time to go—"

"OK, Quinn." Harold stood close, one hand on Evan's waist. "We have such pleasant memories, though, of us in a park together." Harold pulled Evan against him.

Evan pushed back at him, but Harold held him tight with both his arms.

"You better do what you're told, Quinn, or you'll have to answer to me. Understand?" Harold's breath smelled of bratwurst and beer. "I'm your shadow."

"What are you talking about?" He turned his face away from the American.

Harold's breath puffed against his ear. "Your assignment. You better show a return on the investment in you. Or you're dead."

Evan felt his anger rise, and with it, strength. He jerked his body away and pushed the American. Harold lost his grip on him. The surprise on Harold's face satisfied him.

"How did you get into Austria? Was it legal or would the police be interested in you, Harold? I don't want to ever see your ugly face again. Get lost. I have a job to do and *you* are not helping." He pivoted and walked at a brisk pace for the Ring Boulevard. Harold smelled bad. Woody smelled bad. What else bad could happen? He preferred not to go to the park tonight for his Ruger.

He had no other choice, however. In the evening, he forced himself to think of a plan to retrieve the Ruger as he sat cross-legged on his front room floor, canvas spread over the white carpet to protect it, cleaning his CZs. Arrayed on the floor to his right were a long chestnut brown wig, mirror sunglasses, a box of latex gloves, a navy-blue lightweight jacket, and a black gym bag. He couldn't use a light disguise for the park tonight in case a police patrol stopped him. He'd wear his running gear and jog through the park in the cooler midnight air. He wanted them to recognize him, a famous conductor out for a late-night run. The security system panel by the door chimed twice. The male computer voice said, "One male visitor."

Evan wasn't expecting anyone. His stomach soured at the thought of Harold earlier. And Leiner's questions. Sofia. The teen Harold hallucination. The memory lapse. And the disappearing Chinese. He looked down at the disassembled guns. *Schiesse*. Now what? The security panel monitor revealed Bernard Brown at the driveway gate, shifting from one foot to the other.

"Huh." Evan picked up the Georg cell phone, his wallet and went out, muttering to himself, "This is *not* a good time, Brown."

As Evan approached the driveway gate, Brown stopped pacing and flashed his trademark smug grin. "Hey, Evan. I need to talk to you." He glanced around fast.

Evan stood ten feet from the gate and said nothing, his anger flaring.

"Quinn, you could at least say hello. Is she home?" Brown nodded toward Freda's house.

Evan shrugged, shook his head.

"You're not going to invite me in?" Brown's green eyes darted back to Freda's house, to the neighboring houses and the street.

"Let's take a walk." Evan didn't know where Freda was and didn't want to take the chance of her seeing Brown. She asked him about his friends. Brown's nervousness bothered him. He sensed something was wrong.

Out on the sidewalk, he gestured for Brown to walk with him up Sternwartestrasse. "Ever been to Türkenschanz Park?" The American shook his head. "It's a nice family park, lots of people in the evenings."

Brown cleared his throat. "We've got a tail. Saw him following you that evening you visited Dr. Maas." Brown grinned.

Evan checked the street. The shadow turned into a driveway across the street and half a block away. He only caught a glimpse of the shadow's face, the knapsack, the earphones. Not Harold. "Shit, Brown. They see you talking to me, they'll think I work for you."

That smug grin. "Nothing illegal about talking, Maestro. You know Klaus Leiner works on security for the talks with the Chinese?"

Despite his anger, Evan took his time replying. The American had alerted him to the surveillance. Brown's obsession with the Chinese might prove helpful. "Yeah, I'm not surprised. I'd bet other security too."

"Sure," Brown said, nodding his head. "The federal police, maybe private contractors. What do you think of Leiner? He handled your case, right?"

Evan squinted up the street at two children on bicycles. "I'm surprised you haven't researched your object, Brown. Leiner's tough. He's smart. He's cagey. As far as the Chinese talks—"

"*Fuck* the Chinese," Brown said with a vehemence that startled him. "Man, I hate them. I don't get why they all just want to talk, talk, talk, and let the Chinese get away with their dissing power games. You know what they did? They announced this morning that their Vice Chairman will arrive tonight. Then they changed hotels. *Again*. It's the seventh or eighth time in what – not even six months. Jerking us around. And then what do they do? They demand that our delegation stay at the same hotel. They told our delegation the Vice Chairman preferred easy access and communication with *everyone*. Plus better security. Fuck them."

Brown's anger had increased his pace. Trees formed the perimeter of Türkenschanz Park on their right. Ahead, two young women pushed baby strollers toward the park's entrance.

Evan lowered his voice. "It's just a hotel change, Brown. Unless the hotel is far away, like in Klosterneuberg or something."

"Yeah, yeah," Brown said, also keeping his voice low. "I know. But it's their dissin' games." Brown sighed, finger combed his brown hair back from his face. "Not Klosterneuberg. They moved to the Hilton by Stadtpark. Which is a great hotel for the meetings, for security, for the central location. I wish they'd just stay put!"

Evan turned his head so Brown wouldn't see his relieved smile. Brown had saved him with the hotel information. As they entered the park, greeted by the sound of children's voices yelling, laughing, screaming in delight, Evan said, "Surprise them. Maybe the American delegation could thank the Chinese for finally settling at the best hotel in Vienna for the talks and security, and now they're there, finally, there's no reason to move again."

Brown grinned, nodding. "Come work for us. You're good."

"Never."

"Then buy a jazz café with me here. We'd work well together as business partners."

Evan threw his arms up in mock horror as Brown laughed. They approached the park's chess corner, every table occupied by pairs of people, young and old, male and female, concentrated on their next moves, some tables circled by observers. Beyond, near the giant sandbox where children dug holes and built the next generation of skyscrapers, he saw Blonde Man, the guy who'd followed him into the Café Chicago the first time. Blonde Man squatted next to a young boy with an orange plastic shovel and bucket.

"What did you want to talk to me about, Brown? Leiner? One of his men is over there with a kid. We need to leave."

"Sure." Brown pivoted and led him back the way they'd come. "Missed you at the Fischer School this morning. I was worried."

Evan faced him. "That's it? How are you not like the Chinese screwing around with me?"

Brown reached for his arm. "So where were you, Maestro?"

Evan stepped back, avoiding Brown's grasp. "Inspector Leiner invited me out to lunch. He still thinks I'm a CIA spy. And your visit tonight won't help my case."

Brown smirked. "I'll have a talk with him and set him straight."

"You do that. I've got work to do, Brown." Evan pointed back at the entrance they'd used. He spotted the shadow with the knapsack near it, too far away to hear them. "The streetcar stop is there if you didn't drive."

"See you around, Evan," Brown said behind him as Evan walked away, heading for another entrance he remembered as closer to his apartment. Blonde Man glanced at him but continued playing with the young boy.

Outside the park, Evan took out his Georg cell phone to call Woody. "I found them," he told Woody without preamble. "What's their schedule?"

"Good work, Georg," Woody said. "They'll leave the hotel early, sometime between four and five. I've talked with my supplier. He can't fill your order until the day after tomorrow."

"Forget it. I've got an idea." Evan smiled into the phone as he walked. "You'll hear about it, I'm sure." After the disconnecting click, Evan pressed the speed dial number for Vasia's phone. The Russian pianist answered on the second ring.

"Evan! When you come work with me on Caine Piano Concerto? Also Greta wants you to come for dinner."

"Well, can you come to my place tomorrow afternoon, say, around three-thirty? The dinner will have to wait. Ask Greta if the weekend works for her."

"OK, but tomorrow afternoon I have rehearsal with soprano Margareta Baum. We begin at three to prepare Paulus songs for her recital. You have piano now?"

Disappointment lowered the Russian's voice, but Evan wasn't disappointed. "Where are you rehearsing, Vasia? Maybe you could come here after."

"Her apartment in Thirteenth District. Not far from my old apartment in Hietzing. Better we wait, I think."

"Yeah, fine. We can get together later in the week at your place. My piano hasn't arrived yet." Evan felt a surge of relief. Vasia wouldn't be home the next afternoon and into the evening. His apartment was across from the Hilton, a perfect location for a sniper nest.

"Has Greta planted her garden on the roof yet?"

"Greta angry because roof door lock broken. But I tell her it's easier for her to carry plants and things to roof because door open."

"Listen, I'll help you fix it later in the week. No one else knows about it, right? So none of your neighbors are going to sneak in and steal from that pantry Greta loves so much?"

The explosion of laughter in his ear made Evan hold his phone away. After Vasia stopped, he said, "Nobody know, Evan. No neighbors, nobody."

"Great. Talk to you later." Evan flipped his cell phone closed. The next step: tonight case the state bus station next to Vasia's building and plot escape routes. He'd trick the Austrian shadows with a disguise. He could feel in every cell of his body that this plan would work and no one would know he'd done it.

Chapter 23

No one screamed or shouted. No one punched or kicked or brandished weapons. The early morning activity in the First District police station on this Tuesday, August 11, 2048, reassured Bernie for its reserve and courtesy. The place smelled of lemon disinfectant and the pale green walls and wood floor gleamed. The Austrians preferred cleanliness in all things: their streets, buildings, and homes, of their persons, and in their dealings with people. The Austrians were, more than anything else, polite in their dealings with each other and foreigners. Americans often perceived them as aloof. Bernie admired them for their masterful use of courtesy to obscure motive which reminded him of "Minnesota Nice" and the files secure in his briefcase. "Nice" hid secrets.

A uniformed beat cop holding the arm of a raven-haired hooker disappeared through a door to the right freeing the attractive young desk officer. Grinning, Bernie picked up his bulging leather briefcase and olive-green canvas duffel and sidled up to her.

"*Bitte sehr*," she said, her tea brown eyes flicking over his ivory linen suit, pale blue shirt, and blue satin tie.

"*Guten Morgen*," he said and continued in English. "My name is Bernard Brown. I am the Assistant Cultural Attaché at the American Embassy. I request political asylum in Austria." He slid his passport across the counter.

The cop had become a statue, her eyes wide. For a moment, he feared she hadn't understood. "*Haben Sie verstanden?*" he said, his voice soft.

"*Ja, ja, verstanden.* American," she said shaking her head as if to clear it, but she continued in English. "Your request is unusual, Mr. Brown. Are you certain?"

"Totally."

"Will you agree to a blood test, Mr. Brown, to determine if you are under the influence of any mind-altering substance at this time?"

"Yeah, sure. I'd like to speak with Inspector Klaus Leiner as soon as possible."

"I ask you now to state your name, citizenship, and why you are requesting political asylum." She pressed a key on the computer keyboard to her left to record his reply.

"My name is Bernard Brown. I am an American citizen and the Assistant Cultural Attaché at the American Embassy in Vienna. I am also the acting Chief of Station for the CIA at the Embassy. I request political asylum because I want to live in a democratic country. I want freedom. And I have files that I believe the EU countries will find interesting regarding CIA activities in Europe."

Evan jogged at an easy pace. He passed the neighborhood police station. Three uniformed cops nodded to him as he passed. Evan smiled to himself. The cops saw Evan Quinn, symphony orchestra conductor, out for a jog, not Perceval, trained assassin, burning off nervous energy. His cover made him feel invincible for a second. But he couldn't control everything and he knew anything could happen.

The Zentralsparkasse bank appeared to the right and one of his favorite neighborhood cafés across from it where a handful of people sat at tables outdoors in the early morning sunshine. The Lebanese owner brewed the best coffee. He heard his name and waved to the owner's son serving a customer at a sidewalk table. The car traffic had increased and people browsed the green grocer and bakery displays.

Following his usual routine was crucial on this particular day, August 11, 2048, not only for cop surveillance but to calm his nerves and maintain focus. After a cool shower and hearty breakfast accompanied by a Chopin Ballade on Österreich Eins, he played Bach on his violin for an hour to begin work. Bach gave his mind clarity and calmed his nerves. Then he settled into the chair by his front window to tackle more of the Shostakovich Fifth Symphony. He played the second movement on his loaner fiddle, enchanted by the cheeky quality of the theme. Joseph Caine had never talked about his influences or if he preferred one composer's music over another's. When asked, he had stated emphatically that his music spoke for itself and needed nothing further from him. However, Evan recognized echoes of Shostakovich in Caine's Fifth Symphony.

About nine-thirty, he grabbed his blue gym bag to go to the Fischer School. He looked forward to a strenuous workout. Before he'd reached the front door, his Georg cell phone rang from the bookshelf where he'd left it the night before. He'd almost forgotten it.

"Hello."

"Georg. How are you?" Woody said in a slow voice.

"Fine. Is something wrong?"

"I'm calling to wish you good luck."

"Relax, Woody. Don't be such a virgin."

Woody laughed, a dry, raspy sound in his ear. "Good luck."

"Thanks." Evan shut the phone. The old man's voice had sounded more like good-bye than good luck. Woody expected him to fail. Failure was possible, but he'd do whatever it took to succeed and win his freedom. He'd show Woody today the essence of Perceval. He slipped the phone into his denim shorts pocket and left.

The lesson at the Fischer School went well. Okada worked him hard and complimented him on his progress. Brown wasn't at the Fischer School. The American had been concerned about him the day before so where was the guy today?

Evan rode the subway from Westbahnhof to Wien Mitte, the state bus station next to Vasia's apartment building. He strolled down the street, casing the Hilton. Chinese security guards in black suits flanked the front entrance while uniformed Viennese cops walked the perimeter and stopped cars from parking in front of the hotel. He spotted guards on the roofs of the buildings around the hotel. They wanted to be seen.

He wanted to be seen, also. No surveillance detection on his way to the Café Danforth on the Wollzeile. In the café, however, he chose a back corner booth facing the front entrance where he could observe who entered and left but not be easily seen. The café's lunch crowd occupied all the tables and most of the front booths. No one looked familiar and no one took an interest in him except the blonde waitress with a smattering of freckles across her pert nose. She addressed him as "Maestro" and welcomed him back. He ordered the lunch special.

After lunch, he rode the subway from Wien Mitte to the Heiligenstadt station where he waited ten minutes for a Schnellbahn S45 to Gersthof. Both trains traveled faster than streetcars or buses. The Gersthof Schnellbahn station was only a five-minute walk from his apartment. One escape route, the preferred one, had been confirmed. He had plotted two others using alternate subway lines as well as streetcars and cabs.

A kneeling Freda weeded in her back garden and Sasha bounded out to greet him. He waved to Freda but he had no time for a chat. He needed to do a surveillance detection on his way back to the First District. He hadn't spotted any cop shadows so far, but after Brown's warning the night before he assumed they were there.

He called a cab and returned the Georg phone to a shelf in his front room. He packed the black gym bag for Perceval: a set of sweats, a pair of jeans, two plain T-shirts (one blue, one black), the Chinese Vice Chairman's photo from the *Village Spectator*, five pair of latex gloves, one CZ 9mm handgun with silencer and extra clips, the navy-blue lightweight jacket, and the long chestnut brown wig. In a small paper bag that also went into the gym bag he dropped a comb, the black bushy fake moustache that gave him a Mediterranean appearance and black-framed eyeglasses.

In the bathroom, he splashed cold water on his face and changed to jeans, a pastel blue Oxford shirt and running shoes. Passing through the bedroom, he glanced out the back windows. Freda and Sasha had gone into her house. A car horn honked. His taxi.

His surveillance detection began with running out to the waiting cab. The cop shadow, Blonde Man again, stepped out from a hedge half a block down the street and trotted to a parked blue car. The scowling cop flipped open a cell phone as Evan's cab left. The cab dropped him at Robert Waldstein's Ninth District address a block from Palais Liechtenstein where he found a taxi stand on the east side of the palace's modest park. He took another cab (and paid cash this time) to Paulus Platz in the Third District. He considered entering the Central Meat Market to check for following shadows, but after a quick walk around the plaza, he realized he was alone.

For ten minutes he wended through a congenial, quiet neighborhood of apartment buildings, passing a small church and park, until he found a café. Inside he ordered a *mélange* coffee and sat at a window table. No one followed him into the café. He drank his coffee quickly and went to the tiny bathroom: a toilet and small sink and not much room to maneuver but a mirror he used to apply the black bushy moustache. He changed to the black T-shirt. Using the comb and water from the sink, he slicked back his black hair. The black-framed glasses completed his light disguise. As he left the café, no one, not even the waiter serving a table of four, gave him a glance.

He walked a block to Landstrasse Hauptstrasse, black gym bag in hand, and ran to catch a "T" streetcar headed for the First District using a day fare card he'd bought the night before so the cops couldn't track his own fare card. He disembarked at Wien Mitte. No eyes locked on him, moved with him, flashed recognition, as he followed a group of people inside.

Renovated ten years ago, the station's main hall reminded him of bus stations he'd used in America. He passed benches full of waiting travelers and digital boards listing arrivals and departures as public address announcements droned over the cacophony of voices. The subway rumbled below. He glanced at the descending escalator to the subway at the back.

Evan turned toward the service area for employees only, noting the same security he'd observed earlier in the afternoon and the night before. Uniformed police guarded each street entrance to the station, and a duo patrolled the main hall scrutinizing the people waiting there. A crying baby and its mother diverted the cops' attention long enough for Evan to slip past them. He checked the other cops, their eyes focused elsewhere, and he entered the service area.

As he had the night before, he found the utility stairway tucked away beyond the elevator. Covering his hand with the bottom of his T-shirt, he depressed the door handle. Unlocked. How sloppy of the station employees. But the open door alerted him to the possibility of security guards or cops in the stairway. He peeked in to see the first section was clear before entering. At the bottom of the stairs, he held his breath to listen. Not a sound. He climbed to the second floor and, covering his hand again, opened the door two inches to peer at the empty hallway. Voices came from an open doorway on the right twenty-five feet away. Two doors stood open on the left. Evan headed for the first open doorway.

Only a desk-style gray telephone sat on the green-carpeted floor in the room. The air smelled of stale cigar smoke. He closed the door quietly. Squatting down, he opened the black gym bag, took out the latex gloves, the wig, and the CZ 9mm handgun and its silencer. He took off the eyeglasses and dropped them into the bag. The Chinese Vice Chairman's photo went into his jeans pocket. After slipping on a pair of latex gloves, he wiped clean the CZ 9mm, screwed on the silencer, and tucked it into his jeans' back waistband. He put on the navy-blue lightweight jacket, zipping it to his throat and pulling it down over the gun. Last, he stuffed the extra pairs of latex gloves into the jacket's pockets. Ready.

Leaving the black gym bag hidden behind the open office door, he tiptoed back to the stairway door. Voices and laughter came from the open doorway down the hall. He opened the door two inches, checked the stairway. Silence. His rubber-soled running shoes made no noise as he climbed the four flights to the roof. This door, too, was unlocked.

Two Viennese SWAT cops patrolled the roof. Evan wasn't surprised. They wore camouflage, carried crackling radios attached to their shoulders, compact automatic weapons that resembled black Uzis, as well as holstered pistols. Evan hunched down out of sight behind a hooded fan vent, observing them walk the perimeter and survey the roof.

On Vasia's building's roof, two more SWAT cops walked the perimeter. They were all relaxed, expecting no one on the roofs, and, he hoped, bored.

Five minutes later, his two SWAT cops stood at the back while the two SWAT cops on Vasia's roof were at the front, looking down at the noisy Landstrasse Hauptstrasse. Evan sprinted in a crouch across to the two-foot barrier wall from which he leaped over to Vasia's roof, landing in a squat before scurrying over to the hut sheltering the stairs to Vasia's apartment. He hid behind it, one hand on his CZ 9mm. Whatever the noise on the street below, the SWAT cops were riveted on it, moving back and forth in front. The other pair strode to the front of the bus station roof. One of the cops on Vasia's roof pointed down. A shouted chant that sounded like "Free Taiwan!" came from the street.

Evan opened the hut's door. He crabbed inside and closed the door. In darkness, he descended the stairs. The door at the bottom stood half an inch ajar. Evan smiled at it. He pushed the door wide and found the pantry light on. Halfway through the pantry, he heard it, the one sound he didn't want to hear: the piano. He froze.

Someone was in the apartment, someone played the wide angular intervals of the Gigue fugue of J. S. Bach's Sixth Partita. His plan had been shot to hell. He'd failed. He'd chosen no alternate location and he had no time to develop an alternate plan to his plan. The falling sensation of despair and helplessness cascaded through his body.

"Inside want as much as you like..," his father's icy baritone reminded him.

No. He'd take the freedom he wanted, that he'd earned.

Think like Perceval. Whoever was playing the piano stood in his way. He must fulfill his deal with the Americans so they'd disappear from his life.

Look at the facts. He didn't know yet who was in the apartment. The Russian had told him that he had a rehearsal at this time at the soprano's apartment in the Thirteenth District. Greta didn't play the piano. Maybe Vasia had allowed a friend to use his piano to practice. No one could see him or witness the job.

Evan entered the kitchen, the piano much louder and clearer. The last time he'd heard Uncle Joe play the piano, he'd played Bach's Sixth Partita. Vasia's playing had reminded him of Uncle Joe's. Vasia's playing had – Vasia was home, the pianist in the living room, playing the Bach. Evan pivoted and ran back into the pantry.

He stopped at the door to the roof stairs. Vasia. Why was he here? Why wasn't he at the soprano's? He patted his jacket pocket for his phone to call Vasia and lure him out of the apartment. But he'd left the phone at home. What about Vasia's cell phone? Where did he usually leave it when he was home? His bedroom? No, his jeans pocket. Every time he'd been to the Russian's apartment, the cell phone had been in Vasia's pocket. He remembered him taking it out to make a call or to answer it. He looked up at the roof door.

If he opened that door, if he left now, he faced a black abyss. Would they give him another chance? He doubted it. He would not live to conduct Mahler's Fifth Symphony. Harold would kill him. Harold had made certain that he got that message. How could Vasia do this to him? He couldn't walk away and not do the job today. He couldn't throw away his chance to free himself of the Americans once and for all, to be free to live his life as he wanted, to pursue his music career and never need to always look over his shoulder. If he didn't do the job today when they expected it done, they wouldn't trust him. They'd kill him to silence him. Harold would do it. They were ruthless. No second chances. He must be ruthless.

Anger flushed his face. The Russian had pushed him into a corner. No one could witness the job. No one. If the Russian saw him as Perceval, he wouldn't keep his mouth shut. Vasia would call the police. How could Vasia have done this to him? He knew what he must do. The Russian had given him no choice.

He returned to the kitchen. Vasia had stopped playing, but started again a moment later at the beginning of the partita's Toccata. The piano's voice, stately but sorrowful, accompanied Evan into the hallway and through to Vasia's bedroom. From the high shelf in the walk-in closet, he lifted down the hunting rifle case, opened it on the rumpled, unmade bed. He assembled the rifle Vasia had bought for him, brought it up to his shoulder and targeted a far roof chimney outside the window to check the sight. No silencer. The loud gunshot would give witnesses on the street a point of reference for his location. He'd have to move fast afterward. He loaded the rifle, set the action, and dropped extra shells into his jeans pocket.

Maybe he could distract Vasia, lure him out of the living room, and then knock him unconscious. He tiptoed down the hallway toward the living room. Vasia now played the eerie, quiet fugue section of the Toccata with precision. Evan reached back and pulled the CZ 9mm from his waistband.

How to do it? He passed the rectangular cherry dining table with matching chairs where he, Vasia and Greta had eaten dinner together. How could Vasia force him into this impossible position?

Breathing deeply, he focused on the task at hand and detached himself from everything else. He paused in the arched doorway between the dining and living rooms. How to do it?

Oblivious to the world, the Russian sat at the black grand piano near the front windows, his solid wrestler's body visible from the mid-chest up, his curly blonde head bowed. He whisper-sang as he played.

He'd need to sneak up on the Russian. Evan leaned the hunting rifle against the wall by the doorway, behind a chair and out of sight. The Russian continued to play the partita, immersed in the Bach. Evan almost reached him, had lifted the CZ to knock him out. Then Vasia opened his eyes.

The Russian's concentrated expression exploded into a surprised smile. "Evan! I call you hour ago! How you get in? Nice moustache!"

"What are you doing here, Vasia?" Evan said, his tone cold, commanding. Vasia had missed the CZ.

"I call you. Margareta reschedule rehearsal for tomorrow. Let's rehearse Caine Piano Concerto now. How you get in? Why you have moustache?" Vasia swiveled left to grab a music score from the floor.

Evan looked out the front window. Across the wide boulevard in front of the Hilton Hotel, a line of official black limousines waited at the curb, Chinese flags fluttering from short stands on the hoods, their drivers chatting in pairs. The Chinese security guards at the front door paced, their eyes surveying the area. Viennese uniformed cops, twice as many as he'd seen earlier in the afternoon, patrolled the line of limos. SWAT cops guarded the perimeter. On the sidewalk in front of Vasia's building at least one hundred people chanted and waved signs.

"Why you wear hospital gloves, Evan?"

He glared at the Russian. "I used the roof stairs."

Vasia's blue eyes widened. "Why?"

"You're not supposed to be here. Stand up." He pressed the CZ's muzzle against Vasia's right temple. "Now."

The Russian stood slowly, his arms raised to waist height. "Why, Evan? Why you do this? It's crazy!"

Fear gave the Russian's voice a slight tremolo. Evan knew he'd achieved complete control. They cleared the piano. Vasia chopped at Evan's gun hand and punched him in the stomach. Vasia ran for the front foyer.

The security system alarm. Evan regained his breath and bolted after the Russian. He reached the foyer as the Russian's fingers hit two consecutive keys on the security panel. Evan pistol whipped the side of his head.

"How many numbers?!" He aimed the CZ at the Russian on the floor. He hit the reset button on the panel. Vasia's blue eyes stared up at him. "How many numbers?"

"Four numbers, I hit two," Vasia said in a firm voice. "What you do, Evan? I am your friend. Throw gun away. What I do for this?"

"Get up." Evan gestured with the CZ. "You're here. That's what you did."

The Russian struggled to his feet, holding one side of his head. "I live here," he said, pained. "Why *you* here?"

"Living room," Evan said, pushing the Russian's shoulder forward.

With his elbow, Vasia landed a sharp right upper cut to Evan's chin, sending him backward. He hit the wall as Vasia pummeled his stomach and face hard with his fists, knocking him to the floor. The gun clattered across the parquet. Footsteps squeaked away from him. Holding his stomach, he dragged himself to his knees. He must stop the Russian. He'd missed the chance to knock him unconscious. His stomach hurt. Vasia had not hesitated to hurt him. He rose to his feet, found the CZ. He listened. Movement in the kitchen.

Evan strode into the kitchen, aiming the CZ 9mm at the Russian standing at the wall videophone, punching in numbers on the keypad. "Disconnect," he said.

Vasia saw the gun aimed at his head and froze. "You kill me, Evan, you kill music inside you. You kill everything you are."

"No, Vasia. Disconnect."

The Russian pressed the disconnect button. Evan grabbed him, jerked one arm up hard behind his back and with the CZ's muzzle against his head, marched him into the living room. He shoved the Russian onto the sofa and went over to the front window again. The scene at the Hilton had not changed. He checked his watch. He needed to set up.

"Evan Quinn I know is musician. My friend. He not hurt anyone. Evan Quinn I know cares about musicians, about people."

"I'm doing this to be a free musician." He opened the left casement window six inches.

"You already free, Evan! But when you kill, you lose freedom, lose soul. Why you look out window?"

Evan stepped out from behind the piano.

"What's out window? Landstrasse Hauptstrasse. Protests. Hilton Hotel."

Evan touched the CZ to his forehead as the Russian's eyes flashed realization.

"The Chinese at Hilton." In one swift move, Vasia yanked a sofa cushion up and at Evan's gun. The gun flew across the room, thudding on the carpeted floor in the arched doorway. Vasia lunged at him.

He stepped to the side, chopped the Russian's lower back and kidneys with his forearm. The Russian went down. Evan kicked his groin, his stomach, his chest. The Russian grabbed his foot and twisted. Evan twisted with it and stomped his foot down hard on the Russian's face.

The Russian cried out, covered his face with his hands. Evan retrieved the CZ.

"I admire your fight, but you've given me no choice," he said as he bent and lifted the Russian to his feet. "It's time to go." He pushed the Russian up against the wall bookshelves, holding him there with his full weight on his left arm across his chest. "I have a job to do."

"You always have choice!" Vasia struggled, tried to knee Evan's groin. Blood streamed from his nose.

"Stop it!" Evan said, his face inches from the Russian's. "You're only making it harder for yourself."

The Russian opened his mouth to speak and Evan inserted the CZ muzzle into it. Vasia's eyes widened. He wiggled and punched at Evan's body, pulled at his arms. Taking the hits, Evan positioned the gun at a slight upward angle. At the instant he pressed the trigger, Evan stepped back. Blood spattered over him with the chuff of the silencer gunshot. The Russian's body slumped down the wall to the floor, a swathe of blood and gray matter on the books above him. The CZ fell to the floor, bouncing to one side.

Evan turned away with a gasp. His heart pounded in his ears. This time, he felt no exhilaration, no rush of power.

His hands shook. He noticed one of his latex gloves had ripped. He pulled the gloves off, stuffed them into his jacket pocket. The blood spatter. He raced to the bathroom to wash his face and neck. The cold water calmed him, steadied his hands. He rinsed out the sink and let his face and neck air dry rather than use one of the white towels. No fresh DNA for the cops.

Back in the living room, he pulled on a fresh pair of latex gloves and surveyed the room. He returned the sofa cushion to the sofa, plumping all the cushions. He checked the foyer and the kitchen to insure nothing was out of place. Last, without looking at the face, he placed the CZ in the Russian's right hand for the print transfer and removed the silencer, sticking it in his jacket pocket.

He positioned himself with the rifle at the open front casement window. He looked through the sight. The drivers had opened their limo back doors and waited, expectant. The Chinese security guards, joined by Viennese cops, formed two lines leading from the front door to the first limo. The demonstrators shouted and screamed below him. Evan's stomach clutched into a knot. Had he missed the Vice Chairman? Were the other limos already loaded? Three Chinese men in black suits exited the hotel, escorted by the Chinese security guards, and walked to the first limo. Evan pulled out the Vice Chairman's photo from his jeans pocket. He compared it to what he saw in his rifle sight. None of the three were the Vice Chairman. He took a deep breath, studied the photo again.

Vice Chairman Jiang Xu appeared at the hotel's door. His ticket to freedom. Two Chinese security guards flanked him as two more stepped in front of him.

Evan inhaled to the slow count of five as he sighted the Vice Chairman. The Chinese man had thick, black hair that flopped across his forehead. He stood erect, a military bearing, his body lean in a black suit, white shirt, and red tie. Evan aimed at the head. He exhaled to the count of five. The Vice Chairman stepped forward, nodding at the Chinese guard on his left. Evan braced himself for the recoil.

The gunshot cracked louder than he expected. The Vice Chairman's head snapped back. Evan pulled the trigger again, nailing his target's chest. He heard screams and shouts. Chinese guards pointed in his direction and uniformed Viennese cops ran into the street.

He dropped the rifle and sprinted for the pantry, closing the door to the kitchen behind him. He switched off the pantry light, entered the stairway to the roof. In darkness, he scrambled up the steep stairs and paused at the roof door. He was unarmed now – no gun, knife, nothing.

He opened the roof door two inches, nervous that he'd heard no shouting. When he stuck out his head, peering around, the SWAT cops were conferring at the front left corner of Vasia's building's roof. Two peeled away toward the general access doors, one from each team, as he heard more screams from the street and shouting.

Two SWAT cops remained, one on each roof, one at the front, one striding to the back. Voices yelled out of their radios. He slipped out the door, closing it behind him, and waited behind the access hut.

When each SWAT cop squinted down at the street and talked into the radio, Evan scurried in a crouch across Vasia's roof to the wall, leaped onto the bus station roof, and ran on tiptoe for the general access door. As he reached out for it, he heard thunder inside. He ducked to the side behind it. Four uniformed Viennese cops spilled onto the roof, their radios popping and crackling. One SWAT cop turned, waved them forward. When the SWAT cop looked down again at Landstrasse Hauptstrasse, Evan opened the access door and slipped inside.

He listened. No voices, no footsteps. Only the noise and shouting voices outside muffled by the door. Running down the stairs, he unzipped the navy-blue lightweight jacket and took it off. At the second floor, he opened the door two inches. The hallway inside was silent and deserted.

In the empty office, he bent over, his breathing ragged. He'd done it. Tears blurred his vision. He had to work fast now. He needed to escape. He ripped off the latex gloves and opened the black gym bag. Kicking off his running shoes, he stripped off the fake black moustache, his jeans and black T-shirt, and stuffed them into the bag along with the navy-blue jacket and latex gloves. Blood spots on his running shoes caught his eye. Using the jeans he'd taken off, he rubbed off the blood. He dressed in the clean jeans, blue T-shirt, and the running shoes. He put on the long chestnut brown wig, securing it with hairpins, arranging the fringe of long bangs over his forehead and the black-framed eyeglasses. Done.

He headed for the elevator, adopting a slight limp as if he had an arthritic right knee. Anyone coming out of the stairs now who wasn't a cop would be a suspect. Using the bottom of his T-shirt to cover his fingertip, he pressed the call button. The doors slid open.

The elevator doors opened on a deserted service area but he heard muffled shouting in the main hall. As he peeked out the service door, two cops ran past it. With the black gym bag slung over his shoulder, Evan limped into the main hall and dodged running people, saw people sitting on the benches, their eyes wide, mouths open in stunned surprise, and heads swiveling as if their necks had broken.

"Secure the hall! Immediately! Secure the hall!" a male voice shouted in German behind him. Ahead cops blocked the rear street entrance. He stepped onto the descending escalator.

Below, a subway train screeched to a halt. He'd take it, no matter which line it was, and he limped down the moving escalator steps. Two cops, their arms open wide, shouted at the confused and roiling crowd on the platforms.

Evan limped toward the subway train, a Line Four train headed north to Heiligenstadt. Two cops at the back argued whether to clear the area or hold all the people there. They had no description of the assassin. Another pair of cops at the front examined bags and questioned people as they boarded. The middle doors remained closed. He limped to the front. One cop stopped him.

"*Wohin fahren Sie?*" the cop asked.

He coughed. In a raspy voice, his shoulders hunched in deference, Evan said, "*Schwedenplatz für U1, bitte. Ich habe die Grippe. Ich muss zum Arzt gehen.*" They wouldn't refuse a sick man his doctor's appointment. He showed them trembling hands. The other cop opened his black gym bag, rooted around inside, pulled out a corner of Evan's sweatshirt and showed it to the first cop.

The first cop waved him onto the train. He limped down the aisle to an available window seat. With a groan, he sank down onto it. People entered the train at a steady, slow pace. Evan bowed his head, held the gym bag between his knees. In his peripheral vision, he saw the cops wave the last person on board in the front and move away from the train. The doors slammed closed. The train glided forward.

Chapter 24

"You are quite certain Herr Quinn has no employment or other association with any American government agency?" Inspector Leiner said.

Dieter Aschenbeck smiled through his well-trimmed auburn beard. Inspector Hanna Celine of the Bundespolizei frowned.

"As I told you before, Inspector," Bernie said. "I checked with all the American intelligence agencies, military and civilian, as Morgan ordered. Nobody claimed Evan Quinn."

They'd questioned him all day. They'd only begun. He knew what to expect. They'd move him soon to a safe house somewhere in the country. For now, this interview room was standard issue: a gray metal table with remnants of their lunch that scented the room with a pleasant mustard aroma mixed with melon and a one-way mirror spanning one wall. He expected the room was wired for audio and video recording. Nothing on the pale green walls, nothing interesting to look at except Inspector Celine, whose tantalizingly curved body and intense green eyes he'd have found pleasantly arousing in other circumstances.

But they interrogated him. His life depended on a serious demeanor, straightforward manner and complete honesty. Celine's intensity showed him how valuable they believed he was, and he was. He had brought thumb drives filled with the operational details of scientific and corporate espionage as well as the usual military and political stuff. He had brought other thumb drives as well.

"Herr Quinn told me you followed him." Leiner's frown lines deepened around his mouth and across his forehead. "What was your interest?"

"To protect him."

"From whom?"

"From you, Larry Morgan and everyone else." Bernie picked up his orange soda and took a drink.

Dieter Aschenbeck hid another smile. Bernie had the feeling that the government lawyer was enjoying a private joke at Leiner's expense. Inspector Celine shook her head and said, "You planned to recruit Herr Quinn?"

"Not really. To stall for time, I told Larry Morgan we should recruit him. Morgan had requested a transfer and I was waiting for that to come through. As soon as Morgan left, I could delete the termination order he'd issued on Evan Quinn."

"Termination?" Leiner's voice squeaked up the word.

Bernie nodded, feeling his muscles relax even more with each secret he revealed, and a sense of relief flooded his heart.

"But you failed to carry out the order, Herr Brown," Leiner said, his voice normal again. "Why? Why protect him?"

The three of them looked at the door behind Bernie as it opened. A black-haired plainclothes officer in his thirties hurried to Leiner and whispered in his ear. Leiner's face blanched, his mouth tensed into a thin line under his dark blonde moustache.

"What were your plans for Herr Quinn?" Inspector Celine said, leaning forward.

Bernie focused on the darkening storm in Leiner's gray eyes. The black-haired officer moved over to Celine's ear. "To keep him alive," Bernie said. "Beyond that, nothing, although I floated an excellent investment idea with him several times. I was pleased to see him at the Fischer School—"

"You've quite succeeded in protecting Herr Quinn, and with your diversion, Herr Brown," Leiner said, his tone frosty. Celine shook her head, listening to the black-haired officer. Dieter Aschenbeck's smile faded at Leiner's next words. "Marco, I need you and Johann there to ensure the scene is secured. No one speaks to the media, no one. I will come as soon as possible. Send Ellie and her team to secure the Americans at the Bristol."

The black-haired officer nodded. "*Sofort.*"

Inspector Celine gathered her apple green linen suit jacket and black briefcase. "I will call the Prime Minister and meet you there, Marco."

"You wanted Herr Quinn alive why, Herr Brown?" Leiner growled. "Was it a back-channel order from Washington? Something Morgan didn't know? So Herr Quinn could complete his mission? Smoke and mirrors. You have lied to us all day."

Bernie and Aschenbeck spoke at the same time. "What happened?"

Celine and Marco turned back at the door. Bernie heard their breathing behind him.

Leiner said, "Someone has assassinated Vice Chairman Jiang Xu."

Bernie's face turned cold as the blood drained from it. Not Jiang Xu. Not dead. As much as he hated the Chinese and their power games, it would be suicide to knock off the Chinese Vice Chairman. He looked down at the orange soda bottle in his hands. How could he convince them?

"Tell us, Herr Brown, why you wanted Herr Quinn alive?" Leiner said. "Was it for him to assassinate Jiang Xu? That is why you met with him last night – to finalize plans for the assassination? Was your defection a diversionary tactic?"

Bernie shook his head slowly as he listened. He answered in an even, firm voice. "I understand your suspicions, Inspector. Evan Quinn is a symphony orchestra conductor, a musician, nothing else. I can speak with total confidence about that. Morgan and I would have been informed if there had been an operation in place, especially an assassination, but any assassination would be a violation of American policy. We weren't, and there was *no* operation. The Americans had nothing to do with this. Assassinating any member of the Chinese delegation, especially the Vice Chairman, would not serve America's best interests. Last week, Jiang Xu had extended an olive branch. He came to Vienna to seal the deal himself. All the issues would be resolved and the talks would be over within two to three days. Under those conditions, no way does Washington give the Chinese an excuse to attack us or any of our allies and risk war. America did *not* do this. I'd bet the assassin worked for the Taiwanese or Uighurs. You know the Chinese will go after whoever did it." Bernie heard the door open and close behind him. Celine and Marco had left. "As for Quinn...." Bernie looked from Leiner's scowl to

Aschenbeck's thoughtful frown. "Ever heard of a Mr. Red-field?"

"Halt! Wer sind Sie?"

Evan froze. Freda's voice came from his left. Her challenge amused him. She hadn't recognized him in the long chestnut brown wig and black-framed glasses. He carried the black gym bag at his side.

"Evan Quinn," he said, facing her.

"Nein!" Freda held a growling Sasha by the collar. Pruning shears lay at her feet by the five-foot high front hedge that camouflaged the stone wall.

With deliberate movements, Evan set down the bag, took off the wig and glasses, and finger-combed his black hair. Freda's mouth opened in astonishment. "It's me, Freda. Thanks for the challenge, though. Sofia Karalis told me no one would recognize me, not even someone who knew me."

Freda released Sasha who trotted over to him, her tongue lolling out of her mouth. "But why, Evan?"

"For anonymity. People recognize me all the time. It's impossible to go out and to have a normal life. The attention is nice, but I'm really only an ordinary person. I told Inspector Leiner at lunch yesterday that I never had this recognition problem in America. Here, it's different." Sasha sniffed his legs and whined. Had she smelled Vasia's scent, maybe his blood, on him?

"You are famous. A celebrity." She shaded her eyes from

the sun with one hand as she looked up at him. "Inspector Leiner?"

He shrugged as if he dined everyday with the Inspector. "Yeah, the police. I'm on probation. He's my guard, guardian angel, whatever. Anyway, Sofia uses disguises, too, in order to have a more normal life. She helped me create my own. I've tested this one today and it worked like a dream. See?" Playfully, he wagged a finger at her. She nodded and smiled. Sasha whined again, and when he reached down to pet her, she flinched away.

"Sasha, what's wrong with you? It's your friend, Evan."

"It's OK. She may smell another dog on me. I saw a big shaggy dog a couple blocks away and couldn't resist." He hadn't seen another dog, but Freda had no way of knowing that. People believe what they want to believe and she liked him.

Freda watched Sasha lope to the back yard. "She'll forgive you. Have you been to the Fischer School?" She waved at his black gym bag. "I thought you went there in the morning?"

"Yeah, I go in the morning." Evan started up the gravel driveway toward his apartment's outer door, Freda in his wake. "I visited a musician friend. I carried the disguise in the bag and put it on before I left his building. Now, I plan to make that eggplant tomato sauce recipe you gave me."

"Remember to seed the tomatoes." She smiled. "Save a little for me."

Inside, Evan checked his security system. No one had entered his apartment in his absence. He stripped off his clothes and threw them on the pile of dirty laundry in the bedroom. To that pile he added the blood-spattered jeans and navy-blue jacket from the black gym bag, emptying their pockets. In the jeans he found, to his dismay, two shells for the hunting rifle. As far as the Austrians were concerned, he would have no need to possess ammunition. For now, he stuck the shells and 9mm silencer under his mattress and went into the bathroom.

In the mirror over the sink, his reflection revealed red spots on his face and under his chin where Vasia had punched him. Odd that Freda had said nothing about them, although the sun had been in her eyes when she looked up at him. More red spots marked his torso. They'd all turn to purple bruises. His workouts at the Fischer School could explain them. Fortunately, he had no cuts or scratches. He felt confident he had left no fresh DNA in Vasia's apartment.

Turning the water on, Evan stepped into the shower. He hadn't dared allow his mind to acknowledge the feeling until now. His body shuddered with nausea. He sobbed, tears mixing with the spraying hot water as he soaped his body, rinsed, soaped up again, and rinsed, over and over.

Vassily Vladimirovich Bartyakov. Klaus pondered the Russian pianist's body, the blood swathe down the book spines above him. His death made no sense at all. When he'd spoken with the Russian the week before, in the Café Konditorei across from the Staatsoper, he had been full of life, full of the future.

"*Selbstmord?*" Marco said at his left.

"*Gar nicht.*"

Marco squatted next to Bartyakov. "I agree. Look at the hand holding the gun. What do you see?"

Klaus bent for a closer view of Bartyakov's right hand. "Nothing."

"Exactly. If he had shot himself, where is the blood spatter on his hand?"

Klaus nodded. "The hand is clean. Have forensics check it for gunpowder residue. His face. His nose looks broken. And those marks."

Marco leaned in close to Bartyakov's face. "Perhaps bruises. I'll ask the good doctor when he arrives to work with forensics to determine any pattern. And to check for defensive wounds, and under his fingernails, although they are unbelievably short."

Klaus straightened. He raised his voice so all the cops and forensic investigators heard him. "This is a homicide. Someone caused Herr Bartyakov's death. Forensics, please examine this apartment in the closest possible detail, yes? Fingerprints, DNA, trace, everything. Especially concerning the position of the body and the blood spatter. Check for a void area. I want all residents in this building and surrounding buildings interviewed. I want the security system films reviewed." Klaus sighed, rubbing his sternum with his fist. He looked down at Marco. "We will interview all his friends, establish a timeline of his activity."

He glanced out the open door at Hanna Celine talking with the building manager in the front foyer. His memory flashed on the wall calendars in Evan Quinn's kitchen.

"Marco, search for a date book, calendar, or a schedule. He worked as an accompanist. He must have had some way to organize rehearsals and his life."

"I'll tell the computer tech checking the house computer." Marco walked out as Johann came through the arched doorway from the dining room.

"Inspector," Johann said. "We found the rifle case in his bedroom, open on the bed. We also found ammunition and two other hunting rifles in cases in the closet. No case or ammunition for the orphan 9mm."

Klaus sighed. "He told me that he planned to hunt in Romania this autumn with Evan Quinn. Have forensics check all of the rifles and verify the licenses."

He headed for the foyer to ask the building manager for the floor plan to Bartyakov's apartment. In these older renovated buildings, often there were hidden passages, secret rooms, panic rooms, and so on. He suspected they'd not find the assassin on the security camera memory cards. Was there another way to enter the building unseen?

Next to the manager and Hanna Celine, a uniformed cop held a teenage girl by the arm. Skinny and sallow, she had raccoon eyes and black lips, wore black clothes but no visible body piercing. Next to her fidgeted an older woman in a conservative linen business suit.

Hanna's wide eyes met his. "We have a serious problem."

"Witnesses?"

"No, Inspector," the uniformed cop said. He looked familiar to Klaus, but he could not remember his name. "This girl told a journalist who lived in this apartment."

"He paid me one hundred euros!" the girl said.

"Katrina, you know the police asked all of us not to talk to the media," the older woman said. "They have their reasons for that, if you had thought to use your brain."

"And you are?" Klaus said. "Your names?"

"Her mother. Alina Führer. She is my seventeen-year-old daughter, Katrina. We live on the second floor, front apartment."

"*Danke*, Frau Führer. You live directly below this flat?" She nodded. "Were you or your daughter at home between 3:30 and 4:30 this afternoon?"

"I was at work in the Ninth District. Katrina?"

"Lainzer Tiergarten with friends until five."

"*Prima.* Now, Fräulein Führer, which journalist approached you and what did you say? Tell me your exact words."

Katrina wrenched her arm from the uniformed cop's grip. "He said he was from the BBC. He didn't say his name. He said he would pay me one hundred euros for the name of the owner of the front apartment on the top floor. I told him the owner's name was Vassily Bartyakov. He gave me the money and left."

Hanna Celine flipped open her cell phone. "I need to call the Prime Minister." She stepped away from them.

"Was your conversation with the BBC journalist before or after the police told you not to speak with the media?" Klaus said, his tone gentle.

"After."

Klaus sighed. "I am sorry, Frau Führer. We must take your daughter into custody." He nodded to the uniformed cop. "Please escort Fräulein Führer to the Bundespolizei headquarters." The cop nodded and grabbed Katrina's arm again.

She looked as if she'd spit in his face. "Katrina." Klaus spoke low. "Your mother will accompany you."

"Why the Bundespolizei?" Alina said, her face pale.

"Because it is a matter of national security," Klaus said. "I suggest you call a lawyer."

"I haven't committed any crime!" Katrina said, her black lips twisted in a sneer.

"Ah, Katrina. You have interfered with a federal police investigation." He nodded to the uniformed cop who escorted mother and daughter out. Hanna closed her cell phone, her eyes fearful. "Were you able to stop it?" he said.

"No. The BBC had already begun broadcasting the information in special bulletins. Already other media have picked it up. The Prime Minister now prepares a speech for broadcast concerning our investigation in order to try to stop any Chinese military attack on Austria or Russia. I have told him that we are not one hundred percent certain that Bartyakov was involved. We must be allowed to complete our investigation."

Evan tasted the simmering eggplant tomato sauce. Delicious. The basil was more subtle, sweeter, than oregano. He filled another pot with water for the pasta.

"*Fernseher* BBC." The television clicked on in the front room.

After dinner, he would call Woody Lewis and launder

the pile of clothes in his bedroom using Freda's washer and dryer.

"Now, a special bulletin," said the clipped English voice of the male newscaster.

"*Fernseher lauter zweimal*," Evan said as he set the pot of water on the stove and turned on the burner.

"As we have been reporting for the last three hours," the newscaster continued, louder. "Vice Chairman Jiang Xu of China was assassinated this afternoon in Vienna as he left his hotel to attend a meeting at the American Embassy. Suspected in the assassination is Vassily Vladimirovich Bartyakov, a twenty-seven-year-old piano graduate student at Vienna's Academy of Music. The Austrian Federal Police have released a statement in which they urge patience and cooperation as they conduct their investigation. They cannot confirm, without any doubt, whether or not Bartyakov was involved. They have confirmed that the assassin shot from Bartyakov's apartment and Bartyakov was found dead there under suspicious circumstances. When more facts become available, the Austrian Federal Police will issue another statement. Austrian Prime Minister Peter Jäger will address the international community this evening on satellite television. It is expected that he will emphasize the need for a calm, rational approach to this tragic event and request international cooperation with the investigation. Chinese Chairman Li has yet to issue a statement."

They thought Vasia had shot the Vice Chairman. He couldn't believe it.

"*Fernseher abstellan.*" The TV flicked off.

He had expected the police to conclude Vasia had committed suicide. The police were not supposed to figure out who killed the Vice Chairman. The assassin was supposed to remain a mystery forever.

The videophone warbled. Annoyed, he pivoted and said, "Hello!"

The monitor came to life, revealing a tearful Greta Fasching, gold earrings trembling at her ears. He'd forgotten about Greta.

"Greta! What's wrong? Where are you?" Evan moved closer to the monitor so she could see him. He had to be careful. Everyone must believe he knew nothing of what had happened. He was Evan Quinn, orchestra conductor.

"Evan? You have not heard? Vasia is dead." She sobbed, bowing her head.

"Dead? No, he can't be. I talked with him last night. He was fine. He left me a phone message this afternoon while I was out."

"I am at the Bundespolizei. Can you come here?" Her ebony eyes pleaded with him.

"Of course. Right away. I need to…I don't know what to do with…. I'm coming, Greta. Hang in there."

She managed a weak smile before the monitor went black.

The Federal Police, not Leiner. Good news for him or bad? They had Greta call him instead of a federal cop. Nice touch. He turned off the stove, stared at the sauce. He put the pot lid on it, grabbed his wallet, Georg cell phone and beige heather sport jacket to wear with his T-shirt and jeans. He picked up the hot sauce pot with a dishtowel protecting his hands and headed for Freda's in the early dusk.

When she opened her back door, her eyes rested on the pot and her mouth formed a small "o" of surprise.

"I'm sorry to bother you, Freda. I've just heard a musician friend has died and I need to go to the Bundespolizei, his girlfriend's at the Bundespolizei. I have to find out what happened. I don't want to ruin the sauce. What do I do with it?"

"You knew Vassily Bartyakov?" She accepted the hot pot with the dishtowel.

"Was it on the news? I don't believe it. It can't be." Evan's throat tightened and tears welled in his eyes.

"Not to worry about the sauce. I'll drive you there in my car."

"Freda, you don't have to—" She disappeared inside with the pot. He sniffed back the tears, irritated with himself for giving in to the emotion. He had known Uncle Joe all his young life. He hadn't cried for him. He'd known Vasia Bartyakov for only two months. He wiped his eyes as Freda reappeared carrying her purse.

"OK, Evan. Let's go. I am so sorry about the loss of your friend."

"Thank you."

They talked little on the drive into the First District. He remembered the blood-spattered clothes in his bedroom that he'd planned to wash that evening. Would the cops search his apartment while he was gone? Would they find the clothes? His stomach cramped. Think like Perceval. He needed to be careful, focus on his real life as a musician. They mustn't suspect him. He must not get caught. Stop thinking about the clothes. Vasia's blood. Put everything deep in a closet in his mind where no one could touch it as he'd done when he had defected. He was Evan Quinn, conductor.

Freda dropped him off in front of a six-story gray nineteenth century building on the Schottenring. Marco waited for him inside the front door. Evan's stomach fluttered.

"*Guten Abend*, Evan," Marco said and continued in English. "Inspector Leiner asked me to wait for you. We are interviewing Vassily Bartyakov's friends." Marco gestured toward the right and a bank of elevators.

"Where's Greta?" he asked, concern in his voice covering his nervousness.

Marco pushed the elevator call button. "She and Sofia Karalis are in a waiting room upstairs."

Marco took him to the waiting room first. Greta leaped off of the brown leather sofa when she saw him and embraced him hard.

"I'm here, I'm here," he murmured to her. "We'll get this straightened out."

She sighed and stepped back, holding his face in both her hands. "You are a good friend, Evan. Thank you for coming."

Sofia remained seated, her legs crossed at the knee. She did not look at him. Evan spotted a bruise on Sofia's temple. She had said two days ago that he'd hit her. Had he? He couldn't remember. Had she lied to him? Had she told anyone else?

"Hello, Evan," Sofia said, the sound of her smoky voice tightened his throat.

"Hi, Sofia, I'm glad to see you here with Greta."

Greta returned to her seat next to Sofia. "We'll wait here for you, OK?"

"Sure." Evan turned to Marco who extended his left arm toward the door. He stepped out of the room, Marco behind him.

"The first door on the right, Evan. They are waiting for you."

"Inspector Leiner and Aschenbeck?"

"No, Inspector Leiner and Inspector Celine of the Bundespolizei. They are in charge of the investigation into the assassination of Vice Chairman Jiang Xu."

"Wait a minute." Evan faced Marco. "I thought this was about Vasia. What assassination?"

Marco grasped his arm and led him to the door. "Any questions you have, Evan, ask the Inspectors." Marco opened the door and gave him a gentle push inside.

The door closed behind him. He stood in an interview room similar to the one in which he'd first met with Inspector Leiner. He smelled the same lemon disinfectant and heard a low hum from the fluorescent lights above. The woman sitting next to Leiner had pursed her lips as if she'd eaten something sour. Leiner waved him to a gray metal chair opposite them at the table.

"Good evening, Herr Quinn. Thank you for responding so quickly. Have you seen Frau Fasching?" Leiner said.

Evan sat down, using the motion for a moment to think. Leiner's voice was too pleasant and friendly. He must be careful. Don't slip up, don't get caught. He knew nothing. Answer only the questions without volunteering any more information. "Yes, I have," he said.

"May I introduce Inspector Hanna Celine with the Federal Police?" Leiner's left hand, palm up, moved in the direction of the woman.

"Good evening, Herr Quinn," Celine said. Her voice sounded quite ordinary, bland. "We regret having to speak with you under these sad circumstances, but we hope you can help us establish a timeline of activity for Vassily Bartyakov. He was a friend of yours, yes?"

"Yes. I met Vasia – Vassily Bartyakov – in the Musikverein Green Room after my last concert with the Vienna Philharmonic. About two months ago. Him and Greta. He gave me his phone number, which I thought was crazy at the time, but then after my defection, I called him. He and Greta have helped me get settled here in Vienna." He realized as he spoke the last sentence that he'd already broken the rule about not volunteering information. "What's going on? Can I ask? I mean, I don't understand what happened to Vasia. Greta said he's dead. Marco said you're investigating an assassination. What's going on?"

Leiner spoke, smoothing his dark blonde moustache. "You have not seen any news?"

"No. I haven't seen anything."

"I see," Leiner said, bowing his blonde head for a moment before nailing Evan with his gray eyes. "This afternoon at approximately four-ten, someone using Vassily Bartyakov's apartment assassinated the Chinese Vice Chairman Jiang Xu as he left the Hilton Hotel for a meeting. In the apartment, Herr Bartyakov was found dead of a gunshot wound to the head."

"Oh, no." Evan covered his mouth with his right hand. "Who did this?"

"We are investigating, Herr Quinn." Leiner's tone hinted of irritation. "When was the last time you spoke with or saw Herr Bartyakov?"

Evan shook his head like a slow metronome. "I...I called him last night. I invited him to my place to work this afternoon on the Caine Piano Concerto." He stopped, bowed his head. The tears came with little encouragement. "I'm sorry," he said, wiping his eyes. "We have a gig together in Moscow next June. The Caine Piano Concerto."

"You visited him often at his flat?" Celine said.

"Well, yeah, but not often. Maybe three times since he moved to the new place."

"Had you ever seen a person or persons around Herr Bartyakov who made you uncomfortable or suspicious?" Celine said.

"No. I went to his housewarming party and saw a lot of people there. I didn't meet everyone, but those I met were friendly, nice, not suspicious at all."

"What was his mood last night when you called him?" Leiner said.

"Fine. Excited about the Caine. We agreed to work together later in the week."

"Why not this afternoon?"

"He had a rehearsal with a soprano. I thought we could meet after the rehearsal, but she lives in Hietzing and Vasia wanted to schedule another day for our meeting." He sat back abruptly, holding his right jaw, remembering that Vasia had called him. "Oh, yeah. He called me this afternoon while I was out, left a message on my voice mail."

"About what time was that, Herr Quinn?" Celine said, glancing at Leiner.

"The computer recorded it at about two-fifteen, I think. He said if I got the message before four to call him and he'd come out to my apartment. The soprano had cancelled or rescheduled or something. What was her name? Margareta something."

"Yes, Margareta Baum," Celine said. "You called Herr Bartyakov?"

"No. I arrived home just before five, so I planned to call him tonight. But then Greta called." He looked away at the one-way mirror spanning the wall. Leiner's steel gray eyes stabbed him. But they hadn't asked him for an alibi. He decided to offer his opinion of their suspicions of Vasia. He was Vasia's friend, after all, and should be outraged. "Is Vasia a suspect in the assassination? I mean, do you think he did it? Because if you do, I just can't believe it. He couldn't kill another human being. Not the Vasia I know."

"Would he have committed suicide?" Leiner said.

"Suicide? Why? I mean, he was so excited about playing the Caine with me in Moscow, and the recitals coming up, and he told me he felt so lucky...." He realized too late that he'd destroyed his own attempt to make Vasia's death look like a suicide. He shivered. But the Russian pianist hadn't assassinated the Chinese Vice Chairman. The Austrians needed to abandon that theory.

"Herr Quinn, had you saved Herr Bartyakov's voice mail message this afternoon?" Celine said.

He shook his head, no. "But maybe the phone company could retrieve it. I don't know how that works. I could call and ask."

Celine had a sweet smile that crinkled the skin around her eyes. "Thank you, Herr Quinn. We will work with the phone company. You have given us the necessary information for a retrieval. Anything else, Inspector?" Leiner shook his head no. "We understand," she continued, "that with your work you travel often. We would prefer if you remained in Vienna for the next three or four weeks."

The interview was over. He'd made it through. "My next gig is with the Vienna Philharmonic in mid-September. I'll be here preparing for it and my autumn schedule."

They all stood and Leiner walked over to the door by Evan. "We will contact you, if necessary, Herr Quinn," Celine said, offering her hand. "A pleasure meeting you. I'm sorry under these sad circumstances."

"Thanks, Inspector," he said, shaking her hand with a firm, warm grip. He followed Leiner out into the hallway. "I'd like to see Greta before I leave," he said to Leiner. "What will you do, Inspector? Interview everyone Vasia knows? That could take weeks."

Leiner smoothed his moustache. "Not everyone. Only the people he considered friends, people who visited him in his apartment. Frau Fasching has given us a list." Leiner leaned in closer to him, peering at his face. "Those appear to be bruises, Herr Quinn. Why have you bruises all over your face?"

Evan shrugged with an apologetic grin. "I hoped no one

would notice. I'm sore and it looks ugly. I'm learning a lot at the Fischer School."

Leiner frowned, his head at a questioning angle, but after a moment he gestured down the hall.

As they entered the waiting room, both Greta and Sofia stood. Leiner waited by the door. Evan felt the cop scrutinize every move he made, every word he said. Greta hugged him again. She kissed his cheek near his right ear.

"I am pregnant," she whispered in his ear. "The child is Vasia's. He did not know. Only you and Sofia know. Please tell no one."

Evan stepped back, nodding yes, and studied her face. She smiled, tears in her eyes. "You have my phone number, Greta. Call me. I'll do whatever I can to help." He hugged her again hard. His eyes sought Sofia's but she looked away. "I'll call you tomorrow. I'll walk you out."

"Herr Quinn," Leiner said. "A moment, please."

"We'll talk tomorrow," Greta said. She and Sofia left, arm in arm.

"Yes, Inspector."

"Herr Quinn, Bernard Brown would like to speak with you."

"Brown? Why would he tell you that?"

Leiner smiled.

Chapter 25

Evan had no idea how long they'd been traveling or in what direction because of the blindfold, a hood of rough black material that irritated his skin. He scratched his left temple. The hood smelled of moldy potatoes and reminded him of an execution hood.

"You believe his defection is genuine, Inspector?" he said.

Leiner's soft tenor voice came from the seat in front of him. "Yes, Herr Quinn. Bernard Brown made a compelling case for himself."

Brown's defection had left him speechless. When he'd phoned Woody Lewis and told him, the old American had only laughed, called Brown a "Mickey Mouse playing Mickey Mouse games." Brown's request to talk to Evan had surprised Woody into silence, however.

Evan blinked in the blindfold darkness. He recalled the fatigue lines that creased Leiner's face around his nose and mouth. His eyes had turned a dull slate gray. His shoulders stooped. The cop looked like he hadn't slept in days.

All of them – he, Leiner and Marco driving the car – had avoided the most recent news that morning, but he'd noticed their nervous glances to the clear blue sky. In a stunning and decisive move the day before, the Chinese had fired nuclear missiles on Moscow, obliterating the capital city of Russia and everything within a fifty-mile radius. Chinese planes had attacked other Russian cities with non-nuclear ordnance, including St. Petersburg. Chinese ground troops had invaded north across the Amur River and barreled through Kazakhstan (another act of war, like the Chinese cared) toward Volgograd while the Chinese air force continued their attacks on Siberia and cities west of the Urals. Evan had hoped Vasia's family near Nizhniy Novgorod had survived.

The Russian President had been on vacation at his Black Sea dacha, but the rest of the government had perished with Moscow. Military air bases and missile silos had been hardest hit after Moscow, destroying Russia's capability to retaliate. All the Asia-Pacific Coalition nations had declared war on Russia in accordance with their alliance with China. Russia's frightened neighbors, led by Kazakhstan, an Islamist Coalition member, demanded the United Nations Security Council stop China's aggression. Canada, the South American countries, and North African nations had joined them. In accordance with its alliance with Russia, the European Union countries had declared war on China at one-thirteen that morning. The Pacific Alliance declared war on China and APCO an hour later. Two countries so far had declared neutrality: Switzerland and, despite its membership in the EU, Austria. The big question was whether or not the Chinese would respect Austria's neutrality. The Americans had remained silent although their alliances with the EU, Russia and the Pacific Alliance guaranteed they would declare war. The United Nations faced a serious test of its leadership authority and effectiveness in a world enraged by Chinese aggression.

"You may remove the blindfold now, Herr Quinn," Leiner said.

"Thanks." He loosened the ties around his neck and pulled off the hood, blinking in the sunlight. He'd forgotten his sunglasses. He squinted at Leiner who turned toward him.

"How are you feeling, Herr Quinn?"

"Fine. Hot. Could you turn up the AC?"

Marco pressed a button on the dashboard. Leiner faced front again. Evan shifted his gaze to the landscape outside the car. They traveled down an unpaved country road lined with trees whose branches formed a sparse canopy overhead. They passed a cornfield on the left and began to climb a wooded hill. The sun had reached a position over halfway to its noon peak. He estimated they'd driven for approximately two hours and southwest, but he still had no idea where they were.

They turned left onto a rutted dirt road full of jarring bumps and holes. This road led into a clearing in the woods where they pulled up in front of a yellow wood frame house and parked in a line with a midnight blue sedan, two army personnel carriers and a jeep. A burly man clothed in forest camouflage and cradling a gun paced the front porch. The black finger of a headset curled around his face. Other men in camouflage guarded the clearing's perimeter and the dark green barn.

Evan slid out of the silver car and slipped off his beige linen sport jacket. "All right if I leave this in the car?" Leiner nodded. Marco settled on the car's hood, holding a pair of binoculars. "What's with the binoculars, Marco?"

The cop grinned. "Bird watching."

"This way, Herr Quinn," Leiner said.

They entered the house and walked through a modest foyer past a sitting room on the right where three men and two women in camouflage played cards and on into a modern kitchen. The house smelled musty and closed. Through the screen door, Evan could see Brown playing catch in the back yard with Johann on dry dirt decorated with tufts of green weeds and brown grass. The American wore khaki shorts, a short-sleeved white shirt open at the neck and red sneakers. A wide-brimmed straw sunhat protected his head. At least two days' growth of brown beard shadowed his face.

"I will wait in the sitting room, Herr Quinn." Leiner turned to go.

"Is there a radio or internet?" Evan said, surprised that Leiner would leave him alone with Brown. "I'd like to know what happened at the United Nations."

"I have internet on my phone." Leiner gave him a rueful smile.

The screen door squeaked with quaint charm. Brown and Johann heard it and stopped their game.

"Are you a lefty?" Brown called to him. Evan shook his head no. "There's a glove at the top of the steps for you. Johann's a lefty. Later, man," Brown said, waving to Johann who trotted around the house to the front, leaving them alone.

Evan picked up the baseball glove as he descended the steps. "Nice place."

"Yeah, I'm not staying here. It's just for our talk. Stand there, Maestro." Brown pointed to a spot twenty feet away from him. Evan slipped on the glove, punched his right fist into the palm. Brown continued, "I asked for a private, unrecorded conversation with you. The Austrians agreed."

The Austrians must know what Brown planned to say to him. Woody's surveillance detection device on the back of his watch remained quiet. Evan punched his fist harder into the glove's palm. He glanced around at the perimeter guards. "They're not afraid you'll recruit me or something?"

Brown cackled and threw the ball to him. "Little late for that. I've retired from the CIA. I told the Austrians you're not spy material. They've closed your file. I'm still interested in buying that café with you. I think we'd make a good team. We could hire people to run it on a daily basis, of course." His deep-throated laugh was smug. "Now I can have my acting career."

"Haven't you already been acting most of your life?" Evan threw the ball back to him. They settled into a steady rhythm of toss and catch that relaxed Evan. The Austrians had closed his file. About time.

"Oh, sure. I know guys who lost track of the difference between their act and reality. Extremely dangerous. My acting training helped me stay connected to the real world. I'm not acting now, Evan. I never acted with you. Unlike that Russian piano student, that friend of yours. He flew under everyone's radar. Convenient he lived across from the Hilton, huh? He must have just been waiting for his chance. And now the Chinese are more interested in absorbing Russia than collapsing the American economy."

"I don't believe Vasia assassinated the Chinese Vice Chairman," Evan said, throwing the ball harder to Brown.

"Someone else must have been there and that person killed Vasia. That's my theory."

Brown nodded as he listened, holding the ball. "Well, the Chinese got their excuse to add more territory after Taiwan. At least it wasn't America. Let's hope they leave Austria alone. I wanted to give you this." He held out a folded sheet of paper.

As he opened the paper, Evan read "Certificate of Death" in bold black letters at the top and on the first line of filled-in boxes his father's name. "Why are you giving this to me?"

Brown's trademark smirk greeted Evan's eyes. He stepped closer. "He was dead before you arrived in London the first day of your tour. That's the official death certificate, one of five originals. Claim the trust fund his publisher is holding for you. Do it fast, Evan. Today or tomorrow. Before the Americans figure out how much my defection is going to screw them." Brown peered at Evan's face. "Interesting bruises. What'd the other guy look like?"

"About the same. They still want the money?"

"Of course. They figured out how to make a legal claim via a bastard daughter of Randall Quinn."

"My father never had a bastard kid, and I'd have to be dead." Suddenly he understood. "You really *were* protecting me."

"I told you. Morgan hated you beyond hate. He's gone now. The termination order on you no longer exists. But you know, no one in Washington stopped Morgan. You have no friends in D.C."

No friends in D.C. Evan nodded, folding the death certificate and sliding it into a pocket. *They* had wanted him dead for the money. Woody must have known all along. Woody hadn't intended to get him alternate ID documents and the NEP had shirked on his training, giving him only enough to make mistakes to expose himself to capture. They'd set him up to fail and probably to die trying to escape. And then they sent Harold to threaten and shadow him. He hated to admit it but maybe what his father had taught him during the last two years about surveillance, gathering intelligence, counter surveillance and the Underground had saved his life. He understood also that now he was on his own. "Didn't you tell me before that Morgan ordered *you* to kill me?"

"Yeah, wrong guy for the job." Brown grinned. "Now they'll kill me if they ever get the chance." Brown stepped back and tossed the ball to Evan. "Was the guy who bruised your face out to kill you?"

Evan shook his head no. "Some punk jumped me near Westbahnhof. I'd seen him hanging around the Fischer School. He punched and kicked me too many times before I managed to teach him a lesson. He won't bother me again." Evan tossed the ball back to Brown.

"Always somebody playing King of the Mountain, right? Listen, Evan. After you get the money, protect it. Write a will, leave it to anybody but the NEP, right? Don't let them get their hands on it."

"Or on me either."

Brown snorted. "Yeah, you know, I tried to find out from ISS who set up your father, who snitched on him with the concrete evidence they could never get before, but they weren't talking."

"No surprise there." Evan caught Brown's toss.

"So I studied the Quinn file, which I brought with me, by the way. Also, the Caine file. The Austrians have the thumb drives for you. Anyway." Brown punched his fist into his glove. "Your father was a real piece of work. Joe Caine reported him at least twelve times for domestic violence. And you know, your dad wasn't a drunk or junkie, either. Just *mean* and sick, a sociopath. The cops arrested him but the charges were always dropped. Your mother kept believing he'd change, right? Is that what she told you? He promised not to do it again?"

Evan shrugged, tossed the ball. "He beat my mother. He beat me. That's life. No different from what everyone else in America does to each other, one way or another, on a daily basis. Especially the NEP."

Brown gave him a sideways look, his green eyes narrowed, tossing the ball into his own glove. "Well, you see, the person who set Randall up had to be close to him, know about the Underground and his activities in it, know where he hid his secrets. But probably not in the Underground. And probably had an issue with him. Like, it was payback time."

"Toss the ball, Brown."

"*You* set him up, didn't you? I mean, it makes perfect sense. ISS arrests you in '44 because of your involvement with the attempt to re-establish the Chicago Lyric Opera. You're thrown in prison for a couple years. But when you get out, you're not blacklisted like other artists in your situation. No. You resume your conducting career, your job at the Minneapolis State Symphony, while living with your father. And that was the clincher. The Housing Council didn't even have an apartment application from you. They wanted you living with him, observing and reporting. Better than an electronic bug." Brown wagged his index finger at Evan. "What I don't get is why they let you leave the country. They could have killed you easy in America after Randall's death. And they provide the relevant death certificates to Caine's and Randall's London publishers and banks and claim the money. So, what was your deal, Evan?" He tossed the ball to him.

"OK. Yeah. I made a deal. My freedom for my father. But no matter how well you research your object, Brown, you'll always miss something." Yeah, the payback for everything, he thought, an image of his mother coming into his mind. Everything.

"No, I see exactly what you did and I actually understand it in a way. I mean, your father traumatized you for years, right? Probably pushed your mother to kill herself, right? You made a deal with ISS to inform on your father. In return, you got your life back, your clean civic status, and enough power with the Arts Council to wrangle a European tour. Your goal, right? To leave America, defect, live in a free, democratic country for the rest of your life. Brilliant."

"Thanks." Brown was smart. He'd deduced most of it, but not Perceval or Perceval's secret. "Have you told the Austrians?" He tossed the ball to Brown.

"They have no need to know. You can have your revenge against your father. Your secret's safe with me. You deserve a better life. I'm throwing a press conference in a couple days and I don't plan to even mention you. But I plan to chatter away about other things. I'll confirm Randall's death and that I've given official documents concerning his death to the Austrians."

"The Austrians gave me the death certificate." Evan nodded. Brown continued to protect him by ensuring that no one except the Austrian cops knew about their contact, especially not the media. Except Woody Lewis knew, so the NEP knew. Brown was right. He needed to move fast to claim the money and build a legal wall around it to protect it.

"You got it. I won't ask you to go public about the domestic abuse, but I ask you to think about doing it. Silence protects your father and the Americans, like silence protects any abuser of power."

He caught Brown's toss. "At the meeting in Aschenbeck's office, the first time we met, I thought you were a hardcore CIA operative. Why'd you defect, Brown?"

"Finally, the big question." Brown caught the ball. They returned to their easy rhythm of toss and catch. "I grew up in the Bronx. My father was a regular beat cop for years and my mother worked as a secretary for a food distributor. I loved the movies. I was in all the school plays. I dreamed of being an actor. Uncle Danny educated me about politics and the government. The NEP had split off by that time and competed for third party status with the Independents."

Evan threw the ball. "And then the NEP won the presidential election in '16 promising security and economic prosperity."

"Yeah. I was eight." Brown nodded. "Ever hear of a guy named Mr. Redfield?"

"Sure. He smuggled my father's books and Uncle Joe's

music to London. He set up the trust funds. The Brits found his body floating in the Thames in '29."

Brown bowed his head. When he looked up, his eyes flashed anger. "Mr. Redfield's real name was Daniel Blythe, a commerce diplomat who traveled to Moscow via London on a regular basis. He was my—"

"Uncle Danny," Evan said.

"—mother's only brother, her younger brother. One day, he didn't come home from a routine business trip to Moscow. The Commerce Council told us he'd disappeared. Rumors spread that he'd stayed in Europe which hurt my mother, my family. The NEP branded him a traitor."

"Wait a minute," Evan said, squatting and holding his head. "Under those conditions, you couldn't have joined the CIA."

Brown strolled over to him, throwing the ball into his glove and sat cross-legged on the dusty brown dirt in front of him. "I'd wanted to be an actor. I hadn't wanted to work for the NEP in any way, but Danny convinced me that I could be valuable working from within. He encouraged me to sign up my senior year when they came to Cornell to recruit. They wanted people with a facility for foreign languages, which I had, and the ability to be a chameleon, which I also had. I was a good actor."

"You still are, Brown. You're here." Evan sat on the ground opposite him.

Brown grinned. "Thanks. I think that's the first nice thing you've said to me."

"Shut up."

Brown laughed. "The CIA proceeded with a thorough

background check on me. My clean civic status and my father's police service outweighed their suspicions of Danny. Plus, I suspect they wanted me to snitch on Danny. After they told me I'd been accepted, it hit me. If I joined the CIA, I would have a way to protect Danny, right? Six months later, while I was in training, he disappeared. In order to continue with the CIA, I was forced to denounce him. Standard procedure."

"You knew about the smuggling?"

Brown nodded. "I knew he used the name Redfield, too. But I never knew the details of how the stuff got from your father and Caine to him or how it started. Danny wasn't in the Underground."

"He must have had some interesting contacts."

"Yeah, Danny was a great guy. People loved him. Very savvy and intelligent. He knew the score." Brown sighed, took off his baseball glove and placed it on the ground in front of him as if it were fragile. "Nobody in the neighborhood believed he was a traitor."

"You didn't know about the Brits finding him?"

"Not then. I completed training at the Farm, language school for Arabic and German, and got my security clearance. I went to Langley to receive my first foreign assignment. That's where I read Uncle Danny's file. The CIA routinely watches people who travel abroad and they'd suspected him for a long time. Then he must have changed his usual delivery procedure or something. They observed him making a delivery to one of the publishers. The next time he was in London, they murdered him." Brown looked up toward the yellow house. "Leiner's been watching us from the kitchen window."

"Can he hear?"

"He already knows all this."

"Why did you stay in the CIA if they had murdered your uncle?"

"To sabotage them from the inside like Danny suggested. I've been doing it for years. I never became a double agent, but I leaked information anonymously to foreign governments and the media. I lost files, delayed operations, whatever I could do without arousing suspicion. I knew a lot of people, like Danny did." He nodded. "And protecting you, finishing what he started when he set up the trust funds in London."

"Have you helped the Chinese?"

"HELL, NO!"

Evan laughed. In his enjoyment of Brown's outrage, he felt a change, a bond, in his response to the other American. They were both defectors. From the same country. And Brown had protected him.

"Jiang Xu's assassination, though, was the worst thing that could possibly have happened. I can't believe the Russians would start a global war. The Russians, for Christ's sake! They know better."

"I know Vasia, Brown. I am totally convinced he had nothing to do with it."

"The Chinese will never be convinced." Brown took off his sunhat and smoothed back his brown hair, shining clean with streaks of blonde in the sunlight. "The war has already started." He sighed. "Man, I thought now I'd have a quiet, peaceful life." He inhaled sharply. "You know, the CIA shooters who killed Danny never found his last package. You don't happen to know—?"

"The score of Caine's Fifth Symphony on a flash drive sewn into his abandoned trench coat at Heathrow. Someone found it in a restroom, turned it into lost and found. He must have spotted the CIA guys and left the coat there."

"Aaaaah. Your father set up another smuggling operation because he sent out more of his books after '29."

"He hid *that* well. I never found any evidence of it when I was living with him. I didn't know about your uncle until after I defected."

Brown snorted, shaking his head. "People love *image* in America. The NEP uses all kinds of images to manipulate people through the media. You need to tell your story, Evan. Show the world who your father really was despite his genius as a writer. The Americans – the NEP – will do everything they can to protect their own image, you know. You protect yours."

The Toccata of Bach's Sixth Partita played in his mind, the section Vasia had been playing when he'd walked into his living room. His throat constricted painfully at the memory. Exposing his father exposed his own life. It was dangerous to reveal himself, his experience or what he knew. No guarantee the information wouldn't be used against him in some way. Keeping secrets had kept him alive in the past. Paranoia was self-preservation. Self-preservation always won out. He needed to protect Perceval. No one could ever know the truth about him. He remembered something.

"You know, Brown, you can call off the street cleaners. I'm tired of seeing those white vans."

Brown exhaled, frowning, and took off his sunhat again, wiped sweat from his forehead. "No way could I send street cleaners after you here, Evan. It's not America. I wouldn't, anyway. No one at the Embassy could send them after you. So, I don't know what you've seen. Just white vans, maybe."

Just white vans. Evan looked away toward the perimeter guards. Or they weren't real, like Harold and the Vigiciv gang. Hallucinations.

"But look, man," Brown said, putting his hat back on and standing up. "After Amsterdam I feel confident that you can take care of yourself. Are you going to continue at the Fischer School?"

Evan got to his feet. "Yeah. Did you tell the Austrians about Amsterdam?"

Brown grinned. "They have no need to know." Brown slapped Evan on the back. "Come on. I'm thirsty. Let's get out of this blistering sun and have something cold to drink."

Someone had set the kitchen table for lunch. At the stove, Leiner stir-fried chicken with aromatic spices and soy sauce.

Brown opened the refrigerator. "What do we have to drink, Inspector?"

"Beer and lemonade."

"Any news, Inspector?" Evan watched Brown take out a pitcher of lemonade and pour the pale-yellow liquid into two glasses.

"The ambassadors and staffs from China and the APCO nations have left New York."

Brown handed Evan a glass of lemonade. "We have war, gentlemen."

"What about the nuclear option?" Evan said. "Was there agreement not to use weapons of mass destruction again?"

"For the moment, Herr Quinn. Everyone agreed not to use them," Leiner said and added fresh steamed broccoli, peapods, carrots, onion and red pepper strips to the stir-fried chicken.

"The Chinese have already nuked Moscow and invaded Russia. Of course they'll agree not to use them now. The bastards." Brown took off his sunhat and drank half his lemonade in one long swallow.

The five of them ate Leiner's stir-fry lunch in the kitchen, quizzing Marco on his bird-watching hobby and talking about how war would affect the European soccer season.

Evan relaxed. As he looked around the table, he was astonished by how much he enjoyed the company of these four men, threats to him, to Perceval, since his defection. The three cops remained threats. Brown would disappear for weeks, if not months, as the Austrians and other European nations' intelligence agencies interviewed him. He'd miss the guy.

After lunch, Brown walked him and Leiner to the silver car. Marco had opened the car's doors and sat on the hood, waiting for them. He searched the trees with his binoculars.

Leiner handed Evan a small padded brown envelope. "I believe Herr Brown told you to expect this from me."

"The files of the Caines and my family." His eyes met Brown's. "Thanks, Bernie."

"Taken together, they're the landscape of a life," Bernie said with a sad smile. "An American life." They stopped behind the personnel carrier next to the silver car. Brown stuck out his hand. "The war won't last forever. I don't know where I'll end up, but later, maybe we can meet, continue our discussion about buying a jazz café together."

Evan grasped his friend's hand. "Sure. Call me. I plan to stay in Vienna. And thanks for watching out for me, Bernie."

"Take care of yourself, Maestro." Brown glanced at Leiner and headed back to the house.

Leiner smoothed his dark blonde moustache and sighed. "Herr Quinn, we now believe Herr Bartyakov was not the assassin of Vice Chairman Jiang Xu."

Evan's shoulder and neck muscles tensed.

"Forensic investigators have found blood spatter evidence that indicates someone had stood in front of Herr Bartyakov at the moment he was shot. Someone murdered him."

Evan nodded. He'd stepped back but it hadn't been far or fast enough. He said, "I knew it. I knew Vasia couldn't be the assassin. You think the assassin killed Vasia, too?"

Leiner's gray eyes narrowed. "The evidence suggests that, but it's also possible more than one person was there. I mean, two people and Herr Bartyakov. We continue to collect and analyze evidence. For example, your fingerprints were found on the rifle used to kill the Vice Chairman."

"The guy used Vasia's new rifle?" His voice almost squeaked at the end of the question. "Don't assassins usually bring their own weapons?"

Leiner chuckled. "Not if he knew Herr Bartyakov owned suitable weapons."

Their eyes met. Leiner's remained steady, unblinking. So much for the Austrians closing the file on him.

"Vasia invited me over for dinner. He'd just bought a

hunting rifle. He showed it to me, let me hold it, examine it. We'd talked about hunting together in Romania this fall. But then Vasia told me last Sunday that my probationary status prevented the Romanians from issuing me a hunting license." Evan shrugged as if none of it mattered. "I don't know if other friends of his hunted with him or knew about his guns. You'll have to ask Greta."

Leiner smiled. "You're angry. Why?"

"He's *dead*." Evan fisted his hands, punched his thighs. "Vasia's dead. How do you expect me to feel, Inspector?"

Leiner nodded. "He fought his attacker. We found defensive bruises on his hands, bruising on his body and face."

"That's the Vasia I know."

"You, Herr Quinn, have bruises on your face that first appeared on the day of the assassination. Both Frau Fasching and Frau Karalis told us you had no bruises at your picnic in the Vienna Woods on Sunday."

What had he told Leiner before about the bruises? Evan looked over at Marco on the silver car's hood, binoculars extensions of his eyes. "It's embarrassing. A punk jumped me near Westbahnhof. I didn't tell you before because, well, it's embarrassing."

"You reported this attack to the police?"

Evan shook his head, no. "I'd seen him hanging around the Fischer School. I defended myself. Taught him not to mess with me using what Okada had taught me." Evan looked at Leiner whose dispassionate expression told him nothing. "I decided to let it go, spare the guy further humiliation."

Leiner walked a circle around Evan, his arms crossed

over his chest. "Do you know his name? His address? We would like to verify the incident."

Evan shook his head, no. "I didn't make friends with the guy."

Leiner sighed, exasperated. "If you are ever attacked again, no matter the circumstances, Herr Quinn, call the police. Were there any witnesses?"

"Not that I saw." Evan stepped away from Leiner, squinting up at the clear sky. "Sorry."

"For your hunting trip with Herr Bartyakov, had you planned to buy a hunting rifle here or in Romania?"

"You know I couldn't buy a gun until January. Vasia offered to loan me one of his. I'd like to go home now and call Greta to find out if she's heard anything from Vasia's family. We don't know if they survived the attack yesterday." He wanted to get away from Leiner. The Austrian cop had come too close.

Leiner nodded. "One more question, Herr Quinn. Did you know about the pantry?"

"What about it?" Evan said. Leiner waited, saying nothing. "The pantry, the pantry. You want me to guess, Inspector?"

"The stairs from the pantry to the roof."

"Oh, sure. Vasia showed me those stairs the night of his housewarming party. He and Greta showed them to everyone that night."

Leiner's eyes shifted away from Evan to the sky for a second and over to Marco on the car. Evan suspected that Leiner had figured out what he'd done but had no proof, no evidence against him.

Leiner's eyes returned to him. "I am very sorry for the

loss of your friend and colleague, Herr Quinn. Please accept my condolences." He extended his hand.

"Thanks, Inspector." Evan shook Leiner's hand with his usual firm grip. "He was a good friend and a talented pianist. I hope you catch whoever killed him."

Leiner nodded. "Marco. Herr Quinn is ready to leave now. Please wear the hood again, Herr Quinn. I shall be in contact." Leiner turned and headed back to the house, bent from the weight of what he knew and what he didn't know.

Evan folded himself into the car's backseat. Marco handed him the black hood and checked that it was secure on his head before starting the car. He felt them back up and turn toward the road out of the woods.

He'd won. The assassin's identity would remain a mystery forever. Evan smiled in the darkness of the blindfold hood, scratched his neck where the hood's material pressed against his skin. He'd completed the assignment and fulfilled his contract with the NEP. He hadn't gotten caught. He was home free.

Chapter 26

"We need to talk. Come to the café," Woody Lewis's spry voice had said early that morning on the phone.

Evan hadn't expected to ever talk again to Woody after his last call the evening after he'd met with Brown a month ago. Evan had given the old American an abridged version of the meeting. He had not told him about his father's death certificate or that he'd already contacted Henley Martin at King Brothers Publishers in London. Three days later, his father's trust fund money arrived in his investment account. The publisher would continue to pay him the royalties from his father's books. His business lawyer, Christian Bach, referred him to a colleague to draft his will. He named Greta Fasching heir to his entire estate in guardianship for Vasia's child that she carried. An atonement.

The jazz café idea had grown in his mind. He'd heard of two cafés for sale in the Ninth District, a five-minute walk from the University. Brown had held his press conference at Bundespolizei headquarters two days after his meeting with him. Brown's statements sent shock ripples through America's alliances, and media pundits buzzed for weeks that Brown's descriptions of NEP and CIA activities had confirmed their suspicions. America's allies remained silent, however. They had a global war to fight together. As he watched two blocks of bombed out buildings pass outside the streetcar windows, Evan hoped that Bernie was in a safe place and the Austrians would protect him.

He'd squirreled away the Quinn flash drive from Brown in his bedroom closet's secret compartment. He preferred not to relive its contents. The Caine flash drive, however, contained information he hadn't known: Caine had committed suicide in his cell at the Redfield Federal Penitentiary in northern Minnesota a week after his arrest. Brianna and Paul Caine had moved to Grand Forks, North Dakota; a year later, they had slipped over the border into Canada.

Uncle Joe's suicide had not surprised him, but it had profoundly depressed him. He'd believed for twenty-five years that the ISS had murdered him. He had hated them for murdering him. He couldn't hate Uncle Joe for killing himself. Suicide in captivity asserted an individual's will and control, and attacked his captors. His father had told him often that he'd kill himself if arrested to deny his oppressors control of his life and death.

But his father hadn't committed suicide when ISS arrested him. His father had died from a 9mm bullet shot into his brain from ISS Lieutenant Harold Smith, Sr.'s service pistol. He had felt nothing about his father's death beyond relief and a sense of liberation. For once he had had the last word. But now Harold Jr. had re-entered his life, although he'd not seen him since the day before the assassination. He had not seen any more white street cleaner vans or the teen Harold and his Vigiciv gang since that day either. No one could know about those hallucinations. He wondered if they had truly disappeared or if they only waited for him in the dark.

He'd attended a memorial service for Vasia at the Academy of Music two weeks after his murder. He had reassured Greta again that he would be there for her and Vasia's child and do whatever he could to help and protect them. That desire to protect aroused a ferocity in Perceval. Sofia, also at the service, had regarded him with cold eyes and had not spoken to him.

America had declared war against China and APCO the day after his meeting with Brown and had sent troops to Europe and the Pacific. The war declaration triggered a cease fire in the insurgency, and Washington had extracted a promise from the Western secessionist states as part of the cease fire terms that they would not ally themselves with China and APCO. The Western states declared neutrality. America had benefited the most from the war so far: China no longer breathed down its economic neck, most of the world had turned against China, they had a cease fire in the insurgency, they had geared up manufacturing to supply American and allied troops giving the economy a boost, and the country had united in the patriotic war effort. The NEP must be pleased with itself.

The Chinese bombed the Hilton Hotel with remarkable accuracy using a MAO49, an unmanned aerial vehicle, the morning after his meeting with Brown, their first attack on Vienna. Austria abandoned her neutrality. The last month had been filled with night air raids on the city, fires from the bombs, loss of electricity and water for several days at a time, problems with food distribution and the loss of a routine, normal life. To Evan's relief, the Chinese bombers and MAO49s had not found his neighborhood in the Eighteenth

District, or the Staatsoper, Musikverein and Konzerthaus in the First District. The war had bombed his musician's life however. His conducting schedule had suffered cancellations because of it. He hated the war.

The global computer network, including the Internet, remained intact with only periodic interruptions in service. The Chinese needed it as much as everyone else.

The streetcar passed another bombed out area three blocks past the Währinger Gürtel. Pillars of black smoke rose in the east where fires burned after the air raids the night before. Evan had heard on the morning news that the Chinese had targeted two freight railway stations. Traveling around Vienna had become frustrating and slow at times, with unexpected and random interruptions in service. However, the streetcar and bus systems doggedly functioned despite damage in outlying areas to streets and tracks. The subway ran with infrequent interruptions in service. Subway stations also provided shelter during air raids. Evan's Number 41 streetcar passed the Votiv Church and began its descent into the underground Schottentor station.

Ten other people disembarked with him. He lingered in the underground passage, observing the activity in the shop windows, alert for shadows. He hadn't used a disguise for this trip into the inner city but no one paid attention to him. He decided to run a short surveillance detection anyway. Leiner might still have surveillance on him. Or terrorists of any persuasion.

He rode the escalator up to the street. Viennese hurried everywhere, their heads down. Their demeanor and behavior reminded Evan of Americans in Minneapolis, Chicago,

New York City, and other large cities where he'd conducted. That hunch and scurry was the physical manifestation of the primal instinct for survival. Buskers, mimes, food carts, hawkers, Fiacres, and other social activity on Vienna's streets had vanished. He strolled the Ring Boulevard past the University, the city hall which had been bombed once two weeks earlier reducing one side of the Neo-Gothic building to a pile of gray rubble, and the Burgtheater. He stopped at an information kiosk. In this open area on the Ring Boulevard, Evan watched people interested only in their own business, not his.

Fifteen minutes later, he strode into Judenplatz, surprised to see rubble and broken glass where an old Baroque building had stood. Across the square, the Café Chicago remained untouched. Lucky for Woody. He hoped this meeting wouldn't take long. He wanted at least two hours of rest before leaving for the Musikverein with Freda Kirsch who had offered to chauffeur him for a free ticket. He conducted the first of two concerts with the Vienna Philharmonic that evening. Maybe the Chinese bombers would postpone their usual evening sorties until later tonight, after the concert.

The bell above the café's door announced his entrance. The same two old codgers playing chess that he'd seen on his last visit almost three months earlier glanced up from their game at a table by the front windows. They were the café's only customers. Black, heavy drapes held open by loops of gray rope hung at all the windows. A tall, rail-thin waiter disappeared through the kitchen door beyond the pastry counter. Evan slid into a booth on the back side of the large square central column away from both the chess players and the windows.

Woody appeared minutes later carrying a tablet computer. He saluted Evan. "I just realized you have a concert this evening, Maestro." The old American sat opposite him. He looked tired, his hair a roiled white cloud, his clothing rumpled.

"I understood our business was concluded a month ago, Woody."

Woody laughed, dry and raspy. He signaled for the waiter and ordered two cups of tea for them and a slice of *Topfentorte* for Evan. The waiter left. "The *Topfentorte* is fresh today. I don't know how much longer we'll stay open. The war…."

"I thought the war would be over by now," Evan said. "The Chinese have made their point. The air raids—"

"Your neighborhood?" Woody booted the computer.

"No. We've been lucky. I saw Judenplatz took a hit." He really didn't want to chit-chat. He wanted to return home, prepare for the concert.

The waiter served their tea and Evan's cake. Evan squeezed the lemon slice over his steaming cup. Woody opened a file with sound on the tablet computer but stopped it as it began. Brown's voice stopped mid-word.

"No one expected a symphony orchestra conductor to be such a creative assassin," Woody said, turning the tablet so Evan could see the screen. Bernie Brown stood behind a lectern, speaking at his press conference, the picture on pause.

"I wasn't expected to survive the assignment, was I?" Evan twirled the dessert fork on the table next to the cake.

"True." Woody nodded and chuckled. "A brilliant move

deflecting attention away from yourself. Although I understand the Austrian Federal Police have evidence that someone was standing in front of Bartyakov at the moment the
gun went off."

He hadn't told Woody that detail from Leiner, only that
the cops had no evidence linking him to the assassination.
Woody had a police source.

"They have no way of identifying that person. No DNA,
nothing." Woody smiled and nodded. "Good job, Perceval."

"Yeah? Despite incomplete training and shoddy support
from my handler? You set me up to fail."

Woody's smile broadened. "Sometimes learning by experience is the only way. You've transferred control of both trust
funds in London to yourself."

Evan met Woody's blue eyes, his breathing slow against a
stomach spasm. "True."

Woody nodded, his mouth a tense line. "You've received
far more compensation for your work than originally planned.
Our bosses have decided you are a valuable asset, however."

Evan stared at the old man. "I completed the assignment. I fulfilled the contract. I have no further obligation."

"Let's talk this through, Evan. You have a secret. You
killed Jiang Xu and Bartyakov. Your training was docu-
mented, of course." Woody activated the keyboard on the
computer and typed. Another image popped up on the
screen, a soundless video of Evan kneeling in a wooded area,
firing a sniper rifle at a target off screen, Evan in Krav Maga
training, and Evan in small arms training. Instructors stood
with their backs to the camera. Evan was the only identifi-
able person. "We can send this to the EU authorities at any

time through a reliable source, of course, along with audio documentation of your orders and assignment to kill Jiang."

Evan felt the tingling of the blood leaving his face. "It would implicate you and Washington, wouldn't it?"

"We are outside of the government. And inside." Woody nodded. "We are shadows, like you, connected but unconnected. No one in the government knows we exist except the one we serve," Woody said, hitting a key on the computer. The visual returned to a frozen Bernie Brown. "Your training location resembles country in Washington State, doesn't it? Or maybe Wyoming? The Western secessionists will establish their government in November, write a constitution. They established civilian and military intelligence agencies a long time ago." Woody leaned forward. "Do you pick up what I'm laying down, Evan?"

He pushed the untouched cake away as if pushing the American away. "I don't belong to them."

"Your contract, as you call it, was open-ended. You fulfilled only the *first order* under that contract, Evan. Remember what the General's friend said to you?"

He wanted to beat the old guy to a pulp. His stomach clutched into a tight, painful knot and he felt sick. He forced himself to think back to his last evening at the camp in northern Minnesota, the meeting with the General and the Civilian from Washington.

"Congratulations, Evan," the Civilian had said, shaking his hand. "You've done far better than expected with your training. You're a shadow warrior now. Your code name: Perceval. As long as you work for us, you'll be as free as you want to be."

As long as you work for us. Why hadn't he seen it before? He'd accepted their terms. They owned him. They controlled his freedom.

"When the time comes," the Civilian had said, the General grinning next to him, "you'll go to Europe, Evan, and receive your assignment there after your defection." The Civilian had said "Assignment," not the plural, and vague, not specific. He'd believed what he'd wanted to believe. If he wanted to continue living his musician's life in Europe, he had to work for them.

"Inside want as much as you like, but outside do what you're told," his father's icy baritone whispered. They were his father all over again.

"If I refuse?" Evan narrowed his eyes at Woody.

"Refuse away," the old American said, shrugging. "You're not the only shadow warrior out there." Woody pushed the slice of *Topfentorte* to him. "Eat, Maestro."

Harold would kill him. Now he understood what Harold had said, why he was in Vienna. Or worse: they'd expose Perceval and he would end up in prison, without music, without conducting, without his life. He'd lose his mind. His eyes rested on the image of Brown on the computer screen.

"I could arrange for my father's trust fund money to be transferred to Washington." Evan picked up the dessert fork.

Woody laughed, an explosive guffaw. "You're full of surprises, Evan. I know they didn't expect you to say that." He giggled. "Imagine, Evan. You move the money through the international monetary system's computers, millions of dollars noticed by every EU government. How would it look, Maestro, for you to transfer money to Washington?"

"It would look like I worked for the NEP."

"You'd make Inspector Leiner's day." Woody giggled again.

Evan ate a bite of the sponge cake with creamy lemon-flavored cheese filling. He couldn't believe how trapped and powerless the NEP had him. But Perceval gave him power. His anger strengthened him. Perceval could protect his musician's life. Perceval was the instrument he'd play to win his freedom from them, but not at this moment.

"OK. Fine. I'll work for them, fine." Evan took another bite of cake. "I still need alternate ID documents from your forger, remember?"

"That's it?" Woody sat back, his jaw slack.

Evan swallowed and picked up his tea to take a sip.

"You weren't so decisive the first time I met you."

"People change, Woody." He gave Woody one of his public persona smiles, the flashy one he used in the Green Room after concerts. He'd learn their game and play it better, turn it all back on them.

Woody scrutinized him for a full minute before shifting the tablet computer on the table. He pointed at Brown's image on the screen. "Your next assignment."

Evan stared. No. Not Brown.

"You have a choice, Maestro. You can find out where the Austrians are holding him now or you can wait until he's released. Washington prefers you terminate him as soon as possible now. You think you can arrange a fatal accident?"

"Of course." Perceval smiled.

The End

AUTHOR'S NOTE

Perceval's Secret is a work of speculative fiction. All characters, locales, and incidents portrayed in the novel are products of my imagination or have been used fictitiously. Any resemblance to any person, living or dead, is entirely coincidental.

Writing about the near future challenges the imagination to extrapolate current trends in all aspects of human life. I researched futurists and how they work, and read one of the famous books in this area, **A Short History of the Future** by W. Warren Wagar. This gave my imagination the spark and material to build Evan Quinn's future world in the novel.

I chose to focus on the human aspects rather than technological, scientific, or environmental, i.e. on the geopolitical situation, the arts – specifically classical music – and the effects of childhood trauma on adults who've not been treated for it. Other writers in the speculative fiction field have imagined fantastical technology, dire environmental scenarios, or more advanced space travel. Often, these future worlds actually become a character in the stories. My goal was to maintain the focus on Evan Quinn, the human, and the low tech, and not make the future technology a predominant character in the story.

Wherever you go in Europe, you find a blending of the ancient or the merely old with the modern. Vienna, Austria is an excellent example of this. There is a respect for history and for how humans have lived in the past, as well as human accomplishments in architecture, literature, music, art, and the sciences. Europeans seem to look upon the future with a much different eye than Americans because their history has been longer.

In America, questioning has begun about the wisdom of turning over everything to computers and allowing humans to forget how to do things like pilot airplanes, ring up a sale, or type, among other things. Technological progress has its positives, but I think the Europeans have a crucial point regarding human life, i.e. we need to choose not to forget. As a result, I wanted the future world I created to incorporate choices to use objects and systems from the past as well as the present and to *not* be ruled by technology. Classical music and the instruments on which it is played have not changed dramatically for hundreds of years and I don't expect them to change in the next half century.

The composers Joseph Caine, Gerhard Novosti, Owen Te Kumara and Sean Taylor do not exist, but all other composers mentioned are real and their music can be heard on MP3, CD or in concert halls. Characters' homes are not real, but the streets on which they are located are.

Thank you for reading **Perceval's Secret**. If you'd like more information about this novel or the entire **Perceval** series, please visit my blog, *Anatomy of Perceval*, at https://ccyager.wordpress.com. Send messages to me through the "Contact" page there or through the Perceval Novels Facebook page (the link is at the blog). I'd love to hear from readers.

If you enjoyed this novel, please tell everyone you know about it! Or give it as a gift. You could also write a review where you bought your copy or at Goodreads.com.

ACKNOWLEDGEMENTS

Perceval's Secret has had a long journey, measured in years, to publication. Along the way, both strangers and friends have helped and supported me, especially as I pursued my background research for the novel.

First, I would like to thank Professor Emeritus William Wright, the founding Director of the Center for Austrian Studies at the University of Minnesota for talking with me about domestic Austrian law and referring me to the Austrian Cultural Institute in New York City where I connected with Brigitte Agstner-Gehring. She steered me to Wolfram Anders, an international lawyer at Steptoe & Johnson in Washington, D.C. (now Chief Special Operations Officer at International Finance Corporation), who helped me with my questions regarding Austrian law, police, and policies toward refugees and political asylum seekers. I also thank Karen Koepp, former editor of *Showcase* at the Minnesota Orchestral Association for her assistance with an Austrian novel about the police and being a resource for the German language.

Special thanks to Sam Dixon, former artistic administrator at the Minnesota Orchestral Association, for collecting photos and publicity materials at the Concertgebouw in Amsterdam for my reference. I also thank Marian and Ian MacDougall for taking photos for me during their vacation in Amsterdam. Edo de Waart graciously described his home city in loving as well as realistic terms, and gave me details that only someone who lives there would know.

To update my knowledge of the Musikverein Concert Hall in Vienna, Austria, I contacted Dr. Harald Goertz at the Österreichische Gesellschaft für Musik in Vienna, and he provided detailed answers to all my questions about the Musikverein.

Regarding conductors, conducting, and the lives of conductors, I began my research reading articles and books. Three books were outstanding resources: **The Psychology of Conducting** by Peter Paul Fuchs, **The Grammar of Conducting** by Max Rudolf, and **Music and Musical Life in Soviet Russia** by Boris Schwarz. Biographies of conductors also gave me a window into what their lives are like, how being a conductor is more a lifestyle than a job one leaves at an office.

After my preparatory reading, I began interviewing musicians, artistic administrators, public relations directors, and conductors themselves. I would like to thank especially the following for their time and immeasurable help with my research on conductors and conducting: Jim Berdahl for helping me with my conducting technique, Miryam Yardumian for explaining the world of artist managers, Sir Neville and Lady Molly Marriner for describing how European orchestras operate and some of their challenges, Sam Dixon for talking about what life is like on the road for guest conductors, Henry Charles Smith for teaching me how a conductor looks at a music score and studies it, Mimi Keller for introducing me to the musicians of the Seattle Symphony,

Ron Johnson at the Seattle Symphony, Edo de Waart for describing what it is like to conduct at the Concertgebouw in Amsterdam, David Zinman for his insights into Mahler, and Julie Haight-Curran for clarifying the relationship between conductor and modern orchestral musicians, among many other things about the orchestra business. Every conductor has his or her individual way of living the life, and these people helped me to make Evan Quinn unique to himself and authentic.

Finally, a huge thanks and a hug to R. D. Zimmerman for his generous spirit, support, and sharing his publishing experiences. A heartfelt thanks to all my Kickstarter.com supporters. My Kickstarter project failed to meet its funding goal, but I was moved nonetheless by the people who pledged their support. Thanks to Mary Logue and Patricia Weaver Francisco for their insights into writing character, setting, plot, and for their sharp eyes and minds, editing expertise and hearts. And for their unflagging support, patience and understanding, thank you Marie, Niles, Brandy, Julie, and the late Bob Kingwell. *Namaste*.

FOR BOOK CLUBS

Introduction

I love book clubs! Thank you for choosing **Perceval's Secret** to read and discuss. I hope the questions below will stimulate lively and thoughtful discussion. If you would like me to attend your book club by speakerphone or video chat to talk about writing **Perceval's Secret**, you can find my contact information at my blog, *Anatomy of Perceval*, at https://ccyager.wordpress.com. Enjoy!

Questions for Discussion

1. **Perceval's Secret** is set in the summer of 2048. How does the author's vision of 2048 differ from yours? The philosophy that motivates how Europeans have approached the future is mentioned several times. What is it? How does it fit with the current concern regarding humans losing skills, knowledge and expertise that they have had in the past because computers have taken on the tasks that require them?

2. Who is Perceval in the novel? Who was Perceval in history? What do the two share in common?

3. Evan Quinn, the protagonist, is a musician and conductor. What is your reaction to his occupation? Were you surprised by anything Evan Quinn did as a conductor?

4. What makes Evan Quinn a sympathetic character? What makes him unsympathetic?

5. Have you had experience with classical music? How does your experience compare to the classical music world depicted in the novel? If you haven't had experience with classical music, has the novel piqued your interest in it or no? Why or why not?

6. Who was your favorite character and why?

7. At least two characters have experienced psychological trauma in the past. Who are they? What trauma(s) did each experience? How did each deal with the trauma and its aftereffects?

8. What does classical music mean to Evan Quinn? Why?

9. Have you ever lived in another culture where you were unfamiliar with the language and customs? How did your experience compare with Evan Quinn's? If you've never lived in a foreign culture, what did you learn about this experience from the novel?

10. Was Randall Quinn and his best friend Joseph Caine insurgents or terrorists?

11. What did you think of the ending? Is Evan Quinn redeemable or unredeemable?

ABOUT THE AUTHOR

C. C. Yager has worked in advertising and marketing as an account coordinator and as a freelance copywriter. Her advertising copy sold tickets for the Minnesota Orchestra. She has published essays in *Mensa Bulletin,* ClassicalMPR.org, the Minnesota Orchestra website, and writes a bi-monthly column for *Mensagenda*, the publication of Minnesota Mensa. She has a B.A. in Music from Dickinson College, and studied music in Vienna, Austria under the auspices of the Institute for European Studies. While she's not conducted an orchestra since her elementary school orchestra, she has performed, first playing the French horn in school orchestras, bands and as a soloist; singing in school choirs; and then as a pianist in college in chamber music groups and as a soloist. She has taught piano. Her blog, *Anatomy of Perceval* (https://ccyager. wordpress.com), has covered writing fiction, classical music, the future, book, and movie reviews since September 2007. She writes a commentary Substack blog at creobyccyager. substack.com. C. C. Yager lives and writes in Minnesota.